Praise for Unleash

I found *Unleash* such a perfect book. Brock delivers the elements to keep kids—even reluctant readers—engaged and excited, while giving them lessons for life. Any teacher or parent should have this on their bookshelf for their kids.

—**Sigmund Brouwer**, author of the
best-selling Robot Wars series

The title for this book says it all. *Unleash* literally unleashed my kids' hunger for reading. With action on every page, I myself couldn't help but keep the light on a bit longer at night. *Unleash* will make even the most stubborn reader tear into this book from cover to cover.

—**Tricia Goyer**, mother, author, and host of
Living Inspired weekly radio podcast

Warning: Don't pick up this book unless you're ready for a thrill ride that won't let you off until the very end. Join the four Wikk kids as they travel through deep space and encounter enemies right out of your darkest nightmares. This is my kind of story—twists in every chapter, adventures galore, and characters I wish I could hang with. Unleash your imagination and read *Unleash* now.

—**Robert Liparulo**, best-selling author of
The Dreamhouse Kings series,
The 13th Tribe, and *The Judgment Stone*

Praise for The Quest for Truth series

Racing across the galaxy in a stellar ship, the *Phoenix*, you won't be able to put these books down. Be careful not to rip the pages as you tear through the text and devour the adventure. Thrilling scenes, cool gadgets, and memorable characters are all part of what make The Quest for Truth a must-read series.

—**Wayne Thomas Batson**, best-selling author of The Door Within Trilogy, The Berinfell Prophecies, and The Dark Sea Annals

Kids will enjoy the nonstop action, suspense, and excitement in the Wikk family's adventures. Brock Eastman cleverly weaves a thrilling tale that takes young readers on a rollercoaster ride of intrigue and mystery.

—**Jeff Sanders**, fourth grade teacher, Chino, California

The Quest for Truth is a riveting tale of four young kids who have to learn to help and rely on each other. With lives on the line, courage, wit, companionship, and teamwork are vital for Oliver, Tiffany, Austin, and Mason.

—**Hannah Davis**, age 14

It got right to the adventure; it wasn't hard to figure out what was going on. You should read it. . . . Watch out for the Übel!

—**Alex Peterson**, age 9

UNLEASH

THE QUEST FOR TRUTH

UNLEASH

THE THIRD ADVENTURE IN
THE QUEST FOR TRUTH

BROCK EASTMAN

P U B L I S H I N G
P.O. BOX 817 • PHILLIPSBURG • NEW JERSEY 08865-0817

ISBN: 978-1-59638-247-3 (pbk)
ISBN: 978-1-59638-788-1 (ePub)
ISBN: 978-1-59638-789-8 (Mobi)

Printed in the United States of America

Library of Congress Cataloging-in-Publication Data

Eastman, Brock, 1983-
  Unleash / Brock Eastman.
      pages cm. -- (The quest for truth ; 3)
  Summary: The Wikk children face fierce lizards and betrayal by a trusted ally when they return to Obbin's plundered planet, where Oliver and Tiffany slip into a high security laboratory and Mason, Austin, and Obbin take on Corsairs.
    ISBN 978-1-59638-247-3 (pbk.) -- ISBN 978-1-59638-788-1 (ePub) -- ISBN 978-1-59638-789-8 (Mobi)
  [1. Brothers and sisters--Fiction. 2. Pirates--Fiction. 3. Space flight--Fiction. 4. Adventure and adventurers--Fiction.] I. Title.
  PZ7.E126774Unl 2013
  [Fic]--dc23
                                                  2013011725

To Kinley:

You make me smile. With your words. With your laugh. With your kisses and hugs. With your every breath.

You are a gift from our Creator, and every day I get to see the amazing imagination he gave you.

You're just two and a half and yet you make up words and stories; you sing songs with me and do the motions. It won't be long before we'll be writing together.

I'm so blessed to have the pleasure of calling you my daughter, although when I do, you quickly say, "I'm not daughter! I'm Kinley."

I love you.

Contents

Acknowledgments

A few well-deserved thanks.

Ashley, you got me through another one. Your encouragement and your love get me through the long evenings of writing. When I look back at our story, it amazes me how God orchestrated it all. Thanks for standing by me.

Well, I wrote the dedication to you, Kinley, before these acknowledgments. And already you've proven your daddy true. I said we'd be writing together someday soon, and it looks as though it'll be happening shortly after this book releases. You brought me your slinky, and you asked, "Daddy, is this your favorite sound?" From there we wrote a book. I love you, "unruly leader"!

Elsie Mae—or E. C. Mae, as I adore calling you—you grow more every day, and your personality does too. You are so silly and quite the comedian. You certainly know how to make me laugh. You also know how to melt me too. When you stare at me with those eyes and cute frowning face, how can I say no?

Baby Eastman, we just found out days ago, but I know you are growing inside your mommy. I can't wait to find out who you will be. I'm thankful to God for you and can't wait to meet you later this year.

Mom and Dad, I couldn't have done this without you. Your love and support help me on this journey.

Ty and Tiffany, thanks for your ongoing support. Tyler, thanks for giving me the words for the prayer in the back of the book.

Autumn, Maddie, and Hadley, I wish we could see you more but am always thankful to have you as my nieces.

Larry, thanks for helping to make The Quest for Truth a Focus on the Family resource.

Melissa, again your faith in this project has been such a blessing. I appreciate you bringing The Quest for Truth to life, both in story and in art.

Amanda, your edits for this book were a challenge and made *Unleash* a far better book. Your notes were detailed and thought provoking. I couldn't have written this book without you.

Ian, thanks for continuing to put The Quest for Truth on the shelves of stores and therefore into the hands of kids.

Tara, thanks for arranging my PR and for filling all my requests for endorser copies and blog copies.

Ryan, thanks for being so encouraging of my writing. I have appreciated all your chapter-by-chapter coverage on my blog for the books.

David, thanks for your updates to my site and your exuberance for my writing. I enjoy working with you at Focus. You have an awesome career ahead of you no matter what you choose to do because you are so talented.

Most important, thank you to the One who inspired this series. You are the Creator and the one who inspires creativity. I thank you for rescuing us from darkness, and I pray that this series will be used to help those who need to find you.

3.0

Prologue

The moon of Slan Idrac was one of the most hostile he'd ever been on. Razor-sharp rocks jutted from the mineral-laced terrain, making it impassible for the small assortment of craft on their exploration ship, the *XPLR Grazer*. The sky scooters' engines would explode if they sucked the moon's poisonous gases through their intake, and the wheeled vehicles were too wide to navigate the narrow crevices. They had no choice but to travel by foot.

Slan Idrac's poisonous atmosphere required some of the heaviest exploration gear he'd ever worn. He was thankful for the outfit's durability. XPLR Corp provided all he needed—that wasn't what worried him. He wanted to get home. He wanted to see his wife. Her smiling face often came to mind. He missed her so very much.

Slan Idrac was the last stop on the Resource Scouting Tour, also known as RST Mission 1042009. He'd been gone three months. Even now his team was laying markers across the area where the new Ore Crusher would land and begin excavation. Their last mission was to create enough power for the equipment. The sun wouldn't provide enough light for the solar panels, so they would also have to connect a thermal line.

His mission now led him toward a potential thermal vent. The reconnaissance probe's map indicated high temperatures, and the glowing reflection on a spire ahead confirmed its accuracy.

Though it was against company policy, he coveted the times he could explore on his own. XPLR stated the team-exploring policy was for safety, but he'd always felt it was to stop thievery. XPLR sent crews into areas with resources worth billions—if not trillions—of federal credits. The green mineral that dusted the surface of Slan Idrac was worth a thousand credits per gallon once mixed with a solution created by GenTexic, a genetics company.

As he hefted himself up a wide wall of rock, the ledge crumbled. He slid down toward a glowing inferno, a flickering pit of burning ash. Twisting onto his stomach, he scrambled to grab something. Pebbles slipped through his grasp. His right hand hooked something solid; his body jerked to a stop. His legs dangled precariously over the glowing pit. Reddish gas spiraled upward.

After catching his breath, he turned his gaze to his life-line. It was a wooden stake. He pulled himself up onto the slope and dug his boots into the loose stones until he found a solid ledge. He released the stake. It was clearly foreign to the planet. He dug around it, revealing a crossbeam. He dug farther. The wood formed a lowercase *T*. The end of the stake disappeared into a slab of stone.

What had he found? He looked back up at the ledge. It was a wall. He glanced around the pit; it was a good two hundred feet in diameter. There were no other walls. He looked again at the one collapsed wall.

What was that? Something glinted in the rubble. He'd have to get closer to investigate.

He tugged at the piece of wood once more, but it wouldn't come loose. He'd have to come back for it. An artifact like that could be worth a lot. He started up the gravely slope with extreme caution. After a few close calls, he arrived at the crumbled wall. He shifted the pieces of stone and discovered a thin, half-burned box. The metal remains of a latch on the otherwise wooden box had caused the glint. He picked up the box. Inside was a rare find; a shred of paper. It was blackened and burned. A number in the corner indicated that it was a page from a book.

He read the words to himself: "And I give unto them eternal life; and they shall never perish." Eternal life? A powerful concept, but one he knew was impossible. People died. That was the way of it. You lived, you died.

But he didn't discard the scrap of paper. It was as valuable as the cross. Maybe even more so, because it contained text. This page was an artifact from the past. Some people still paid handsomely for a scrap like this. And he'd once heard a rumor about a group searching for the secret of eternal life.

If he could sell this, he would never have to work another day in his life. He and his wife could travel and spend every moment together. They could see the galaxy.

The problem was selling it. He would have to smuggle it back onto the *XPLR Grazer*, which wouldn't be too difficult, but then he would have to slip it past the inspection teams that scoured the returning crews and ships to prevent this sort of thievery. Any discoveries were considered corporation property. This was no different. If he could get past the search, he'd have to wait a few months before quitting. If he quit and suddenly came into a large sum of credits, he would raise suspicion and be investigated. He had to do this right. He had to be patient.

Then he'd seek a buyer on the Dark Market. It shouldn't be too hard, but he wasn't accustomed to dealing with those sorts of people. What would he tell Sylvia? How would he explain their sudden wealth? He couldn't tell her about the paper; she'd not approve of his stealing it. Guilt churned in his stomach. He should just turn it over to XPLR Corp.

He sighed and sifted through the rest of the rubble, as well as the rocks covering the slope. He found nothing else. If only he could free the stake.

He looked back at the pit. The crater was not a source of thermal energy. The destroyed wall, the smoldering ash in the pit—this was the site of an explosion. Something had blown up, destroying the building and creating the fire below. How long ago? It was impossible to tell. The ore on the planet could burn for hundreds of years, which was one reason it was so valuable.

He didn't understand why anyone would live there, though.

A second thought crossed his mind. He'd read about the atmosphere: some of the gases were unusual, not naturally occurring. Observing the crater again, he noticed the similarities it had to a missile impact crater. Understanding rushed over him.

This site had been attacked, and gases had been released on the moon. Someone had wanted the place destroyed and uninhabitable. The explosion had likely happened some time ago. This scrap of paper could be dangerous to its owner or . . . worth a whole lot of money.

He knew what would happen if he reported that the thermal vent was actually an explosion crater. XPLR would terminate their activity on Slan Idrac until the Federation investigated and cleared the moon. The moon would be quarantined. XPLR would not place corporation equipment in a hostile zone. It was too valuable, and they'd dealt with too many ransom situations on personnel in the past.

It could be years before XPLR would be able to return, or before he could. He tucked the scrap of paper in a pouch and climbed back over the remnants of the wall. He would return to the *XPLR Grazer* and somehow smuggle the scrap back with him. He'd find a way to make Sylvia see that he deserved to cash in on the relic's value.

GEN- TEXIC

Life

BIOTRONICS INTERVENTION UNIT

FILE AQUIRED
5.6.85
CLEARANCE 9

PLAN VERSION 11.21.20.13

Holographic Mapping Sequencer

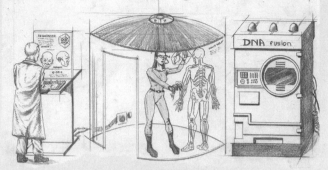

Cubix Modeler

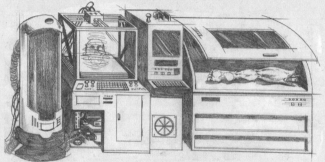

Reassemblance and Configuration Lab

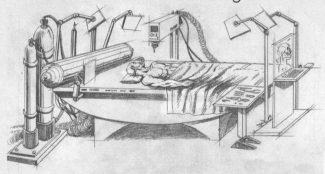

Body Assemblance Components

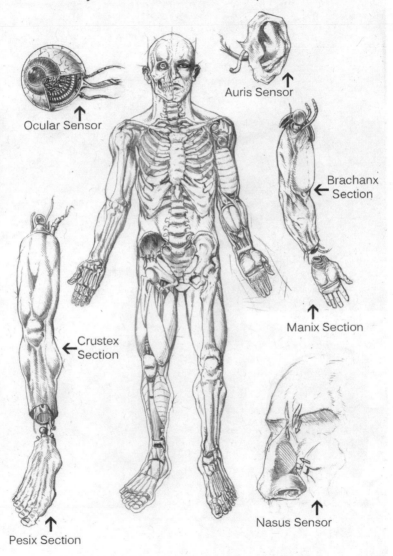

Ocular Sensor

Auris Sensor

Brachanx Section

Manix Section

Crustex Section

Pesix Section

Nasus Sensor

INSTALLATION SCHEDULED
7.10.85
LEVEL 9; MEDICAL WARD

BIOTRONICS INTERVENTION UNIT
PLAN VERSION 11.21.20.13

3.1

Parting Gift

The *Phoenix* blasted through the sky, barreling toward the remaining storm clouds. Lightning flashed inside them.

Oliver blinked at a dark silhouette within the cloud. Had the Übel waited for them? His hands gripped the controls, ready for action. His body grew rigid in the pilot's seat.

When he looked again, the mysterious shape was gone. Relief escaped his lips in a heavy breath. He stroked back his usually spiky brown hair. He'd not spiked it for several days now.

The ship's altitude increased, and the sky grew darker. They were nearly free of Evad and on to Jahr des Eises, where they would return Obbin and locate Mr. O'Farrell. Oliver had so many things to ask the Wikks' benefactor and fellow explorer. He seemed like the most likely source of information for them, the only one who might know the truth about their parents' work.

The *Phoenix* pitched forward, and a thundering explosion echoed all around. Green light enveloped the ship. Oliver shielded his eyes. The displays on the *Phoenix* flashed. Warnings erupted on every screen.

"What was that?" cried Tiffany from the copilot's chair, her brown eyes wide and alert. Yet she never stopped working the screens before her, swiping and tapping her fingers as if playing a piano. Her brown ponytail swished back and forth with her movements.

The ship jolted again.

Tiffany pulled Midnight, her new pet cat, close. "There's something wrong with the generators. And the navigation information for Jahr des Eises has disappeared."

"I see that." Oliver glanced at the radar screen. A red dot flashed on, then off again. The systems were on the fritz. He was blind to anything not in his line of sight.

He felt an urging in his gut. He twisted the controls of the ship, and the silver craft dove, then spun. The structure of the ship groaned under the maneuver. "Hold on!" The words had become all too familiar to his siblings.

"Whoa! Go, Oliver!" shouted Mason and Austin from the second row.

A ball of green light encapsulated by glowing blue mist sailed past them. Oliver hadn't known the shot had been fired, but he'd sensed the need to barrel roll.

As Oliver jerked the controls back, a piercing pain shot through his body like a knife thrust into his ribs. His arm went numb, and he lost his grip on the controls. He grimaced at the tearing sensation in his side.

Something was wrong. When and how had he been hurt? He gasped in a shallow and painful breath. He didn't have time to feel pain, let alone do anything about it. They were under attack.

Gritting his teeth, Oliver pulled back the controls. The *Phoenix* shot up, then rolled onto its back. Like prisoners, the kids were locked into their chairs by the extreme g-force of the tight turn.

"Obbin, it's okay," Austin said.

"Yeah, Oliver is a great pilot," Mason said.

"That's not why I'm closing my eyes," Obbin explained.

Oliver increased the thrust and turned the controls. For a split second, he saw their attacker: a gray ship unlike the black Übel fighters. This one had a globular canopy, set on a fuselage with short, rounded wings and three tailfins. The enemy fighter twisted and slipped out of sight like a phantom.

Oliver tried to follow. As far as he knew, the *Phoenix* was unarmed. He hoped to keep the ship behind the enemy until they could escape, but how to do that was unclear. Far from any canyon, cave, or obstacle, he had nowhere to take cover.

The new pain continued in his right side. Oliver was still wearing his wetsuit from his underwater dive, and its tight fabric wasn't helping. It rubbed against the injury with every movement.

"Oliver, what was that?" Austin asked, brushing his sandy-colored bangs clear of his green eyes. The youngest Wikk was always alert and ready for action.

"A fighter. Not sure whose."

"Aren't we cloaked?" Mason called out.

Oliver shook his head. He glanced at the silver ball still engaged with the system, then clicked the remote.

No confirmation message flashed on the screen. "It isn't working."

"Whatever hit us earlier damaged something in our electronics," Tiffany said. "The systems are still sporadic."

Oliver couldn't believe his slipup. After uncloaking the ship so the kids could reboard, he'd forgotten to reactivate the device. The failure added to his dismal feeling of helplessness. If he'd taken his time and turned it on, they'd have been invisible and unable to be attacked.

The fighter zipped into view again. No time for regrets. Oliver had one choice: stay on its tail.

Fiery pain shot through his side. It felt like a knife was being dragged along his skin. The unknown injury threatened his ability to fly.

How long could he keep this up?

Oliver released the controls, but not in defeat. His left arm flew to shield his eyes. A blinding purple orb came from out of his field of vision and struck the small tri-finned fighter. A brilliant flash blasted out in a ring of violet plasma.

The ship glowed and dropped in altitude, falling through the sky.

Oliver turned the *Phoenix*. Could he get a glimpse of the new entry to the sky battle?

The arrival was a ship identical to his.

"The *Eagle*," said Mason.

"Brother Sam!" Obbin exclaimed. "Thank Creator!"

Oliver turned to look at them. "What?" *The* Eagle? *Brother Sam? Creator?*

"There he goes!" called Tiffany, pulling Oliver's attention back.

The *Eagle* turned and dove. Oliver followed. The phantom enemy ship twisted toward Evad's surface. Oliver was just about to turn the ship away to spare his siblings the sight of a pilot slamming into the jungle below when the canopy of the crashing craft popped free and the man ejected. Instead of using a parachute, he zipped through the air on a jetpack.

The saving silver ship flew after the pilot. Much as Oliver wanted to meet this Brother Sam, he had other priorities. The Übel had just departed for Enaid with the Wikks' imprisoned parents, and he had a detour to make before he could follow. He had no time to waste at the present. Oliver pulled the controls, and the *Phoenix* again pointed toward space.

They passed free of Evad's gravitational pull. Oliver brought the ship into an orbital holding pattern above Evad. "Everyone watch for anything unusual. With our systems down, we have to do this ourselves."

The *Phoenix* flew in a wide circle. Oliver scoured the black space around them.

"Over there," called Austin.

The *Phoenix* jerked as Oliver stopped its turn. Everyone searched for Austin's sighting with bated breath. A red light blinked in the distance. Oliver strained his eyes. Should he speed away or wait?

A golden ball grew in size as they coasted toward it. The red light flashed.

"Most likely it's Evad's planetary beacon," Mason said. "At least, that's what it looks like."

Oliver sighed. "You're right. The Federation placed beacons near every known planet within its borders."

"What now?" asked Austin.

"We have to fix the NavCom," Tiffany said. "We can't launch into hyper flight when it's offline and our other systems are malfunctioning."

Oliver knew she was right, but he wasn't a mechanic or systems technician. He had basic knowledge of what needed to be fixed, but he'd have to rely on the manual and schematics to actually do it.

"You're right, Tiff," he said. "Austin, Mason, and Obbin, when we get into space, I need you to check the NavCom servers. They're in the room next to the engine room. The status screen on the server rack should normally read *100 percent online*. My guess is it's far from that. I think we were hit by some sort of EMP. We might need to restart."

Obbin's green eyebrows raised on his blue forehead. "EM—what?"

"An electromagnetic pulse," Mason said, his blue eyes twinkling. "They're used to short out electronic systems."

"The *Phoenix* is somewhat shielded from that sort of attack, but it seems the weapon did some damage. Anyhow, I need you guys to see—" Oliver paused, hiding a gasp as his injury throbbed. Before he did anything else, he needed to find the source of his pain.

He was still facing the windshield and knew his brothers and Obbin could not see his pained expression he wore. If Tiffany had, she was holding her tongue. "See if the systems need to be reset, then report back," he said.

"Shouldn't you be the one to—?" Mason started, but Austin stepped in.

"I'll be glad to take on this mission," he said. "Obbin, let's go."

Mason sighed as Austin and Obbin released themselves from their harnesses. "I'm coming. This mission needs more than brute strength. It's going to require someone with a brain."

Austin scoffed but didn't argue. The three left through the hatchway, their shoes clattering down the staircase to the lower floor, and Oliver let out a groan.

"Oliver, what happened?" Tiffany asked, releasing Midnight. The black cat jumped from her lap and tucked itself under her chair.

"It's my side. I think I'm cut." Oliver twisted, trying to lift his arm.

"Don't," Tiffany cautioned him. "Keep still. I'll get the medic kit from the galley. Meet me in your room."

Oliver nodded, and they departed.

3.2

Blood-red Ruby

Oliver started to take off his diving suit. The tight-fitting outfit placed an uncomfortable pressure on his wound. Every twist sent an excruciating jab into his right side. His arm was nearly incapacitated, slowing his progress.

Reaching in a drawer near his bed, Oliver pulled out a long-bladed knife. Carefully he slit the sides of the suit and rolled it down to his waist, leaving his chest bare. Warm crimson liquid oozed down his right side. As much as it had hurt, the suit had acted like a bandage to compress the wound.

He took a shirt from his drawer and wiped away the blood. He grimaced as something rough caught under the shirt. He pulled the shirt away. A piece of glass sparkled in his skin. He looked closer.

It wasn't glass at all. A shard of ruby had torn through the suit and lodged itself in his right side about halfway up his rib cage. If not for his ribs, the shard might have torn farther through him, damaging organs or causing internal bleeding.

When and how had the fragment of jewel found him? He hadn't felt anything until flying the *Phoenix*. Hadn't he been long clear of the underwater tunnel when it had been destroyed? Oliver sighed. Perhaps this was a stray piece of debris from the Übel missile strike.

Either way, he was injured, and unless Tiffany could do something about it, he'd be limited in his physical ability to lead the mission.

Oliver looked at the shard. It was as big as the top of his thumb. Were any other pieces still buried in his skin? Blood trickled down his side. He reached for the extra shirt and gently wiped the wound.

There was a knock on the door.

"Come in." Oliver was ready to get this over with.

"I've got the kit," Tiffany said.

Oliver pulled the blood-soaked shirt away from his side. Tiffany frowned as she saw the wound and its cause.

"A ruby," she said. "We'll have to get that out first."

"I know," Oliver said with gritted teeth. "Just . . . just make it quick." He winced as he moved.

"We need to numb it first." Tiffany took out a couple of strips of NumbaGlu and laid the tacky numbing agent along each side of the wound. A piece of her long hair tickled Oliver's side, and he flinched.

"Ouch," he said.

"Don't move."

"Your hair tickled me."

"Sorry." Tiffany pulled her hair up into a bun and rewrapped her hair tie to secure it into place. She leaned in again and lightly touched his side. "Now do you feel that?"

Oliver shook his head.

Tiffany held a pair of tweezers over the exposed portion of the jewel. She leaned in, looking closely at the wound. "The fragment is jagged. I can't tell how long it is. I'm not sure that the NumbaGlu will be effective that deep."

Her talking wasn't helping Oliver, though he knew it wasn't for him. It was something his sister did while she concentrated. It was how she reassured herself during a difficult task.

"In other words," Tiffany said, "this might still hurt."

"I sort of figured." Oliver clenched his fists as he tensed his body.

"Don't do that," Tiffany said. "That will make it bleed more. Try to relax."

"Tiffany, there's a piece of ruby in my side that's as big as my thumb. And you said it's jagged. How can I relax?" Sarcasm saturated his voice.

Tiffany sat up straight. "Oliver, I . . . just take a deep breath . . . I know you are in pain. I'm sorry. I've not done something like this before. The biggest thing I've removed was a pine needle from Austin's cheek."

Oliver closed his eyes. He tried thinking about something peaceful. His mind went to the pine forest behind their home on Tragiws. He placed himself on a stone outcropping just above the gorge.

A twinge in his side reminded him of Tiffany's work. He concentrated harder. A lone eagle glided through the air along the stone cliffs.

Suddenly a black spacecraft dove into view.

Oliver opened his eyes. Even his imagination had been tainted by the Übel.

Searing pain wracked his side as he felt Tiffany draw out the ruby. He gripped the edge of his bed. His knuckles turned white.

"Done," Tiffany said. Oliver looked at the red jewel lying next to him on the mattress. His blood stained the white sheet.

"Oliver, since this is a puncture, you will need a couple of stitches."

"Can you do that?" Oliver asked. The pain in his side had been reduced considerably. He didn't like the idea of getting stitches, but he knew his sister was right. The wound would move a lot because it was on his side. Stitches were the only thing that could keep it closed from infection.

"I've never attempted it before." She swallowed. "But I . . . I'll try."

"That's the best I can ask for," Oliver said. His slight laugh was a futile attempt to lighten the mood. "You got the jewel out."

"First we should use some FlexSkyn to help the wound heal quicker," Tiffany said.

Oliver was familiar with FlexSkyn: a faux skin patch made of plasma. It contained nano-bots that took the patient's DNA and embedded it into the skin-cell framework within the patch. This caused damaged skin tissue to mend far quicker. FlexSkyn had transformed the medical science field nearly a hundred years ago.

Tiffany took a patch of FlexSkyn and laid it across the wound. The wound was long enough that she had to lay a second patch below it. "That should do it."

She took out a small hooked needle, some sterile string, and two more strips of NumbaGlu. "I want to make sure it stays numb."

Oliver nodded.

"Do you feel that?" she asked, her fingers pressing the area near his wound.

"No. Go ahead. We can't delay too long," he said bravely.

Tiffany frowned. "Don't rush me."

For the next five minutes, Tiffany meticulously stitched up the wound. Oliver only grunted in pain a couple of times. In all, twelve stitches were needed. Tiffany wrapped a long stretch of gauze around Oliver to enclose the wound.

"I don't want to mention this to the twins," Oliver said.

Tiffany nodded in agreement as she put the unused supplies back into the kit. "I'll stick this in the laundry," she said, taking his blood-soaked shirt in hand. "Are you going to be okay?"

"I'll be fine," he promised. "Can you check on the boys? I really only sent them ahead so I could have you look at this without making them worry. I don't really think they'll be able to figure the servers out. It's a complex system."

"Oliver, you underestimate them, I think," Tiffany countered. "I think they're more capable than we give them credit for. And you don't always have to appear strong. You're our brother. We know you have weaknesses." She hadn't said it in a way to offend him.

Oliver grunted, a painful twinge reminding him of his wound. "Maybe."

A brief silence ensued.

"Also have them clean up the engine room while they're down there."

Tiffany nodded.

"I'm going to change, and then I'll be down."

Tiffany left, and Oliver gathered a fresh set of clothes. It hurt to remove the rest of the wetsuit, and he knew he'd have to be very careful over the next few days so as to not tear open the stitched wound. He put on some comfy Academy sweatpants and his hoodie.

As Oliver passed the engine room, he saw Obbin and Austin diligently putting things away. He poked his head in.

"It seems someone was messing around the *Phoenix* while we were in the basin." Oliver looked at Obbin.

"I was bored," Obbin said with a shrug. His spiky green hair bounced.

Austin raised his eyebrows. "Were you bored right before we took off from your planet?"

"I wasn't as ready to leave as I thought," Obbin admitted.

"Cold feet?" Austin asked. He worked a wrench on a bolt as he secured the ventilation cover back into place.

Obbin nodded.

"Well, you'll be home soon enough," Oliver said. He noticed several fur-covered satchels piled nearby. "Looks like you brought plenty of supplies for the trip. Was that where you stowed away?"

Obbin nodded. "I used some harnesses. Even though I'd never flown before, my father had told me stories of the ancient days when our people explored the universe. I wasn't sure what to expect, but I knew I'd better be ready."

"You continue to impress me," Oliver said. "You've proven to be both brave and smart." Oliver caught a jealous scowl on Austin's face. "You'll do well with my brothers. You all have a lot in common." He hoped the compliment would keep Austin from sinking into rebellion again.

"Yeah, you can share my bunk with me, Obbin," Austin offered. "It'll be better than an air duct."

"Thanks," Obbin said, lifting his fur packs onto his shoulders.

"I'm going to check on Tiffany and Mason. You guys head up to the bridge and wait for us there," Oliver said.

"Can we drop off his stuff in our cabin first?" Austin requested.

Oliver liked being asked. "Yes, of course." He stepped out of view but paused when he overheard Austin.

"Obbin, I'll help you carry your stuff to Mason's and my cabin," he said. "When you packed all this before the escape, I didn't realize you meant you were coming with us right off the planet."

"I wanted to fly, and after helping you escape I decided it'd be best to go away for a little while. It seemed like a better option than being grounded for the rest of my life."

"What if you'd never made it back to your home?" Austin asked.

"I would have," Obbin said.

"Wouldn't you still have gotten in trouble?"

"Yeah . . . probably, but I'd be bringing back great stories and news of the outside world, so maybe not."

"Are you worried about going back now?"

There was a second of silence. "No . . . I mean, I miss my family and . . . and it was wrong of me to do what I did. Creator would be unhappy. I need to go back and ask my family to forgive me."

Who was Creator? Was it another name for the king?

Austin sighed. "I need to do that too."

His confession made Oliver's concern about insubordination seem irrelevant.

Footsteps told Oliver that the boys were leaving. Not wanting to be caught eavesdropping, he darted forward quietly.

Tiffany had the e-journal out and connected to one of the servers. Mason had a large silver box out on a counter. Several wires connected it to a display. Austin might have been the tinkerer, but he worked primarily with gadgets. Mason and Tiffany were the brains when it came to operating systems or applications.

"So how bad is it?" Oliver asked over the sound of humming servers.

Mason shook his head. "Not that bad. We had to restart the system and transfer the prime-boot file to the journal, wipe the current server file, and reload it."

Mason's lingo and explanation were far more than Oliver needed or expected. Maybe Tiffany was right. Mason sounded like one of the guys headed into tech-ops at the Academy, always talking about servers and transfers. Oliver was on the path for pilot, captain, and admiral. Of course he didn't trouble himself with the tech stuff. Perhaps Mason would end up serving under him on a star-frigate someday.

Oliver knew the basics of spaceship server systems from a course at the Academy, but he didn't have the depth of knowledge Mason and Tiffany did. He was thankful for their detail-oriented personalities. He was thankful they paid attention in their courses.

"How long?" Oliver asked.

"Ten minutes at most," Mason answered. "Just have to sync this server back to the system once it's in the server rack."

"Great. Tiffany, will you be able to get Jahr des Eises reloaded into the NavCom?" Oliver asked. "We need to get there right away. I don't want to delay any longer than we must. The Übel are off to Enaid, I'm sure." He left out mentioning their parents.

She nodded. "Right away."

Footsteps on the metal stairs echoed in the corridor. Running. Oliver turned to see Austin enter the server room.

"Oliver," he said, slightly out of breath. "It's that guy you and Tiffany met. Mr. O'Farrell. He sent a message; it sounded like a distress call or something. He mentioned an attack."

Oliver charged for the bridge, blowing past Austin, who followed. They raced up the stairs. Obbin stood by the console. Oliver took his seat in the pilot's chair and pulled up the communications log. He replayed the message.

"Oliver and Tiffany, please. They've come for me. I've barricaded myself into a tunnel. I don't have long. Use my signal to find me." Something rumbled in the background. "Hurry!"

The message cut to static.

"That's it," Austin said.

Oliver heard Tiffany and Mason enter the bridge.

Who had come? The old man's voice no longer held the calm, steady tone Oliver had known from before. He was in serious danger. If there had been any doubt that they should go to Jahr des Eises and not head immediately for Enaid, it was gone now.

Oliver had seen Vedrik's treatment of the last set of clues. Obliteration. Although their destination was a highly populated planet, Oliver didn't think the Übel would hesitate to blow up artifacts. Perhaps they might destroy the clues with a lesser display of power. In the end, that wouldn't give Oliver and his siblings the information they needed to continue the quest or to keep up with their parents. This had been his concern all along, but Mr. O'Farrell's plea was even more urgent.

Mr. O'Farrell was the key to understanding more of their parents' mission. If he were captured and the Übel destroyed the clues, there would be no hope of ever finding them.

Oliver recalled the note his dad had left. He'd swiped it from the shelf in the chamber just before the entire underground cavern on Evad had been detonated. He recalled the Übel soldier Pyrock's maniacal laugh.

"Austin, stay here. If we get another message, call me over the intercom," Oliver said. "Is the server fixed?"

"Not qui—" Mason started.

"Then do it, Mason," Oliver commanded, sounding exactly like a general.

"Yes, sir." Mason saluted.

"I need to get something from my cabin. Tiffany, meet me in the library."

3.3

Encouragement

Tiffany waited for her brother in the library. Midnight had followed her and was curled up on a couch under one of the portholes. White glitter sparkled like diamonds in the pitch black outside the window. There were so many stars out there. How grand and expansive the universe was.

Oliver came into the library, interrupting Tiffany's thoughts. He handed her a slip of paper and smiled.

"What is this?" she asked.

"It's the note Dad left in the chess chamber," Oliver explained. "Read it."

The crisp paper crinkled in Tiffany's fingers. Her heartbeat surged as she held the link to her dad. His own handwriting marked the page.

"'Good job with the mTalk. You're doing great. Check the entry on the Valley of the Shadows. Keep safe. We're doing well and will see you soon,'" she read aloud. She looked at Oliver with a smile. "He saw the mTalk. He knew we were there."

Oliver nodded. "I wonder how they reacted when Vedrik ordered the room destroyed, and then the entire basin?"

"I hope they don't think we're dead."

"Me too," Oliver said. "But we mustn't get caught in those thoughts. I didn't know what the note was going to say, if it'd be a clue. This was better." Oliver forced a smile, but it quickly disappeared. "It's been tough, you know. I mean, I believe we can do this, and this note is a huge encouragement to me. But there were . . ." Oliver sighed, and Tiffany knew he was fighting to open himself up. "There were several times when I was ready to give up," he admitted.

"Me too," Tiffany said. "Before you found me, I was ready to do just that."

Tiffany expected Oliver to be frustrated. He'd given her instructions, and she'd not followed them. But he surprised her. He wasn't mad; he simply gave her a smile.

"Sis, we're going to do this. Dad and Mom know we're coming, and Dad thinks we're doing a good job. That's all we need to keep pushing ahead," Oliver said proudly. "But the note isn't the only reason I wanted to speak to you. It's Mr. O'Farrell's message."

She nodded.

"His last location in the transmission placed him in a tunnel along the maglev rail. I'd intended to contact him before we received the message . . ." Oliver hesitated. "Now, with him in immediate danger, I feel we have no choice. But I'm worried about putting us in danger too. We don't know who is after him. Attempting to save him puts our mission and our parents' rescue at risk. Still, I think we need him and the information he has. What do you think?"

Tiffany felt a surge of pride that Oliver would consider her counsel valuable. To her this meant that she had an equal voice in the leadership of their quest. She wasn't just a passenger: she was an asset.

"If Mr. O'Farrell is truly in danger . . ." Tiffany looked out the window. She had a nagging feeling that she should be cautious when it came to Mr. O'Farrell. "I mean, he was helpful before, and he's been supporting Dad and Mom's expeditions. Most of all, like you said, he does know a lot about what our parents were up to, more than we do."

"What is it?" Oliver asked.

"Didn't Mr. Krank warn us to be careful of Mr. O'Farrell?"

"Sort of."

"Why would he say that?"

Oliver shrugged. "Do we know that we can trust anyone?"

"We know we can trust each other," Tiffany said with a smile.

Oliver grinned. "I'm learning that more and more. So what do you want to do?"

Tiffany thought. She wanted to believe they had friends to rely on, that there were more experienced people whom they could trust. But this had all happened so quickly. Their world had been flipped on its head.

"Let's just play it close. We'll be careful of what we reveal to Mr. O'Farrell." Tiffany ran her hand through her thick brown hair. "We need to have a contingency plan in case things aren't what we expect."

"Plan B." Oliver smirked. "My sister, the special agent." His eyebrows rose. "Contingency plans."

"The one thing I've learned is that everything can change in the blink of an eye. Nothing is certain," Tiffany admitted. "I mean . . ." But she didn't finish her thought. It wasn't time to discuss philosophy.

The uncertainty of their quest was exactly why they needed to return Obbin to his home. The boy had rescued the twins, but they didn't know where the quest was taking them. Would they ever have another opportunity to return him? He was so young. Had he truly considered leaving his family forever? She doubted he had. If he were at all like Austin, he lived more in the moment than in the future.

"So we'll take Obbin back after we rescue Mr. O'Farrell?" Tiffany asked.

"Yes, assuming we can rescue him. Obbin belongs with his family."

"Good. They're probably very worried about him," Tiffany said. "Besides, it's one thing to have two young boys to keep track of, but a third? The boys have been the most unpredict-able variable of the whole quest."

"That's something we've got to get a hold on," Oliver said.

Again he'd said "we," and a sense of honor filled her. "We can do it."

"Let's go to the bridge before the boys get suspicious," Oliver suggested. "Mason should be about done with his project."

Tiffany folded her dad's note and started to tuck it into the pocket of her jacket, then hesitated. Her clothes were still damp from the rainstorm on Evad.

"I'm going to change," she said, looking at the note scrawled in her dad's handwriting. She would hold on to this scrap of paper for a long time.

3.4

Cathedral of the Star

Mason sat in the copilot's chair. The NavCom glowed before him. He'd dug out some clean Ultra-Wear clothing after fixing the server. Now he and Tiffany were testing their work, Tiffany looking over his shoulder. She too had changed, dressed now in a purple hoodie and gray pants.

A map of the city-planet Enaid was loading. It rotated on the screen. No buildingless gaps existed in the metropolis, save for one massive crater: an extinct volcano called Peipomi. The city spread out across the globe.

Although Enaid was not their first destination, Tiffany and Mason were determining where they would go on the planet. They didn't want to lose time exploring or researching once they arrived when they could use the spare time they had now.

"It could take years to search a city of this size. Are you sure there wasn't a clue in the message from the cloaked guy in the chamber on Evad?" Mason asked. "Nothing?"

Tiffany shook her head. "Let's watch the video again. As far as I remember, no one mentioned a location on Enaid."

Mason uploaded the video from the chess chamber into the *Phoenix's* computers. They skipped past nearly all the game, only stopping if their parents spoke. Mason watched intently, taking in the images of his parents and the few words they said. Their voices drew strange feelings within him: sadness and a measure of comfort at the same time.

The video zipped by a second time, then a third.

"You're right. Nothing. Just the planet's solar coordinates," Mason said when the clip ended.

Tiffany patted his head. "Perhaps Mr. O'Farrell will know."

"Do we really have time to go to Jahr des Eises?" asked Mason.

"Mr. O'Farrell is in trouble. He needs us," Tiffany said. "We can't leave him to be captured."

"But by the time we get there, it might already be too late," Mason said. "Is it wise to risk us all getting captured to save one person?"

Tiffany smiled. "We're a strong team, Mason. We've gotten through some pretty tight spots. Together we have proven that we have what it takes to survive."

Mason sighed. He looked out the window before him. Pinpricks of light littered the darkness of space. Space would seem so lonely and hopeless if not for the distant stars.

Stars. It hit him. He'd read something important.

"I'll be right back."

Mason took off for his cabin and found his bulging pack. He pulled out the first of the four-volume series, *The Veritas Nachfolger on Evad*. In the short time he'd read through it, Mason had found something about the origins of the people called the Veritas Nachfolger.

He tucked the book under his arm and ran. He passed Austin and Obbin, who were headed for the twins' cabin.

"Ready for more adventure?" Austin asked.

"I think so," Mason replied.

"Awesome. We'll see you in a minute," Austin said, and he and Obbin disappeared into the twins' cabin.

When Mason returned to the bridge, Oliver was busy working the pilot's screens. They'd be headed into hyper flight soon.

"Thanks for fixing the servers," Oliver said. "You're quite good at techno stuff."

Mason smiled, then set the book on the console and started flipping through it.

"Is that from Evad?" Tiffany asked.

"Yes, I read something about a star," Mason explained. "It had to do with the Veritas Nachfolger. I just have to find it."

"The Veritas Nachfolger?" Tiffany asked. "Oh, yes. They're the ones who used the cross as a symbol of Truth. Remember, Oliver?"

Oliver nodded.

"Brother Sam said he was part of a group called the Veritas Nachfolger," Austin said as he and Obbin entered the bridge.

"You know of them too?" Tiffany asked.

Austin nodded. "The guy who rescued me—us—everyone. He told me a little about them."

"Found it!" Mason exclaimed.

Austin and Obbin gathered around. Oliver kept working.

"Okay, the Veritas Nachfolger settled on Evad after the Empire annexed their planet and began enforcing its laws. In order to avoid compromising their beliefs, they fled Ynobe and abandoned their architectural masterpiece, the Cathedral of the Star." Mason stopped reading. "The entry goes on from there."

"I don't get it," Austin said.

"I do." Tiffany spoke excitedly. "The Cathedral of the Star was destroyed by a large explosion on Enaid hundreds of years ago. Ynobe and Enaid are the same place; the Federation renamed the planet. As for the Cathedral, the Federation allowed people to build on top of it. Layers of old tunnels and buildings are buried below the present city. Rumors say there are tunnels more than a thousand feet below the surface."

"Archeos has requested access to the ruins several times," Mason said. "The cathedral specifically. Dad and Mom were even on a team preparing to go. But each time, something changed at the last minute and the teams were denied entry."

"How are we going to get in then?" Austin asked.

Mason shook his head. "I don't know, but my guess is that's where we need to go."

"I agree," Tiffany said. "And look at this."

Mason and Austin leaned over her shoulder to see a listing of their parents' contacts on the screen. Tiffany had highlighted a name, and a series of information stemmed from it.

Name: Casper
Location: Casper's Stage, Performer's Alcove, Section 5712, Floor 15, Level 12, Enaid.
Transmission Code: No longer in service.
Notes: Must contact when on Enaid.

"So who is this guy?" Mason asked.

"This is all we know," Tiffany said. "But Mom and Dad made a note to contact him. That must mean something."

Mason agreed. "Casper . . . ?"

"I know. It doesn't sound familiar," Tiffany said. "I just hope he has helpful information."

"Just because Mom noted that he should be contacted doesn't mean we should go," Austin said. "They weren't planning to go to Enaid. Maybe she just wanted to say a casual hi next time they visited."

"When has anything related to our parents' work been casual?" Mason asked. "Enaid is the location of the Cathedral of the Star. Our parents tried getting access to its ruins many times and failed."

"Exactly, Mason. That's why we need to follow our parents' note and contact him. I am wondering if he has a connection to get us into the Cathedral," Tiffany said.

"How do we reach him with no transmission code?" Austin asked.

"We'll have to go to this address," Mason said.

"After we go to Jahr des Eises," Oliver interrupted. "Everyone strap in. We'll have plenty of time to discuss this in hyper flight. It's time to rescue our friend and take another one home."

As Oliver and Tiffany made the final preparations for hyper flight to Jahr des Eises, Oliver's mind buzzed with thoughts of the dangers of returning to the ice-laden planet. His previous experience hadn't been all that great. Now he was specifically taking his family there to rescue someone under siege by enemies Oliver didn't even know.

Tiffany changed their destination and entered the correct coordinates into the NavCom.

"Please confirm the coordinates: 123.34 X, 342.30 Y, 863.22 Z, Jahr des Eises," the *Phoenix*'s flight control system said.

"Yes," Tiffany confirmed.

"Hyper flight sequence engaged. Plotting course," the computer said.

Several applications popped up on the screen, displaying the final steps the flight computer was taking for the *Phoenix*'s jump into hyper flight.

"Everyone strapped in securely?" Oliver asked as a red strobe light began to flash. A chorus of "yeses" filled the room.

"Confirm hyper flight sequence initialization. Projected course is clear," the computer said.

Oliver touched an icon that flashed the word *jump*. Instantly, large blue numbers appeared on the screens, starting a count-down. Oliver's first jump to Jahr des Eises had been his first jump ever. It hadn't even been a week ago. This time Oliver was confident the jump to Jahr des Eises would be a success.

The computer spoke again. "Ten seconds to jump."

Oliver tapped the screen again, and titanium heat shields slid down to cover the three sections of the windshield.

"Eight seconds . . . "

"Here we go again," Mason called from the back row.

"And this time I get to enjoy it in a seat, not strapped inside a vent," Obbin admitted with excitement.

The twins laughed. Any anxiety from last time seemed to have passed.

So many things flashed across Oliver's mind: the past days, the possibilities of the future, the riddles and clues they needed to solve.

"Four seconds . . . "

"All right; here we go." Oliver looked at the screen.

"Three . . . two . . . one."

Oliver pressed against his seat under the force of the jump. A whistling noise filled the cabin momentarily and then ceased. The pressure slackened, and the invisible hold released him.

"Hyper flight stabilized," the computer informed them.

"You're getting good at this," Tiffany said.

Oliver smiled. "I guess I am."

"Home, here I come," Obbin said.

3.5

Intertwined

Once they were safely into hyper flight, Mason reminded Austin that he needed to fill them in on Brother Sam's revelations. The five gathered in the library.

"Our knowledge of the Übel barely scratches the surface," Austin said. "These guys are far more dangerous than we could have imagined."

He walked to the center table and sat in one of the chairs. The gazes of Obbin and his siblings were on him. "Brother Sam said he has information we need for our quest. He was very clear about that, that we were on a 'quest.' He gave me a cross necklace and said it was a key but also just one of the tools we need. He said he'd give all the keys to me, but we ran out of time. He was tracking our movements in the basin on Evad. He knew where we were at every moment, which makes me wonder if we were ever actually in any danger."

"The danger sure felt real to me," Mason said.

Austin looked at Tiffany and Oliver. "Our conversation ended because he had to rescue you. He said he would tell me more later and sent me through the tunnels. That's when I found Mason."

"Like I said, the danger was real," Mason said.

"So that's all you know?" Tiffany asked.

"No, not at all. Brother Sam told me the true history of the Übel, and he mentioned the Truth and what it is," Austin said. "We're in the middle of a battle between two forces with power beyond our understanding."

"What the Truth is?" asked Oliver.

"I have to get there," Austin said.

Oliver smiled and let Austin speak.

"A long time ago, a group of men attempted to wipe out the story of the Truth. Their goal was to 'cleanse humanity of its greatest weakness.' They acquired power and ruled the Federation—or Empire at that time. They became untouchable. The emperor was in the clutches of the men, though Brother Sam didn't say if he was one of them. Soon they became known as the Übel.

"Their wealth grew and so did their knowledge, until they believed they knew all they needed. At least, that's what Brother Sam said. They became paranoid. In order to maintain their position and control, they rewrote history. They created a past that reflected only peace, prosperity, and equality, and it became widely accepted as the truth. Apparently it was easier to wipe history clean than anyone would have expected. They changed it all with a few keystrokes."

"Like a virus?" Mason asked.

Austin shrugged. "Maybe. But it didn't end there. They set out to destroy any written text, any artifacts that remained to contradict their version of the truth. That was their greatest mistake."

"But what about everyone else? Didn't they reject the new history?" Tiffany asked.

"Brother Sam didn't say much about that."

"So how was destroying artifacts their greatest mistake?" Mason asked.

"The Übel's worst enemy wasn't an uprising but their very own bodies. They were aging and needed a way to live forever."

"Live forever?" Tiffany muttered. "Oliver, didn't you say something about that?"

"Vedrick said, 'And I give unto them eternal life; and they shall never perish,'" Mason quoted.

"That's it," Tiffany said.

"But how—" Oliver started.

"I'm getting there," Austin said impatiently. "Brother Sam said something I can't forget: 'This was not something they could discover with money or wisdom.' I think he meant eternal life. Brother Sam said the Übel had hidden the information that could grant them their desire."

"So there really is a way to live forever?" asked Oliver.

"Yes, according to Brother Sam," Austin said. "The Übel used technology to extend their lives, but it wasn't enough. New Übel leaders wanted eternal life so much that they let go of their control of the Empire to put all their effort into discovering the secret. That was when the Federation was born."

"Empire, Federation," Obbin said. "I think this has something to do with my people settling in the gorge."

"Brother Sam spoke of a battle for the Truth, one that started at the beginning."

"Beginning of what?" asked Mason.

"He didn't say, but he mentioned that darkness was winning. At least, that's how it seemed. The Veritas Nachfolger remained loyal to the Truth. And here is the part related to Vedrik's phrase. Brother Sam said, 'Eternal life is attainable but not in the form the Übel are seeking.' I didn't understand that."

Obbin cleared his throat. Austin looked at him, but the prince shook his head. Apparently the interruption was unintentional.

Austin continued. "Brother Sam also said the Übel will stop at nothing to find the secret and that the Übel's supreme commander has found a promising artifact. It'd been almost a hundred years since the last discovery, and apparently it was a good find because the Übel went all out. They even allowed archeological research to restart—under their supervision, of course. Brother Sam was clear that their reach and influence saturates every corner of the Federation."

"Our parents," Tiffany said.

"The Übel knew of their discovery at Dabnis Castle," Oliver added.

"I wonder if Mr. O'Farrell knows any of this?" asked Tiffany.

"How could he? He would have warned our parents if he had," Mason said.

"Yes, but Dad mentioned they knew the Übel were coming and that Vedrik had arrived slightly earlier than expected," Oliver said. "Vedrik even acknowledged it, like it was a game of cat and mouse."

"So if they knew . . ." Tiffany started.

Austin cleared his throat. "I'm not finished."

"Oh, sorry," his siblings said in unison.

"Thanks. Next Brother Sam told me about a friend he had tried to tell the Truth to, but the friend wouldn't listen and I guess went crazy."

A gasp escaped Obbin's lips.

"What's wrong?" Tiffany asked.

"Nothing," Obbin said. "Nothing."

"Brother Sam told me he would teach me how to discover the Truth for myself. He said he would give me the keys to do so. Then he said the most interesting thing. He said the Truth is a *who*, not a what."

"The Truth is a person?" asked Mason.

"I guess," Austin said.

"How would that be possible?" Tiffany asked. "He or she would have to be really old—at least thousands of years!"

"If the Truth knows the secret to eternal life, he's probably using it. So he could be thousands or millions of years old."

"I wouldn't want to live that long," Mason said.

"Did he say anything else about the person?" asked Tiffany.

Austin pushed back his bangs. "No, he only said that faith leads to the Truth. That's when we had to go. He needed to rescue you and sent me to find Mason." Austin stopped, remembering. "The number."

"What number?" Tiffany asked.

"There was a number and a letter on the slip of paper Brother Sam gave me," Austin said.

"He gave me a slip of paper with a number too," Obbin said. "Remember, I gave it to you." He looked at Mason.

"That's right," Mason said. "Did Brother Sam say anything to you? Did he reveal anything else?"

Obbin shook his head. "He only gave me the task to rescue you and get you the note. He led me to where I would find you. Then I waited."

That was a bit disappointing, but Austin knew a lot had been happening in the gorge and that Brother Samuel had been trying to help where he could.

"We have a note as well," Tiffany said. "Oliver found it after some Übel soldiers were trapped."

"Brother Sam," Oliver said. "He must have been the one who restrained all those soldiers in the net."

"And left the note," Tiffany said.

"A coordinate, if I remember right," Oliver said.

Tiffany nodded. "If we each got one, perhaps it's the location of something."

"Where is yours?" Austin asked.

"In my pack in my room," Tiffany said.

"And yours?" Austin looked at Mason.

"Right here," Mason said, lifting his pack from beside the chair.

"I left mine in my room," Austin said.

"You two, get your notes and meet back on the bridge," Oliver said. "If these are coordinates, we will want to check them on the NavCom."

Empty Space

O liver sat at the NavCom. Mason looked over his shoulder. They had already entered his coordinate: 120.1995 Y. The paper remained on the console. Now they awaited Tiffany and Austin.

Obbin sat in the back row of seats. He had a little book open on his lap and was reading. Mason had asked what it was, but the prince said he needed more time.

Obbin seemed very deep in thought, and Mason didn't want to pry any further. He knew what it was like to be bugged while trying to figure out something. If Obbin were like him, too many questions would distract him from coming to a conclusion.

Oliver hadn't noticed. He was busy rechecking the status of the *Phoenix* systems.

Austin was first back on the bridge. "112.1990 X," he said.

Mason watched as Oliver tapped in the second number. The star map closed in on two intersecting axes. However, this left an infinite number of possibilities on the third axis.

Austin bounced next to Oliver. He set his paper atop Mason's.

Mason smiled. His younger brother was always excited about adventure. He knew that in Austin's mind, the three coordinates, the unknown location, were an adventure waiting to happen.

Tiffany's soft footsteps told them of her arrival. "620.2011 Z," she said as she set the note on the console, the final in the stack.

An excited laugh slipped out of Austin.

Oliver tapped in the coordinate, and the intersect point slid across the third axis. Mason took a deep breath. What hidden or long-lost planet were they about to discover?

A red circle pulsed around the intersect spot on the screen. But in the center was . . . nothing.

"I don't see anything," Austin said.

Mason knew something was wrong. The circle around the intersect point should have been green, and there should have been a listing of statistics about the planet at that location. There was nothing.

"There has to be a reason Brother Samuel gave us these coordinates," Tiffany said.

"Of course, but what?" Mason asked.

"We could go there and see," Austin said. "Just because there isn't a planet there doesn't mean there isn't something else."

"Like what?" Mason asked.

"I don't know. A space station, a satellite, a beacon," Austin said. "Anything. The point is that Brother Sam is sending us there. So we should go."

"We don't have time to waste now," Oliver said. "We know we need to get to Jahr des Eises to rescue Mr. O'Farrell. Then we need to head to the coordinates one of Brother Sam's comrades gave us for Enaid. That's where our parents are headed now. Whatever is at these three coordinates will have to wait."

"What if the Übel get there first?" asked Austin.

"The Übel aren't going there. They're headed to Enaid," Oliver said. "They don't have these coordinates."

"If only Brother Sam had told you or Obbin more," Mason said.

"We could have tried to meet up with him before we left Evad," Austin said. "He did stop that fighter from shooting us down. Maybe he wanted to talk to us."

"We have to stay with our plan," Oliver said. "We don't know enough. Plus, I can't stop us in the middle of hyper flight."

"If he had wanted us to go to these coordinates, he would have told Obbin or said so in the note," Tiffany said. "Obbin?"

Everyone looked at the prince. He shook his head as he came to attention. "Yeah?"

"Brother Sam didn't say anything else to you about the coordinate he gave you?" Oliver asked.

"No. Nothing."

"Are you okay?" asked Tiffany.

"Yeah, yeah, I'm fine," Obbin said with a half smile.

"He's probably just nervous about facing his parents," Oliver whispered to his sister and brothers. "Let's just let him alone for now."

Tiffany nodded. "I think everyone should get some rest," she said. "One thing we have learned is this adventure—"

"Quest," interjected Austin.

"Thanks, Austin," Tiffany said, but her voice wasn't appreciative. "We have learned that this quest is unpredictable. We should take advantage of the downtime we have. These planets have entirely different days and nights. The Übel have numerous soldiers to take shifts. We don't. We need to rest."

"Good idea, sis," Oliver said. "Everyone to their bunks. Try to get some sleep." He stretched his arms as he stood.

Mason was the last Wikk on the bridge. Obbin still sat in the last row of seats.

"Obbin, are you coming?" Mason asked.

He looked up, startled from his thoughts. "Uh . . . yeah."

"What are you reading?" Mason asked, hoping the boy had had enough time to think.

"Well, it's just"—Obbin sighed—"do you really think Brother Sam's friend went crazy?"

"I guess. I mean, that's what Austin said the guy told him," Mason said. "We don't have any reason to not believe Brother Sam."

"Okay," Obbin said. "Then I guess it's nothing." He stretched, but Mason wasn't sure what Obbin was really thinking. "Let's get some rest."

3.7

Mr. Fixit

The *Phoenix* was in hyper flight, cruising back to the planet they had visited just two days ago. Austin understood why Oliver wanted to take Obbin home—he didn't like it, but he understood. Technically he was a bystander: a kid who had got more than he had expected. At the same time, he and Obbin had formed a friendship. The prince had an equally adventurous side; he was brave, skilled, and smart, just like Austin. The only real difference was their age and the fact that Obbin was blue. Still, Austin knew Obbin's return was for the best.

Even though this was a detour from their real quest, it was also important for them to rescue Mr. O'Farrell. After all, he had contributed so much to Austin's parents' research. He had even picked up the tab for the parts to fix the *Phoenix*. That was pretty cool.

Austin was ready to meet the old man, but first they had to save him from an unknown assailant. His mind raced through the possibilities. It might be Übel of course, or Corsairs, or the Federation, or bandits, or even that warehouse guy, Schlamm. Any group was a possibility. The distress call hadn't given them much to go on. They only knew he was in danger and that he was in a tunnel in the vast woods along the maglev rail.

Austin wasn't ready to rest. This segment of hyper flight was short compared to some of the others: only two hours and a few minutes. The first flight to Jahr des Eises from their home planet, Tragiws, had been five hours. He smiled. The distance they could travel in only a few hours was unbelievable.

Obbin lay next to him in his bunk. Though the prince was out cold, Austin doubted he'd be able to sleep. Even Mason had dozed off in his bunk below. Usually he kept Austin up late because he was reading.

Austin's mind raced. They'd already used up most of this trip talking about Brother Samuel's story and tracking the three coordinates. Now they were returning to a planet they'd barely escaped the first time. He had to be ready, especially since they knew they were heading directly for a confrontation. For once they were on the attack!

Not only were they possibly going into battle, but the weather would be against them as well. The entire planet would be covered in ice. From what he'd been told, the winters were so long and cold that the city of Brighton was under lockdown for the duration of Eises. No one was allowed out or in. If Mr. O'Farrell were trapped, how long could he survive the bitter cold? They had to hurry.

What if there was more to the distress call? What if it was a trap? The Übel might know the Wikks would come back for Mr. O'Farrell. Had they trapped him just to lure the kids back? Or were the Corsairs involved? Oliver had mentioned that Corsairs had traded the McGregors' ship, the *Griffin*, to the parts trader. That meant they had attacked and captured Rand and Jenn McGregor. The Corsairs might have discovered that the Wikks and McGregors had discovered the path back to Ursprung. Maybe they wanted to find the fabled planet and the secrets it held.

Thinking of the McGregors, Austin wondered where Tiffany's friend was. Had Ashley been with her parents when their ship had been attacked? She'd tutored Austin back at Bewaldeter. He'd never have passed Planetary Linguistics without her help. Now it seemed no one was safe.

There was also Brother Sam's tale. It had revealed a huge, secretive society that spiderwebbed the Federation. Surely the Übel had spies on Jahr des Eises as well. It made sense for them to have been behind Mr. O'Farrell's call.

How could his family trust anyone? How could they know the truth? Or Truth, as Brother Sam had said. A person. That interested Austin the most. This Truth was someone great, someone powerful. Talking about Brother Sam had made Austin ponder his story further. Brother Sam had said that faith was the way to the Truth. Faith in what, though? He hadn't explained that part. Faith in a man who knew how to live forever?

Austin's head hurt. Too much thinking. He needed to distract himself. He looked across the cabin. If he stayed in bed, he'd only grow more anxious. There were too many questions. He wasn't like Mason. Thinking and solving riddles was stressful to him, not fun.

What might he do?

He could try to fix something. Maybe the mTalks.

The three devices that had been in the underground chamber were unusable, probably fried by the explosion. Working on the devices would occupy Austin's wandering mind.

Austin climbed from his bunk and found Mason and Obbin's mTalks inside a drawer. He located his stashed tool belt. Having things securely stored was important. If the interior pressure dropped or the internalized-gravity stabilizers failed, things would fly all over the cabin. With all the evasive flight maneuvers Oliver had been using, that was a real possibility.

Hyper flight wasn't such a case. The ship could still maneuver, but if ever you felt a twisting while in hyper flight, you weren't likely to feel anything else after. An image of the *Phoenix* disintegrating flashed in his mind. A dreadful thought indeed.

Austin gathered the wrist-worn devices and his tools and headed for the library. He poked his head into Oliver's cabin. His older brother was asleep, but his broken mTalk remained on his wrist. He'd fix it later. Disturbing Oliver would only let his older brother know he wasn't resting.

In the library Austin sat on a stool in front of the long countertop where artifacts were analyzed—or, in this instance, gadgets fixed.

First, the basics. Austin tried to turn on the device.

Nothing.

The mTalk simply wouldn't come to life. Austin flipped it over and looked for a way to get inside. He found a hatch on the back that needed to be released.

Austin waved a small wand called a Magnilox across the back of the hatch, and it popped open. He began by removing all the components: the storage disk, camera, speaker, microphone, receiver, transmitter, screen, and power supply. All minute in size. All vital to the mTalk's operation.

Austin would have to test each component separately to see if one or multiple systems had failed. He suspected that the explosion in the underground chamber had been caused by an electromagnetic pulse like the one that had damaged the *Phoenix*. The pulse would have shorted out anything within range, including the mTalks. He'd probably have to reinstall the operating application.

Only when he was inventing or working on gadgets could Austin tolerate this much attention to detail. It wasn't work to him. It was exciting.

As he tested each piece, he found that the power supply and transmitter had been damaged. The operating software also needed a reboot. Extra components might be stored in the cargo bay, but he doubted there would be enough to fix all three damaged devices.

Maybe there were extra mTalks in storage. That was a real possibility. Austin slipped the pieces of the mTalk into a drawer along with his tool kit and headed for the cargo bay. He was careful to be quiet as he passed each cabin, although their hatches were shut.

As he looked over the large storage bay, a guilty feeling swept over him when he saw the damaged sky scooter still lying on its side. Though he'd tried to blame Mason, Austin knew he was equally responsible for its destruction.

What if he could repair it? When it had fallen over, its wing and rudder had been damaged. Those things, he could fix. A crack slithered across the windshield as well. He would need to find a sealant compound.

With a new task in mind, Austin skipped down the steps, putting the search for extra mTalks on hold. Fixing the sky scooter was more important.

Circling the flying craft, he confirmed that his memory had served him well. The damage appeared to be superficial. None of the systems appeared damaged.

He could do this. He could fix the ship for his family. He could make up for his earlier mistake. His time apart from them on Evad had made Austin realize that his attitude and actions had been wrong. Brother Sam had revealed the plot of those who had taken his parents and even now sought the rest of his family. Austin had no one but his brothers and sister. They were the only three he could truly rely on. Though everyone was getting along now, he still needed to own up to his wrongs. Obbin had mentioned apologizing to his family; Austin needed to apologize to his.

Austin glanced at the black sky scooter. Fixing the craft would be part of his apology: a peace offering. But it still wouldn't be enough. He'd have to verbalize his apology too. It was the right thing to do.

How long did he have? Austin checked the clock on the computer console used for accessing the *Phoenix*'s cargo manifest. He had about three quarters of an hour before they'd arrive at Jahr des Eises.

It was plenty of time to make the repairs, or at least most of them. Austin located sealant for the windshield and liquid welding-calk for the wing. After a quick search, he discovered the cargo indeed contained another ten mTalks, more than enough for him and his siblings.

After finding some heavy-duty tools from the maintenance cabinet, Austin set to work. He moved the service crane into position and unstrapped the sky scooter from where it had been fastened down. The crane lifted the damaged craft off the cargo bay floor. Austin could now access the damaged areas easily.

It was time to get busy.

3.8

Awakened

The passage was black as night. The light from his mTalk bounced off the walls of the cave as he ran. He knew they were close, but he had no idea where the tunnel led, no idea how to escape. His ankle twisted as the tip of his shoe struck a rise in the cave floor.

He stumbled. Though his ankle throbbed, he kept going. He'd never seen anything like the creatures that chased him. They were closing in. They would tear him apart when they caught up.

"Oliver!" cried Tiffany.

His sister's face glowed in the passage ahead.

"Oliver," Tiffany called again. His shoulders shuddered.

Then his eyes opened. Oliver looked up at his sister. Her hair was still in a bun, she was wearing a purple hoodie, and they were in his cabin.

He'd been having a nightmare. He felt something on his chest. Midnight padded off him and stretched out on her back beside him.

"You look terrible," Tiffany continued. "I was coming from the galley when I heard you scre—shout out."

Beads of sweat dripped off his forehead as he sat up "I . . . it. There were these creatures. They were after me. I couldn't escape." His voice rose; his breathing came fast. He had to get control.

"Oliver, it's okay. It was just a dream."

He looked at his sister. Her expression was calming.

"We're still on the *Phoenix*," she said. Midnight mewed, Tiffany opened her arms, and the cat jumped into them. "It's nearly time for us to come out of hyper flight. We should get the boys and get to the bridge."

"You're right." Oliver looked toward the porthole in his cabin. "I just need a minute. I need to change." The collar of his shirt was soaked with sweat. He turned, grunting as the wound on his side stung.

"Are you okay?" asked Tiffany.

"It's this cut," Oliver said. "Is there anything we can do to numb it?"

Tiffany shook her head. "No. I mean, yes, but we wouldn't want to."

"Why?"

"You're so active that you'd likely tear it open or do serious damage if the pain didn't warn you that you were putting too much strain on your injury."

Oliver touched his side tenderly. "You're right."

Tiffany stood up. "I'll tuck you into my cabin," she said to Midnight as she snuggled her nose against the cat's head. Her purr thrummed loudly.

Tiffany left, and Oliver took in a deep breath, covering his face with his hands. He had to get a hold on himself. The dream had been so vivid. In the back of his mind, he could still hear the screeches of the creatures. He shivered.

A series of small beeps rang from an alarm built into the communications console near the door. He'd set it for fifteen minutes before the hyper flight disengaged. He had to go.

He was ready to get on with the mission and put the sleep-invading visions out of his mind. He grimaced as he removed the sweat-soaked shirt and again as he slipped on a clean one.

The injury in his side continued to impede his abilities, a stubborn reminder of the dangers of the tasks ahead.

He nearly fell over as he crossed into the corridor, but not because of his injury. Mason and Obbin ran toward the cargo bay, sweeping him aside. He looked after them and saw Tiffany already on the overlooking balcony.

"What's going on?" Oliver asked, but they were too committed to their destination to answer. He dashed after them.

In the cargo bay, he found Austin standing next to two sky scooters. The craft sat side by side, both secured and plugged in to their respective charging cables. Two? Had Austin fixed the damaged scooter? The once-broken craft even looked better than the other. Oliver and Tiffany's trip to Brighton had put many dents and scratches into the sky scooter they had used. The unused one sat ready for action.

"Austin, did you do this?" Oliver asked. He already knew the answer. The youngest Wikk looked up at his three siblings and Obbin and smiled, beaming with pride at everyone's admiration.

"Wow!" Mason said as he started down the stairs. "It looks perfect."

"It's not perfect," Austin admitted, "but it will fly."

Oliver, Tiffany, and Obbin were quick to join the twins on the deck of the cargo bay.

"This is great," Tiffany said. "We'll need these."

Oliver was about to speak again, but Austin stopped him. "Look, I'm really sorry for how I acted." He paused. "I know I was wrong. I know that it was my fault this thing got broken and that Mason and I got captured. Running off on Evad was wrong. I shouldn't have abandoned you. I've been trying to be someone I'm not." Austin looked down at his feet. "At least, someone I can't be without working with you guys. I really am sorry."

Mason hugged his brother. "It's okay. I forgive you."

"As do I," said Tiffany, joining in the hug.

Oliver smirked. "Brother, I forgive you too. I'm glad that you want to be part of the team. We've all made mistakes, but—"

"Oliver, just give us a hug," Tiffany said. He obeyed.

"I'm actually glad you left the ship. Otherwise I might not have met you guys or come along on this adventure," Obbin said.

The four Wikks turned to look at the blue prince.

Oliver smiled. It was true. Things had worked out for the best. It was clear that something greater was at work. It seemed that regardless of what happened, bad or good, a path lay ahead of them—a path they themselves could not control.

"It's not that I want to break this up, but we do need to get to the bridge. We'll be coming out of hyper flight very soon," Oliver reminded them.

One by one they started up the stairs.

"I'm glad you fixed the scooter. And I am sorry too," Mason told Austin. "Your experience in the jungle must have been something."

"Why? Because I apologized?" Austin asked.

Oliver heard the older of the twins grunt his approval.

Numbers flashed on the pilot's screen as Oliver entered the bridge. They were getting very close to their destination, although they might be many light years away if they dropped out of hyper flight at that moment.

"Take your seats please," Oliver said. A series of clicks let him know they were all getting settled.

"Oliver, do you want me to try to contact Mr. O'Farrell when we come out of hyper flight?" Tiffany asked.

"Not right away. Let's assess the situation first, see what condition the planet is in and also if we get any transmissions from Brighton. Then we'll scan the area. See if we pick up anything. Any sort of enemy ship."

"We're cloaked," Mason reminded them.

"That's true. Still, I want to wait to see if we receive any new transmissions before we act," Oliver decided. "Or if we can pick up any chatter."

"Chatter?" Tiffany asked.

"Communications between other people," Austin said.

"We'll have to be careful as we approach Mr. O'Farrell's location," Oliver said.

"What if it's a trap? Maybe the Übel expect us to come to his rescue, and they're using him to lure us in," Austin said.

Oliver turned and smiled at Austin. The kid knew his stuff. He'd make a good strategist. "My thoughts exactly. We'll be careful."

The seconds counted down.

"Everyone ready? Here we go," Oliver warned.

3.9

Into the Midst

T he controls slipped under Oliver's hands. He'd done this several times in the last few days, but the maneuver still brought perspiration to his brow and palms. It was time, but he stalled.

Numbers blinked on the screen before him as the *Phoenix* raced toward its destination.

Their first task was to rescue Mr. O'Farrell, but their second was to go to Cobalt Gorge. Oliver had not seen the home of Obbin's people, the Blauwe Mensen, but his brothers had. He'd heard of the blue soldiers capturing the boys and now sat just a row in front of one of their princes.

It was time.

The *Phoenix* dropped out of hyper flight at Oliver's command. His body felt as if it were being sucked forward by an invisible force. The straps of his harness pressed into his chest, but the feeling soon ended.

They were out of hyper flight.

A flurry of information cast across the displays of the *Phoenix*. Red squares flashed, highlighting other spacecraft.

Close spacecraft.

Oliver tapped the screen. The large heat shields slid clear of the windows, revealing a sight that struck fear and confusion into his mind.

Oliver jerked the controls right. "Hold on!" he called as he spun the *Phoenix*, then dropped it ninety degrees.

"What—?" Austin started, but stopped as a brilliant orange glow exploded before them.

A gray ship of massive size passed in front of them, large enough that a dozen ziggurats from Evad could have fit within it. It was ablaze with activity. Zips of purple lasers, orange streaks of fire flaming from the tails of hyperion torpedoes, and bright red orbs fired out from the cruiser in all directions.

Smaller ships twisted out of the barrage, firing their own arsenals of lasers, missiles, and torpedoes.

Oliver twisted the *Phoenix* the other way as a series of glowing red globes thundered their direction. He looked at the status of the cloaking device. It seemed to be active and working. The ships' fire was not targeted at them.

"Can they see us?" Austin asked.

"No, the cloak is working," Oliver promised. He jerked back on the controls to miss a stream of purple streaks. This time he felt something tear in his side. He couldn't stop with his family's lives hanging in the balance. The battle was too near, whether it was aimed at them or not.

Oliver noticed Vor Eis in the distance. The sister planet to Jahr des Eises had not been colonized due to its inhospitable atmosphere. Should he make course for the empty planet in an attempt to find a safe haven? They could wait out the confrontation on the *Phoenix*.

"What's going on?" Tiffany asked.

"A battle, of course," Austin said.

"I can see that. I meant that the NavCom isn't identifying the ships."

The *Phoenix* was now flying away from the battle.

"I'm getting us a safe distance away, but we're not leaving . . . not yet, anyway," Oliver explained. He'd dismissed his idea of fleeing to Vor Eis. "I think that ship is a Corsair ship, and those fighters look just like the ones the Übel used to chase us off Tragiws and to patrol Evad."

"The Übel and Corsairs are fighting?" Mason asked.

"That's how it appears," Oliver said.

One of the alleged Übel fighters took a direct hit from a torpedo, and the pilot's protective capsule jettisoned away from the fuselage.

"Got him!" Austin cheered.

"How do you know the Corsairs are on our side?" Mason asked.

"I don't, but at least one of the enemy is down," Austin admitted.

The prince hadn't spoken at all. "Obbin, are you all right?" Oliver asked.

Obbin shook his head. "Something is wrong with my family." His body was rigid as he sat up. A frown marred his face.

Tiffany looked back at him. "I'm sure they're fine. This battle doesn't have anything to do with them," she assured the prince.

"Besides, I'll have you there very soon," Oliver promised. "We'll stay cloaked and sneak around the battle."

That seemed to relax Obbin slightly. He sat back in his seat and released a captive breath.

As they flew a wide arc outside the firefight, another Übel fighter was taken out. A large explosion rocked the massive cruiser.

There was no sign of the *Skull*. Oddly enough, Oliver would have liked to see it. The large black cruiser's presence would have meant that the Übel were not on their way to Enaid. Now he assumed the worst: Vedrik and his parents were on their way to the next clue.

The *Phoenix* slipped completely past the battle. Now it was time for Oliver to take on the next key maneuver: entry into the Jahr des Eises atmosphere.

A shiver coursed his body as he recalled the first time he'd landed on the icy planet. The winter storm had just begun to stretch over the world, beckoning forth a yearlong winter. Accompanying lightning and powerful updrafts had struck the *Phoenix* and nearly brought the kids to a disastrous end. Oliver had curtailed the ship's plummeting spin and brought the *Phoenix* down safely, but barely. He hoped the storm's violent onset had subsided into something like the peaceful winters of the planet Noxaj.

"Commencing entry into Jahr des Eises," Oliver said. "Tiffany, the moment we cross into the atmosphere, I need you to run a scan of the coordinates from Mr. O'Farrell's transmission."

"Will do," Tiffany said.

The entry was uneventful. The *Phoenix* glided through the now-clear sky. White snow blanketed the barren forest below. Tall leafless trees stretched for miles like brown needles. Only groves of pines added color to the landscape.

"Oliver, I've sent the scan to your screen," Tiffany said.

He looked at the screen, taking his eyes from the wintery terrain.

"Nothing . . ." Oliver said. "Is that what you have, Tiffany?"

"The scans didn't pick up anything," Tiffany said. "Should we try to contact him?"

Oliver shook his head. "We'll have to go ourselves. Our transmissions could be picked up. Just because our scan isn't revealing anything doesn't mean someone isn't there. They could be cloaked like us."

"So what do we do?" asked Mason.

"We're going in on foot," Oliver said.

"We?" Tiffany asked.

"I am taking Obbin with me," Oliver said.

"Obbin?" Austin asked, his voice edgy.

"I assume you know these woods well?" Oliver said. His comment was directed at the prince but meant to hold off Austin's opposition.

"Yes," Obbin said. "My brother Rylin and I explored it a lot."

"Good," Oliver said. "We'll land near Mr. O'Farrell's last known location and leave the ship cloaked."

"How will you find the ship when you come back?" Mason asked.

"I'll store the coordinates in the mTalk," Oliver said.

"And if they use an electromagnetic pulse to wipe out your gear?" Mason asked.

"Then I doubt we'll be coming back alone, in which case you should escape," Oliver said.

"Oliver," Tiffany said.

"I'll leave a LuminOrb outside," Oliver said. "They're inconspicuous."

"That's better," Mason said.

"How long will you be?" Tiffany asked.

"An hour at most," Oliver said. "If we can't find Mr. O'Farrell quickly, we'll come back. Austin, you're in charge of security while we are gone." Oliver hoped this would reconcile Austin to not being on the rescue mission. "I'll take a Zinger for me and Zapp-It for Obbin."

"Should I get one of the Übel rifles you captured?" Austin asked.

Oliver nodded. "Thanks for reminding me. I'll take one and leave you the Zinger."

Austin snorted.

"The StunShot Rifle SI can be lethal, so I'd rather you not use one until I show you how to handle it," Oliver explained.

"Can they be unlethalized?" asked Mason.

"Maybe," Oliver said. "Obbin, I still want you to take the Zapp-It."

"Do we have any other weapons?" asked Tiffany.

"I didn't really check, come to think of it," Oliver admitted. "On Jahr des Eises I saw the Zapp-It in a crate when I was searching for the tents and sleeping bags. On Evad I was looking for some tools for our expedition when I happened on a case with the Zinger in it. I never searched for more weapons."

"We'll check for them while you're out with Obbin," Austin said.

"Can you also look at the electronics we captured from the Übel?" Oliver asked. "I've not taken the time to see what we got. There might be something of use."

"Will do," said Mason.

"You two be careful," said Tiffany.

"We will," said Austin.

"Not you two. Oliver and Obbin."

"I'll secure the ship," Austin said. "We need a reentry pass phrase."

"How about 'the Übel lose'?" suggested Mason.

"Perfect," Austin said.

Rescue

The side hatch opened. A gust of icy wind and snow flurries greeted them, accompanied by a few feet of snow that had piled against the outside of the hatch. Obbin and Oliver were outfitted in Bliz-Zero gear. A white and gray camouflage pattern covered their parkas, pants, and facemasks. The outfits were thick and protected the wearer from the cold and dampness of snow. If proper eye-, hand-, and foot-gear were worn, one could survive in sub-100 degrees if necessary. Not for long, of course, but long enough to be rescued. A set of IZEE-150 boots and gloves and RetinaX goggles were also needed. Oliver knew his grandfather's Ultra-Wear clothing wouldn't stand against the frigid temperatures outside; otherwise he'd have worn it.

Fortunately an extra set of Bliz-Zero gear had been packed for each for the Wikks, and one of the twins' sets fit the prince just right. Obbin's blue face stood out brightly against the stark white of the outfit.

The Bliz-Zero gear would keep Oliver and Obbin warm and dry, but it would equally impede their ability to fight if they were confronted by an enemy. The heavy gear on top of Oliver's injured side compounded the danger of the mission.

He and Tiffany had sneaked off to his room to check on the injury. Thankfully the stitches had held despite the twinge during the space battle. Tiffany had agreed to apply some more NumbaGlu to ease the pain, deciding that it was necessary. It would be on Oliver to safeguard his side and not exert himself too far.

Obbin's knowledge of the area and his outdoor survival skills would hopefully help them avoid any lurking danger.

Oliver checked the weapon in his hand. The StunShot Rifle SI could kill someone if he set it wrong. He checked and double-checked to make sure it was on stun. The thought of ending someone's life made him shiver. He almost wanted to go back to the *Phoenix* and take the Zinger instead, but he didn't want to leave his sister and brothers defenseless, and he didn't want Austin to be handling the rifle. Not yet, at least.

"Ready?" Oliver asked.

Obbin nodded and flashed his Zapp-It. A sizzle of blue electricity glowed between the two metal tips. That was the sort of firepower Oliver liked: enough to subdue his opponent temporarily so he could get in control of the situation. It seemed the escalating danger of the quest meant a need for more powerful weapons.

Oliver remembered a history lesson from his pre-Academy days at Bewaldeter. In an arms race between two warring factions, the Eurekanites and the Roanokians had eventually weakened each other so much with their ever-increasingly powerful weapons that they had never stood a chance when the Federation had moved in to annex them.

"Are we going?" asked Obbin. "It's not getting any warmer."

Oliver had been staring off into the trees as he thought. "Sorry."

He looked down at his mTalk. Austin had found ten of them in the cargo, and everyone had been given a new one. The small wrist devices were invaluable. Each small gadget held so much information, the best means of communication, and many tactical uses.

Oliver started out. The snow came up to his waist. This was going to be harder than he had expected. They couldn't use a sky scooter because its black exterior would stand out against the white surroundings. Plus, navigating around the many trees had proven to be an arduous task for him and Tiffany last time.

Oliver turned back. His eyebrows rose. The *Phoenix* was truly invisible with the cloak on. The only sign of its existence was a rectangle of light and the metallic interior of the ship where Obbin stood. The prince appeared to float in an open door. The only other signs of the ship's presence were the deep indentions where the *Phoenix*'s landing gear rested in the snow.

Obbin smirked at Oliver. "What?"

"If the door were closed and I were walking, I would run right into the side of the ship," Oliver said. He reentered the ship and shut the hatch. "We need a better way through the snow."

Oliver and Obbin headed for the cargo bay.

"What's wrong?" Mason asked.

"You two look like a couple of snowmen," Austin laughed.

"Ha ha," Oliver said. "The snow is too deep, Mason. It'll take hours to wade through it. Do we have any gear to help us move quicker?"

"Why not go over it?" Austin said. "We have hover boards."

"Why didn't you suggest them before?" Oliver asked.

"Just noticed them on the cargo manifest," Austin said.

Oliver grunted. He needed to take some time to see what they had available. He'd started to look a few times, but something had always came up.

"Do you know where they are?" Oliver asked.

Austin let the Zinger hang across his back as he pulled up the cargo manifest on the computer. "Crate 29."

"Have you found any other Zingers or Zapp-Its?" Oliver asked. He wanted to abandon the rifle if at all possible.

Austin shook his head. "No, none came up when I searched. Not even the ones you found."

"That's odd, isn't it?" Oliver said.

"Not really," Mason said. "If Dad and Mom knew they might be attacked, they wouldn't have listed weapons so their enemies could find them. My guess is Dad just remembered what crates they were in."

"Then this will have to do." Oliver lifted the rifle carefully. "Let's try this again."

A few minutes later, Oliver and Obbin stood at the open hatch, each with a hover board in hand. This time Austin joined them. He wore a hoodie and his Ultra-Wear pants, but he still looked cold.

"Do you know how to use these?" Austin's lips quivered.

"Yes, I do," said Oliver, his voice testy. He was warm in the gear, and the delay was getting to him. He was ready to be on Enaid, yet they had to rescue the old man and go to Obbin's home.

"I wasn't talking to you," Austin said. "I meant Obbin." He crossed his arms over his chest and rubbed.

Oliver sighed. Of course. "Sorry."

"I've used a board before. Rylin and I mudslide in the gorge if too much rain soaks the valley. But those boards touch the ground unless we hit a jump."

"You'll have to tell me more about that later! It sounds cool," Austin said. "But at least you understand how to balance. I'll just explain how to hover. Tap this pressure sensor at the front of the board, and it will accelerate." Austin pointed to a series of black rings. "Then let off to slow. They don't go very high off the ground, but you can gain altitude by leaning back and accelerating. Lean forward to go back down." Austin made the motion, and Obbin nodded. "Twist your ankle whichever direction you want to go. That should be it."

"I think I got it. Thanks, Austin," Obbin said.

"Good. I'll lock the ship down when you leave," Austin said. "Remember the reentry pass phrase."

"All right," Oliver said. "Thanks. Now go and get warm."

Austin nodded, his teeth chattering.

"Obbin, are you ready?" Oliver asked.

"Yep."

"I almost forgot." Oliver took out a LuminOrb and squeezed it once. He tossed it outside the ship. The small globe glowed blue as it fell into the snow. "Let's go."

Tiffany sat before the NavCom. She tried to widen the radius of space around the three intersect points, but nothing came up within a light year. What could have been at the coordinates?

She wished there was a way to contact Brother Sam or the *Eagle*. Since the ships were the same model, she searched through the *Phoenix* contact logs in hope of some past reference or transmission between them, but there was nothing.

"Why would he give us three coordinates to nothing?" asked Tiffany. She stroked Midnight's thick black fur. She'd brought the cat back out from her room since they would be waiting for a little while.

"He wouldn't," Mason said. He sat in the second row of seats, a stack of Übel electronics next to him.

"Did you meet him?"

"Well, no, but from what I know about him, it doesn't seem like something he would do."

"Perhaps," Tiffany said. "But based on what we know, a lot of people are trying to discover this secret. It seems many are willing to go to extreme lengths. I wouldn't put anything past anyone at this point."

Mason shrugged. He lifted an oval-shaped device and looked at it closely. Tiffany looked back at the stars.

Mason spoke up again. "Brother Sam did say he would tell Austin more. And he found us on Evad. He'll find us again."

"Yes, but what if we were supposed to go there first?" asked Tiffany.

"I think Oliver was right," Mason said. "We got direct coordinates from the red-cloaked guy in the chess chamber. Our parents are headed there, and we should head there too."

Midnight meowed. She stood and rubbed her head against Tiffany's chin. "My friend Ashley would have liked you," Tiffany told her. "We always wanted to have a cat in our dorm, but pets were strictly forbidden." She laughed as Midnight's tail tickled her. "Ashley once tried to keep a lizard she'd found in the forest. But it escaped right into the floor chaperone's room. We had to serve in the cafeteria for a month after that, and our lizard was released back into the wild."

"I didn't know that," said Mason. "You said you were volunteering."

Tiffany blushed. "It was less voluntary than we would have liked."

"Tiffany, my sister, a rule breaker?"

"I told Ashley we'd get in trouble."

"But you still let her keep it."

"Well, it was cute. I mean, for a lizard. It had big bulgy eyes and purple spots all across its back. And it had the longest pink tongue."

Midnight started licking her front paw.

"You are a good cat," Tiffany said.

"You know, that thing isn't really a cat. It's a cub to whatever those creatures were on Evad," Mason reminded her. "That means it's going to get a lot bigger."

Tiffany pulled Midnight close. "You'll always be nice, won't you?" she said in her best baby talk.

The cat meowed in answer.

Oliver swept a branch aside. This was the location of the distress call. It appeared that Mr. O'Farrell had hunkered down within a maglev tunnel.

Oliver followed Obbin toward Mr. O'Farrell's hideout. The prince had told Oliver he had indeed explored the area with his brother, Rylin. Though the terrain looked different with most of the foliage dormant, he knew a way into the tunnel without going directly along the magnetized railway.

There was no sign of an enemy present. No evidence of a struggle or fight. This should have made Oliver relax but instead suggested that this might very well be a trap with the old man as the bait. Übel or Corsairs were probably waiting.

Oliver double-checked his weapon. It was set to stun and held a full charge. He was ready.

Obbin pointed to two large boulders. "There's an air shaft behind those. We can climb down it without too much trouble. Rylin and I used to drop onto maglev trains. They're the quickest way to get to places that would take us days to walk to."

"How fast do they go?" Oliver asked. "The one Tiffany and I nearly collided with was blazing fast."

Obbin shrugged. "Pretty fast."

Oliver grunted, recalling the amazing speed of the train.

"We did have a plan," Obbin admitted. "We always dropped a tree across the tracks so the maglev had to stop inside the tunnel."

"Didn't they ever wonder why trees always fell at that spot?"

"The trains are primarily automated. They have retractable blades and a scoop to clear the rail."

The two climbed up the sloping rock surface, abandoning their hover boards behind a tree, but not their weapons. The stone was slick, and Oliver lost his footing several times. The tip of his rifle bounced against the rock, sizzling as the electrified prongs touched snow.

The two boulders split apart, leaving the narrowest gap of entry. Oliver turned sideways and raised his arms and rifle above his head. The puffy jacket made it difficult to squeeze through. "Obbin, I've got to take this off."

"But it's freezing out," Obbin said. He'd barely gotten through the crevice himself.

"I can't make it otherwise." Oliver backed out and began unzipping the Bliz-Zero Gear.

"Why don't I just go on my own?"

"It's too dangerous. We don't know what might be in there," Oliver said. "Besides, you've not met Mr. O'Farrell. He might think it's a trick."

"I'll just go far enough to see if he's there," Obbin said. "If he is, I'll come back and get you."

Oliver hesitated.

"You won't be any good if you freeze to death," Obbin said. "Besides, I have my Zapp-It."

Oliver looked at the mTalk. It was negative five degrees.

"Okay, but once you see him, stop," Oliver said. "Don't make contact. Just come back."

Oliver stood behind the boulders, keeping his eyes on the wide tree trunks with glances at the mTalk. He kept his rifle at the ready. It hummed from the high level of charge. Oliver constantly updated the scans of the surrounding area on his mTalk. He wasn't going to be caught off guard by any enemy.

"Oliver." Obbin's voice echoed up the airshaft.

"I'm here."

"He's not," Obbin said.

Oliver looked at his mTalk. "We're right at the spot. Did your signal overlap with the transmission coordinates?"

"Yes. I even moved around it. I called for him in case he had moved."

"It doesn't make sense," Oliver said.

"No, it doesn't," Obbin agreed. "There was no sign of a fight, and his location was widely exposed. The only barricades I saw were some rocks piled up. But anyone could have climbed over them."

Oliver wanted to check the spot himself, but it would only waste more time. If O'Farrell wasn't there, he wasn't there. He had to trust that Obbin had been thorough in his search.

Oliver lifted his mTalk. He knew using it was a risk, but before they left he had to know if there had been any new transmissions from Mr. O'Farrell. "Tiffany, there is no sign of Mr. O'Farrell. Have you received any new messages?"

A few seconds passed before her voice broke over the speaker. "No, nothing. Are you sure he isn't there?"

"Yes, no sign. We're on our way back. We should be there in fifteen minutes."

He and Obbin retrieved their hover boards and floated inches above the heavy snow. As they traveled around trees and over boulders, a stunt competition soon began. With no strangers in sight, Oliver let loose, allowing himself some fun. He felt no pain in his side.

Obbin twisted up and around a thick oak trunk, using the board's levitating ability to gain altitude. Oliver jumped a boulder, grabbing the board and flipping in the air.

The boys continued this as they made their way back, twisting, flipping, and jumping, always seeing whose trick was better. Oliver was impressed with the young prince's athletic ability.

Austin's mTalk flashed. "It's us," came Oliver's voice. "We're at the side hatch."

He glanced at the time. They had been supposed to be fifteen minutes; it'd taken twenty-one. Had they been ambushed, compromised?

"I'll be right back," Austin said to Tiffany and Mason. "You two stay here. I'm going to lock the hatch to the bridge. Don't let anyone back in unless they use the pass phrase 'Energen is awesome.'"

Austin dashed down the staircase and to the side hatch. He held up his mTalk. "Pass phrase?" he asked.

"'The Übel lose,'" said Oliver. Someone laughed in the background.

Austin hesitated. The pass phrase was right. Why was he nervous? He touched the keypad.

As he touched the keypad, he realized he'd left the Zinger on the bridge. His heart sank. Then he stumbled back as he was struck in the chest.

3.11

Absence of Mist

Austin shook flecks of snow and ice from his shaggy hair. He growled at his attackers. "Not cool. That wasn't even a fair fight."

Oliver and Obbin had ambushed him with more than a dozen snowballs. He'd shed the hoodie and Ultra-Wear pants and was wearing only shorts and a short-sleeved shirt. His bare limbs seemed to have attracted the brunt of the attack. He shivered.

"You should always be ready for an attack," teased Oliver, tossing a glowing blue LuminOrb at his brother.

"You knew the pass phrase."

"You let your guard down," Oliver said as he and Obbin hovered into the ship. "You could have looked out of the *Phoenix* from any of the cameras."

"True," Austin said. "You got me this time, but you won't next time. No, you won't."

Oliver hopped off his board and gave Austin a half hug, ruffling his damp hair. "You're a good sport, bro."

Austin grunted. "Yeah, well." He liked his brother like this. His favorite memories from home were of the days Oliver had taken the time to play . . . no, to *spend time* with him. Going on adventures with Oliver was always fun.

Obbin pulled back his hood. His bright green hair exploded from a buildup of static electricity in the Bliz-Zero fabric.

"Whoa," Austin said, pointing. "Nice hair."

Obbin stroked it back. "I need a trim."

"Austin, where is your Zinger?" asked Oliver, his tone serious.

Austin swallowed. "I left it on the bridge."

"A lot of good it would have done you there," Oliver said.

Austin turned and looked at his brother. Obbin had dropped a few more steps behind them. "You knew the password."

"Doesn't matter. We could have been compromised," Oliver said.

Austin continued toward the bridge, angry with himself. Oliver was right, and Austin looked careless.

"I'm sorry, Oliver."

"Just don't let it happen again," Oliver said.

"I won't."

Oliver sat at the pilot's seat. "You wouldn't happen to know the coordinates for your city, would you?" he asked.

"No. Sorry," Obbin said.

"I suspect I could guide you from where we'd previously landed," Austin offered. "I might need to sit where Tiffany is, though."

"There will be landmarks to guide us," Obbin said. "I think I'll recognize the path home."

"Then we'll sit together," Austin said.

Oliver was skeptical. The desolate forest looked very different from before, and neither Austin nor Obbin had seen the path from above. The forest stretched on and on with little differentiation in appearance as far as he could tell.

But why not let them try? He didn't have a better idea.

"Sounds like a plan. Tiffany, can you load our coordinates from the first time we landed here?" Oliver asked. "I'll fly us there, and then we can start."

Tiffany did, then switched seats with Austin and Obbin. Austin's excitement at getting a shot to lead his family was emblazoned on his face; Obbin looked as though he were simply along for the ride. Oliver wondered at his recent changes in temperament. He'd seemed okay about heading home, he'd done some deep thinking at the story of Austin's time with Brother Sam, and most recently he'd had fun with their hover board competition on the way back.

"Here we go," Oliver said as he engaged the thrusters. A dusting of snow cascaded across the windshield. With no foliage on the trees, Oliver had a clear view of his surroundings. Taking off was even easier than landing. Part of that was because he was mastering the flight systems. He smiled.

The *Phoenix* soared over the seemingly lifeless forest. All foliage save the dark green needles of the pine trees had vanished, and those were coated in a glaze of ice. Only empty branches and piles of snow remained on the oaks and willows.

Austin stood before the copilot's seat, too excited to sit. Obbin was at his side, leaning forward. Oliver urged them to take a seat several times, and Mason reminded Austin of his painful experience on their previous entry to Jahr des Eises, but neither of them listened.

This was different. They were coasting along, and Austin was directing them. He was sure of where he was going. While the forest looked starkly different from before, he knew which direction to go.

A few moments later, however, Austin grew anxious. The blue clouds he had expected to see had not appeared. Had he been wrong? Before him was a tall cliff face, but no steam masked it from view. Beside him, Obbin gasped.

"Something is wrong." Obbin spoke softly as the ship cruised closer to the cliff.

Austin pointed. "There's the door and bridge."

The large double doors that protected the entrance to the caves stood together, sealed as they'd been the first day the twins had arrived. The drawbridge angled into the air. The guard towers were empty. The large bowl-shaped lanterns were unlit.

"The waterfall and steam . . . stopped?" Obbin said. "It's impossible."

"Go over that," Austin said. "We have to fly to the other side."

Only the hum of the systems on the bridge and the low rumble of the engines existed as the five kids remained silent with bated breath.

Oliver flew the *Phoenix* up and over the cliffs. The height and width of the ridge was extensive. The tall trees paled in comparison to the mountain ridge they were flying along.

They cleared the summit. Austin's knees wobbled, and he nearly sat back. But Obbin needed him. He gripped Austin's shoulder for balance and averted his eyes from the scene ahead. Austin guided him into the copilot's chair and took a second look.

The thick blue cloud that had covered the gorge was gone. The entire city lay exposed to the powerful chill of Eises. The narrow valley stretched out before them, the central river shallow and frozen. The many blue buildings stood still and vacant. Several of the fire towers had been destroyed, and the few that remained were no longer lit. No longer did thick steam billow from the many vents that crisscrossed the city.

Oliver brought the *Phoenix* lower into the valley. The snow-covered walls of the gorge swept up around them. Ahead of them, the palace stood on a large cliff. Its tall, wispy waterfall no longer flowed. Part of the palace had collapsed, damming the river's current.

Mason and Tiffany were now at Obbin's side. Each had a hand on his shoulder as they whispered words of comfort to the boy.

Austin's stomach churned. Cobalt Gorge was barren, its buildings covered in ten or more feet of snow. Many of the roofs had collapsed from the unfamiliar weight. The once-lush tropical trees were shriveled and hardly poked through the layer of white.

"Oliver . . . this is not how it's supposed to be," Austin said softly.

"I gathered as much," Oliver said, but his tone was sympathetic. "The scanners don't show any sign of other ships. Perhaps we should head for Brighton."

"No, my people are here," Obbin said. "They'll have gone to Cavern Haven."

"Cavern Haven?" Mason asked. "How many people can fit in there?"

"A few thousand," Obbin said. "Twelve or so."

"Is it safe for us to be here?" Tiffany asked. "Whoever did this may still be around."

"We're still cloaked. No one will see us," Oliver promised.

"We have to find his people," Austin said.

"Yes, please." Obbin sounded choked up. "I must."

"I agree," Oliver added.

Tiffany nodded solemnly.

"Is there somewhere to land up there?" Oliver asked, motioning toward the palace.

"There are gardens and some fields, but I think you should land in the amphitheater to the left," Austin said. "It is dug deep into the ground. It will protect us."

Oliver followed Austin's directions and put the *Phoenix* into a vertical descent. The ship's nose disappeared into the snow. The snow here was even deeper than where they'd landed to search for Mr. O'Farrell.

"Obbin, we're going to find your family," Austin said.

The prince forced a smile and nodded.

3.12

Snow

"**N**o life forms in our immediate vicinity," Tiffany confirmed as she came down the stairs to the cargo bay. Oliver had sent her to double check.

"I want to scout ahead with Obbin," Oliver explained. "Who knows what sort of cloaking ability the enemy has."

There might have been resistance before, but not now. A few days ago, one of his siblings might have said, "What if you're captured, Oliver? Then we'll be alone." But Oliver knew they were growing into determined, capable partners on this mission. Each seemed ready to fill the gap that would be left if Oliver were removed from the equation.

They outfitted themselves with packs of supplies, food, H_2O, gadgets, and other essentials for the mission. Oliver had the StunShot Rifle SI, Austin was armed with the Zinger, and Tiffany had taken the Zapp-It with some reluctance. Oliver wasn't ready to arm anyone else with the other Übel rifles. The risk of someone being fatally shot was too high.

Oliver tightened the wrist straps on his gloves and shifted his thermal cap into place, then lowered his goggles. He put his rifle across his back. "Obbin, are you ready?"

A tuft of Obbin's green hair bounced out from under his hood as he nodded.

"Austin, you're in charge of security while I am gone." This wasn't another gesture to pacify Austin. No, the kid was quickly proving himself to be the best boy for the job.

Austin straightened, shoulders squared, and saluted. "Yes, sir." He patted his Zinger. "This won't leave my side."

Oliver's fingers tapped out the code on the keypad. The corner of his mouth peaked into a smile. The code consisted of the last two digits in each of the kids' birth year, a reminder to him of what he, his sister, and his brothers meant to their parents.

The hatch slid open, and a blistering breath of cold air swept into the bay.

"Let's go." Oliver tossed the board across the threshold of the *Phoenix* and jumped on. The board dipped but didn't drop into the snow. Obbin followed, looking like a natural. That was impressive, seeing as his first hover had been hardly more than an hour ago. With a wave goodbye, the two were off.

Obbin might have known where to go, but Oliver stayed in the lead. He wanted to control their pace based on his instincts and his visual analysis of their surroundings.

Oliver leaned back to gain altitude as they started up the steep embankment of the amphitheater. He imagined rows of seats just below the deep snow. Obbin had pointed out their destination: two tall pillars capped with an ornately carved arch.

He stopped before cresting the top. He peered over the horizon toward the palace, then jerked back and ducked, motioning for Obbin to get low. He'd seen a man dressed in white surrounded by children. He slipped the rifle into his hands.

The wind whistled as it picked up and blew a gust of flurries his direction. As the wind abated, Oliver edged upward, squatting low on his board. He leaned around the pillar.

A statue! The danger had been nothing more than a statue of a man talking to children. It was half buried in the snow.

"Obbin, let's go," Oliver said, just loud enough to overcome the whistling winter wind.

The pair zigzagged through the desolate maze of statues and empty fountains. What had the place been like when the twins had been there just days before? Green and lush, he'd been told, but could hardly believe it.

"Over there!" Obbin shouted, pointing. Oliver winced but didn't reprimand the boy. He saw no entrance.

Obbin led him along a low wall. "I want to use a hidden entrance. The main ones could be watched."

"Good call," Oliver said.

Obbin hauled himself onto the wall. "Hand me the boards," he said as he straddled the stone barrier.

Oliver obeyed, then followed Obbin over. A tall, shriveled hedge blocked their way. Obbin dropped off his board; the snow was nearly to his chest.

They squeezed through the spiny branches of the bushes. Oliver's glove caught and slipped off. The air bit his skin. He grabbed for his glove and slipped it back on. His last check had placed the temperature at negative eleven degrees.

"It's much easier without snow," Obbin said. He hopped back onto his board, and they started toward the palace again. A high wall edged them on their left. Obbin followed the exterior of the palace and then went into a grove of barren trees with long scraggly branches. Covered with thick green foliage, they would have cloaked the entrance. Obbin continued to a tall tower.

"We're here," Obbin said. A wooden door was set into the base of the stone tower.

Obbin took hold of a silver ring hanging from the door like a handle, but instead of pulling on it, he began to twist it. The ring wound outward an entire foot before Oliver heard a click. Instead of swinging out, Obbin pressed the door inward. Snow poured into the entrance, filling the first several feet of the hall.

Oliver gathered the hover boards and stepped inside. He lifted his goggles and dropped his hood back, putting the boards aside so he could hold his weapon again. In these uncertain times, it was beginning to feel like a security blanket.

The palace was dark and eerie. The lights from their mTalks illuminated the way as Oliver followed Obbin farther inside. The passage led them through a side entrance to a great hall with a large unlit hearth.

"The hearth was once lit," Obbin said.

Oliver shrugged. "Well, it is a fireplace."

"This fireplace is only to be lit if our people face danger," Obbin explained. "It warns everyone to alert the others, who then evacuate to the caves."

Oliver thought of a silent alarm at a financial center. "Is this a good sign?"

"Hopeful," Obbin said. "They'll go to Cavern Haven."

"Let's get the others. Then we can find your people."

"No." Obbin stepped back from the fireplace and away from Oliver. "I must go now."

"Obbin, I can't leave my—"

"I won't leave here until I'm sure of my people's safety," Obbin interrupted. "Go if you must, but I won't."

Oliver's face flushed. He felt his temper rise, but he couldn't lose it on Obbin. First, he'd only just met the boy and didn't know how he'd react. Second, he understood and respected Obbin's position.

"Then I'm going with you," Oliver said. "Just let me call Tiffany."

Oliver didn't really want to use the mTalk. Each time he did, it threatened to alert others to their presence. Though encrypted, the transmissions could be detected, and those they fought against were probably savvy enough to decrypt the messages anyway. But if he was going to go with Obbin, he didn't have a choice.

"That would be good," Obbin said. "The caves are deep underground."

Oliver nodded. He stepped toward the door and tapped the screen of his mTalk. "Tiffany, come in," he said, his voice no more than a whisper.

A second passed.

"I'm here. Is everything okay?"

"Sort of. We're inside the palace. We didn't run into any soldiers," Oliver said. "I have to go with Obbin to find his people."

"You're not coming back for us?"

"He says he'll go without me."

"Why can't we come meet you?" Tiffany said.

Oliver grunted. "Just because we didn't—"

Obbin's hand on Oliver's arm stopped him.

"What?" Oliver asked.

"Why not let them come here, while we go? Mason and Austin can show her the library. There may be information you need," Obbin suggested.

Oliver considered this. Would he be wise to expose his siblings to the potential dangers of lurking Übel soldiers or Corsairs? Just because they hadn't seen any didn't mean there weren't any. Was it worth it?

Oliver remembered Tiffany telling him he couldn't do it all himself. That was true, of course. Did she think he was trying to do it all? Discarding her opinion would tell the others they were on their own. That was not the message he wanted to give anyone, especially the twins.

Oliver took a deep breath. "All right," he said.

Obbin smiled.

"Tiffany, you're right. You and the twins should make your way into the palace and go to the library," Oliver said. "I'll place some LuminOrbs to show you the way in . . . What's that?"

Silence. "I didn't hear anything," Tiffany said.

"I thought I heard the twins arguing."

"Nope, Austin is dictating his experience with Brother Sam to Mason, who is putting it all into the e-journal."

Oliver stroked his chin. His stubble was rough under his fingers. "Probably just interference on the radio. Still, someone might be monitoring our transmissions."

If the Übel were listening in, they would already have pinpointed their location from the signal.

"Obbin says the twins know the way to the library. If you don't hear from me for a while, don't worry. We're headed deep underground. It may affect my mTalk signal."

"Okay. We'll set out immediately," Tiffany replied. "Thanks."

Oliver heard shouts on the other end. The twins were clearly excited that they'd be reentering the palace.

"If you don't hear from me in two hours, go back to the ship. If you don't hear from me for an hour after that . . ." Oliver hesitated. "Get help. Contact Archeos."

"Archeos? But we don't know if we can—"

"Who else do we have? Mr. O'Farrell sent us a distress signal, and we couldn't find him. The McGregors' ship has been captured, so we don't know where they are. Mom and Dad are prisoners," Oliver said. "Who else is there?"

"Enough, Oliver. You've made your point. We have no one left. No family, no friends . . ." Tiffany's voice wasn't mournful but accepting—even capable.

Oliver swallowed. Her words hit him hard, though Tiffany seemed unaffected. *No one left.* Was there really no one out there who could help?

"I'll set the timer on my mTalk for three hours," Tiffany said. "If we don't hear from you, we'll contact Archeos."

Oliver couldn't fall into hopelessness, which would lead to helplessness. He had to stay positive. He had to maintain control of his emotions. They were on a mission.

"If you didn't already, make sure your tracking signals are off," Oliver said. "I don't want the Übel or whoever invaded here to pick up your location."

"Will do."

"Over and out," Oliver said.

He knew he'd ended the conversation quickly and hoped it wouldn't send the wrong signal to Tiffany. But he needed to get going, get his mind wrapped around the task at hand:

taking Obbin to his people. He needed to leave behind the notion that they were all alone.

First things first.

"Obbin, we need to place markers along the path to get here so my siblings can find your secret entrance." Oliver pulled five LuminOrbs from his pack. "We'll make it quick."

Obbin frowned but agreed.

3.13

Terra Originem

"Ready?" asked Austin anxiously. He was at the keypad, ready to type in the code. His Zinger was strapped to his back; he'd wrapped the weapon in white material to camouflage it against the snow.

"Almost," Tiffany said as she tucked a special scanner into her pack. She'd known her parents would have a LibrixCaptex, and after coming across the overwhelming tomes on Evad, she'd known she'd need one too. There had been so much there, yet she'd only been able to see . . . to save a few items. The Übel had completely destroyed Yth Orod. She wasn't going to lose so much knowledge so easily again.

What would stop those evil men from wiping out the gorge? Even now missiles might be cruising toward them. She shook off the worry; she couldn't live in fear. It would neutralize her as an asset to the mission—or "quest" as Austin had said.

"What is that?" asked Austin, bringing Tiffany back to attention.

"A LibrixCaptex. By setting a book on the scanner, we can record each of its pages instantly," Tiffany said.

"Really? Doesn't it miss stuff?" Austin asked.

"The scanner could garble or miss something, but overall it captures a higher percentage of information more quickly," Mason said.

"Our other options are to use the mTalk camera or type information into the e-journal like we did on Evad," Tiffany said.

"And seeing as we didn't get through even a small percentage of the books before the Übel incinerated them, I don't think that's a viable option," Mason said.

"Besides, once we've scanned everything, a simple transfer will load all the information into the e-journal or anywhere else."

"Can we go?" asked Austin. Tiffany knew dumping details on him was exhausting to him. He'd probably heard nothing beyond "garble or miss something." He hefted the Zinger higher on his shoulder and pulled his mask up and goggles down.

"I've got my Zapp-It ready," Tiffany said, "though I hope I don't have to use it."

Austin raised an eyebrow. "Last resort, Tiff," he said. "I'll handle any confrontations that arise." His tone was confident and a bit macho.

Tiffany looked at Mason, who rolled his blue eyes. He faked a smile and lowered his snow goggles.

The hatch opened. Chill wind swept into the cargo bay once again. The storm had picked up, and a heavy snowfall was ahead of them. With their surroundings entirely white and no mTalk tracking, Tiffany wasn't sure how they'd find their way.

Tiffany's pack clung to her back, and her Zapp-It was holstered at her side. She was ready. She'd never felt the way she did at this moment. With each challenge thrown their way, they'd worked together and claimed victory. This mission would be no different. Whatever they might find in the palace, they could overcome. They would overcome everything until they were reunited with their parents.

They had no one to turn to but themselves. Oliver's words had ignited a spark in her that had been waiting to be unleashed. She'd felt it on Evad when she had believed her brothers dead. She felt it now as they prepared to enter the ransacked palace. She'd felt it all along, but now she let it free. She had nothing to lose. It was time to go all in.

Tiffany held her hover board awkwardly in her hands. Riding the device would be a challenge in itself, but she was ready. "Well, here goes."

Austin laughed. "Just follow my lead and you'll do fine."

Austin had stepped up to the challenge. He had embraced the adventure they were on. Oliver hadn't let up since he'd saved them all on Tragiws. Now she was joining their ranks.

Tiffany tossed the board before her and hopped lightly onto the board. She threw out her arms to catch her balance and realized it wasn't really that bad.

She looked back at the twins. Though their mouths were hidden behind facemasks, she knew they were wide open.

"What are you waiting for? Let's go!" she said.

At the bottom of a wide stone staircase were two arched entranceways, both dark, with extinguished torch sconces beside them. The doors looked unforgiving. Dark tunnels led into the unknown.

Obbin stopped. "Fun or boring?"

An odd question. "Either," Oliver said.

"Fun then." Without hesitation, Obbin stripped off the Bliz-Zero gear and undershirt and stood in his shorts.

"Can I choose boring?"

Obbin shook his head. "We're getting wet either way."

"Wet?"

Obbin nodded. Oliver shrugged and took off his gear. As he pulled off his shirt, he was careful not to disturb his injury. He'd not felt pain from it for a while. Was the NumbaGlu still working? It hadn't lasted this long before. Perhaps he'd just not moved as much.

"That looks bad," Obbin commented.

"It's fine," Oliver said. "Nearly healed." The FlexSkyn and stitches were helping his skin mend quickly. The wound already looked better.

Obbin nodded and began stuffing his clothing into his pack. But it became obvious the Bliz-Zero set would not fit. "We'll have to leave the cold weather stuff," he said. He lifted the pack and put it on backward, over his chest. "You'll have to leave that," he added, pointing at the StunShot Rifle SI. "It'll fry us if it hits the water."

Oliver shook his head. "Once I turn it off, the power source discharges. The charge-pack is liquid-proof. It won't be dangerous."

He knew this from weapons training at the Academy. He'd assembled and disassembled this type of weapon more than a hundred times. The rifle could be used lethally underwater if needed. It was one of the most flexible weapons in the federal forces' arsenal.

When Obbin still looked doubtful, Oliver said, "I don't want to leave our only defense behind. We don't want to be unprotected. Someone raided your palace."

Obbin nodded. He looked as if Oliver had dashed his hope that his people were safe in Cavern Haven. If they ran into soldiers, it would mean the enemy had infiltrated the underground sanctuary of the Blauwe Mensen.

Oliver wasn't sure what to say. He rubbed his bare shoulders as a cool breeze swept down the stairway behind them. "There's certainly a draft in here."

"The destroyed area of the palace is just down that hall," Obbin explained, his tone still melancholy. "There's no protection against the freezing temperatures anymore. Everything is destroyed."

"Not everything. You must have hope," Oliver said. "My sister and brothers and I have hope we will find our parents."

Obbin shifted his feet. "I know. You're right."

"Then let's get going," Oliver said. He slipped the Zinger over his shoulder.

"I wouldn't do that," Obbin warned. "Just hold on to it tightly."

Oliver didn't ask why. He wrapped the strap around his hand a few times.

"Follow me," Obbin said. He sprinted through the second arch and disappeared.

Again Oliver had to trust his companion. He had no choice but to follow.

Oliver started forward. He heard the sound of water. Then his feet flew out from under him. His injured side jammed against the stone floor. It hurt this time but didn't feel as though he'd torn the wound open. Perhaps he should have told Obbin the injury wasn't completely okay. Couldn't Obbin have explained a bit better? A simple "it's slick" would have been nice.

It was too late now. Away in the darkness he slid, surrounded by streaming water. Warm water?

He heard a gleeful cry ahead and below him, yet without knowing where they were headed, he didn't have the same sense of joy Obbin seemed to be feeling.

The river curved several times in a spiral, then dropped steeply. The StunShot clanked against the walls of the slide, and his grip loosened. He struggled to regain it. The slide turned back, then dipped suddenly before spiraling again. The darkness faded, and Oliver heard the thrashing of falling water. The slide disappeared. His body free fell momentarily before he was engulfed in water.

As Oliver bobbed to the surface, he caught sight of Obbin. The prince was swimming away.

Oliver looked around. They were in a massive cavern. Were those the diving boards the twins had mentioned? This must have been the natural swimming pool he'd heard so much about. The water was hot. He looked back the way he'd just come, realizing he'd ridden one of the waterslides. What had the boys called it? The Aqua Palace . . . no, Aqua Cavern . . . no, that wasn't it either. It didn't matter. He'd tell them it was as awesome as they'd said.

"Come on!" called Obbin from the far side. He bobbed near the wall, waiting. Oliver swam to catch up.

"The entrance is just a few feet below," Obbin explained. "Dive down and swim right up into the chamber."

Oliver nodded. He was in the prince's domain now.

The air in the chamber was unexpectedly warm. Oliver saw the source: a large fire burning in a hearth. The room itself was sizeable. Along one wall stood a series of wooden lockers. Most hung open.

Obbin opened one of the lockers and took out a bag. Inside were a pair of brown pants and a silver shirt. He took a similar set of clothes from another locker. Then he stepped onto a large silver disc on the ground. A blast of air streamed from a hole in the ceiling. Obbin's green hair fluffed up. "Your turn."

Warm air engulfed Oliver, drying him nearly instantly. Oliver carefully slipped on his new shirt. He'd not noticed any trickles of blood from his side. The wound had remained sealed after his fall in the slide. He turned on the charge for his rifle and strapped it across his back.

Obbin had already changed and was twisting a wheel set in the wall. A section of the wall lifted open. The door was only a couple of feet off the ground when Obbin ducked under it and out of sight. Oliver followed.

Obbin took off in a dead sprint, the pack bouncing on his back as he ran. Oliver ran behind him through passages that twisted and turned every few feet. The constant change of direction was not only confusing but tiring. This was a maze designed to protect Obbin's people, and Oliver knew he would never find his way out on his own.

Obbin darted around corners, through doorways, and up sets of rickety stairs. They came to a dizzying spiral staircase hewn right out of the stone. Down, down they went.

"How much farther?" Oliver asked, nearly gagging as he got the last syllable past his lips.

"Not much," Obbin promised.

"Not much" seemed like forever by the time they arrived at the base of the staircase. Two passages branched off into pitch black either way. Obbin stopped. Oliver bent over, his hands on his knees, trying to overcome the dizzy feeling that had consumed him.

"Which . . . way?" he asked.

"Neither," Obbin said.

Oliver lifted his head just slightly to see.

Obbin pressed his hand against a white stone on the rock wall, a stone that might have been easily overlooked. His fingers were spread out, his palm flat. Oliver looked at his feet, then forced himself to look up again.

The tips of Obbin's fingers started to glow as a red light lit under each one. The light began to flash, but Obbin held still.

Schwoop.

The red light changed to green. A grinding noise erupted at the base of the wall, and Obbin stepped back. The entire wall sank into the ground.

This was the first time Oliver had seen this type of technology used in the Blauwe Mensen's kingdom. There was more to these people than met the eye.

Austin led his sister and brother into the palace, then turned and shut the secret door. The snow had piled high, so the task wasn't easy.

To the library. Austin remembered the way. He held the Zinger at the ready. A gallery of images in his mind served as a map, just as when he had guided Oliver in piloting the *Phoenix* through Cobalt Gorge.

"This way," Austin said. Tiffany and Mason followed him up several flights of stairs and down a long hall. Paintings of wild animals confirmed they were on the right path. They went down another staircase and across another hall. A large wooden door stood at the end: the door to the library.

"Mason, would you like to do the honors?"

Mason jumped forward, then immediately calmed himself. "Absolutely." He pressed on the doors, but they didn't move. "They're stuck."

Austin joined his brother and pushed. The doors groaned. A scraping sound echoed on the other side as the doors painfully shifted forward. "Harder," Austin said, and Tiffany joined them.

When the door opened, a mournful cry escaped Mason's lips. "What happened? It's been destroyed!"

The sight on the other side was unfathomable. The four-story room had been ransacked. A table had obstructed the door. The remnants of books—covers, spines, pages—were strewn across the floor. The windows of the topmost floor were shattered. Snow piled throughout the library and the two narrow balconies that skirted the second and third floors. "You two stay here!" Austin said, dashing forward with the Zinger ready for action.

"Austin, you—" Tiffany started.

"Oliver left me in charge of security in his absence. Just wait here," Austin commanded. "Get your Zapp-It ready."

Tiffany fingered the weapon in its holster. "But . . ."

Austin waved his hand and darted straight for the entrance Obbin had led them through days ago. Only a remnant of the tapestry that had once hung over the archway remained, the fabric shredded and torn.

Austin's breath caught as he twisted into a stairwell, aiming his weapon at whatever might be above.

Nothing.

He followed the staircase to an arched exit. The hall beyond was dark. The "forbidden library" Mr. Thule had mentioned had been turned inside out.

Austin had forgotten the old man who'd been assigned to their transition into the Blauwe Mensen. Now he wondered if Mr. Thule was angry that the twins had escaped without him. He wasn't a Blauwe Mensen by birth. He'd been captured like the twins had. Perhaps they should have let him go with them.

Austin returned to where his sister and brother remained. He had searched far enough to feel confident that they were alone.

"It's clear," he announced. "We won't have much time, though. I assume Oliver will be returning soon." Austin noticed Tiffany's Zapp-It was in its holster. Had she even obeyed him and taken it out? He was about to say something but decided against it.

"There isn't much left," Mason cried. "They've destroyed it all."

"Not all," Tiffany said, her arm around Mason. "There are still many books to look through."

"But anything helpful will be gone," Mason said.

"You don't know that," she assured him. "This library is so large."

"Look, we're alone. That means the bad guys have been and gone," Austin said soberly. "So get it together and let's hurry." He pointed at the third floor. "There are some books up there. I'll get them."

Mason scowled at Austin's buck-up statement.

"Together, Mason. We can do this together," Austin promised.

Plink. Plink. Plop.

Water droplets splashed out of sight. They'd entered an empty dark cavern. Oliver hoped this wasn't Cavern Haven.

"Do you smell that?" Obbin asked.

Oliver sniffed. The scent of burning wood was in the air.

"They're here," Obbin said, yet Oliver could see no one. "Thank Creator!"

"Who?"

But the prince was off again, leaving the question in his dust. Oliver slipped on the damp stone floor as he jumped after him. The cave stretched into the darkness, following a shallow stream. Soon the cavern narrowed, and the stream occupied its entire width. Obbin didn't hesitate, splashing forward. Oliver flinched as water sprayed his face as Obbin ran.

The passage twisted once more. Then, as if someone had lit a flare, it became brightly lit with a bluish light. The tunnel opened up, and the water disappeared over a ledge. A single rope dropped from the ceiling, its end disappearing from view.

"Are we there?" Oliver asked.

"Yes," Obbin said. They were still a few hundred feet above the ground.

Oliver looked out into a massive cavern. It was at least as wide as the basin on Evad, and its ceiling disappeared into the darkness high overhead. The columns supporting the ceiling were nearly as wide as the observatory tower in the basin.

Large bowls of blue flames sat atop pillars of their own, pro-viding flickering light.

This was not what stole his attention. Thousands of blue people inhabited the space below. It was clear they were still unpacking from their escape into Cavern Haven. Hundreds of structures stood in the empty spaces surrounding the col-umns. They would be homes for the Blauwe Mensen for the foreseeable future.

The smile on the prince's face said everything.

"You're telling me all these people went through the same passage we did?" Oliver asked.

"Oh, no. There are many other passages," Obbin said.

"So how do we get down?"

"There's a lift," Obbin said, "but I'm not waiting."

Without warning, Obbin leaped off the cliff. Oliver's heart skipped a beat as he watched. But Obbin was not without a plan; he grabbed onto the rope and started down like a monkey.

Oliver looked for a way to call the lift, but Obbin was cur-rently occupying its rope. Normally he would have attempted the descent down the rope, but he still felt exhausted from his run. With a deep sigh, he sat down. He had no choice but to wait for the prince to send the lift.

A narrow ladder provided the access Austin needed to reach the third floor of the library from the second balcony. The shelves of the top level had been searched, but more tomes remained intact than on the other floors. Had the ransackers run out of time? What had run them off?

Tiffany and Mason were making quick work of the many discarded books. Mason collected each and delivered them to

Tiffany, who placed them in the LibrixCaptex for scanning. They'd developed a speedy system.

Austin grabbed a stack and leaned over the balcony rail. "Mason, watch out!" he shouted as he dropped the books from the third floor.

"No!" shouted Mason.

It was too late. Gravity was in control.

The books smashed into the ground. Covers and pages exploded across the polished stone floor.

"Austin! What are you doing?" Tiffany cried out. "You can't throw them!"

Austin scowled. "How did you expect me to get them to you? Carry them one by one down a two-story ladder?"

"You could have used the lift," Mason said sharply, pointing at a small wooden box attached to a rope and pulley.

"Besides, you can't be positive that no one else is here!" Tiffany added. "If there are soldiers in the palace, they surely will have heard that racket."

Austin shrank back out of sight so his siblings couldn't see the red glow that had overtaken his face. He hadn't been thinking. He'd been reckless with their safety and lazy with the artifacts. He was sure his sister and brother were shaking their heads and thinking, "Why did Oliver put someone so irresponsible in charge of security?"

Unready to step back into view, Austin wandered along the balcony. A window provided a view of the demolished gorge. It'd been a warm refuge from the wintery storm, thriving with lush plants. Now it was nothing more than a barren stretch of snow-covered rock.

As he turned back, Austin saw a shelf dislodged from the wall. It hung at an angle that should have toppled it over. Yet it hung in place.

"Austin? What are you doing?" Tiffany called.

He waited until he was sure his suspicion was correct. "I . . . I think I've found a hidden passage."

Obbin had led them down many secret passages, so discovering one wasn't a surprise. He only wished to see where this one led, if only just to do something more in his skill set.

He squeezed through the narrow gap behind the door.

"Whoa!" he shouted without thought.

Several dozen books lined a single seven-shelf bookcase. The spines were similar in appearance, but their colors varied. Each shelf had its own color set. There was a gap among the green spines as if a few books had been removed.

A scrap of paper lay in the vacated space.

Austin lifted it. "Voltan, I have taken *The Chronicles of Terra Originem*. I will trade them for our family's release. Forgive me." The note was signed by Rylin, Obbin's brother.

Footsteps just outside the room caused him to turn.

"Austin, are you in there?" came Tiffany's voice.

"Yes, I'm in here."

Tiffany entered with the Zapp-It out before her. Austin liked seeing that. Perhaps she was ready for this after all.

He moved aside, revealing the books. "I've found something."

"Yes, you have," Mason said admiringly.

"Not just those, but this." Austin held out the note. "It's from Obbin's brother Rylin. Obbin's family must have gotten kidnapped like our parents. Rylin must have escaped, because he's going after them to make a trade."

"Going after them?" Mason asked. "They don't have any spaceships."

"You don't think he stowed away on a shuttle and returned to the *Skull*?" asked Tiffany.

"Obbin did it successfully on the *Phoenix*," Austin reminded them.

"We can't be sure it was the Übel," Tiffany interjected. "This might be the work of the Corsairs. Remember the battle off-planet?" She tucked the Zapp-It back into its holster.

She was right. They couldn't be sure who had attacked or what they had been after. Maybe it had nothing to do with

the Übel and the quest the Wikks were on. But maybe it had
everything to do with it. Austin hadn't been taught to believe
in coincidences.

As the lift touched down, two soldiers approached with
spears at the ready. Oliver noticed a dozen more just ten feet
away, some armed with spears, some with bows and arrows.
All were aimed directly at his heart.

"Place your weapon on the ground," one of the approaching soldiers commanded.

Oliver obeyed. He had no choice unless he wanted a fight,
and he believed Obbin's people meant him no harm. He assumed
the soldiers only wanted to ensure the safety of their people
after such a devastating attack. He was an outsider, and from
the twins' stories, it sounded as though these people did not
take intrusion lightly.

"Now back away," the soldier ordered.

Oliver did. The second soldier rushed forward and scooped
up the rifle.

Oliver's mind blinked. He thought of three ways he could
take down the soldier. He knew the confiscation of his weapon
had triggered the reaction. It seemed automatic. He clenched
his fists and looked at the ground. Something flashed in his
mind: the room for his physical examination, the probes and
connectors attached to him. Then the image was gone.

The men who'd had their weapons trained on Oliver
moved back to their guard posts. Oliver looked at the two
who remained. They could not have been much older than
him. Each wore fur shorts with leather straps crisscrossed
over his chest. Spears were the only weapons they held.

They seemed to think Oliver was no longer a threat without his rifle, though he knew many ways he could harm them with his bare hands.

Oliver shook his head. It was time to get to business: find Obbin and return to his sister and brothers.

"I'm Semaj, and this is At Okad," the taller of the soldiers said.

"Nice to meet you. I'm Ol—"

"Oh, we know your name," At Okad said with a smirk.

Semaj smiled. "We've heard of your run-in with Crown Prince Voltan."

Oliver wasn't sure if he should be embarrassed or proud. "Is that so?" Is that why they'd taken his weapon?

"You defeated him and tossed him from the top of your ship," At Okad said admiringly. "Apparently you are quite the hand-to-hand fighter."

"At least, that's how Prince Rylin told it," Semaj added.

They had to know that if he wanted to harm them, he could. That meant they must trust him a little.

"Where's Obbin?" asked Oliver.

Semaj cleared his throat, getting back to official business. "Prince Obbin did not wish to wait on you. He has headed for the council. He wishes for us to take you to meet him."

"Lead the way."

At Okad leaned in. "He also said that you should be ready with a solid reason for him to stay with you on your quest."

"What do you mean?" Oliver asked.

"The moment I told him that his family had been taken and Prince Voltan had gone to rescue them, he knew the council would resist his departure. Should no one from his family return, he is the last in line for the throne." Semaj frowned. "The council will never let him leave."

"Perfect," Oliver mumbled under his breath.

"What was that?" Semaj asked.

"Nothing. Let's go."

Semaj and At Okad led Oliver along the main thoroughfare of the underground city. It seemed just like the downtown of any city, except it was deep under the surface of Jahr des Eises. It almost seemed odd for the buildings to have roofs. What were they stopping? Rain? Snow? No precipitation could occur down here. Perhaps they were to create a sense of the ordinary and privacy.

Oliver had only seen the blue people as he and his siblings had escaped from the planet, when the apparently famous fight between himself and Prince Voltan had occurred. If any of these people were unhappy with Oliver's rough handling of the crown prince, he could be in trouble. He'd visited places with his parents where royalty was held in such high esteem that merely mentioning names in the wrong tone could get you thrown into a prison cell.

Now he was surrounded by Blauwe Mensen. His pale skin stood out like a fire in twilight.

The farther they walked, the more his theory that they despised him proved untrue. No one gave him dirty looks; they stared curiously perhaps, but without glaring. No one shouted names at him. Instead people waved and greeted him. A few children even bowed; one little girl offered him a small, jeweled bracelet, which he accepted. It was almost as if he were some sort of celebrity to the youth.

The people of the city seemed to be in good spirits even after vacating their homes and being attacked. The smell of baking bread and roasting meat filled the air. Fresh vegetables and fruit lined the street in large bins. The Blauwe Mensen were selling and buying goods already, trying to live with some sense of routine and adapt to their new homes.

Oliver had learned about the importance of maintaining normalcy in a society through and after a crisis. A civilization only remains civil as long as it maintains regularity. Once everyday goings-on cease, society begins to unravel, and it isn't long before unrest and chaos occur.

"How long ago did you come here?" Oliver asked.

"Immediately after we were attacked," Semaj said.

"And when was that?"

"Last night."

"But there must be more than ten feet of snow out there," Oliver said. "Some of the buildings have collapsed."

At Okad grunted, his eyes narrowed. "They came at the worst time. We knew a blizzard was striking because heavy rainfall had broken through our protective layer of warm clouds," he explained. "Flying crafts swept down through the cloud and destroyed the Towers of Fire, then attacked the palace, collapsing part of it into the river."

"The river produces the steam that creates the protective cloud," Semaj said. "When the fallen palace dammed the river, it stopped flowing. Steam stopped filling the gorge. Our cover was gone, and the blizzard swept into the city. Some shuttles landed. We were outmatched in weapons, though our numbers were far greater."

"We did our best to fend them off," At Okad said, raising his spear.

"We also helped move our people into Cavern Haven," Semaj said. He waved his hand at the city around them. "It was quickly clear that they were here for two things."

"The traitor!" At Okad interrupted.

Semaj nodded. "And the royal family."

"The traitor had given them all the knowledge to destroy our city and capture our king," At Okad said.

"We were able to hide the crown prince," Semaj said. "He has now taken our best warriors to rescue his parents and siblings."

They arrived at the center of the cavernous room. A domed building several stories high rose up before him.

"This is the council building. We'll be leaving you here," Semaj said. "We're not palace guards."

"It was nice meeting the one who defeated Prince Voltan. It isn't often he's bested." At Okad laughed.

The two young soldiers hit their chests with their empty fists, then bowed their heads. Two large double doors opened, and a new set of guards stepped forward. The younger guards bowed, then turned and left the way they had come without looking back. Oliver was sure he heard one of them say, "We just met *the Oliver!*"

The palace guards were armed with swords and wore jeweled helms. They wore full body armor inlaid with bright blue stones, the very same that were prevalent throughout the gorge.

"This way," one of the men said. "The prince wishes for you to join him."

Oliver obeyed without question, though he had preferred the previous guards. These were far tougher looking, and he didn't get the feeling they were much for small talk or ones to recognize his fighting abilities. He forced himself to stand straighter.

Mason retrieved the LibrixCaptex to scan the books remaining on the shelves in the secret room. Tiffany started deciphering the title of the book collection that had been taken by Rylin. *Chronicles* was easy. It meant two or more books. *Terra* stood for *land*, but *Originem* . . . ? She supposed it meant *origin*, but the word wouldn't come up in her searches so she couldn't be certain. Her conclusion seemed off: *The Books of Land Origin?*

Maybe it was a deed to the gorge. The land and the blue jewels she'd been hearing about would be worth a fortune. Of course, the Übel were unbelievably wealthy, but Rylin probably didn't know that. Why else would he use the books as a bargaining chip to free his family? Did he know what the Übel were after? If he did, then was this book a history of where humanity had originated?

The thought almost took her breath away. Could the answer to their search have been right in this room? Had the twins been that close a few days before?

Her stomach turned over with the sickening realization that perhaps the books were now in the hands of the Übel. She grasped the shelf to steady herself.

Mason noticed. "What's wrong?"

"The books that Rylin took . . . I think . . . I think they're the key," Tiffany said. "I think the books have the information to find Ursprung."

Mason shook his head. "But . . ."

"And now they're with the Übel. They have the key!" Tiffany said.

"You don't know that for sure."

"It's as likely as anything," Tiffany said.

"Then we should get going," Mason said. "We'll want to be ready when Oliver returns. We need to find out everything we can about our next destination."

"Are you finished scanning?" asked Tiffany.

"Yes, that was my last one," Mason said quickly.

Tiffany slipped the e-journal back into her pack. Mason lifted the LibrixCaptex and tucked it away.

Austin was tugging on a bookshelf as Tiffany and Mason stepped from the room. "I don't think you're going to find another room," Tiffany said.

"We need to go," Mason added. Tiffany knew his mind was likely racing with concern. That made her feel bad, but she'd told him the truth.

Austin sighed and released the shelf. "You're probably right." He peered over the balcony, Zinger in hand. "Still clear. Let's go."

As they climbed down the ladder, Tiffany took in the ransacked library once more. What must it have been like when the twins had first seen it, so grand and filled with wonder on every shelf? If only they'd had their mTalks to take a picture or two for her.

Once on the ground, Tiffany took a few pictures of her own but wondered if they might only make her sad when she looked at them later. Still, they'd be something to show her parents whenever they were back together.

Austin led Mason and Tiffany the way they'd come. When they reached the Great Hall, he stopped dead in his tracks. Mason and Tiffany stumbled around him.

Tiffany regained her balance. Then she saw what had halted their flight.

A soldier garbed in black and gray camo and a black beret stood just before them, his weapon poised to fire, a smug smile on his lips.

3.14

Council

Ornate decorations of silver and blue crystals marked the walls of the large room, showing it to be a place of significance and power. It was also cool, almost frigid in comparison to the rest of the city, though torches lit sconces every five feet around the room.

Oliver followed the guards through a gap between the tiered seats lining one half of the room. Before him was a raised table. Nearly a dozen men and women sat behind it. They wore long blue robes and odd blue-domed hats. This was the council.

Obbin stood before the table, shaking his head, two guards at his side. "Speaker Ovon El, you cannot make me stay," Obbin argued. "If I'm the last of my family here, that makes me interim king until my parents are rescued."

Ovon El, a man near the table's center, scowled down at the prince . . . or king. "Young prince, like you, we believe your father is indeed alive. Furthermore, Crown Prince Voltan has already started a rescue mission and has commanded us to maintain order." His tone became stern. "Therefore you are not the interim king. The council remains a protector of the people until the king or crown prince returns."

A councilwoman to the Speaker's left cleared her throat.

Prompted, the Speaker continued. "Should the worse come to pass—we pray to Creator that it does not—we will turn over the kingship to you."

Obbin's shoulders dropped. Oliver didn't know if he were responding with acceptance of his current position or with grief at the possibility of his father's and brother's demise. Though it was not the time to ask, Oliver really wanted to find out what this talk of *Creator* meant. And the Speaker was praying to it? Was it a person?

"Should such a time come, I will be ready to take up my role," Obbin said. "But we must not let this happen. I must continue with the Wikk family under Captain Oliver's command."

Oliver's mouth dropped open. Obbin had called him a captain! It was true, he supposed—he'd just not thought of himself that way. He was also impressed, albeit surprised, that Obbin could speak in such a regal tone and with such clear articulation to the council. The boy had always seemed nothing but carefree and playful, not educated on kingdom rules or procedures. Then again, challenging authority seemed in tune to what Oliver knew about him.

"Young prince—" Speaker Ovon El started, but he stopped as Oliver's arrival became apparent.

From the looks on the council members' faces, Oliver's arrival was unwelcome. A few expressions also seemed puzzled. He wondered if talk of him as a captain had misled the council members' perception of his age. If the story of his fight with the crown prince had made its rounds through the city, they would have known his age. Maybe they just didn't like him for defeating their future king.

"This is Oliver," Obbin said. "He is the captain of the *Phoenix*, the same ship our soldiers raided several days ago."

The word *raided* stuck in Oliver's ears. Obbin had used the word to put the Blauwe Mensen at fault for the confrontation in the woods.

A councilman coughed. "Everything happened as soon as they left," he grumbled. "They set this in motion."

"I knew that Thule was no good," a second councilman cried. "If only!" He slammed his fist on the table.

"How do we know this Oliver isn't working for him?" asked the councilwoman who had prompted Speaker Ovon El. She looked at Obbin. "And now you have shown him our last sanctuary?" She looked exasperated, but her eyes were wide. "Surely those soldiers will arrive any moment."

Soon all the members of the council were talking over each other, until Speaker Ovon El stood and waved his arms. "Enough! We're all tired. We have had a very chaotic day—or two." He sighed, clearly not sure how much time had slipped past. "Let us hear from this Captain Oliver." His tone dropped with the mention of Oliver's newly assigned title, and he sat down to a few resistant grunts from the others.

Oliver swallowed the lump in his throat. Silence ensued, while he gathered how to begin.

"Greetings, sirs . . . and ladies. Council." Oliver took a deep breath. *Confidence.* He cleared his throat, taking a sensible tone. "First, to ease your fears, I can promise that we are not in league with the soldiers who attacked your city. We came here looking for our parents, whom soldiers have also taken."

He looked at the council members who'd accused them of starting everything.

"My brothers were to remain in our ship and not leave. They disobeyed my orders. Their capture put our rescue mission in jeopardy. In escaping they had no intention of causing you harm." He paused for effect. "They returned to our ship so we could continue our quest to find our parents."

Oliver looked at Obbin. "We came to bring your prince home before continuing on our journey. We hadn't known he was on board the ship when we left."

Out of the corner of his eye, Oliver saw Obbin sink back. The councilwoman and a few others looked as if they'd won a small victory with this statement. Oliver knew why. He'd wanted the prince to be here as well, perhaps not for the same reasons. But Oliver had known nothing of the destruction of Cobalt Gorge.

"When we arrived here, we found the city destroyed. We would have left immediately, but the prince hoped to find his family safe and intact, so we came into your sanctuary. It would seem that the men who did this to your city are somehow connected to those who have my parents."

Obbin perked up slightly.

"Together the prince and I might find and rescue both of our families," Oliver said and cast a smile at Obbin.

The council remained quiet until the Speaker stood again. "If the prince has been with you these past few days and he wishes to continue with you, it is plausible that your intentions are what you say they are." He looked at his colleagues. "That said, I will put it to a vote of this council whether you shall be released on your quest or whether further discussion is needed."

The words caught Oliver off guard. They were considering forcing him to stay? He flinched. A desperate need to escape *that very second* crossed his mind.

He glanced around at the armed guards. He'd not escape without a fight. What if he told them that his siblings would contact Archeos if he did not return?

Threats never worked, he reminded himself. They only served to anger one's opponent.

Perhaps he could just allude to the fact that holding him here would cause his siblings to contact the outside. This could bring the members of the Archeos Alliance and possibly federal soldiers from Brighton into the basin. Then again, the council might send soldiers to look for his sister and brothers instead. It'd be better not to even mention his siblings again. He'd wait and hear the decision of the council.

The council stood and began to depart through a door directly behind the table. Oliver wanted to tap out a message to his brothers and sister, but the mTalk had no reception. The clock on the device showed that he was nearing his time limit. Much longer, and his siblings would call Archeos and set off a chain reaction that would be out of his control. Soldiers would come again.

Time was not on his side.

3.15

Giraffe

The soldier was all too familiar to the twins. Oliver had called him Drex.

"So we meet again." A short laugh accented Drex's victory.

Austin was startled at how similar Drex was to Oliver—at least in age and size. He'd not noticed this in the underground chamber on Evad. Yet Drex was unlike Oliver at the same time; he seemed vile and threatening.

"You know the drill. Put down your weapon, and come to me," Drex ordered, shaking his rifle at them.

Mason put his hands in the air, and Tiffany slipped the Zapp-It from her holster. She set it on the ground, then raised her hands. Austin did neither. He held the Zinger tighter. One shock would be enough to knock Drex out cold.

"You too!" Drex commanded. "*Now!*"

"Oliver, get him!" Austin shouted. He lifted his Zinger and fired at one of the large unlit bowls that hung from the ceiling.

Drex turned to defend himself against the named attacker.

Austin pressed his sister and brother back the way they had come. There was no Oliver. It would only be a moment before Drex realized that.

A resounding boom echoed in the hall as the large silver bowl crashed into the marbled floor.

Austin glanced back to see Drex lying on the floor a few feet away. He fired a second shot toward the enemy, but it sparked as it hit the bowl instead.

"Go!" he shouted as Tiffany and Mason dashed through the arched exit from the hall.

Whoomp!

Austin heard the sickening blast of the soldier's rifle. The shot hit the top of the arch.

"That way," Austin commanded, directing his siblings down an unknown path. He fired a third shot behind them but didn't stop to see where it hit. He heard rapid fire behind them. Austin was outclassed in skill, and he knew it. They had to run.

Neither Mason nor Tiffany hesitated. Austin was in charge, and they obeyed his every order. Soon they'd find out if those orders were the right ones.

Austin kept glancing back as they went, then looking forward to order a new direction: left, right, sometimes up or down. The pounding of boots on the stone floor told Austin that Drex was still in pursuit. Austin initially knocked over chairs and tables in the halls, even stopping to push over a few cabinets. Soon he realized that this would only show Drex the direction they'd headed.

He was sweating from the Bliz-Zero gear's heavy insulation. The outfit wasn't meant for sprinting through the interior of a palace. He wished he could shed it, but he didn't know when they'd find themselves outside again. Better hot inside than frozen outside.

Austin stopped. This painting looked familiar: a floor-to-ceiling canvas of a waterfall. It hit him. Obbin had taken the twins through this secret passage on their way to be presented to the Blauwe Mensen.

"Stop!" he called to his siblings, his voice hushed.

Mason and Tiffany stumbled as they fought the momentum they'd accumulated.

"This way." Austin grabbed the frame and pulled it open. "Hurry."

Footsteps echoed just around the corner.

Tiffany and Mason dashed in, and Austin pulled the frame shut. Ten seconds later, boots clumped past. The ruse had worked.

Another minute passed before anyone dared to speak.

"I think we're safe," Tiffany said.

"For the moment," Austin added. He unzipped the front of his jacket.

They were in pitch darkness until Mason turned on his mTalk light. "That's better," he whispered. Austin and Tiffany turned their lights on.

Tiffany and Mason also unzipped their coats. They removed their hoods, facemasks, and gloves. The chilly draft from outside didn't haunt this area of the palace.

"Follow me," Austin said.

The trio started down the secret path. "This will lead us to the banquet hall where we met the rest of the royal family," Mason explained.

The passage curved. They arrived at their first split.

"Mason?" Austin asked.

"Uh, don't look at me," he said. "We were in this tunnel many tunnels ago."

Austin looked at his sister. She shook her head. "First time."

"We could go back," Mason suggested.

No one spoke. Austin closed his eyes and focused.

"It's right," he said. "I'm seventy-five percent sure."

Tiffany shrugged. "Good enough for me. It won't be long before Drex realizes he's lost us and backtracks. I'd rather not get into a path he'll cross."

Austin took the right, then a left, another left, and a right. The path continued to curve. Overall, it seemed familiar. At one point he asked for the others to turn off their lights. Having only one light gave them the level of illumination they'd had in the previous trip.

The path abruptly ended. "Wait here," Austin said as he backtracked fifty feet down the tunnel to see if he'd missed anything.

He returned. "Seventy-five percent?" Mason asked.

Austin grunted. Then it hit him. He shone his light at the wall. A piece of shiny fabric was tucked between two stones. He shifted the beam, and it caught a white stone.

"Ninety-nine percent," Austin said as he touched the white stone.

A section of the wall before them began to move. Light crept into the secret passage as the door opened into another hallway.

The three stepped into the hall. Austin pushed the door shut. It was a floor-to-ceiling painting of a tall animal.

"That's a giraffe," Mason said.

Austin started down the corridor.

Tiffany didn't follow. She was digging in her pack. "There is . . . I just remember something familiar about this."

"We should keep going," Austin said.

Too late. Tiffany was searching through the e-journal, tapping a few keywords on the screen.

"What's she doing?" Austin asked.

"This picture must have triggered something," Mason said.

"No, not that," Tiffany said. Her finger slid up and down the screen. "Nope. Hmm, not that one. No. So close. Yes! I found it!"

"What?" asked Mason.

"Keep it down," Austin reminded them.

"Here," Tiffany said. "Mom wrote about this, only she didn't know what it was called. These animals were supposed to have died on Ursprung during the exodus, but she saw one while flying away from a dig on Evad. She wrote, 'We didn't have time to search for the animal, but someday I hope to return to Evad to find it.' This picture is that animal," Tiffany finished.

"It sure sounds like it," Mason admitted, "but we can't be sure. I didn't see any on Evad."

"We didn't travel very far outside the basin, did we?" retorted Tiffany. "The basin, these people—they're all connected."

"Haven't we already established that?" Austin asked.

"This is just further proof," Tiffany said. She lifted her mTalk and took a picture. "I can't wait to ask Mom if this is what she saw."

"If we want to rescue Mom and Dad, we should get going," Austin reminded her.

"You're right. Sorry."

"I thought it was a good discovery," Mason said.

Tiffany smiled, tucking the e-journal back into her pack. "Lead the way."

They crossed out onto a balcony that overlooked a large circular room. Tiffany and Mason took pictures of the ceiling and floor. The fresco of clouds and sun that adorned the domed ceiling had been unscathed by the attackers. The ornate mosaic of trees and animals that spread out across the floor had fared well, though it was scuffed as though hundreds—if not thousands—of feet had trampled across it. Austin eyed the banister but decided not to slide down it as Obbin had.

Austin approached the large doors that would lead them through the shriveled gardens and back to the amphitheater. He pulled on the doors, but they didn't move. He pushed, but still they did not budge. "Mason, Tiffany, would you give me a hand?"

The trio pushed and pulled. Nothing worked.

"I'd say they're stuck," Mason said. "Even the ones in the library gave after we all worked together."

"But this is the quickest way back," Austin said. "Almost a sure way to avoid Drex."

"Austin, they don't seem to be moving," Tiffany said. "There has to be another way. The palace is huge; Drex could be anywhere by now."

"I'm not scared of Drex," Austin started.

"She didn't say that," Mason said.

Austin realized his temper had risen too quickly. "Let's just get out of here." He pointed toward an arched door. "This way."

3.16

Painted Puzzle

Obbin came to Oliver's side. "Thank you for your words."

Oliver forced a smile and nod. "Do you think they'll make us stay?"

"Perhaps," Obbin said. "But don't worry. Rylin and I have explored the caverns many times before. There are other ways out."

Oliver exhaled. He wouldn't be trapped here forever.

"I don't think they'll keep us," Obbin continued. "The council has never disregarded the wishes of a member of the royal family. Should . . . " His voice trailed off, and he took a deep breath. "Should my family not return, the council will fall under my kingship. They will be careful not to make an enemy of me."

That was good news, but it seemed contradictory to a council's purpose. Councils were meant to provide wisdom even in opposition to the will of the ruler.

"I hope you're right," Oliver answered. "How long might they be?"

"Moments or hours. There are eleven members on the council. Each will no doubt argue his or her point."

"We don't have long," Oliver reminded him.

"What will Archeos do when contacted?"

"I'm not actually sure," Oliver said. "It's not a military organization. My guess is Archeos will call on the Federal Fleet."

"Have you spoken to Archeos since your parents were taken?"

"No," Oliver admitted. "We weren't sure who to trust."

"Why trust it now?"

"It seems we have no other choice."

"You have me," Obbin said. "And you have Creator." The words seemed unusual, but his tone was genuine. He spoke with complete truth.

"Who is Creator?"

Obbin smiled. "You don't know him?"

Oliver shook his head.

"Creator is the one who watches over us. He is the one whom we can trust with all our cares," Obbin said. "He gives us peace."

The cryptic words rang oddly true in Oliver's ears.

"Creator loves each of us," Obbin continued.

"But I don't know him."

"He knows you," Obbin promised.

"Prince Obbin, a word with you, please," said a palace guard.

Obbin held up his hand, signaling he'd be right there. "We have much to talk about if you don't know Creator." His tone was serious, yet hopeful. "I'll be right back."

The prince went to the guard. The two spoke in hushed whispers. Oliver noticed a lot of nodding. Whatever they were saying, the two seemed to be getting along.

He thought about what Obbin had said. So this guy called Creator watched over him and loved everyone? Oliver could trust him? Who was this guy? Some king of old? A scientist who could live forever and spy on whomever he wanted? It seemed almost comical to consider. Or frighteningly similar to what they were dealing with at that very moment. The Übel seemed to know everything, and indeed Vedrik had mentioned eternal life when he had taken Oliver's parents. Oliver shivered, his breath drawing short. Creator, Übel? Were they the same?

No, absolutely not. He shook off the idea. The word *love* did not belong in the same sentence as the Übel, and Obbin had said Creator loved him.

Oliver rubbed his head. Perhaps he'd lay off deep discussions until they were out of this tense situation.

"What was that about?" asked Oliver as Obbin started his way.

"Apparently one of my father's most trusted guards was taken with my family," Obbin said.

"How is that good?" asked Oliver.

"Feng would give his life for any member of my family. He's also a skilled warrior. If he's with my family, then they're safe," Obbin said.

"His name is Feng?"

Obbin nodded.

The name was oddly familiar, yet Oliver couldn't place where he'd heard it before. Had the twins and Obbin spoken of him? No, that wasn't it. He snapped his fingers. When the Blauwe Mensen had surrounded the *Phoenix*, Feng had been there.

"I've met Feng," Oliver said. "I mean, he told me to surrender when your people surrounded us."

"He is a great captain," Obbin said. "He tolerates me."

Oliver thought that was an odd choice of words for someone Obbin admired so much, but he didn't question them.

Mason held up his mTalk. He was trying to record everything he could. He hoped to capture as much of this hidden world as he could and catalog what he discovered. Whether the Blauwe Mensen could ever return to their past life of secrecy or were exposed to the entire Federation, Mason wanted to protect some of what once was.

Tiffany was using the e-journal's sonar to help them find their way out. She was building a map of the palace to find the exit.

Austin was leading, his Zinger at the ready. Though they'd not seen or heard anyone in nearly a half hour, Austin wasn't taking any chances. He'd halted Mason and Tiffany several times to scout ahead and often hushed them when they talked too loudly.

They'd seen a lot more of the palace than they had before. Mason hadn't fathomed its immense size. He started counting rooms but eventually gave up.

Mason stopped. The paintings on the wall of this particular corridor seemed different from the décor of the rest of the palace. The paintings had bright, almost gaudy, colors: neon greens and yellows interspersed with metallic inks of silver and gold. They seemed to jump out of their canvases.

Austin and Tiffany had turned the corner, but Mason didn't follow. He was held in place by the artwork. Twelve paintings were lined in a row. The strokes of paint seemed to carry from frame to frame in the first six, and then again in the last six. It looked as if the two sets were part of a connected painting.

"Mason?" Austin's voice echoed from the connecting passages. "Mason, where are you?"

He heard them returning but didn't look for their arrival. He was trying to figure it out.

"Mason! You can't just stop like that," Tiffany scolded.

"No, you can't," Austin said.

Mason looked at his brother. The end of the Zinger glowed with bright blue energy.

"That Drex guy could still be around here somewhere." Austin looked around protectively. "Probably is."

"I'm sorry," Mason said, "but there's something here. There's something about this art."

Tiffany and Austin stared at it.

"I don't see anything," Austin said. "It's just some funky colors. Let's go. Oliver would want us to be back at the ship by now."

"I don't see it either," Tiffany said. "Austin's right. We need to go."

"Has Oliver called yet?" Mason asked.

"No," Tiffany admitted.

"Then we have time." Mason's voice rose defensively. He had a feeling that this series of paintings was something. A clue to their quest? He couldn't be sure without better examination. His mom had written about a giraffe on Evad, and they'd found a picture of one hanging in the palace. It wasn't a coincidence.

"We were supposed to return in case he'd been captured," Austin said, "not so we'd be ready for him."

Mason ignored him. "It's like a puzzle. Each painting is a piece." Hand on chin, he tried formulating a pattern in his mind.

"Drex—"

"Drex isn't here, nor are any other Übel soldiers. We haven't seen anyone for almost an hour," Mason said. "He's probably given up searching for us."

"Maybe he's found the *Phoenix*."

"It's cloaked, remember?"

"Wait . . . I see something," Tiffany interrupted. "The images aren't laid out right. The bottom six need to go above."

"You're right," Mason agreed.

Austin started for the wall, pulling some tools from his pouch. "Let's get them down then."

"Not necessary," Tiffany said. "Look." She held up the e-journal. She'd spliced an image she'd taken of the pictures and was using her finger to arrange them six over six on the screen.

Austin looked disappointed, but he continued toward the paintings and set down his pouch. His Zinger was slung across his back.

Mason stared at the e-journal screen with Tiffany. The strokes in the paintings were lining up, but nothing discernible was being revealed. Long lines of neon colors intersected and crisscrossed.

"Maybe it was one big painting once, but they couldn't fit it anywhere so they cut it up," Austin proposed. He was holding a long wand in his hand.

Mason didn't buy that. "You don't do that with art." He smiled. His twin was intrigued enough by the art that he'd dropped his agenda of getting back to the ship and was now helping to unravel the mystery.

"I'm running a cryptographic cipher," Tiffany explained. Small red lines zigzagged across the e-journal's screen.

A bright flash lit the wall behind him. Mason turned and saw Austin holding his wand near one of the paintings. It flashed again.

In that instant, Mason saw a word. Then it was gone.

"Did you see that?"

"No." Tiffany still stared at the e-journal screen. "Nothing has been detected."

"Not there, on the wall." Mason pointed. "When Austin flashed that thing, I saw something." He traced the spot where the text had been.

"It's a Spectrum Scope," Austin said. "It's a useful tool to have." He patted his pouch.

"There's some sort of invisible ink on the painting," Mason said.

"Let's see." Austin pressed a button on the Spectrum Scope several times; its beam flashed. There it was again: the words Mason had seen.

"That's the one." Mason moved toward the beginning of the paintings.

Austin stepped back and searched for the beginning of the text. Tiffany and Mason's eyes followed. This painting had stolen their attention entirely.

"There," Tiffany said. "Stop there."

3.17

Decision

The doors opened, and the council members filed out and took their seats. Some looked angry and others sorrowful. Oliver tried to recall which ones had opposed Obbin. Were they the angry ones? Had they not gotten their way? The suspicious councilwoman's expression was unreadable, which seemed odd considering how clear she'd been with her feelings in the beginning. The Speaker was last to enter. He didn't sit.

A door opened at the chamber's side, and twelve additional palace guards entered the room.

The guards were there to make sure Oliver didn't escape as he had last time. It seemed like a bad sign for their verdict. The guards' jeweled helms and armor sparkled under the firelight, making them look as if they themselves were aflame.

The Speaker cleared his throat.

"We have come to our decision." He folded his hands before him. "Prince Obbin, you have brought us an unusual dilemma, and you, Captain Oliver, have compounded that dilemma." The Speaker shook his head. "The council's first priority has always been to protect our way of life, our people. We retreated into Cavern Haven for that reason. But now we have been exposed to outsiders."

Oliver's throat constricted.

"Secrecy is no longer an option. We must leave here. To do that, we must have our king."

Hope trickled into Oliver's heart as the Speaker eyed him, a smile twitching the man's lips.

"You are our best hope for that." Oliver bowed his head but held his tongue. "Your technology far exceeds ours, and you have the means to seek out the royal family. Those who have taken your parents are very likely the same who have taken our king."

The Speaker's expression became mournful as he stared at Oliver. "One of our guards has told us that the name *Wikk* was mentioned by an enemy soldier. Thule appeared to be in command of the raid. He orchestrated the capture of the royal family by pretending to lead them to safety. All but Crown Prince Voltan were imprisoned."

Oliver pictured the prince. Voltan wasn't much older than he. Now he too was on a quest to rescue his family. Though they'd fought, Oliver felt a sort of camaraderie with him at the new information.

"We shall provide you with necessary supplies for your journey. Ask, and we shall give it, if it is at our disposal," the man promised. "We ask only that you take the Oath of Secrecy and Protection. Is that acceptable?"

"It is," Oliver said. "And I may have whatever I need to continue my quest?"

The Speaker nodded. "If it is at our disposal, then yes. You have my word."

Oliver glanced at Obbin.

"What of me?" Obbin asked.

"You are to remain here in the caverns. We—"

"I will not!" Obbin cried. "You cannot make me."

The Speaker leaned forward. "Prince Obbin, I have known you since the day you were born. I have known your family much longer and served not only your father, but his. You will be obedient in this matter and trust that I am looking to your very best interests." The man's words were swift and clear. "The council believes this is what your father would want."

The twelve guards edged closer to Obbin like a snake tightening around its prey. This was not going to be good.

"Within the depths, we do leave the keys to passage safe and free. We hope in time the Truth will reign freely, when man again sees the way. Until the time when darkness is unveiled for what it is, we shall protect the path. We pray only that redemption again is clear to the masses, for so long it has been overlooked as something valueless." Mason read the words aloud, but that only made it more complicated in Tiffany's mind.

She tapped the text into the e-journal and read it again and again. This enigmatic message had such depth to it. Its underlying message might unleash the clue they'd been looking for. With all the information they'd been collecting, the pieces to this puzzle were slowly coming together.

The message stretched across the six pictures that made up the lower half of the painting. Austin passed the light over every segment of the frames, revealing new lines. These had the makings of a map. Combined with the words, this was quite possibly a find of great significance.

"The only way we're going to see this map clearly is if we take the pictures off the wall," Austin said. "We need to line them all up."

"But even then the cameras on our mTalks won't pick up the invisible ink," Mason argued.

"Do you have a better idea?" Austin asked.

Tiffany only noticed the ensuing silence because their discussion had distracted her from the riddle.

"We'll remove them from the frames and take them with us," Mason suggested.

"Seriously?" Austin asked. "We don't have that kind of time."

"Seriously. This might be the thing that unlocks the secrets of our quest."

"*Might*," Austin retorted.

"This is a secret message hidden in the palace of a secret people who were suddenly raided by either the Übel or Corsairs just after we were here. I don't believe in coincidences," Mason scoffed.

"Fine," Austin said. "But let's make it snappy."

"I need to sit somewhere quiet and think about this message," Tiffany said.

Austin was already working on the frames. "Mason, get ready to take the painting out as I loosen the frame."

They'd not even heard her, but she didn't mind. It'd take them a while to complete their task. Tiffany walked around the corner and looked for a place to sit against the wall.

"No, not yet!" she heard Austin shout. "You'll tear it."

"I'm not doing anything!" Mason shouted back, his voice echoing into her hall.

"That's the problem! You never . . . "

She had to find somewhere quieter. She took another left and entered a well-furnished hallway. She wished she still had her Zapp-It with her, though she wasn't sure she could actually use it. But they'd not seen Drex for nearly an hour, and there'd never been a sign of other soldiers. She felt sure they were alone in this part of the palace, and perhaps in all of it.

Opening a door, Tiffany found a small sitting room with several plants. Their leaves had begun to shrivel. She re-zipped her parka. Wearing the Bliz-Zero gear had kept her warm; she'd not noticed the temperature within the drafty palace.

She listened. Silence. She took a deep breath and let it out slowly. She hadn't realized how much she needed a second to herself.

She found a high-backed chair and removed her pack, then sat down. She set the e-journal on her lap. All this exploring and running had worn her out more than she could have imagined. Could she take a quick ten-minute nap? The boys would be a while getting all the paintings down.

She shook her head and forced her eyes open. There was no time. And nodding off was just irresponsible.

She had to do her part. It was time to solve the riddle; it was time to see if the words from the painting were connected to other discoveries her parents had made.

Although shorter than the council's table, Obbin stared up at the Speaker with an intensity that made him appear bigger.

"What will you do? Restrain me? Imprison me?" he cried out.

Three guards moved forward.

"If we must," the suspicious councilwoman said. "It's for your own good and the good of our people."

As one of the guards reached for the prince, Obbin twisted and kicked at the man. The guard barely dodged the strike. Two more rushed toward the chaos.

"Stop," Oliver cried. "Stop!" The guards and the council seemed confused at his command. "Sir," Oliver directed his words to the Speaker. "You said I might request anything at your disposal. I would like Obbin to join us on our quest."

The man's eyebrows rose. "Why?"

Oliver looked at the council, then at the prince. "Because he has already proven to be resourceful and courageous. He led my brothers to freedom on the planet Evad, and he survived on our ship in secrecy. He succeeded in escaping from your guards with my brothers before."

"And I will try every day, again and again, until I succeed," Obbin boasted.

Oliver shook his head. "Obbin, I'm not asking this of the council as an alternative to your disobedience. I am asking because I think you will bring real value to our mission."

Obbin seemed surprised. His mouth closed.

"Speaker Ovon El, Obbin has been around your Mr. Thule for some time. His knowledge of the man might be an asset in the future. Also, if I go alone, why would your king trust me?"

Ovon El opened his mouth, but Oliver had one last thing to add.

"You gave your word that I could have whatever I needed as long as it was available to you," Oliver reminded him. "I need Obbin."

3.18

Rescue

With the paintings free of their frames, the boys laid them out in the arrangement they'd discovered. The neon paint strokes lined up perfectly. As Austin moved the light across the reunited painting, a map of halls and rooms came into view. "A maze!" Austin exclaimed. "Tiffany, it's a maze!"

Silence. The hall was empty.

"Mason, did you see Tiffany leave?"

"No." Mason looked down the hall in each direction. "Tiffany?"

Austin held his finger to his lips and shook his head. "Send a message to her mTalk instead." He took the Zinger from where it'd been propped against the wall and turned on its charge.

Mason tapped a message into his mTalk. "Sent."

A moment passed with no response. Something was wrong.

"Why would she go off on her own?" Austin asked. "Doesn't she realize the danger?"

"We did sort of get caught up in our discovery."

"We've got to find her," Austin said.

"And the paintings?"

"Roll them up. We're taking them with us."

The twins stacked the paintings and rolled them up together. The bundle was too big to fit in a pack, so Mason carried it. Austin held his weapon at the ready. Blue energy sparked along its end.

They traveled down several halls, checking every door along the way. It was frustrating that Oliver had ordered them to turn off their tracking signals. They'd have found Tiffany by now with the beacons on.

There'd still been no word from Oliver. It was far past the time he'd told them to remain in the palace, and it was quickly approaching the point when they were to call Archeos. Yet they still weren't at the *Phoenix*.

The weight of the entire mission settled on Austin's shoulders. He closed his eyes and took a deep breath but was interrupted when Mason bumped into him.

"Why'd you stop?"

"You don't think Drex came back, do you?"

"That's exactly what happened," came the undesired voice from behind them. "Drop the weapon before you turn around, kid, or I'll blast you both right where you stand."

Austin started to turn.

"I'm warning you!" Drex shouted.

POW!

Stone clattered to the ground as Drex fired a warning shot at the wall. That hadn't been the sound of the stun setting. That had been a kill shot.

"He's serious," Mason warned. "Put it down, Austin!"

Austin started to bend.

"No! Toss it in front of you," Drex ordered.

Austin threw the Zinger onto the stone floor ahead. The weapon clattered, and several sparks erupted from it. Austin hoped it wasn't damaged.

"Now, what is it that you have there?" Drex called to Mason.

"Art!" exclaimed Austin. "It's art."

"Ah, and you liked it so much you decided to take it with you?" Drex asked. "Ha. Hand it over."

Mason looked at his brother. Austin shook his head. "Where is she?"

"You expect me to tell you?"

Austin scowled. "You'll regret touching her."

Drex fired another shot at the wall near the twins, sending a spray of debris to the floor. Austin flinched as shards struck his arm.

"The power is in my hands. I'm making the rules," Drex warned. "I've not harmed your sister." As if he'd given way to weakness, he added, "Yet. Now turn around slowly."

Mason turned. Austin resisted only a second, knowing he didn't have a choice. The twins stood in plain view.

"Good. I guess you two can obey orders. Your brother said otherwise when we were at the Academy," Drex said.

Austin swallowed. The words stung. Had Oliver said such things about him to this guy?

"Hand over those paintings and your mTalks."

Austin nodded to Mason, and the twins began to remove their devices. "You'll not get away with this," he warned.

"Yeah, wait until our brother finds out," Mason added.

"Ha, I know your brother. Weakling! He doesn't have the guts to take me on face to face. In the underground chamber, he was only brave enough to sneak up behind me."

"Like you just did to us?" Austin said.

Drex scowled. "Whatever. Set down your mTalks and the paintings and back away."

Slowly they moved away from their opponent. Austin thought about grabbing the discarded Zinger, dive rolling, popping up, and firing at Drex, but thought better of it. The soldier's weapon was trained on the twins. One shot and one of them would be dead.

Austin felt useless. He felt like a failure.

The twins were near a door when Drex started to approach. A good twenty yards separated them. The paintings had unrolled, revealing bright neon strokes. Drex gathered the art together again.

Could Austin cover the distance and tackle his enemy before he saw the attack coming?

"Not a chance," whispered Mason as if reading his thoughts.

Drex backed away from the twins, his weapon trained, his eyes locked on theirs. "Stay right there," he warned. Then he slipped through an archway, taking the paintings and mTalks with him.

Austin started forward for the Zinger. Mason put out a hand to stop him, but Austin shook it off. The indicator light that showed the Zinger's power charge was black. The fall had rendered it useless.

"Mason, you find Tiffany! I'm going after Drex!"

"You can't! It's not safe," Mason said.

"He has our stuff! I have to!"

"It's too dangerous."

But Austin wasn't listening. Sheer determination drove him. He had to get back the paintings and mTalks. He had to make Drex pay for attacking his sister. Drex had said he hadn't harmed her, but was Austin really going to trust the word of someone like him?

He tore down the hall, catching sight of Drex darting around a corner. He pursued his enemy like a predator intent on its evening meal. Drex hadn't noticed Austin, or he would have fired at him.

Drex's footfalls echoed in a stairwell, leading Austin up a spiral staircase.

A door slammed shut. Austin burst through the exit. Atop the open tower sat a small ship. It was exactly like the one that had attacked them as they'd left Evad. The cockpit lowered into place. The front of the ship faced away from him.

Only a second to act. What could he do? A coil of rope attached to a pulley system disappeared over the tower's edge. Its use was unimportant. Austin grabbed a section and pulled. A length of rope came loose, and he dashed toward the craft. The engines switched on, firing a blast of engine exhaust.

Austin dove out of the way; his elbows striking the stone pavers of the tower roof.

Mason watched his brother disappear around the corner, brave or out of his mind. He shook himself. He had to find Tiffany. Where had Drex stashed her? Was she awake, scared?

He started in the direction Drex had come from. "Tiffany!" he shouted. A shiver of fear turned his thoughts to other soldiers, but he convinced himself there were none. They'd not seen any other than Drex. Besides that, his sister needed him.

"Tiffany! Tiffany, where are you?" he shouted. He opened door after door after door.

He flung open another door, and his heart skipped. There she was, lying on her side next to a chair, eyes closed. There was no blood. He knelt down beside her and rolled her onto her back.

"Tiffany, Tiffany, Tiffany, wake up," he said.

She didn't stir. He swung his pack to the floor and started digging. Why hadn't he brought any H_2O? He pulled out a can of Energen. This would have to do; at least it was cold. He popped the top and poured the fizzy drink on her face.

Tiffany spluttered and tried to sit up. Mason supported her back with his hand.

"Tiffany," he said. "You're awake."

She groaned and placed a hand to her forehead. She shuddered as she licked her lips. "What was that?"

"Drex knocked you out," Mason started.

"No, I mean, what did you pour on me?" Tiffany asked. "I remember Drex."

"Energen," Mason said. "What did Drex do to you?"

"He came in from that other door," Tiffany said. "He put his hand over my mouth before I could scream. When I refused to cooperate, he used this powder to knock me out. I must have fallen out of the chair after that."

"He's horrible, attacking a girl," Mason said.

"How long have I been out?"

Mason lowered his head. "I'm not sure. We didn't see you leave. Then we ran into Drex. It's been a while."

"Where is Austin? Is he still looking?"

"No, he went after Drex."

"He *what*?"

"Drex took all our stuff, mTalks, the paintings, and it looks like he took your stuff too."

Tiffany searched around her. Her pack and the e-journal were gone.

"Can you stand?" asked Mason. "We need to help Austin."

An ear-shattering rumble echoed all around. The walls shook. A painting slipped from the wall; a vase fell from a mantle over a fireplace. Shriveled leaves dropped from the plants.

"What was that?" Tiffany asked.

Had the soldiers come back, or had a new enemy arrived?

Austin swung the rope, launching it toward the tri-tailfins of the ship. The loop caught as the ship began to rise. Austin dove to the ground as Drex engaged the full thrust of the ship. The rope uncoiled as the craft flew away.

Austin's heart sank. His plan had failed.

The rope snapped tight. There was a terrible creak, and wood splintered. The pulley system broke free of the tower wall.

A resounding clang echoed below.

Something crashed against the tower's exterior. Austin peered over the side. A huge metal disc had caught inside an archway that connected his tower to an adjoining one.

He looked toward Drex's ship. It was bucking wildly in the sky, the rope holding tight around the tailfins. Suddenly one of the tailfins splintered. The ship spun onto its back, and its nose dove forward. It plummeted through a nearby tower. Flames burst across the roof as the engines spurted blasts of red fire.

Austin had to get their stuff before the clues were destroyed forever.

He ran down the stairs, skipping two and three steps at a time. Where was the door to the archway that connected the towers? Halfway down, he tried a door. Wrong one. Another, then another.

The fifth door opened to the bridge between the towers. Smoke billowed from the top of the tower. He was running out of time.

He ran across the bridge, throwing his weight against the closed door at its end. He raced up the stairs with all the ferocity of a wildcat. The air became smokier with every step. Soon he could hardly see.

He stood on something soft and reached down. Drex's body. Blood streaked the young man's face. Austin lowered his ear to listen for any breathing. A soft wheeze. Drex was still alive.

Austin looked toward the ship. The front half was in view. The canopy glass had shattered from taking the brunt of the impact. The other half of the ship stuck out through the top of the tower.

The flames hadn't engulfed the cockpit yet. There was still time. Austin reached through the canopy and took the tattered paintings from the copilot's seat. A satchel sat on the floor. Inside were not only the three mTalks, but also the e-journal. He'd not even thought that Drex might have taken the device from Tiffany. Without it, the Wikks would have been completely in the dark.

Drex groaned, then gasped. Austin looked at him with anger. This guy had almost stolen their only link to their parents and the only information they had to drive them forward on their quest. Plus, he'd fought them, threatened their lives, and probably tied up Tiffany.

A sharp cough wheezed from his mouth. His throat had begun to burn with the thick acrid smoke.

Austin slung the satchel over his back and wedged the paintings into it as best he could. An explosion echoed above them. The tower shuddered.

It wouldn't be long before the ship exploded and destroyed the tower. A dark thought crossed Austin's mind; he could leave Drex and let fate decide whether the soldier would live or die.

No. That wasn't fate. That was Austin playing judge. He was not ready to decide whether someone lived or died. Even though Drex was a villain, Austin couldn't stand by and watch him die. He grabbed him under the arms and pulled him backward down the stairs.

The tower shook as another explosion rocked its structure. Drex groaned with every bounce of his body against the stone stairs. It was the best Austin could do.

Finally Austin pressed through the door at the base of the tower, releasing Drex. He bent over. His arms ached. Quick shallow breaths rewarded his efforts. His hair clung to his forehead, soaked in sweat. Dirt, grime, and soot covered his body.

The entire hall began to shake. It wasn't over.

Austin grabbed Drex's limp arm and pulled. He dragged him down the corridor as quickly as he could. As he stepped into the next hall, the ceiling nearest the tower entrance collapsed. Stones filled the passage. A billow of dust flowed toward them.

A second later, debris blocked the hall. The tower collapsed completely, caving in the surrounding section of the palace.

Tiffany? Mason? Where were they? He'd run through the palace in pursuit of his target without thought to his direction. Now he was alone with an injured prisoner and no idea of his family's well-being. It was likely his sister and brother would think he was buried in the collapse.

Technology

Oliver and Obbin followed Speaker Ovon El out of the council chamber, escorted by two palace guards. The Speaker placed his hand on a white stone next to a metal door at the end of the hall.

His hand glowed red, then green, and the door slid upward. He, Obbin, and Oliver entered a room with paintings of men and women covering every inch of the four walls. Not all had blue skin.

"These are portraits of the past kings and queens of the Blauwe Mensen," the Speaker said. He touched a white stone beside the door, and it closed, leaving the two guards outside.

"Follow me," he said. He walked to a tall painting of a man and gripped its frame. The picture swung out from the wall, revealing a white stone. The Speaker placed his hand on it. The portion of wall behind the painting sank into the ground, only a foot or so remaining visible.

They stepped over the short wall and into a hall. The hall was dark, but Oliver's boots made a metallic thump as they struck the floor. Two lines of bright lights flashed along the top of the hall, leading toward another room.

"What's this?" asked Obbin.

Oliver looked at him in surprise. He'd been sure Obbin had explored every nook and cranny of Cobalt Gorge.

"This is a very special chamber," Speaker Ovon El said.

Oliver and Obbin followed him to the end of the hall.

"This room was built by the twelfth king of the Blauwe Mensen when the first foreign settlers came to this planet. He knew our people's secret way of life would not last forever. Eventually we would be discovered and become dependent on the settlers' plans for the planet."

The chamber was square, no wider than ten feet across. A blue crystal statue of a man stood in the center. He wore a crown and held a long silver sword that pointed outward. A basin sat at his feet. An inscription had been etched into the stone.

"Oliver, this is where you will take the blood oath of protection," Ovon El said.

"I made your brothers do this before they left," Obbin said, "only with a statue in the upper halls."

"Our secret is out. Once the soldiers landed, all hope of secrecy ended for our location, but . . ." The Speaker paused and looked toward the wall. Oliver noticed a cross-shaped pattern of white stones. "There is one last secret for you to keep. Obbin is already under the oath, and that extends to what I am about to show you."

Oliver nodded.

"Repeat after me," Speaker Ovon El said. He walked to the statue and placed his left hand on the sword hilt. "I promise to uphold the code of the gorge."

"I promise to uphold the code of the gorge," Oliver repeated.

"I will hold the secrets of this place in my heart and mind but never on my tongue, from this day forward, unless released by one of the royal family. This I promise and seal with my own blood." Speaker Ovon El guided Oliver line by line, then held out his right palm. "Now press your hand against the end of the sword."

Oliver eyed the silver point. He pressed his hand against the sword's tip. A drop of blood rolled down his palm and into the stone basin below.

Obbin grinned and embraced him. "Welcome, my brother."

The Speaker handed him a square of cloth for the cut. "You are now bonded to us as a protector of the Blauwe Mensen people," he said. "The gorge itself will have to be abandoned."

"Can't you coexist with the settlers?" Oliver asked.

Speaker Ovon El gave a polite smile but shook his head. "The same persecution that led us to flee our previous home still exists."

Persecution? Oliver didn't quite understand that.

"Now, let me show you what I brought you here to see." The Speaker walked to the cross of white stones. It was identical to the ruby pool on Evad. He touched the top and bottom stone of the vertical line, then the two outside stones of the horizontal line. Each lit green. A strong gasp of air came from the bottom of the wall as it slid upward. It groaned as it disappeared into the ceiling.

Oliver was not ready for what he saw next. Obbin stumbled back, equally shocked.

Before them sat a spaceship.

The bronze ship was several times larger than the *Phoenix* but not as large as the *Skull*. It sat in a large bay. Dust covered the domed windshield of its nose. Large landing skids swept out from the side of the craft like wings but curved toward the ground, holding the ship upright. Five engines ran along the underside of the ship, and a towering tailfin sprouted at the very back. Another glass dome sat toward the front.

"This is the *Ontdekking*," Speaker Ovon El said. "It brought our people here long ago."

Obbin scratched his shaggy green hair. "I never thought this still existed. I figured it'd been destroyed or dismantled."

"No, we put it here for safekeeping."

"Why didn't you show it to Voltan?" asked Obbin.

"We are not sure that the *Ontdekking* can even fly, nor is there a pilot among our people." The Speaker looked toward the ceiling. "That's something we failed to maintain, our knowledge of flight.

"However," he continued, "I do believe the communications on the *Ontdekking* still work, though using them risks having our transmissions be intercepted or our position triangulated by the Federation. I want us to have a way to communicate with you and the prince. Should we be forced to leave or should"—Speaker Ovon El hesitated—"should Prince Obbin become king, we will need to contact you, Captain Oliver."

Oliver nodded. Obbin's head was bowed, the direness of the situation clearly sinking in. Oliver found himself unexpectedly reaching out. He put his arm around the boy, pulling him in. Obbin looked at Oliver and smiled, seemingly comforted.

Followed by Obbin and Oliver, Ovon El started toward a walkway that extended from an open hatch halfway up the side of the ship. He touched a button as he entered the ship. Overhead lights flickered on with an electrical hum. A few went out immediately, and several burst with sparks, but enough remained on to see by.

The floor was a metallic grate, allowing them to see below. They moved quickly up several spiral staircases and entered a large bridge with a domed windshield. The crew had a 360-degree view of their surroundings. A pole in the room's center held a small platform near the peak of the dome. A narrow ladder led to its top.

"Up we go," Speaker Ovon El said.

They climbed to the platform. Two chairs sat back to back, low panels of controls before them. Two crewmembers could sit there with a view of everything around them. The controls probably fed them information and allowed them to communicate with the captain.

"Here it is," the Speaker said. Only a few of the screens and indicator lights glowed on the panels. He tapped a metal placard on the front panel. "Can you put this information in your watch?" he asked Oliver.

"Of course," Oliver said. He tapped the screen on his mTalk. "5002-01-TCO-7002-60-NUJ."

"Got it."

"That's the serial code for the ship. It should also act as our transmission locator code," Ovon El said.

"That is how it usually works," Oliver said, "though we should test it when I get to the surface and can pick up a signal with my mTalk."

"For now we must have hope," the Speaker said. "I will come here daily and check for messages."

"This is quite the ship," Oliver said admiringly.

"I can't believe it's been here all this time," Obbin said. "Rylin and I have searched every bit of this gorge. We've uncovered many secrets, yet this one eluded us."

The Speaker smiled. "We hoped your adventures on the outside would satisfy your craving for adventure and occupy your time."

"You knew?" asked Obbin.

"Your father, your mother, and I," the Speaker said. "But we've spent enough time here. We must get you on your way."

As the Speaker lowered the wall to the landing bay, he said, "Prince Obbin and Captain Oliver, tell no one about the ship. Only in the direst of circumstances should you breathe word of its existence."

"What about my sister and brothers?" asked Oliver. "They'll be on the ship. It would be hard to communicate with you without their knowing."

"Yes, I can see that," Ovon El said. "You may tell them. All but your sister have taken the oath. Help her understand why she must keep the *Ontdekking* secret."

Oliver and Obbin agreed.

Once they returned to the portrait room, the Speaker placed a hand on Obbin and Oliver's shoulders. "Let us pray to Creator."

He spoke as if direct communication were possible. When they had a moment to sit down and catch their breath and Oliver had an Energen in hand, he would ask Obbin to explain it all.

Speaker Ovon El and Obbin bowed their heads, so Oliver mimicked them.

"We ask for your protection over these boys and their families during this quest. We pray for strength and courage, for safety and skill, for wit and discovery. May they have success and your guidance as they seek to save those who have been wrongly taken. Amen."

The Speaker lifted his head, tears rolling from his eyes. "Now you must go."

The two palace guards awaited them outside.

"Take Captain Oliver to speak with Guard Ssej," Speaker Ovon El said. "He needs to be told everything we know about our enemies."

The palace guards handed Oliver and Obbin off to the young soldiers Semaj and At Okad, who took them to Guard Ssej at his post near the lift.

"Hey, Dad," Semaj blurted out.

Guard Ssej half smiled. "Son."

"Sorry. Greetings, Guard Ssej," Semaj corrected himself.

"Greetings."

"This is Captain Oliver," At Okad explained. "The Speaker has requested that you tell him what you heard."

Guard Ssej nodded. "I'll tell you what I know, but my recall may not be perfect. Please use what I am about to tell you with that in mind."

Oliver agreed.

"My men confronted the attackers in the library. They had begun to ransack it," Ssej explained. Obbin gasped. "I and three of my men charged into the battle, but they had weapons that rendered my three comrades unconscious. I must not have received a full blast because I remained awake. I'd been knocked to the ground and couldn't move, but I could hear everything around me."

Oliver shuddered as his memory of Vedrik shocking his dad replayed in his mind. He looked at Semaj, but his expression was unreadable. Of course, Semaj's dad was right before them. He'd not been taken prisoner.

Guard Ssej continued. "I heard Thule's voice as he entered the library. It was clear he was in charge, always being referred to as 'sir.' I heard one of the soldiers say, 'The ship is ready for launch and Professor Norton is awaiting our arrival at the GenTexic facility.' Thule asked about the Wikks. 'Are the Wikk archeologists secure? I've just met their children.' 'Yes, we have them. They will be rendezvousing with us near Yeldah so that you can escort them to the laboratories.' 'Have the soldiers retrieved my notes from the underwater cavern?' 'Yes.' 'Excellent. We're finished here. Let us leave this icy prison.' That was the last I heard before they moved on."

"Do you know anything about the notes they retrieved?"

"I do not," Ssej said.

"Thanks for your help," Oliver said. "We should be going."

"Captain, be careful. These men are very dangerous," Ssej said, just as a father would to a son. Oliver noticed his eyes flick to Semaj.

"We will continue to use caution," Oliver said. "Obbin, let's go."

Palace guards brought packs of supplies containing fresh food, several books about the history of the Blauwe Mensen, and a few maps. They also returned the StunShot rifle to Oliver.

"Give the council my thanks," Oliver said.

The guards bowed and left.

"We've been tasked with escorting you to your ship with the supplies," At Okad said. Semaj held up his fist as if showing his strength.

"Good, we could use the help," Oliver said.

The two guards wore thick furry hats, coats, and pants as well as gloves and boots made of animal hide. They also had wide, woven discs to wear on their feet for crossing the snow. Oliver and Obbin were offered the outfits as well, but Oliver explained that he wanted to pick up their Bliz-Zero gear.

The lift stopped at the entrance to the tunnel that led away from the cavern. At Okad and Semaj took Oliver and Obbin a different way from the way they'd come before. It avoided the water and instead crossed several narrow stone bridges over deep chasms. Oliver would have preferred the water.

They collected their Bliz-Zero gear from where they'd left it. Oliver was tempted to take a second look at the underground pool, but if the soldiers had already taken the notes, there would be nothing left to find. He would only be squandering more time.

One Lost

"Oliver!" Tiffany cried as she and Mason ran over to him.

Worry overcame Oliver at their desperate looks.

"Where's Austin?" he asked.

"We don't know," Mason said. His words were choked. "Drex . . . he came back. Austin chased him. There was a . . ." Mason's voice trailed off.

Oliver grabbed his brother's shoulders, an uncontrollable fear surging over him. "There was a *what*? Mason?"

"A collapse," Mason said, his eyes lowered.

Oliver hadn't heard or felt anything of the sort. Surely a collapse would have shaken the ground or created a loud rumble.

"We searched, but we didn't see him," Mason said. "We called out, but we couldn't hear anything."

Tiffany began to sob. "It's my fault. I shouldn't have left them. If I hadn't, then . . ."

"Tiffany . . ." Oliver looked at his sister, then back to Mason. "Show me where," he said.

Mason turned to go.

"Leave the supplies," Obbin told Semaj and At Okad. "Come with us."

Rubble blocked the entire hall. There was no way through. Oliver had to admit the truth to himself. No one could survive such a collapse. Sorrow swept over him. For the first time since the quest had begun, his tears rolled freely.

Tiffany and Mason gathered around him as he dropped into a squat. They sobbed alongside him. Obbin and the guards faded into the distance. The entire world seemed to come to a crashing halt.

How could he continue from here? Yes, their parents were still missing, but their brother was dead.

Death—the thought of it . . . what came after?

"Austin?" came Obbin's surprised voice.

Oliver looked toward the prince. In an instant, he and his sister and brother were embracing Austin. The youngest Wikk didn't seem surprised at their reaction. He'd come from a side hall.

"I hoped I'd find you before you thought the worst," he said.

Oliver stepped back. "You're alive." He smiled at his brother, wiping tears from his eyes.

"You really thought you'd lost me?" Austin said.

"We did," Tiffany admitted. "I'll never leave again, I promise. It's my fault that—"

"Tiffany, it's not your fault," Mason said.

Austin hugged his sister again. "No, it's not."

"We were here not long ago," Mason said. "We called out for you. Why didn't you answer?"

"We had to go a long way to get around the collapse. The tower took out several floors," Austin said.

"We?" asked Mason.

"I had to drag him." Austin raised his hand and moved to the side.

Drex's body lay at the end of the hall. Oliver's temper rose at the sight. Drex was the one who'd caused this.

"He's hurt badly," Austin explained. "We need to get him medical attention right away."

Austin's compassion surprised Oliver. Was he seriously concerned for the attacker? This enemy who'd caused so many problems for them?

"Why?" he asked.

Austin's next words shocked Oliver further. "Because we're better than that."

Oliver looked at his sister and sighed. She nodded in agreement. "Fine, we'll turn him over to At Okad and Semaj. They can take him to their people and treat him, then keep him prisoner until our quest is over."

"No, we have to take him with us," Austin interjected.

"He'd be a danger to our mission," Oliver argued.

"Austin's right," Mason interrupted. "We need to find out who he's working for. Find out what they're after and search for a weakness in their plans."

"Interrogate him?" Tiffany asked.

The twins nodded.

Oliver hesitated. Once Drex recovered, he would be a formidable opponent. They couldn't keep him locked up indefinitely or guard him every moment. And once they had what they wanted from him, they couldn't release him or abandon him. Keeping Drex posed significant problems. Whereas leaving him in the care of the Blauwe Mensen meant he was out of their hair.

Then again, the twins had a good point. Drex's knowledge could be useful—if they could even pry it out of him. Perhaps the Blauwe Mensen could interrogate him. The Speaker could relay information to them via the *Ontdekking's* communication.

"Tiffany?" Oliver asked. She looked toward the unconscious prisoner. Her hand moved to her chin. Oliver hoped that she would side with him. That way the decision would be mutual and he wouldn't be overpowering the twins.

"Well . . . I think I must agree with Mason and Austin," Tiffany said.

Oliver was surprised.

"We have much to gain from what he knows. I say we bring him along."

Oliver surveyed his family. Three to one.

"Okay, Drex comes with," he said. "At Okad and Semaj, will you carry him?"

"We are at your service," At Okad said with a bow. Oliver noticed him smile at Tiffany.

Oliver cleared his throat. "Yes, let me introduce At Okad and Semaj. They're two soldiers of the Blauwe Mensen and will be escorting us to the *Phoenix*."

"It is our pleasure," Semaj said and stepped forward to take Tiffany's hand. He bowed his head to her. At Okad grunted an interruption.

"Nice to meet you," Tiffany said as Semaj dropped her hand.

"The pleasure is mine," Semaj said.

At Okad stepped closer.

"Hi, guys," Austin said. "You'll want to be careful with Drex. One of his arms is pretty burned, and his leg has a deep gash. I tried to wrap it with my shirt as best I could."

Oliver realized Austin was playing interference between the young men and his sister.

"Let's go then," Oliver said. "Mason and Obbin, will you gather the supplies At Okad and Semaj were carrying?" They agreed. "Obbin, lead us out of here."

Oliver heard the prisoner groan and begin to murmur in his waking sleep. "Must be relit . . . hatch . . . too many tries . . ."

None of it made sense, and Drex went silent again. Tiffany dug a sedative from her pack and injected Drex with it. "This should relax him until we can give him better care. His burns look bad, but I can't treat them until we're back in the *Phoenix*."

Obbin stood over Drex as Tiffany administered the shot. Oliver heard him again pray to Creator. Mason must have noticed as well, because he was staring at the prince and scratching his head.

Now it was time to go.

Through the halls and back to the secret entrance they went. The cold air swept in as Austin opened the door. The piles of snow had melted but turned to ice from the freezing blast.

At Okad and Semaj fastened their discs to the bottom of their animal-hide boots. They'd been created specifically for traversing the deep snow.

The Wikks and Obbin located their hover boards. They wrapped Drex in three layers of thick curtains they ripped from a few windows. They hoped the heavy fabric would keep him warm. The soldier's thermal wear had been badly burned, and Austin had peeled off most of it so that Tiffany could treat his wounds. Dragging the prisoner became a significant challenge as he continued to sink into the snow, slowing their progress. Oliver and Obbin tried balancing him while riding their hover boards, but it didn't work.

Finally Oliver, Tiffany, and Mason went ahead to prepare the ship, leaving Austin and Obbin to guide At Okad and Semaj.

They found the *Phoenix*, and Oliver uncloaked it. After entering the code, they stepped into the relative warmth and protection of the ship.

"Mason, would you load the coordinates for Enaid?" Oliver said.

"So we are still heading to the Cathedral of the Star?" Mason asked.

"Yes," Oliver answered. "That will be our primary destination."

"Will do," Mason said and started up the stairs to the bridge.

"Tiffany, I want you to look at my wound. Then I'm going to find a place in the cargo bay where we can restrain Drex during the flight. We'll have to figure out more secure accommodations later."

"I'm out of gauze and NumbaGlu after attending to Drex," Tiffany said. "I can get some more from the galley."

They headed up the stairs. Oliver went to his cabin. He pulled off his coat, lifted his shirt, and pulled back the wrapping. The wound in his side looked a whole lot better. He looked in the mirror. Other than the injury, his body was in good shape. If anything, his abs and muscles had become more toned.

Tiffany walked in, and Oliver let his shirt down, slightly embarrassed that he was admiring himself. She smiled knowingly.

"Go ahead and take off your shirt, then sit on the bed," she said. The undertone in her voice meant she was laughing inside. Oliver removed his shirt. "Wow, it looks like it's healing pretty well," she said. "That FlexSkyn really helps."

Oliver laughed. "Yeah, I can almost feel the little nano-bots crawling along my skin."

His sister shivered at the thought.

"I can't actually feel them," he admitted.

Tiffany smiled. She took a cloth dampened with some sterilized gel and wiped it over the wound to clean it. "This is looking great, Oliver. You should be back to normal soon."

"The power of a well-trained mind and physically fit boy," Oliver said with a laugh.

"The power of nano-biology," Tiffany said.

"Your great stitching held it together," Oliver said. He slid his shirt back on. "Well, I'm off to the cargo bay."

"I'll be there in a minute. I want to check on Midnight and wash the Energen out of my hair."

"Energen?"

She sighed. "Don't ask."

He didn't.

"I'll see you after I check if Mason got the coordinates loaded," Tiffany said.

"Sounds good," Oliver said. "Thanks for taking care of me."

Tiffany smiled. "I try."

The wind had picked up in the gorge, and snow had begun to fall. Austin hovered close to Drex. The prisoner was still out, though he moaned on occasion and mumbled partial phrases.

Obbin guided the procession, Austin beside him.

"Obbin, we found a note from Rylin in the library," Austin said. "He's attempting to trade some books for your family's release."

"You found the Chamber of Cranium?" Obbin asked in surprise. "Why didn't you tell me?"

"Sorry," Austin said. "A tower nearly fell on me."

"I'm sorry. I didn't mean to jump on you. It's just . . ." Obbin's voice trailed off.

"You miss your family," Austin said. "I do too."

The blizzard whipped around them, nearly knocking Austin from his hover board.

"Do you know what books he took?"

"Some chronicle books about Terra," Austin said.

Obbin didn't say anything.

"Is that bad?"

"I'm not entirely sure," Obbin said. "The books in that chamber are very secret, known to very few. I'm not exactly sure why he chose those."

A rumble alerted Austin to the *Phoenix*'s engines igniting. "How close are we?" he asked.

"Five minutes at most," Obbin said.

Austin looked back at At Okad and Semaj, who were fighting against the deep snow. "You sure?"

"Maybe fifteen," Obbin admitted.

Twelve minutes passed before they made it down the sloping sides of the amphitheater.

The cargo bay was open, waiting for their arrival. The Blauwe Mensen dragged Drex into a holding cell constructed of building panels used for archeological base camps. Cargo straps served as shackles. For the time being, this would be Drex's prison.

The guards waited while Drex was secured into his make-shift cell. Tiffany stood by with a medical kit to dress the prisoner's wounds.

"I hope to see you again someday," At Okad told her. Austin thought his tone was far too sweet.

"Me too," Austin interjected.

Tiffany blushed. "Yes, it would nice to return under different circumstances."

Semaj made his way over. "Please return when you can. I would enjoy showing you around our gorge."

The cold wind whistled through the open cargo bay as if to remind Semaj of the gorge's destruction.

"Or Cavern Haven," he corrected himself.

"Yes, I—" Tiffany started.

"Well, time to go," Austin said, ushering the soldiers toward the open door.

"Prince Obbin, be brave," At Okad said.

"You will make your people proud," added Semaj. "May Creator guide you."

"Thank you," Obbin said.

The soldiers said goodbye and disappeared into the blowing snow.

The door closed. It was time to go.

"Everyone to the bridge," Oliver ordered.

"I'll stay here and guard Drex?" asked Austin.

"It's too risky during takeoff. If something goes wrong or we're attacked, I want you with us," Oliver said. "He's restrained and won't get hurt. We'll come down as soon as we're in hyper flight."

It wasn't exactly what Austin wanted, but it was agreeable.

"Were there any new messages? Anything from Mr. O'Farrell?" Austin asked as Tiffany sat down. His sister had retrieved her cat from her room.

"Nope, nothing," Tiffany admitted. "I only hope Schlamm didn't get him." She stroked Midnight's fur.

Austin hadn't ever met the parts trader, but Tiffany had said he was a tough-looking guy who dealt with Corsairs. That in itself made him an enemy in Austin's opinion. Corsairs were nothing but a bunch of pirates.

"Or Spike," Mason added. Tiffany had also told the twins about Schlamm's genetically engineered guard lizard.

"Mason, don't be morbid," Tiffany warned.

"I'm sure he's fine," Oliver said. "He's resourceful . . . and cunning."

"So we're leaving without him?" Austin asked.

"We can't wait any longer," Tiffany said.

"Oliver, did the Blauwe Mensen know anything about who attacked them?" Austin asked. "Was it the Corsairs or the Übel?"

"The Übel, I think. A guard overheard a brief exchange between a soldier and Mr. Thule. Apparently they mentioned our parents and said they'd rendezvous somewhere." Oliver stopped and frowned, trying to think. He snapped his fingers. "Yeldah! It was called Yeldah."

"I'm not sure where that is. I'll check the e-journal," Tiffany said.

"There's more. They're headed to pick up a professor at some laboratory . . ."

"GenTexic or something," Obbin finished.

"That's right," Oliver said. "They were going to rendezvous with our parents first. The Übel are headed to the GenTexic facility before they go to Enaid and pick this guy up."

"The night I was separated from everyone"—Austin's voice cracked—"I heard a soldier mention some Übel being dispatched to get a Zebra Xavier guy. Could this be him?"

"That's right, Austin," Tiffany said. "I heard mention of Zebra Xavier too. Vedrik seemed fearful of him. He was worried about facing the man's wrath over losing us."

"Why would they try to kill us if they were worried about our escaping? I mean, if we'd been killed, wouldn't this Zebra guy be even more angry?" Mason suggested.

"Good point," Oliver said.

"Zebra is not a very scary name," Obbin added.

Oliver and Mason laughed.

"Do you think the Übel think we're dead?" Austin asked.

"I don't think so," Mason said. "Remember, Drex works for Vedrik. He chased us off Evad until Brother Sam intervened."

"That's right," Oliver said. "And they left Drex here again to clean up or to wait for us. They must have known we'd come here. But how?"

"Mr. Thule would have known Obbin disappeared with Austin and me," Mason said, "and he was communicating with them and is with them now."

"Seems like a long shot. We might have kept Obbin with us and not returned," Oliver retorted.

"I'm not sure it matters much at the moment," Tiffany said. "We need to decide where we're headed. I've found Yeldah. It's one of three moons that revolve around the planet Re Lyt. It's in the Ppank System."

"You don't think we should head for Enaid?" asked Mason.

"Not if the Übel are heading to Re Lyt for a rendezvous," Austin said. "We should go there first and head to Enaid if we don't find them."

"Hold on," Oliver said. "Did you hear Drex mumbling?"

"Yeah, just a bunch of random thoughts about lighting something and hatching something," Obbin said.

"The lighting part—he said *relit*, but I think he meant *Re Lyt*, the place," Oliver said.

"But hatching?" asked Austin.

"Chickens?" Obbin suggested.

"Not sure about that part," Oliver said. "But this means we should be heading to Re Lyt as well."

"If Drex was saying *Re Lyt*, it must somehow be connected," Tiffany said.

"Or he just knew that was where his team was headed next," Mason said. "Maybe he was supposed to rendezvous there as well. Which means we have no additional information to what we had before."

Everyone stared at Mason. Again he'd come to a solid conclusion.

Oliver looked at the windshield. "Let's vote. Enaid?"

Mason's hand rose.

"Re Lyt?"

The other four voted for Re Lyt.

"Re Lyt it is," Oliver said. He breathed an unexpected sigh of relief. Making decisions as a team had taken some of the burden of the quest off his shoulders. He wasn't solely responsible for their success or failure; everyone was taking ownership.

"I'm still not sure how chickens fit into the equation," Obbin said.

Austin smiled. "Chickens . . ."

3.21

Uncloaked

"Everyone secured?" Oliver asked. "Engaging thrusters."

The rumble echoed through the air. A blur of white snow swirled around the *Phoenix* as it rose. The wall of the gorge ahead disappeared from view, and the range of mountains stretched out before them, cloaked in white.

The sky grew darker and darker the higher they flew. Soon only the two moons of Jahr des Eises were visible.

"Tiffany, can you check our trajectory and see if the Corsair or Übel ships are still here?" Oliver asked. "I don't want to fly right into the middle of a battle again. We may need to fly around the planet and leave from the other side."

Midnight nestled on Tiffany's lap as she tapped the Nav-Com before her. "Scanning."

Oliver looked at the flight systems. Everything was in check. The work on the servers had been sufficient.

"We're clear," Tiffany said. She leaned over and tucked the cat into a pack under her seat.

The ship shuddered as it broke free of Jahr des Eises' gravitational hold.

"Preparing for hyper flight." As Oliver's fingers slipped across the screen, the lights in the bridge went dark.

"What happened?" Mason asked.

"I don't know," Oliver admitted. The screen before him was still on.

The lights flickered back on.

"Oliver! There's a ship! It just appeared," Tiffany warned him. "It's the gray one from before."

"You said there wasn't anything," Austin accused.

"It must have been cloaked too," Mason said.

Oliver's heart sank. They were not cloaked. He'd not activated the cloaking device. He reached for the remote, tucked in a compartment in the console. Hoping it wasn't too late, he clicked the button

Nothing happened. The application for the device wasn't running. The system didn't seem to be recognizing the small silver sphere. Oliver ejected it, then plugged it back in. He hit the remote again.

Still nothing.

"It's turning toward us," Tiffany cried out.

Oliver looked out at the large ship. It now faced them.

"It fired something!" Austin yelled.

"Engaging hyper flight sequence," Oliver said.

Two silvery balls of light surged toward them.

"We're not going to make it!" yelled Mason.

It was true. Oliver yanked the controls to the left and hammered the thrust. The *Phoenix* twisted. The controls in his hand stiffened.

The entire ship shuddered, and a blinding light burst through the windshield.

3.22

Prisoners

Mason rubbed his eyes. He forced them open, squinting in the overly bright light.

"Huhhh . . ." he groaned. He was lying down? He forced himself to look around. He saw three gray walls and one of smoky glass. A single light hung overhead.

This was not the bridge of the *Phoenix*.

"Tiffany?" he asked.

No sound but the hum of the overhead light. He was alone in a small room.

The last thing he could remember was a blinding flash and the *Phoenix* spinning around him. They'd just taken off from Jahr des Eises when the bright light had struck. But why?

What had happened just before?

His mind was like the static on the mTalks. Fuzzy.

. . . Corsairs . . .

They'd been attacked. Surprised by the enemy.

Mason stumbled toward the glass wall. He could make out a corridor on the other side. A bar of lights stretched along the hall about midway up the wall. He saw no signs or doors or guards.

Mason knocked on the glass. His arm jerked back in shock—quite literally. The wall flashed silver, and a spark of electricity snapped his fingers.

The wall was energized. He was a prisoner, and this was his cell.

Mason's legs were heavy, as were his arms and eyes. He plopped back onto the bunk and waited. His mTalk had been removed. He was barefoot.

Hours or minutes passed before the glass wall sank into the floor. A guard dressed in a gray jumpsuit stepped into view. Every bit of the Corsair was concealed. He wore black goggles, a mask, a gray tricorne hat, black boots, and gloves. The only identifying mark on the guard was a name badge that read *Trexter*.

He held a baton, or perhaps a sword. Its black handle had a silvery glow. The guard didn't speak but motioned Mason out of the cell.

He hesitantly came forward and stood near the wall. To his relief, four other people had just done the same, each with his or her own assigned guard. Mason eyed his siblings and friend. He was glad to see they were all alive. It seemed a casual thought, given the seriousness of life and death. Since they'd faced death so often, it seemed less and less frightening. That couldn't be a good thing. That wasn't being fearless; that meant he was becoming numb.

"Maso—" *ZAP!* Austin's guard tapped his shoulder with the glowing silver sword, cutting his call short. "Ouch, you—!" Austin silenced as the guard motioned to tap him again.

Suddenly red arrows lit up in the floor and blinked, pointing the prisoners down the hall. The guards directed Oliver first, followed by Tiffany, Mason, Austin, and Obbin last.

There was no sign of Drex. He'd been on the ship as well. Perhaps he had been taken to a medical ward—if these people had one.

Or maybe they'd not discovered him in his cell.

After marching through nearly a dozen doors, they entered a large, round room. Corridors branched from it in every direction. At the center, guarded by three men, sat an old man. He wore a brown tweed suit and an emerald flat cap.

Was this Mr. O'Farrell?

The guards stepped away from their captives and exited through the door. The hatch closed behind them.

Oliver spoke immediately. "Mr. O'Farrell, how . . . I mean, we lost you. We got your distress call and came right away. We searched the location of your transmission, but you weren't there."

The old man nodded toward the door and grimaced. "Yes, my boy, I believe you did. Only they got to me first." He looked at the others. "You must be Mason and Austin. I've seen your pictures." His eyes twinkled. "But you . . . you must be one of the Blauwe Mensen."

"My name is Obbin," the blue prince said.

"Obbin, nice to meet you. Your kin—people have long eluded the citizens of Brighton . . . and Mudo for that matter," Mr. O'Farrell said with a curious smile. "I have many questions to ask you."

"We found their city destroyed," Mason interjected. "The Übel attacked and took his family."

Mr. O'Farrell frowned deeply and stared at the prince.

Oliver cleared his throat.

"Yes, my dear boy." Mr. O'Farrell sighed. "Schlamm chased me quite a ways. I was able to lose him by slipping beneath one of the maglev bridges. He sailed right over me." Mr. O'Farrell stopped, removed a piece of emerald cloth from his pocket, and wiped his forehead. "These ships are so hot inside."

Mason shivered. He actually felt cold.

"Thinking I'd lost him, I tried to reach you with my location. Alas, I couldn't contact you, so I determined to fly back to Brighton and get hold of Samuel . . . or Mr. Krank. He's resourceful, and I thought he'd take me in his ship to find you."

Mason remembered what Oliver and Tiffany had told him about Mr. Krank. The man had run a parts shop in Brighton. He'd appeared to be Mr. O'Farrell's friend, but maybe not. He'd given them the silver sphere to cloak the ship and told them to wait until they were rid of their wealthy benefactor before using it. Perhaps he was working for the Übel like Drex.

Mr. O'Farrell continued his story. "As I went, the snow became heavier and heavier. I couldn't see but ten feet before me. I holed up in a maglev tunnel. That's when I was ambushed." Mr. O'Farrell closed his eyes. He looked exhausted.

"Who ambushed you?" Austin asked. "Schlamm?"

"Not quite." Mr. O'Farrell's words had a sharp edge to them. "He'd called his friends, the Corsairs. They were still in the area and were more than happy for an excuse to do a little kidnapping."

"You're not a kid," Obbin said. This made Mr. O'Farrell laugh, but Tiffany looked taken aback.

"It's just a term," she corrected.

"Indeed, I am not a kid. But they captured me and brought me here. Schlamm told them I had a sizeable fortune."

"Pirates!" Austin exclaimed. "Always after money."

Mr. O'Farrell nodded. "Not long after that, there was a large battle with the Übel. This ship, the *Black Ranger*, was damaged, but so were several of the Übel's fighters. Then I got word of your capture. I immediately requested to speak with you. They declined, of course, but I offered a lucrative financial deal the Corsairs couldn't pass up." This sounded a bit like a boast. "They'd better understand the quest we are on and the magnificent rewards at stake."

Mason didn't like the sound of that. An alliance with pirates couldn't be good. Plus, Mr. O'Farrell had seemed angry with the Corsairs only moments ago. Now he seemed pleased after his successful negotiations.

"That brings us to this very moment. You'll be able to move freely about level thirteen, the prison sector of the ship."

Austin scoffed. "Sounds like fun."

"Austin, be thankful. It's better than the small cell you were in," Tiffany reprimanded. "Besides, it was kind of Mr. O'Farrell to negotiate on our behalf."

"Thank you, dear. Now, why don't we head down to the dining hall for some food?" Mr. O'Farrell said. "It's actually not that horrible."

"I thought Corsairs were pirates," Austin said.

"Well ... yes, that's the reputation they have," Mr. O'Farrell admitted. "But there's more to them than that. Like many other groups, they don't want to adhere to the Federation's governance. Some might call them freedom fighters."

"Like who?" Austin asked.

Mason interrupted. "Mr. O'Farrell, have you ever heard of the Veri—"

A swift kick to his shin from his eldest brother stopped him. "Have you verified the McGregors' disappearance or the Übel's involvement with Archeos at all?" Oliver asked as cover.

Mr. O'Farrell pulled his eyes from Mason. "No, I've been here. I've had no time." His words were slow and measured. It seemed he was curious about what Mason had been about to ask.

"Have you put together an escape plan?" Austin blurted.

"Shhh!" Tiffany warned.

Mr. O'Farrell smiled. "I'm working on other means of negotiation. Give it time."

Mason sighed. His twin was not known for patience.

"Mr. O'Farrell, there was another aboard our ship. His name was Drex. Do you know his whereabouts?" Tiffany asked.

"Yes, the young man had serious injuries. He's been taken to the medical ward for treatment. The Corsairs might be considered pirates, but they aren't merciless. They are a community. Families live on this ship, you know."

"I didn't. I mean, I wouldn't have thought," Tiffany said.

Mason's stomach grumbled. He touched his tummy.

Oliver must have had the same feeling. "So, about that food?"

3.23

Ashley

Level thirteen was expansive. Austin estimated you could fit fifty or more *Phoenix*-sized ships within the prison floor—sliced into pieces, of course. As Mr. O'Farrell had said, they could move about the level, although there were a few doors that were closed off and marked with glowing red Xs. Non-marked doors simply opened as he and Obbin neared. The few guards on the floor stood still as stone, mostly next to marked doors. However, not all the doors had guards. Austin supposed guarded doors were exits. The others probably hid violent criminals or maybe even nasty beasts. Austin's imagination began to run away with him. The marked doors were the ones he most wanted to get behind. What things were terrible enough to be locked in solitary confinement?

Mr. O'Farrell, Oliver, Tiffany, and Mason had returned to a conference room to discuss all that had happened in the time between their separations. Not wanting to sit through a boring, detailed account of the past days' events, Austin and Obbin had requested permission to explore.

It'd been granted.

Within the prison level, they'd found a workout center, dining hall, library, recreation room, and cinema. They'd spent some time in the rec room and even in the workout center. The cinema was playing some documentary on a now-extinct species. They'd come across other prisoners, but they were few in comparison to the expansiveness of the thirteenth floor. All were barefoot and wore bright green jumpsuits.

One of the prisoners was being escorted by two guards; his hands were bound, and a green hood covered his head. Obbin and Austin kept a safe distance from him. Another prisoner turned and walked in the opposite direction the moment the boys came into view, seeming shocked to see the blue boy. The last prisoner they encountered was a woman. The boys waved, and she returned the gesture. She spoke with them briefly, but her eyes never left Obbin. Apparently she'd been taken from a trader ship. The Corsairs had not yet freed her.

She explained that the Corsairs took prisoners when they captured ships but tended to release them when they next had the opportunity. They weren't ones to keep extra mouths to feed. Sometimes they held someone of great value until a ransom was paid, but she was only a lowly trader's wife, she said. Her husband was in the dining hall with two of the crew from their ship, the *Comet Catcher*. It had already been sold off as parts; its cargo had also been sold or distributed among the Corsairs.

As they continued to wander, Austin began to itch for adventure. The marked doors teased him at every turn. They called out to him, "Just try me. Come on in."

Austin stared at the glowing crimson X. The double door at the end of the hall had no guard. "Think we could get through one of those?"

Obbin grunted. "How?"

Austin pointed at the floor.

"The grate?" Obbin asked. A rectangular vent cover was set into the wall beside the door.

Austin shrugged. "Why not? You hid in one on the *Phoenix*."

"True," Obbin said. "The grate won't just come off, you know. Don't you think there will be some sort of security on it?"

"Listen to you. I thought you were brave."

"I am." Obbin looked Austin over. "Braver than you."

"Only one way to find out. What are they going to do? Throw us in prison?" Austin laughed. "As for getting it off . . . can I see one of your earrings?"

Obbin frowned. "What?"

"I just need it for a minute," Austin said.

Obbin touched the curved white bones in his ears. "I don't think so. I made these from—"

"I'll give it right back. I'm not going to hurt it, brave guy. Promise." Obbin sighed, slipped his right earring free, and handed it over to Austin. "Let's go!"

The boys ran toward the grate. Austin dropped to the floor and slid to a stop. The move wasn't necessary, just a way of adding flare to the mission. He used the bone earring to loosen the set of nuts holding the bolts in place. Within a minute, the bolts were free and so was the grate.

Best yet, no alarms sounded and no guards came. Austin assumed this was because they weren't actually escaping from the prison level but moving to another section of it. What would be the use of extra security?

Austin and Obbin wiggled through the narrow vent, and Austin worked the next grate loose. It was more difficult to do from the inside. He ended up kicking the grate free, resulting in a loud clatter of metal.

Fortunately there were no guards in the cordoned-off corridor before them. Another X-marked door was at the end of the hall. Gray-shadowed glass walls were on either side.

Austin swallowed a lump in his throat as he approached the first cell. What would he find? A violent criminal? A deformed beast? His mind was racing. He jumped as Obbin touched his shoulder.

"Don't do that!" Austin warned. "You'll give me a heart attack."

"Brave . . . ha!" Obbin laughed. "Can I have my earring back?"

Austin handed it over. "What do you think is in here?"

"Beats me. They're probably empty."

"Then why lock them off?" asked Austin. "No, there's something good—or really bad—in here."

Austin and Obbin slowly stepped toward the first cell.

Empty.

The one across from it was empty as well.

But what they found in the next cell shocked and confused them.

A girl.

Alone.

No older than Tiffany. Her long brown hair hid her face from them. She was sitting against one of the walls, her attention fixed on a book. She didn't notice them outside.

"She doesn't look very scary," Austin said. "Why would they lock her in here all alone?"

"Maybe she's some sort of unassuming assassin," Obbin said.

Austin laughed. "Reading a book?"

"Assassins read," Obbin said. "Let's find out. Use the intercom."

A small speaker was on the wall next to the door. It had a screen above and a keypad below. The first two rows of buttons were numbers, but the third row looked like actions. One button had a mouth with curved lines, as if someone were talking. Two more showed an open door and a closed door. The fourth had a lightning bolt and the last a single raindrop.

Austin pressed the open-door button. The words *Access Denied* appeared on the screen. Perhaps he needed the code. He touched the talking button next. The word *Talk* appeared on the screen, accompanied by a humming on the speaker.

The girl was humming a tune.

"Hello?" he said.

The girl started and twisted to see who had interrupted her reading. Her expression was one of surprise, but it immediately turned to happiness. That was when Austin realized who it was. He looked right into her hopeful blue eyes.

Ashley McGregor. At Bewaldeter, she'd helped him with his schoolwork. She was his sister's best friend and roommate. The two were nearly inseparable. Not only were Ashley's parents coworkers with Austin's parents, but Ashley had come on several expeditions with the four Wikk children. She and Austin were friends of sorts.

Austin momentarily forgot about the electro-shocking glass and stepped forward, placing his hands on the wall. He jerked back, but nothing had happened. He tapped the glass again to double check. No shock.

So the walls' electrified property was limited to one side. That made sense. Why energize the guard's side?

Austin jumped back to the speaker. "Ashley, are you okay?"

Her voice sent a shiver through him. "Yes. Other than being locked in here."

"Wait until I tell Oliver and Tiffany," Austin exclaimed.

"Are they here?" she asked.

"Yes, they're telling Mr. O'Farrell about the past few days."

Ashley's face went pale. "Austin! You have to go. Tell them not to tell him anything. It's him," she said. "He's the one behind this. He captured my parents and me. He took our ship. The Corsairs work for him!"

"What?"

"Just go!"

Austin hesitated. He didn't want to leave Ashley there alone.

"It's not like she's going anywhere," Obbin called as he bent down to crawl through the vent. He'd already obeyed Ashley's command.

It seemed inconsiderate, un-heroic even, but Obbin was right. "I'll be back for you," Austin promised her and ran to catch up with Obbin.

3.24

Game Over

Tiffany was trying to remember every detail she could from the adventure, but it was tough without the e-journal in hand. It'd been confiscated along with her mTalk and everything else. This was the second time the e-journal had been taken today. Mr. O'Farrell had assured her that he would try to get it back.

Mason was invaluable in remembering the things she forgot. They'd exchanged much information in their few moments of free time aboard the *Phoenix*, and now it was coming in useful. Mason was able to fill in the gaps as she recounted the story of their journey since they'd lost Mr. O'Farrell in the woods.

"When Austin ran away, he ended up meeting a man who—"

Suddenly the door burst open, and Austin and Obbin came charging in. A guard closed in behind them but said nothing. He held his sword high.

"Tiffany, stop! Don't say anything else!" Austin cried out. Mr. O'Farrell raised his arm. The guard surged at Austin, who ducked, then rolled to the right.

Obbin picked up for Austin. "This guy isn't what he says! He's bad. He's in charge—"

Another guard burst into the room. Mr. O'Farrell was on his feet. "Silence them!" he shouted.

Austin cried out, still avoiding the guard's glowing silver weapon. "Ashley . . . we saw Ashley. She's here, her parents . . ." The sword flashed as it struck Austin in the back. The youngest twin fell to the floor in a heap.

"What have you done?" screamed Tiffany, shooting to her feet. Her attention turned to Obbin.

The prince was still on the move. "We found them. We saw them. They're in a cell just down the hall . . ." Then Obbin met the same fate as Austin and fell to the floor like a wet noodle.

"*Stop!*" Tiffany screamed. Tears surged from her eyes. She swept her arm behind her, knocking the chair backward. It hit Obbin's attacker in the legs, causing the guard to buckle over. Tiffany dove toward Austin, gathering his head and shoulders into her arms. She tucked her ear to his mouth; he was still breathing.

Oliver charged the guard who'd struck Austin, knocking the Corsair to the ground, the tricorne hat falling free. The second guard recovered and charged forward, bringing his sword down in a wide arc.

"*Stop!*" shouted Mr. O'Farrell. "Enough!"

The guard stayed his hand and withdrew the sword. Oliver rolled to his back, staring up at the guard who'd almost struck him.

The guard Oliver had attacked grunted, then picked up himself and his hat. He glared at Oliver and grumbled under his breath, twitching his sword at the boy in warning.

"Enough." Mr. O'Farrell exhaled deeply.

Tiffany stared at him. Could all this be true? She was in shock; she stroked back Austin's shaggy hair.

Mason knelt over Obbin. Oliver pushed himself to his feet and brushed himself off.

"You three, sit!" Mr. O'Farrell removed his cap and set it on the table, then rubbed his knuckles. "I suppose the game is over now."

Under the threat of a renewed attack from the guards, Mason and Oliver returned to their seats. Tiffany gently laid Austin's head back down, then took her place at the table. She looked back at her little brother.

"It's true?" she said sorrowfully. "About the McGregors?"

Mr. O'Farrell shrugged. "Indeed. It is as they said."

Oliver shifted in his seat. He stared at Obbin, then Austin. "What have you done?" Tiffany heard the anger in his voice; she wasn't sure he wouldn't renew his attack on the guards. Perhaps he would go right for Mr. O'Farrell.

"They'll be fine in a moment. The shock is quick to knock them out, but the recovery can be equally quick."

Tiffany recognized the "can be" as a warning not to try anything.

Mr. O'Farrell nodded to the guards. They removed small pouches from their pockets and waved them before the shock victims' noses.

Almost instantly the boys began to stir. Austin's eyes opened first. "Don't tell him anything!" he burst out, then stopped when he saw Obbin on the ground nearby and the guards at attention again.

"They know, Austin," Mr. O'Farrell warned. "You've done what you set out to do. Take a seat." His near-instant return to calm seemed unusual given the events that had just taken place.

Austin and Obbin did as asked, albeit shakily. Tiffany could tell it was taking every ounce of control the boys had to obey the villain. Yes, villain. That was what this man had become to her.

She looked at Mason. His face was white, his eyes mournful. He looked sick, and she knew why. They'd just divulged a wealth of information. It didn't matter what they had told Mr. O'Farrell, though. They'd catalogued it all in the e-journal, which was now in his possession.

Tiffany whimpered; her friend Ashley had been locked up for how long? They'd seen the *Griffin* in Schlamm's warehouse how many days ago? She tried to picture the man's face when they had seen the *Griffin*. Had his shock at the sight of the ship been real? Of course not.

"You! Check that the McGregors are still securely in their cells. Have a guard posted to each cell from now until we leave," Mr. O'Farrell ordered.

The assigned Corsair left.

"Leave? Tiffany asked.

"We'll be continuing together on the next leg of the journey," Mr. O'Farrell explained. "You've discovered where we're headed, and I intend to take the *Phoenix* and the information your parents and the McGregors have gathered and continue the quest. After all, the *Phoenix* is my ship."

When Mr. Krank had given Oliver and Tiffany the cloaking device, he had said, "Don't open that until you're rid of O'Farrell." Now his words made sense. Of course he hadn't wanted Mr. O'Farrell to know they could cloak their ship. It had probably been Mr. Krank's way of helping them permanently escape Mr. O'Farrell. If only he'd been more clear.

Why hadn't she figured it out before? She and Oliver had spent a fair amount of time with him. Then again, her parents and the McGregors hadn't known either—or had they? Maybe they had known without being able to do anything about it. Clearly they'd been stuck between two towering, powerful enemies: the Übel and the Corsairs. They were just collateral damage in a desperate quest.

"Why?" Tiffany asked. "Why did you take the McGregors prisoner? Don't they work for you? You've funded all their recent digs. Couldn't you have asked for the information? Why didn't you take us right away? Why did you wait until we came back?" Her questions spilled from her lips. She was mad; she felt betrayed; she was now facing an enemy.

"Ahh, yes." Mr. O'Farrell looked pleased with himself. "You see, when I was alerted to your parents' capture by the Übel, I had to ensure the McGregors would not meet a similar fate.

I had to know that at least one of my investments was secure and under my contr—protection."

"Investments!" Oliver scoffed. "That's what our parents were to you? Not people, just investments."

The old man looked at Oliver but didn't acknowledge the analogy.

"It was a desperate move," he admitted. "I wasn't sure I could protect the McGregors in the *Griffin* without the full force of the *Black Ranger* and the rest of my Corsair armada. By now you've seen the Übel's *Skull*."

"But why didn't you take us the moment we came to Brighton?" Tiffany asked.

"There was no need to alert you to my entire operation. I wanted you to work with me, to share things your parents might not have told me. If you were prisoners, all you knew would be imprisoned as well. I'd already placed the McGregors in that position. I couldn't risk alienating you too." Mr. O'Farrell shook his head. "It's really too bad it turned out this way."

"Clearly you weren't ambushed by Corsairs. You simply had them pick you up," Oliver accused.

"When you first left, I assumed you'd figured out more about me than you should have. I thought you were trying to escape me," Mr. O'Farrell said. "Once the Übel struck the Blauwe Mensen, I became concerned. The Übel were actively preparing for a long-term mission. All my informants had made that clear. When you returned in answer to my emergency transmission, I didn't have time to reinsert myself onto the planet while the Übel were attacking the *Black Ranger*."

Tiffany wondered how he'd known they'd returned. Had he been tracking them?

"By the time the battle was over, you were already headed off the planet—without me, I might add." It sounded as if he were accusing them of betraying him. The audacity of the statement made Tiffany angry. Mr. O'Farrell continued, "I had no choice but to stop you. We hardly had enough time to intercept you." Now it sounded as though he expected her and her brothers to feel bad that they had inconvenienced him and the Corsairs. "Clearly you had new information, information that the McGregors did not. We'd have been left behind. Now we'll go to the next clue together."

"The McGregors too?" Tiffany asked.

"Ashley and her parents will stay here," Mr. O'Farrell said. "I know the two of you are close." His words seemed to be misplaced on Oliver, instead of directed at Tiffany.

Tiffany hated the idea of leaving her friend behind. Yet she could not think of a plausible reason to argue for her to come—at least, not one that wouldn't give Mr. O'Farrell more information.

"We'll be off right away," Mr. O'Farrell said.

"Not until I see Ashley," Tiffany demanded.

Mr. O'Farrell contemplated her, then shrugged. "It's of no consequence to me. There's nothing they can tell you that you don't already know."

"I'm going with her," Oliver said.

"Fine. The guards will escort you." Mr. O'Farrell's eyes darkened. "Don't try anything, or these three will pay. They'll remain with me."

Tiffany looked at Oliver, but his eyes were on Austin.

"We wouldn't think of it. Let's go, Tiffany." Oliver took his sister's hand as they left the twins and Obbin in the old man's care.

Austin and Obbin leaned against the wall, talking to each other. Mason sat across from Mr. O'Farrell. He'd not known the man at all. He'd only heard of him from his parents and most recently from Tiffany and Oliver. Any credibility or trust that had been built through those mentions was now lost.

This guy was bad. Just plain bad.

What was he really after? He'd hidden his relationship with the Corsairs. He'd had his own ship attacked and captured. He'd taken the Wikks and McGregors prisoner.

"So, O'Farrell," Mason began, "can you explain what we're really searching for?"

O'Farrell smiled. "I'm not sure that it's time to reveal such information to you. What I will tell you is that I do respect your parents and—"

"Ha! Respect!" Austin scoffed. "You don't know the meaning of the word."

Austin had moved to the table and was standing next to his twin. Mason stretched out his hand to calm him.

"I respect your parents and the McGregors and their work. When this is over and we've found the secret, I will make this right by all of you."

Mason heard something in those words that could have been truth. Then again, all he knew about this man had been secondhand, and that was all out the door now.

"Tiffany and Oliver mentioned that you used some tricky trading methods with that Schlamm guy," Austin recalled. "It seems you're accustomed to misleading people."

O'Farrell glared at Austin. "And trading with Corsairs for stolen ships and parts is an honest man's behavior? Ha! Schlamm's not exactly an upstanding person."

"You command the Corsairs!" Mason accused.

"I do indeed, but there is far more to our organization than you know. We've created our persona for a reason," O'Farrell admitted.

"To pillage and steal!" Austin said.

"No . . . to collect evidence and information," O'Farrell said.

"Evidence and information? You mean toward the quest?" Mason asked.

O'Farrell nodded. "And other uses."

"Like what?" Mason asked.

"Leverage," O'Farrell said.

"Blackmail," said Austin.

O'Farrell smiled. He seemed to enjoy this banter. The notion gave Mason the creeps. This guy wasn't right. Perhaps betraying and searching had taken its toll on him. Maybe he was so deep in lies that he could no longer see the truth. Clearly he was lost in a world of deception unlike any Mason had ever imagined could exist in his parents' line of work.

3.25

McGregors

Oliver and Tiffany walked into the prison corridor and waited. As Mr. O'Farrell had commanded, guards had been placed at each cell.

"Open the cells," one of the guards commanded. His voice had a computerized rhythm to it.

The guards obeyed, releasing the McGregor family one by one. The moment Ashley was free, she dashed past the guards and embraced Tiffany. Tears streamed down her cheeks. Tiffany's tears joined her friend's.

"Oh, Ashley," Tiffany cried. "I'm so glad to see you. Are you okay?"

Ashley stepped back. "I'm okay given the circumstances."

Oliver looked on with an ache in his chest. This girl whom he'd grown up with, whom he cared for, had been locked away by herself. She'd probably just been reunited with her parents for the first time since their capture. She looked his way, and the corner of his mouth curled into a smile.

Mr. and Mrs. McGregor hurried over to their daughter. They reunited in an embrace. Mr. McGregor pulled his daughter close and whispered in her ear. Oliver was sure he was speaking words of encouragement.

Mrs. McGregor didn't waste any time before taking Tiffany and Oliver into her arms.

"My dear children." Her voice cracked. "I've been so worried for you. For your parents. Are they here?"

Oliver couldn't speak. He only shook his head. He sniffled. His eyes burned as he fought back the tears that desperately wanted to pour from his eyes. Emotion had been building and now was coming over him without control. Mr. McGregor seemed to notice and took Oliver to his side, placing his arm firmly around his shoulder.

"Oliver, it's okay. It's going to be okay," he promised.

Oliver nodded and looked back at his sister. Her face was already a mess. Her eyes were swollen and red, her hair matted to her cheeks. He couldn't hold it in any longer. He tucked his head against Mr. McGregor and let it out. He'd wanted to be strong, to keep up his façade of toughness, especially in Ashley's presence. But no more.

Mr. McGregor held him close. His dad would have done the same. His dad had always said, "Strength is allowing your emotions to show without letting them take control." Oliver took a deep breath. He pulled his head from Mr. McGregor's chest, his eyes puffy, his nose running. He felt better in spite of their circumstances. He'd left nothing bottled inside, and a new sense of calm came over him.

"We learned that you'd been captured a few days ago," Tiffany said, addressing Mr. and Mrs. McGregor. She looked at Ashley. "But we weren't sure if you were on board the *Griffin* or still at school."

"We saw the ship on Jahr des Eises," Oliver added.

"We're thankful that Ashley is with us." Mrs. McGregor took a breath. "I couldn't bear the thought of her being alone at Bewaldeter with no trace of what had happened to us."

Ashley looked at Tiffany solemnly.

Oliver thought back to Mr. O'Farrell in Schlamm's warehouse. He'd said he'd send someone to retrieve Ashley from

Bewaldeter, knowing all along that she was already a prisoner. Anger burned inside him at the lies, all the lies he'd been fed.

"The Übel came to our compound and took our parents in the dead of night," Oliver said. "We barely escaped."

Mr. McGregor looked at his wife. "We shouldn't have waited," he said.

"Honey, you and Elliot didn't know. None of us could have known that the book from Dabnis Castle would be the final trigger," Mrs. McGregor consoled him.

"The book!" Oliver said. "What do you know of it?"

"Where is it?" Mr. McGregor said instead of answering. "Please don't tell me they have it."

Guilt overcame Oliver. He couldn't form words.

"They do," Tiffany said. "There was nothing we could do. They came in a large shuttle with many soldiers and ambushed our home. We would have been captured, if not for Oliver's heroic flying and bravery."

Some of the guilt slipped away but wasn't erased.

Mr. McGregor patted Oliver's back, and he caught a smile on Ashley's tear-streaked face. A sort of pride filled him for a second.

"It's not your fault," Mr. McGregor said. "I'm glad you got your sister and brothers to safety. That was no small feat, I'm sure. I know who was tracking you."

The door opened, and three guards walked in, Mr. O'Farrell in the lead.

"It's time to go. Guards, put the McGregors back in their cells," he ordered. "You two come with me. We're leaving."

Oliver considered resistance; after all, there were five of them. But he knew it was futile. The guards had their flashy shocker swords. Plus, they were in the middle of the *Black Ranger* with no knowledge of where the *Phoenix* was or if they could even escape.

"Oliver, take care," Mr. McGregor said and pulled him close. He quickly whispered into Oliver's ear. "GenTexic, Re Lyt, Building 6, code 11, 19, 82."

It was an odd statement. Oliver quickly repeated it to himself to lock it in his mind. One of the guards pulled Mr. McGregor away. Oliver saw Ashley release his sister; Mrs. McGregor stepped forward and took Tiffany in her arms.

Before Oliver realized it, Ashley had embraced him. Her head was on his shoulder. "Be brave."

Her hair smelled soft and flowery. He hugged her and smiled when she stepped back. Ashley moved to her cell peacefully before a guard could force her. Oliver was thankful for that. Odd feelings were swirling within him, and he was sure that if a guard had laid a finger on her he would have attacked him.

Mrs. McGregor returned to her cell as well, and he wondered if she'd told Tiffany a clue like Mr. McGregor's. He repeated the message in his mind again. There was Re Lyt again. He was now sure it was their destination.

He leaned over to Tiffany as she walked past and hugged her, whispering in her ear, "GenTexic, Re Lyt, Building 6, code 11, 19, 82. Remember that, Tiffany."

He pulled away, and she looked at him curiously.

"We're going to be just fine," he said.

She gave him a fake sympathetic smile. Her eyes told the truth; they were full of thought.

3.26

Bravery

The lift stopped, and the party stepped into a brightly lit corridor ten times the height and width of any they'd seen before. At the end of the hall, a large hatch peeled open like the petals of a blackened flower, revealing a massive flight deck. Nearly fifty fighter craft sat idle. Another two-dozen shuttles and an array of other ships were assembled in the gargantuan bay.

To the farthest side of the bay sat the *Phoenix*, gleaming under the bright overhead lights. Corsairs were loading it with supplies. Others were atop the ship, sparks shooting as they made exterior repairs. Large cables and tubes attached to multiple points of the silver craft.

Austin saw a damaged ship that resembled the *Phoenix*. Was it the *Griffin*? Had the Corsairs taken it back from Schlamm?

The expedition was about to begin again, and Austin felt an odd sense of belonging—not to O'Farrell, but to the quest. He was part of the search for something great, something that men had invested their entire lives and fortunes into finding.

SNAP! WHOOSH!

HSSSS!

Austin turned to see a man-sized lizard whipping its tail back and forth. Two guards lay on the floor beside it. Sharp spikes lined the ridge of the beast's back. Its skin was red and bumpy, shining under the bright lights of the bay with a slippery sheen. Then it disappeared. Only a stiff metal collar remained, and a harsh, guttural hiss echoed from the empty spot.

The lizard reappeared, but now its head was aimed at Austin. It hissed again; a black forked tongue shot forward. Its bright green eyes bulged. It felt as though they were drilling right into Austin's soul. Its nostrils flared, and it hissed again.

It charged.

"Shoot it!" O'Farrell called to no one in particular.

Austin took in their surroundings. There was no one near. No one could intervene before the massive creature reached them. Adrenaline surged through Austin. An odd fact about animal attacks rushed through his mind. But did it hold true for lizards?

Austin charged head-on at the lizard. A deadly game of chicken was underway; the lizard's legs pounded on the bay floor as it neared.

THUD, THUMP, THUD.

Austin could see every scale on its leathery body. The sharp spikes tilted to aim at Austin. Its mouth opened wide in a snarl—he could see rows of saliva-dripping, razor-sharp teeth. This beast was surely a trained killer.

Austin looked back. Oliver was yelling. Tiffany was shaking her head. Mason and Obbin were in shock. O'Farrell was darting away.

Austin returned his gaze to the oncoming predator, raising his arms and yelling at the top of his lungs. "*AHHHHHHHHHHH!*"

The lizard jerked awkwardly, surprised by the small human's actions. It pulled its head back, attempting to stop, but between its speed and the metallic floor, its legs got tangled. The beast tumbled forward, its head slamming into the ground. Austin dove to the left, just as the reptile rolled past. The spikes on its back tore gashes into the floor.

A collision would have turned out badly. Austin doubted he would have survived.

Before the beast could recover, four guards were on it. They cast a large metal net over it and jabbed its side with long pronged staffs. Sparks of silver energy surged into the scaly beast, silencing it.

Austin sat, his heart pounding, his chest heaving. What had he just done? Where had the courage come from?

A second later, his family was around him. Obbin pulled him to his feet. Tiffany hugged him. Oliver and Mason patted his back and squeezed his shoulders. All praised his reckless bravery and courage, his selfless act that had saved them. Even O'Farrell thanked him, though Austin wasn't sure he'd have done it if only the old man had been in jeopardy.

The whirr of praises subsided, and Austin's mind came back into focus. He bent over, hands on knees, and hurled as the adrenaline released and his nerves broke.

"Someone clean that up," O'Farrell called to a nearby Corsair. "Ridiculous beasts."

"What was that?" Mason asked.

"That was a wartock, a genetically engineered lizard. Your sister and brother will remember my mentioning Spike when we were in Mudo. This one is five versions newer and far more deadly. Wartocks were created to hunt, not just guard. They seek out their prey on command and don't relent until their task is complete. However, you can see they have several flaws in their intelligence and design. Human error no doubt muddled this creation," O'Farrell admitted.

Austin was thankful for each of those flaws. Tiffany knelt next to him, her hand on his back. Mason offered him an H_2O bottle, which he accepted gladly in hopes of removing the taste of bile from his mouth.

"We acquired a dozen of them recently." O'Farrell grunted. "They've proved more trouble than they're worth. I'd have the whole lot exterminated, but we may yet need them."

"That's right. I remember," Oliver said. "RepFuse."

Mason and Obbin helped Austin to his feet.

"Yes, RepFuse—a subsidiary for a genetics company. I invested millions in the parent company, and what has it gotten me? A bunch of monstrous lizards."

Oliver put his arm on Austin. "Are you okay?" Austin nodded. "That sure was something awesome you just did, buddy."

Austin felt a surge of pride. "I had to. There wasn't anything else to be done. Someone had to . . ." Austin trailed off. He didn't want to sound as though he was still stuck on Oliver's misstep the first night with the Übel. That wasn't what he'd meant.

"You sure aren't afraid to throw yourself into danger without thinking," Obbin said.

"That can be a good and a bad thing," Austin admitted.

"This time it was good," Mason said. He patted Austin on the back.

"Enough. I think Austin's deed has been repaid with enough accolades," O'Farrell said.

Austin looked at Tiffany.

"He means you've been praised enough," she said.

"Everyone to the *Phoenix*. We leave in fifteen minutes," O'Farrell said.

"Why the *Phoenix*?" asked Oliver. "Your shuttles look more powerful."

"The *Phoenix* holds all your parents' artifacts and information."

"Couldn't you just transfer everything over?" Mason asked. "You have enough men. The e-journal has all the information from their expeditions."

"No, my boy, not all."

Austin looked at Mason. He knew what his twin was thinking: the kids hadn't searched deep enough. Their parents had backed up information on the *Phoenix*. Probably they had locked certain information away in a more secure location than the e-journal.

O'Farrell glanced at the silver ship. "I have other reasons," he said. But it was clear he was not going to reveal them.

The seats on the bridge were nearly filled with the new Corsair crew.

The engines of the *Phoenix* rumbled. The liftoff from the flight deck was hardly noticeable. Before them, huge bay doors opened, revealing the desolate black of space. Several other craft rose around them, hovering. A whole squadron had been assigned to escort the mission: seven fighters, five shuttles, and three bombers. Apparently Mr. O'Farrell wasn't taking any chance of being captured by the Übel.

The pilot tapped on the console. "E4:32 *Phoenix* requesting takeoff clearance."

A scratch of static. "Flight Bridge Command to E4:32. You are clear for takeoff in ten . . ."

A countdown continued. On "one," the pilot pressed the throttle forward smoothly. The *Phoenix* glided toward the gaping hole.

Space surrounded them, small white stars all around.

An elbow jabbed Oliver in the side. "Wow, now that's how you take off." It was Austin. He smiled, assuring Oliver he'd meant it as a joke.

"Yeah, not hard when you're not being gunned down, chased, or thrown into the midst of a storm." Oliver ruffled his brother's hair. "We'll see how you do some time."

"Really?" Austin asked.

Oliver smirked. "Yeah, if we ever get the ship back to ourselves," he whispered.

Three of the space fighters moved to a position ahead of the *Phoenix*. The rest of the squadron remained out of sight.

"Echo Squadron in formation, prepare for synchronized hyper flight," the copilot said. "Destination: Re Lyt. Flight time: eleven hours and twelve minutes."

"Confirmed," the pilot responded. "On my count."

After another countdown, the hyper flight sequence began. By now Oliver was used to the flashing red numbers and the computer's voice announcing the sequence, but this was the first time he'd not been in the pilot's seat since the quest had begun.

Supremo Admiral

Everyone had been sent to get some rest for the first seven hours of the flight. Tiffany still had her cabin, but the four boys were sharing Oliver's room because the twins' room had been given to the guards to use. Mr. O'Farrell had taken their parents' room. So Oliver and Mason shared the bed, while Austin and Obbin took to the floor on two hovermats provided by the Corsairs.

After they woke, the kids gathered in the galley for a bite to eat. Mr. O'Farrell had given them permission to move about the *Phoenix* but had warned them not to cause any problems. After all, he'd told them, they were really all on the same side.

As an extra precaution, Mr. O'Farrell had stationed Corsairs throughout the *Phoenix*. One guard patrolled the cargo bay, another patrolled the upper corridor, and a third was in the lower corridor near the server and generator rooms.

Austin and Obbin had returned to Oliver's room, but it was clear to the rest of the Wikks that it wasn't their actual destination. Mason knew they would go for the cargo bay. Mason, Tiffany, and Oliver stayed in the galley after Mr. O'Farrell returned to the bridge. The Corsair guard had been standing near the bridge and hadn't walked past for a while.

Oliver leaned low over the table. His sister and brother leaned in. "Mr. McGregor whispered something to me," he said a hushed tone. "GenTexic, Re Lyt, Building 6—"

"Code 11, 19, 82," finished Tiffany. "I've been waiting to ask you about that."

"When we were in Cobalt Gorge, we learned that the Übel were most likely going to Re Lyt. Drex also mentioned it. Isn't it interesting that Mr. McGregor gave us a specific building number? Though I don't know what the code is for."

"Probably it's the code to get in," Tiffany said. Oliver and Mason nodded agreement.

"This GenTexic place, RepFuse, must be connected to the quest. But why would the Übel and O'Farrell have so much interest in genetics?" Mason wondered. "O'Farrell said he invested a chunk of his wealth in it."

Oliver noticed he'd dropped the *mister*.

"Genetics is a lucrative science," Tiffany said. "More than half the seniors at Bewaldeter graduate with some form of genetics initiative embedded in their career paths."

Mason took a swig of the Energen he'd claimed from the fridge. "Yeah, but this isn't about money. It's something else."

Oliver looked at his sister. "Did I tell you what Captain Vedrik said the night our parents were taken about living forever?"

"You said the Übel had discovered an artifact that suggested that possibility."

"The words went something like this: 'I give unto them eternal life, and they shall never perish,'" Oliver said. "I remember because the statement seemed encoded in Vedrik. It was like it was permanently etched into his brain."

Tiffany repeated the phrase. Mason looked at her. "Eternal life? Genetics makes perfect sense then."

"Lifespan extension research has been the top priority of many institutions for centuries," Tiffany said. "It's also one of the most financially depleting fields."

"No one can live forever," Mason said.

"Or can they?" Oliver asked. "Eternal life would be a great enough prize for many to waste their entire lives on finding the secret."

"Isn't that a quandary? Waste what you have to get something that would give what you lost back to you. Yet you might never get it back." Tiffany's words were a puzzle themselves. Oliver had heard his sister speak like this before, when she was pondering great mysteries.

Footsteps echoed in the hall. Oliver laughed. Mason and Tiffany looked at him oddly. "Pretend we're just telling stories and having fun."

Mason and Tiffany laughed.

"Then the monkey leaped onto Oliver's back," Tiffany said.

Oliver grunted. He'd opened himself up to this one.

"He turned and shouted," Tiffany continued, "and I'm pretty sure I heard a high-pitched squeal."

Now she was just exaggerating, but this time Mason's laugh was real.

The guard looked in on them. At least, he turned his masked head toward them. What was behind the mask?

"I believe his words were, 'Get it off! Get if off! Get it off!'" Tiffany said.

The guard continued past.

"Okay, I think you can stop," Oliver said.

Tiffany smiled at Mason, who was still laughing.

"You know, it did bite and scratch me," Oliver added.

Tiffany gave him big puppy-dog eyes as if to express her condolences.

Oliver sighed. "Has O'Farrell given back the e-journal yet?"

"No. They copied everything off it. I think he was searching to see if there is any hidden information locked away from the transfer."

"Think he'll find anything?" asked Mason.

"I hope not, but there were several notations I myself could not unlock," Tiffany said. She sighed. "How's it feel not flying?"

"Weird. I mean, it shouldn't." Oliver scratched his head. "I didn't fly when Dad was here. But I've gotten used to being in control."

"It's odd having so many extra bodies aboard," Mason said. "Two pilots, five guards, and one *supremo* admiral." He finished with a sneer.

"Supremo admiral?" asked Tiffany.

"O'Farrell," Oliver explained. "I guess his real title is *supreme admiral.*"

"Eight of them, the three of us, plus Austin and Obbin," Mason said. "Final count: thirteen people, which is more than there are sleeping quarters for."

"And the remaining flight time?" Tiffany asked.

"About three and a half hours, I think?" Oliver said.

"This is one of the longer jumps we've made, right?" Mason asked.

"Yeah, except for that one time Dad and Mom took us to Daht," Tiffany said.

"Oh, that was miserable. The twins cried the whole time," Oliver said.

Mason looked semi-resentful. "I was just four."

"I think Dad and Mom spent most of their time walking you two in opposite directions down the aisle of the space barge," Tiffany said.

"Oh, the days of traveling on overcrowded barges," Oliver said. "Nice to have a ship like the *Phoenix*."

"Or even the *Lance*. That wasn't a bad ship," Tiffany admitted.

"Not for you," Oliver teased. "You didn't have to share a room with the twins."

"Hey now," Mason grunted. "We're . . . *I'm* not that bad."

"No, Mas, you're not. Neither is Austin. You've really proved yourselves," Tiffany said. "But when you were younger . . ."

Oliver laughed. "Daht was one of our longer flights, probably because we were on a barge and tightly packed like sardines."

"Do you remember the summer on Daht, though?" Tiffany asked.

"I don't," Mason said.

"I do. Amazing tidal-surf beaches. That's where I first got to roller surf," Oliver recalled. "It was great."

"I can almost feel the soft pink sand under my feet," Tiffany said. "Ashley and I tried to fill as many bags as we could. She wanted to cover her bedroom floor with it, but her mom objected. So instead we had fun exploring underwater caverns in the *Aqua Tortoise*."

"Our submersible," Oliver told Mason.

"They called it the *Tortoise*?" asked Mason.

"Dad let *someone* name it."

"I liked sea tortoises then!" Tiffany said.

"Speaking of underwater caverns," Oliver said, "apparently Thule had hidden his notes in the cavern under the palace. My guess is he was taking notes on the Blauwe Mensen during his time with them. Mason, you mentioned him being an outsider? Do you know how long he was there?"

"Nine years, I think."

"Nine years to investigate, to research the people," Oliver said. "Isn't it obvious? This was part of their plan all along."

"He wasn't captured—he was planted," Mason said.

"Exactly," Oliver said.

"The Blauwe Mensen must be very deeply connected to the quest for Thule to spy on them for nine years," Tiffany said. "That's a significant commitment."

"Oliver!" Mason exclaimed, then ducked his head as he remembered the Corsair outside. "We never told you what we found. Austin uncovered a secret room of books in the library. And there was a note from Obbin's brother. Apparently Rylin thought some of the books would be valuable enough to barter for his family's release."

"*The Chronicles of Terra Originem*," Tiffany interjected.

"We scanned the rest into the LibrixCaptex," Mason said.

"Why did you wait until now to tell me this?" Oliver asked.

Tiffany frowned. "We haven't had a chance to discuss our discoveries, have we?"

"And thankfully we didn't get this far when recounting everything to O'Farrell," Mason said.

"You're right. I haven't even told you about Cavern Haven," Oliver said. "You finish your tale, and then I'll tell you what I discovered."

"The only other thing we found was a set of paintings that create a map," Tiffany added. "We had to bring those along because they had invisible ink on them."

"Where are they now?" Oliver asked.

"They were in my cabin," Mason said. "I wonder if any of the Corsair goons found them."

"Why don't you see if you can sneak in and get them?" Oliver said. "Tiffany and I will go to the cargo bay. The Blauwe Mensen gave me a collection of maps and books. Perhaps the information is similar."

"At the very least, we should take a look at them," Tiffany said.

"I wonder if Austin and Obbin could distract the guard in the bay long enough for me to grab the stuff."

"Sounds like a plan," Tiffany said. "Mason, check your room in case the guards have left."

Mason nodded. "I'll get them even if they're still sleeping."

Tiffany smiled. "Great. We'll meet you in the library."

"Way to take charge, sis," Oliver said.

"What are you two doing?" called the Corsair on guard. "Step away from the scooter and put that tool down."

Austin and Obbin had gone after one of the scooters the Corsairs had brought on board. The craft were slightly larger than the two the Wikks had and also silver like the *Phoenix*.

"Right now!" the guard shouted.

Austin stepped back, and Obbin set the tool on a nearby crate. The Corsair marched toward them, his silver sword flashing. He looked over the flying craft, then grunted under his mask. "Run along!"

Obbin and Austin had just reached the balcony when Oliver and Tiffany neared the door to the bay.

"What are you doing?" asked Oliver.

Austin looked over his shoulder at the Corsair, then back to his brother and sister. "Not much."

"Staying out of trouble, of course," Obbin added with a smirk at Austin.

"Well, I have a mission for you," Oliver said quietly. "I need something from the cargo bay."

Austin's ears pricked up. "Yes?"

"Can you two distract the guard for a minute?"

"Of course." Obbin punched Austin's shoulder playfully. "It'll be a piece of scotcharoo."

"Scotcha-what?" Austin asked.

"It's a dessert my mom makes."

"Discuss that later. Can you guys do it?" Oliver asked.

"Yes, we're on it," Austin agreed.

"Meet back in the library," Oliver said.

"Come on."

They slipped back onto the balcony. The guard had already disappeared behind a stack of crates. The cargo bay had become twice as full as before with the addition of the Corsairs' supplies.

Austin rode the staircase railing down, followed by Obbin. They wandered among the many stacks of cargo crates. Each one was labeled and strapped down.

"Let me get up there," Obbin said. "Then toss me that chain."

Austin nodded and gathered the suggested item.

Obbin scrambled from crate to crate until he stood on top of the stack. "He's near the bay door."

"Here it comes," Austin said and slung the bundle of chain at him. Obbin's arms dipped from the weight of the chain as he grabbed it.

"Got it!" He quickly unwound the bundle.

"Hey, pirate dude! Over here!" he shouted as he started to swing the chain in circles over his head.

Austin couldn't see the guard, but he heard him.

"Get down from there!" the soldier shouted.

"Come and make me!" Obbin called back.

"Now!" the Corsair cried out.

Obbin let go of the chain, and it flew across the bay, clattering loudly as it struck a set of crates. Austin heard a shattering sound and wondered what had been in the chain's path.

Obbin made a face with his hands and tongue. The clanking of boots on the bay floor started coming their way.

"Better go," Obbin said offhandedly and hopped down a level of crates, then another.

Austin led Obbin around another crate, then through the maze of stacked crates in the bay. They heard the Corsair stomping around in his search, but they were soon up the stairs and on their way to the library. The man would eventually find them, but what could he possibly do? Lock them up? O'Farrell had taken them prisoner, but it didn't seem as though he'd do them permanent bodily harm.

Would he?

Mason sat at the research counter with the LibrixCaptex before him. The screen set into the counter's console showed the progress of the transfer. Mason had set up a secured hidden folder on the mainframe and was transferring the scanned book files there. Though he knew that O'Farrell would be looking for just that sort of hidden information, he needed a way to read the files without the journal. He hoped creating security barriers and burying the files in several layers of information would be enough. It was worth the risk: if he couldn't read the files, they wouldn't be of any use.

The door creaked, and Mason jumped, but it was only Tiffany and Oliver. Oliver set an armful of things down on the table, then went back to the door and shut it. He tapped a code into a nearby keypad, and the door locked with a soft click.

"Won't the guard wonder why we shut the door?" asked Mason.

"He's eating," said Oliver, "and he'll soon be asleep."

"Why's that?" asked Mason.

"Ask your sister."

Tiffany smiled and stoked Midnight, who purred in her arms. "When I went to retrieve Midnight from my room, I noticed the guard was in the galley. I retrieved a sleeping agent from the medical kit in my room, the same I used on Drex, then returned to the galley. I went to get a dish of H_2O for Midnight and asked the guard if he would like something to drink. He said yes. So I squeezed some of the sleeping liquid into his glass. He should be sound asleep right now."

"Good work, Tiffany," Mason said.

"Some crack force O'Farrell has," Oliver said. "Austin and Obbin's distraction worked perfectly, and Tiffany just took out one of the guards."

"O'Farrell never saw us coming," Mason said.

"No, he didn't," Oliver said.

"Looks like you were successful as well," Tiffany said.

"The pilot had just left for the lavatory. I sneaked in and out really quickly," Mason admitted.

"And we got what we needed from the bay," Oliver said.

"How will we keep this a secret from O'Farrell?" asked Mason.

"Very carefully."

"We'll have to get through it as fast as we can and hide whatever we aren't using," Tiffany said. "We can use my room for that. I'll bury the stuff beneath my clothing. It seems none of the guards want anything to do with a girl's cabin."

"Good."

There was a bump on the door.

"Quick, hide it all!" Oliver warned and moved toward the door.

Midnight hopped from Tiffany's lap as she and Mason sprang into action. They ripped open drawers and compartments and shoved things inside as carefully as possible.

Oliver stood next to the keypad. "Ready?"

They gave him four thumbs up in answer. Oliver tapped the keypad, and the lock released.

The arrivals were Austin and Obbin. Oliver resecured the door once they'd entered.

"Did you get it?" Austin asked.

Oliver nodded. "We have very little time and a lot of stuff to look through. Everyone needs to chip in."

3.28

Info Overload

As an extra hurdle to an intruder, Oliver wedged a chair against the door. Still, Tiffany doubted it would delay anyone long enough for them to hide all the artifacts.

Mason was skimming the index of titles they had scanned on the LibrixCaptex, looking for anything that might stand out as a good place to start reading. Obbin flipped through the physical books the Blauwe Mensen had given him and Oliver. The sound of turning pages was still new to Tiffany's ear. Books weren't common in the Federation.

Oliver scoured the maps they'd been given by the council. Midnight lay on a chair, purring loudly. Tiffany and Austin went over the row of paintings, trying to piece the hidden map together. Austin copied the image onto an e-papyrus so they could hide the actual maps. He had adjusted the Spectrum Scope to the correct electromagnetic wavelength and hung it over the paintings. The invisible ink glowed, revealed by ultraviolet rays.

Immediately after starting, Tiffany realized a significant message had fallen into O'Farrell's hands. It'd been on the paintings, and she'd put it into the e-journal. All O'Farrell would have to do was check the most recent entries, and it would be right there. She recorded it again, this time into the e-papyrus:

Within the depths, we do leave the keys to passage safe and free. We hope in time the Truth will reign freely, when man again sees the way. Until the time when darkness is unveiled for what it is, we shall protect the path. We pray only that redemption again is clear to the masses, for so long it has been overlooked as something valueless.

If O'Farrell checked the recent entries, surely he'd wonder where they'd discovered the message.

The paintings were laid out across the longest wall of the library, six over six. As Austin sketched out the image that otherwise would have been invisible, excitement came over Tiffany. She'd seen this before—at least, part of it.

On Jahr des Eises, Tiffany and Oliver had visited O'Farrell's condo for a brief time. When she'd flipped through a book on the living room table, she'd discovered a sketch called *Valley of Shadows*. She had always intended on looking it up but had forgotten.

Tiffany was almost positive that she'd seen a portion of the map hidden in the paintings. But the map across the paintings was bigger. There had been more to the drawing in the book, and now they had it.

"Oliver, come here," she called.

Austin stopped sketching. Oliver stood up from the maps he was looking over and stretched.

"What'd you find?" he asked.

"Do you remember the book at O'Farrell's place?" Tiffany asked. "The one on the living room table?"

Oliver shook his head.

"There was a sketch in it labeled *Valley of Shadows*. It looked like this section here." Tiffany pointed to an area of Austin's sketch on the e-papyrus.

"Are you sure?" Oliver asked.

"Positive."

"Is there anything about the valley in the e-journal?" Mason asked, having joined the discovery.

"I never looked. I'd meant to, but . . ." Tiffany trailed off, feeling guilty. She needed to act on her instincts right away, especially since things changed so quickly. No more waiting.

"Maybe the books we scanned mentioned it," suggested Austin. "It did appear in paintings that were in the Blauwe Mensen's palace."

"We'll just have to wait until we get it back from O'Farrell," Oliver said. "I'm not seeing anything too revealing in these maps yet." He pointed to the stack he'd been going through. "At least, not in connection to anything we've discovered."

"I've highlighted a few titles for further reading," Mason said. "I'll look for the Valley of Shadows."

"I heard you found the Chamber of Cranium," Obbin said. "If only Rylin had waited. He could be with us now."

"We all miss our families." Tiffany put her arm around the prince. She'd begun to see him as a little brother like the twins.

A moment of quiet passed.

"What was it you said? Chamber of Cranium?" Mason asked.

"A hidden room in the library. Rylin came up with the name. My father visited it on occasion, always in the dead of night and in secret. Rylin and I once followed him there. We got in once and saw the strangely titled books, but neither of us was big on reading."

"Did Thule know about it?" Austin asked.

"I don't think so. Not even Voltan knew. Only my mom, I think. Maybe Speaker Ovon El."

"We'll have to read them," Mason said.

"Have at it," Austin said. "I'm going to keep working on this map."

"Mason, I'll help," Tiffany said.

"Me too," Obbin offered. "Though I'm not especially fast."

They set about their tasks again. Several minutes passed. Books, maps, notes—they reviewed everything.

"Eureka!" cried Oliver. Tiffany turned. Her brother held up a large map.

"What did you find?" asked Austin.

"It's the blueprints for the Cathedral of the Star!"

"What?" exclaimed Mason. "Are you serious?"

"Mason, where are the books you found on Evad?" Oliver asked.

"*The Veritas Nachfolger on Evad*?" asked Mason. "They're in our cabin."

"Go and get them," Oliver ordered.

Tiffany looked at Oliver.

"Please," Oliver added.

"The pilot might be back," Mason said.

"I'll go with you." Austin removed the chair from the door.

Oliver typed in the code. The twins ducked out, checking to see if any Corsairs were in the corridor.

"Tiffany, this is where you and Mason suggested we were headed," Oliver said. "Look at these blueprints."

Several pages were attached to each other. Each page contained forty separate floor plans.

"There must be a hundred floors to this building," Oliver said.

"Not anymore. The building was destroyed," Tiffany reminded him. "We need plans for the tunnels beneath."

"Half of the floors are underground," Oliver said. "See, it says these are subterranean levels." He pointed to some text on the blueprints. "Everything—the building, the Blauwe Mensen, Evad—are connected."

Obbin smiled. "Often some of the elders in our city gather and tell fantastic stories of our past. No one ever believes any of it." He looked at the paintings lined up across the floor. "To think all this was around me all my life, and I never knew. Well, I knew, I guess. I saw the books. I saw Cavern Haven. But I took it all for granted."

"It is something. My parents have been uncovering lost truth all their lives. Until now, I never realized how important their work was or what it was actually leading to," Oliver admitted. "I just thought they were adventurers. They were . . . are . . . truth seekers. That's what they are."

Tiffany smiled. "I've always been interested, but I never realized the stakes. Mom and Dad have been at this since before we were born. While they took us along, we never saw their work in this much detail."

"Do you think the Übel have been after them from the beginning?" Oliver asked.

"Perhaps not after our parents, but it's clear this search has crossed many centuries," Tiffany said.

There was a knock at the door.

"That was quick!" Oliver said as he started to tap the key code into the keypad. He jumped back as he saw O'Farrell's face.

"What are you all doing in here?" the old man asked.

3.29

Caught

Tiffany and Obbin hopped into action as Oliver threw his body against the door. She heard O'Farrell give a painful grunt. A small smile of satisfaction crossed her lips. Someone getting hurt wouldn't ordinarily cause her even a remote twinge of joy, but O'Farrell's reaction was okay with her. Probably it had to do with his betrayal of them all, especially Ashley.

Oliver's interference with the door had made it clear they were trying to hide something. They didn't have much time. Tiffany scooped the paintings into a stack. Obbin was at the counter; he swept his arm across the table, knocking the books and maps to the ground.

The hatch thumped, and O'Farrell shouted, "Let me in this instant!" Oliver redoubled his efforts, throwing his shoulder into the door. It snapped shut with a click.

"I can't lock it!" Oliver said, straining to get one hand to the keypad.

Tiffany shoved the paintings into a cabinet, then went back for the e-papyrus. Obbin shifted one of the chairs from the center of the room and angled it to block the view of the pile of books and maps.

"He knows we were looking at something," Tiffany said. "Obbin, take a few artifacts from the cabinet. Hide them under the table, and leave the cabinet door ajar."

If they didn't pretend to hide something, O'Farrell would search the room and discover everything. This wasn't a great plan, but better than making it obvious. Tiffany pulled a stack of old maps out from under the long desk where the LibrixCaptex sat and tossed them onto the couch under the porthole. She quickly moved the LibrixCaptex to a different location, hiding it in one of the cabinets.

Obbin haphazardly placed some artifacts throughout nooks and crannies in the library, as if they were meant to be hidden. He hid two beneath the table, then sat in one of the chairs. Tiffany used the pillows on the couch to "hide" some extra maps she'd gotten out and sat in front of them. Oliver shifted his weight to let the door open a bit more.

"Uh . . . sorry . . ." Oliver stumbled. "We were, um . . ."

"I know what you were doing," O'Farrell snarled.

The kids remained silent as the old man moved into the room. He shook his head and sighed. He motioned for Tiffany to move and took the maps from their hiding place.

"Hiding something?" O'Farrell asked, to no answer. "And these?"

He swept his arm at Midnight, startling the cat and causing her to jump from her chair. Tiffany scowled at him, then picked up the cat.

O'Farrell set down a black case he'd carried into the room and began walking about. One by one he collected the artifacts and set them on the table. "Tsk, tsk. There's no need to sneak around. We can work together." He looked over the things he'd gathered. "Besides, I've already seen all these. I've been working with your parents for a long time. These have been investigated and reveal nothing. There's no need to waste your time."

Oliver looked at him and nodded. Tiffany gave him an innocent smile, and Obbin shrugged.

"It's time we discussed our plan of action for landing on Re Lyt."

At that moment, the twins popped in through the door. Tiffany held Midnight close, but the boys didn't have any books with them. Her shoulders relaxed.

"And where were you two?" O'Farrell asked.

Austin grinned. "We were hungry."

Would the old man buy the story?

To her relief, Mason revealed a box of animal-shaped crackers. "Obbin, do you want some?"

Of course the twins had stopped for food. They were always eating. But where had the books gone, and how had they known to hide them?

"Why don't you three children head to the galley to eat your crackers? I need to talk to Oliver and Tiffany," O'Farrell said.

"Why can't I stay?" Austin protested.

"This doesn't apply to you," O'Farrell said. "Now run along."

Austin seemed ready to take a stand, but the previously sleeping Corsair appeared at the door, his sword glowing.

"Where have you been?" asked O'Farrell.

"I . . . I was in the—" the Corsair started.

"Never mind. Just take these three to the galley," O'Farrell said angrily. "I'll deal with you later."

The Corsair bowed his head and made way for the three boys. Like a puppy whose master has denied it a bone, Austin turned and left. Mason and Obbin followed.

"Now to business," O'Farrell said. He opened the black case he'd brought with him and removed a translucent purple disc. When he let go of the disc, it floated level with his chest.

"Re Lyt," he said. The purple disc dissolved, and in its place appeared a glowing orb, its color changing to a deep blue. Small orange specks glowed across its surface. Three smaller orbs appeared around it.

One of Tiffany's professors at Bewaldeter had used one of these devices in her astronomy class. It was a GlobeX Glowmap.

"This is our destination, Re Lyt, and its moons. The planet is unstable; it's known for its violent volcanic explosions and seismic activity. There are no permanent civilian settlements. It's the perfect place for a secret genetics facility."

Tiffany watched the blue orb grow.

O'Farrell placed his hands a few inches from the orb and pulled his arms back. The glowing blue globe expanded fivefold.

"We'll have to be very careful with our approach to the planet. It's well guarded. Our descent to the surface is the most risky part of infiltrating the GenTexic security forces surveillance. The atmospheric disruption caused by entry will show up on any tracking arrays they have. I've been here before, but I went as an investor. They won't be allowing any visitors if the Übel are there."

"So we're flying into a trap?" Oliver asked him.

"I've taken care of that. I wouldn't risk capture," O'Farrell said, almost swelling with pride. Tiffany realized he'd set up Oliver to ask the question so he could show his strategic preparation. "We have fate on our side. It so happens the three moons of the planet are nearly in alignment, causing all sorts of atmospheric and gravitational disruption."

Fate. What did that word even mean? Tiffany didn't like the thought that her future was predetermined by some natural cosmic order. She scratched Midnight under the chin.

"The one variable I've not been able to control is the two of you." O'Farrell eyed Tiffany and Oliver. "I need to know that you're working with me and not against me."

The audacity of his words angered her. How could he even for a moment think Tiffany would help him in any way, especially after his capture and mistreatment of her best friend?

Oliver remained equally silent.

"For many years, your parents and I worked together hand in hand, side by side. Many of their discoveries were only made possible through my financial contributions. I don't say this to brag on myself but to show you that we were truly a team.

Without your parents' knowledge, skill, and hard work, we would have not made the progress toward Ursprung that we have. You see together *was* the only way. Once again, together *is* the only way. Our mutual goal is to save your parents. Can we work together? Can we be a team?"

Oliver glanced from his sister to the old man. "I'm not sure what to say. It's hard to trust you. But"—he saw Tiffany looking at him—"I do want to free our parents. I'll assist you in that effort."

O'Farrell considered this. He seemed unsure if Oliver's words were a riddle.

"And I will obey my brother as the leader of our mission," Tiffany added in an effort to direct O'Farrell's focus from Oliver.

"Supreme Admiral, please report to the bridge. Preparing to disengage hyper flight," a voice called over the intercom.

O'Farrell grunted.

Tiffany felt relief. This was indeed an escape from further scrutiny.

"That's that. Let's go," O'Farrell said.

"I'm going to put Midnight in my cabin first," Tiffany said.

The old man nodded and left.

That wasn't all she would do; Tiffany also wanted to know where the boys had stashed the books.

She and Oliver headed to the galley after she placed Midnight safely into her room. They found the three boys eating . . . or playing with their crackers. The different animals were scattered across the table, some missing legs, some heads, some halfway eaten. Clearly a fierce battle was playing out.

The Corsair guard stood against one wall, holding an Energen in his hand. He hadn't said anything about the drugged water. Either he didn't know or he didn't want to admit his carelessness.

Tiffany sat next to Mason and leaned in. "Where did you put the books?"

Mason hummed. "They're safe," he said. "We heard O'Farrell so we dashed into Oliver's room and tossed them into his laundry hamper."

She smiled. "A good place indeed."

"Yeah, you should have smelled it," Mason said.

There was a growl from Austin as a lion lost its tail.

"We'd better head to the bridge," Oliver said. "The supreme admiral will be getting anxious."

Tiffany looked at the Corsair guard who was still just standing there. Why wasn't he rushing them off to the bridge? Well, she wasn't about to tell the guard how to do a better job for O'Farrell.

3.30

Re Lyt

nly moments remained before the *Phoenix* would come out of hyper flight on the far side of the moon, Nos Idam. O'Farrell had told them there was a guard outpost on the moon Nmutu-A, and Guard Ssej had told Oliver that the Übel cruiser, the *Skull*, was rendezvousing with Thule and his men near the third moon, Yeldah. This left Nos Idam as the only safe preentry to Re Lyt. Once around Nos Idam, the *Phoenix* would speed toward Re Lyt, drop into the atmosphere, and covertly land on the planet.

"Initialize cloak," O'Farrell said.

Oliver saw the cloaking device plugged into the console of the *Phoenix*. Now O'Farrell controlled Mr. Krank's device. How had the Corsairs made it work again? Did O'Farrell wonder how'd they come by the device? Would he suspect Mr. Krank? Maybe he thought it was part of some master plan by the Wikks and McGregors to escape and leave him behind.

The Corsair pilot worked quickly. "Cloak initialized. Cloak active. Thirty seconds to hyper flight disengage."

O'Farrell turned to look at the five kids, all seated in the back two rows. "Remember, no attempts at treachery. We're going to work together and rescue your parents," he said, forcibly kind. His gaze returned to the pilots.

229

"Treachery," mumbled Austin. "What would he call his actions?"

Obbin and Mason nodded.

"Boys, don't try anything. We"—Oliver pointed to the boys and Tiffany—"will work together. As for him"—Oliver looked at O'Farrell's back—"you leave that move up to me." Austin smiled his approval and agreement.

There was a sharp bump, but the *Phoenix* otherwise remained steady. The star for this system was directly behind them. A large purple moon glowed before them, and just beyond it shone two others, one pink and one orange. Re Lyt was an orb of deep blue in the distance. The blue was not water, but stone. Small orange freckles glowed across the surface, marking fissures where magma blasted to the surface and settled in lava pools.

"We've got a lock on the enemy cruiser, the *Skull*," stated the Corsair copilot.

"Navigating to designated moon, Nos Idam," the pilot said.

"Very good," O'Farrell said.

"Echo Squadron is in position," the copilot said.

"Have them on standby near Nos Idam, awaiting my orders to engage if necessary. Activate communication silence and have them only break it if they receive the scenario four pass code," O'Farrell commanded. The copilot repeated the instructions to the squadron, and it separated from the formation and flew closer to Nos Idam. O'Farrell wasn't taking any risks.

The fiery glow of Nos Idam took on a deeper orange, like embers in a hearth, as the *Phoenix* rounded to the sunless side.

"Prepare for atmospheric entry," announced the pilot.

"Heat shields activated," the copilot called. The view of the moon disappeared behind the two titanium plates.

The ship's engines rumbled loudly. "Boosters active," the pilot said.

Boosters? Oliver hadn't known the *Phoenix* had astro-boost capable engines. They'd have come in handy several times over the last few days if he'd known. This also explained why they'd traveled to the far side of the moon before heading to Re Lyt. Astro-blasters used the smallest of space particles as accelerants and created a blazing trail of pink light during the initial blast. The momentary glow would be easy to spot from the bridge of the *Skull* or the outpost on Nmutu-A, even though the ship was cloaked.

"Ten seconds." The countdown had begun.

They checked their harnesses once more. "We'll see how the professionals do it," Austin teased Oliver.

He smiled.

The *Phoenix* shuddered, twisting violently. Then nothing. Nos Idam clearly had a shallow atmosphere. The titanium shields retracted, and the pilot took control of the spacecraft.

"You two, prepare our gear for a night journey." Two Corsairs released themselves and headed from the bridge.

The copilot spoke up again. "No activity on Nmutu-A. Cloak seems to be 100 percent effective."

"Ten minutes until arrival at destination," the pilot said.

"Oliver, you and Tiffany will be going with me. The three boys will remain in their cabin," O'Farrell said. His voice took on a dark inflection, one the kids had not heard before. "Any funny business at all and the results will not be pleasant," he warned. The real O'Farrell was showing through. He was like a wolf, ready to feed on anyone who crossed him.

"Oliver and Tiffany, special suits have been placed in your cabins. Change into them and meet in the cargo bay. You have fifteen minutes."

Tiffany looked at Oliver, and he nodded. The man was all business now. They released themselves and started for the door.

"Oliver, what about the boys?" she whispered.

"They'll be safer on the ship than with us, I am sure," he said. "I overheard a couple guards chatting about this planet. It's not a place I'd volunteer to go."

Tiffany took a deep breath and continued to her cabin.

Oliver stepped into his cabin, shut the door, and closed his eyes. This quest had been nonstop. If he wasn't flying a ship through a cavern, he was fighting wild vines or representing his family before a council of blue people or sifting through pages and pages of ancient documents. Nothing was as it should be: O'Farrell had betrayed them, plants could come alive, and the Federation had a dark past. What could he put his trust in? What could he know was true?

He noticed the suit on his bed: long pants and a long-sleeved jacket. It was made of black rubbery-looking material, almost like a body suit. He undressed. He felt the area where his ruby-inflicted wound was. The injury was ninety percent gone, and the FlexSkyn was flaking off. He picked at it. He was impressed at how well his sister had patched him up. Having his body nearly back to normal boosted his confidence. He'd once again be able to handle any challenge thrown his way.

Oliver pulled on the assigned outfit. He didn't like that O'Farrell knew his clothing size. This guy knew way too much about him and his family.

The fabric clung to his skin, forming to his body like a glove. He zipped up the jacket. A pair of black shoes sat on the floor. When he slipped them on and took a step, he seemed to bounce. He flexed his arms, then dropped to the ground for three quick push-ups. He rolled into a somersault, popping into a defensive stance. The suit was a snug fit, but not to the detriment of his agility. Better yet, his wound no longer pained him.

What he'd said to his sister about the planet's dangerous terrain was true, and the outfits would help with that. But he was testing his abilities because he was going to turn the tables on O'Farrell. The old man had not seen the extent of his moves; it was time for him to learn. He only hoped this mission presented the opportunity.

Oliver opened a drawer of his dresser and took out a tube of hair cream. He'd not messed with his looks since the beginning of the journey. He eyed his reflection in the mirror: stubble across his chin, dark circles around his eyes, cuts and bruises across his face. He looked like a warrior.

He glopped cream into the palm of his hand and in one swift move streaked it through his hair, bringing it to a point in the front. It looked like a horn sprouting from his head. He was ready for battle. He took a pair of webbed gloves from the bed and put them on. Small pinprick-sized lights glowed at each fingertip and at several points across his palm and wrist. These he'd not seen before, but they were cool. What did they do?

In the corridor he found his sister. Her outfit mirrored his.

"Tight, isn't it?" she asked, holding up a gloved hand.

"A bit." He shook out his arms and legs.

In the cargo bay, four Corsair guards stood near a pile of packs. Three were dressed in similar gear to Oliver's with the addition of their always-worn facemasks; one remained in the standard-issue gray jumpsuit uniform, tricorne hat, and mask. Why were these soldiers' faces always hidden? Oliver thought back over the last several hours. Had he ever seen their eyes? Mouths? Noses? He hadn't.

"Are we ready?" came the voice of O'Farrell from atop the balcony. Oliver looked toward the supremo admiral. He too wore black rubbery attire. "Orion, man the door!" he commanded as he pulled the hatch shut. He stepped down the stairs, then closed the hatch to the lower level of the *Phoenix*. "Everyone gear up."

He was sealing the bay.

The three remaining Corsairs lifted their packs and fastened the straps into place on their backs, double checking that they were secure. In unison the trio spoke, "Ready." Their voices were rhythmic.

O'Farrell wasted no time and lifted a pack to his back. Oliver and Tiffany followed his lead, taking the remaining two.

A sickening thought crossed Oliver's mind, but it wasn't for his sake. It was for his sister's. He knew what they were about to do.

One of the Corsairs opened a silver crate of goggles and masks. He handed one of each to Oliver, Tiffany, and O'Farrell.

Orion, who remained by the door, latched himself to a hook with a long tether.

"Prepare," O'Farrell ordered. They pulled on their masks. Tiffany hesitated, but Oliver nodded with a soft smile.

"You'll not want to remove these. The atmosphere isn't deadly, but it's not welcoming. The air is highly sulfuric and doesn't suit human lungs well." O'Farrell's voice was clear even behind the mask. "An hour of breathing it will cause great pain."

A Corsair checked over Oliver and Tiffany, then gave a thumbs up to the old man. "Set," he said.

"Open the door," ordered O'Farrell.

Oliver looked at his sister, knowing she'd realized what was about to happen. They were headed out the door while the *Phoenix* was still flying. Through the visor in the mask, he could see terror in his sister's eyes. She began shaking her head.

A swoosh erupted as the door opened, and a chilly blast of air swept into the cabin, then sucked outward. Oliver stumbled to get his footing.

Tiffany was shaking her head more quickly; Oliver could almost hear her frantic breaths as she backed away from the gaping hole. It pained him.

Before he could calm her, a Corsair grabbed her and moved swiftly to the door.

Adrenaline surged through Oliver, and he leaped forward. It was too late. Tiffany and the man were through the door, swept away into the darkness. A second man scrambled toward Oliver to stop him, but he didn't need assistance. He'd done this before at the Academy.

He jumped without hesitation. No more than two seconds later, the wings on his pack opened. Without any need to control his descent, the wings and small rudder on the pack guided him in a wide arc toward the surface of the planet below. A minute screen displayed a decreasing red number as his altitude dropped.

The destination had been set. There was nothing to do but let the pack do the work. If only he'd been able to tell his sister. Oliver's heart ached for the fear he was sure Tiffany had felt the moment the guard had taken her unwillingly from the ship to plunge thousands of feet to the ground.

Tiffany's breathing finally slowed. The sight below would have been inspiring if not for the knots in her stomach. The glowing lava fissures looked like rings of fire against the stark blue earth. The pack attached to her back swung her in a wide, spiraling arc.

The Corsair who'd rudely thrown her from the safety of the ship was just twenty or so feet below her. Every so often, she saw his silhouette as he passed over the orange glow of a lava pool; otherwise, he was nearly invisible in the darkness.

She tried but could not look above her. She had faith that Oliver was there.

Ten minutes later, her body pulled back as the wings adjusted and brought her to the ground in a standing position. Her feet touched down on the solid surface of the planet. Immediately the lead Corsair came to her. He slipped off his pack.

"Remove it," he said. She did, and he took it, pressing the wings back into the pack.

The two other Corsairs, Oliver, and O'Farrell touched down seconds later.

The packs were stashed next to a large spire that jutted from the earth as if magma had shot upward, then frozen instantly into place.

"Megus, you're with Tiffany. Zemba, you have Oliver. Cogan, take the rear. Let's move." O'Farrell sounded more like a general than the generous old benefactor he'd been when Tiffany had first met him.

The guards slipped their swords from sheaths at their sides. O'Farrell carried some sort of pistol in a holster at his side. Escaping was not a possibility at that moment.

The team moved quickly. They stayed wide of the many lava geysers, but Tiffany was enthralled by the spray of glowing liquid rock and couldn't help but pause each time one erupted. Megus pushed her along impatiently, and Oliver made a few threats about not touching his sister. He was silenced by a warning wave of Zemba's sword.

A large cliff crested before them. It should have been a dead end, but instead it was time for Tiffany to learn about the features of her suit, including the glowing spots on her gloves.

"Megus, lead," O'Farrell commanded. The Corsair took off at a sprint toward the cliff. It looked as though he were going to run right into it, but then he threw himself into the air. The shoes added an extra bounce, propelling him up. His gloves and shoes stuck to the rock face as he clung like a spider. The image was complete when he began to climb, just like a spider would—minus four legs, of course.

Oliver was at Tiffany's side. "Looks easy, sis."

She half laughed, her confidence surprising even to herself. "After that jump, I'm not worried about climbing a wall."

"You first, then," Oliver said.

Tiffany didn't run. She walked to the wall, placed her hands and feet, and started up. She looked back at her brother, who tested the full abilities of the shoes and suit by leaping into the air and flipping. His feet touched the wall first, then his hands.

"That was awesome," he said.

Tiffany cheered him. He waited for her to climb up next to him before continuing up the rock wall.

Oliver stayed beside her as Zemba and O'Farrell followed. Cogan remained at the base until all five were atop the cliff. Then he ran at the wall and leaped, making short work of the rest of the climb.

The party walked through a forest of spires until they came to a lookout point. A plain stretched out before them, pools of lava bubbling and erupting across the blue expanse. Centered in the horizon stood arched pylons topped with a massive oval building. Its white exterior flashed with the reflection of each explosion of lava.

"Scout it," O'Farrell ordered. The three Corsairs spread out among the rock and lay flat to the ground.

Tiffany watched as they messed with their goggles. "Oliver, what are they doing?"

"Adjusting their range," he said and tapped the upper part of his goggles. "They can zoom in and out, focus, use night vision, and so on."

Tiffany pressed the uppermost part of the goggle rims, and the oval building expanded in size. She could make out the shadows of people in the many windows. It put their distance in perspective: the building was much farther away than she'd thought. The lava field before them was deceptive in size.

The Corsair escorts called their confirmations: "Clear left!" "Clear center!" "Clear right!"

"Launch the LOCA-drone. Then call it in," O'Farrell said. Cogan slipped back through the stone spires.

"When he returns, we move," O'Farrell explained. He opened a second holster and slipped out the e-journal.

Tiffany nudged Oliver, then spoke under her breath. "He brought it."

"We'll get it," Oliver whispered.

3.31

GenTexic

rossing the field of fissures took more than two hours. Oliver felt for his sister. She wasn't built for this sort of arduous trekking, though she didn't complain once. The rocky surface was treacherous. Worse, they constantly had to drop low as small black orbs crisscrossed the area, searching for trespassers. O'Farrell had already assured them that their suits would keep them undetected. But Oliver was still on edge, jolted each time one of the Corsairs called, "Down!"

O'Farrell led, moving from spot to spot as he followed the map built into his goggles.

Oliver counted at least twenty stories in the building ahead, assuming each row of windows marked its own. Below the large building were high fences. A labyrinth of tubes wove along and around the fences, connecting to each other at domed nodes.

"That's the Hatchery," O'Farrell explained. "Our access point is just over there." He turned to Oliver and Tiffany. "You must understand. I'm trusting you by bringing you with me. Please hear me, I want what you want. I want your parents safely returned to us. I want us all to work together and complete this quest." He seemed to be pleading with them, his voice genuine.

"Sir, the signal," Cogan said. Oliver turned. A brief green glow pulsed once more and was gone.

"Do we have an understanding?" O'Farrell asked.

Neither Oliver nor Tiffany moved.

"Do we?" The old man's voice was stronger.

Oliver nodded, then mumbled to himself. "To defy, yes."

Clearly O'Farrell had not heard. "Good. Then let's go."

Oliver felt like a spy as they slunk in a tight line toward the green light. He gasped as their rendezvous came into view. "Drex?"

"Yep." Oliver couldn't see Drex's smirk behind his mask, but he still wanted to wipe it right off his face. "Isn't this a nice surprise, seeing the two of you again? Especially you." The young man's last words were meant for Tiffany.

Oliver was ready to say something when Megus's impatience erupted.

"Enough," he snarled. "Show us."

"Drex works for O'Farrell?" Tiffany whispered.

"I guess. I don't know," Oliver said. "I thought he worked for Vedrik."

"He must be a double agent," Tiffany said.

The term made Oliver scowl. Double agents never served anyone but themselves. They took whatever mission was most convenient at any given moment. They gave their loyalty to no one. This would make Drex an even more dangerous opponent.

If Drex worked for O'Farrell, how had he infiltrated the Übel? Everything Oliver knew about the group, which was very little, indicated that they were highly secretive. Not even their existence was common knowledge. He doubted just anyone could be a member.

Drex led them through a hatch in one of the nodes and sealed them in. "You can remove your masks and goggles," he said.

Oliver pulled the mask down around his neck and lifted his goggles over his forehead, as did his sister.

"Great work," O'Farrell confirmed. "Have you located the Wikks?"

"Yes, sir. They're being held on floor twenty-one," Drex said. "They're heavily guarded by twelve soldiers and seven celtyx."

"Celtyx? You expect the seven of us to overcome not one but seven celtyx? Not to mention twelve soldiers?" Megus asked.

"Silence," O'Farrell warned him. "Drex? I assume you have a plan. While I don't like cowards, Megus does have a point."

"We'll be climbing. The central elevator bank has been shut down for maintenance." Drex smiled. "I've already secured two grapple lines," he explained. "The two operable elevator banks on opposite ends of the Hatchery are under guard. Only Captain Vedrik and one celtyx remain with the Wikks and Zebra Xavier. As for the celtyx, this will take care of them." Drex flashed a red globe. "Kinetic plasma laced with polkin powder."

Oliver didn't know what either of those things were, but apparently they were enough to subdue or kill the celtyx. From the fear Megus had displayed, it was clear these were not beasts to be tangled with.

"Good work. You continue to impress me. You three had better step it up or you'll soon be reporting to him," O'Farrell said.

"Thank you, sir," Drex said. "Welcome to the Hatchery."

The name of the facility sounded familiar coming from Drex. Oliver suddenly recalled Drex's murmuring at the palace. He'd mentioned "hatch," and they'd joked that he was talking about chickens.

Drex led the invaders through a cylindrical tunnel. The interior was stark white. The groups' black uniforms stood out like the moon in a starless night sky.

"Security cameras?" Cogan challenged.

"Taken care of," Drex said proudly. "I've looped the feeds to the cameras we'll pass to show yesterday's recording. Everything here is highly regimented, especially security patrols. The arrival of Zebra Xavier will affect certain passages and levels. Those I left off the loop, and we won't use them."

Oliver didn't look, but he was pretty sure O'Farrell was smiling. Was this a son, nephew, grandson? If Drex was related to O'Farrell, the double-agent theory might be out the door.

The passage was lit by powerful overhead lights. There were no windows, only a few vents. A soft hum was the only noise aside from their footfalls. Oliver paid attention as Drex entered two separate codes at each door. "Did you see that?" he asked Tiffany under his breath.

She nodded, then repeated quietly, "18, 00, 23 and 26, 45, 90."

He thought back to the code Mr. McGregor had told him. He only had three numbers: 11, 19, 82. What was the second part of the code needed for Building 6? And where was Building 6?

"We're almost to the lifts," Drex explained. "I'll make sure the area is clear of any maintenance workers. They aren't scheduled to attend to it for another three hours, but with Zebra Xavier here, things get done faster."

O'Farrell nodded. Drex slipped through the open door. The hatch sealed.

"Cogan, contact the *Phoenix*. See that it's landed," O'Farrell said. "Then have them initiate communication silence. They are only to act if they see one of us."

"Yes, sir." Cogan stepped away and made the call.

"Zemba, you and Megus keep close to these two. I don't want anything happening to them. Their parents must see they are safe . . . and we don't want them falling into the Übel's hands."

"Yes, sir."

The hatch reopened, and Drex motioned them through. The lift's doors were open with two lines already strung up inside them. Drex handed out clips.

"The *Phoenix* is at the designated rendezvous point. They'll be ready for immediate launch on our return," Cogan informed them. "Communication silence initiated."

"Excellent," O'Farrell said.

Drex took the left line, Megus the right, Cogan the left, Tiffany the right, O'Farrell the left, Oliver the right, followed by Zemba, also on the right. The elevator chute was clear. Oliver could see the underside of the lift hanging high overhead.

Hand over hand, they climbed the cables. The clips prevented them from slipping back down the lines. Oliver watched his sister ahead, hoping she was all right. This was hard work even for him. She showed no sign of tiring, nor did she voice any complaints. Tiffany was far tougher than he had given her credit for, and she was growing stronger every day.

When Oliver's gloved hands were nearly numb from the vibrating chord they climbed, he saw it.

Building 6. The words were stamped across a set of closed doors. They were six floors up from what he'd counted. Instead of *floor*, it read *building* just like Mr. McGregor had said. Was this the place?

He paused and considered it.

Zemba prodded him upward. "Keep moving. We have a long way to go."

O'Farrell was just across from him. His climbing ability and endurance were impressive for someone his age. A challenge formed in Oliver's subconscious; he'd beat the old man to the top. With a grunt, he increased his pace.

Seven more floors passed. Eight to go.

Down Jump

ZJJJJIPPP!

The sound of spasming energy rang out overhead, followed by a thud and several clicks. Oliver craned his neck to look around Tiffany. A yellow light pulsed on the underside of the elevator high overhead.

"The lift!" called out Megus. "It's on."

"Impossi . . ." Drex's voice trailed off. The elevator jerked, then began to lower. The cables they clung to remained taut as the canisters from which the cord had been fired retracted any slack in the line.

"The maintenance ledge!" O'Farrell shouted.

Oliver was just above O'Farrell, having surpassed him.

Megus leaped to the right, grabbing the ledge of the nearest floor, fourteen. Oliver looked down. Zemba did the same to thirteen, but Oliver and Tiffany were between floors. Cogan reached up and grabbed the nearby ledge. Drex jumped down to it, his feet barely missing Cogan's fingers.

The elevator halted for a moment.

O'Farrell was between floors as well. "Oliver, Tiffany, release your clips! Slide!" He unclipped and dropped down the line, using his gloved hands as guides. He threw himself onto the ledge directly across from Zemba. "Be ready to help them!" he called to the Corsair.

An idea zipped through Oliver's mind. His hand was on his clip. "Tiffany, don't stop until you reach me!" he shouted. The words seemed innocent enough: the cry of a brother looking out for his sister.

She looked down at him, her eyes wide.

"Until you reach me!" he said again. The grinding wheels of the lift creaked overhead, and the elevator began to lower.

Oliver unlocked his clip and let himself plummet, jumping not toward Zemba but toward O'Farrell on the opposite side of the thirteenth floor. Tiffany was just behind him but hadn't jumped to the ledge yet. Oliver shoved his arm into the old man, knocking him backward. He swept his free hand toward the e-journal and ripped the holster from O'Farrell.

He leaped back onto the cables. "Down!"

The lift started dropping again. Was it moving even faster now?

Zemba hadn't had time to react. O'Farrell struggled to get his balance.

The lift wasn't stopping.

The elevator car passed Cogan, Drex, and Megus, hiding them.

Tiffany was directly across from Oliver.

Tenth floor.

They had to drop quicker.

"Stop them! Zemba, go!" But O'Farrell's voice was muffled as the lift passed level thirteen.

"Oliver!" cried Tiffany. The lift passed level twelve; they were on eight.

"Almost there!"

Oliver and Tiffany passed level seven. The lift was at level ten and gaining speed.

"Here!" Oliver leaped onto the ledge of the sixth floor: Building 6. His sister jumped; he reached out and pulled her to him. Three seconds later, the elevator zipped past. Oliver looked up. The Corsairs were attempting to get onto the actual elevator cables.

He slunk around the ledge. There was a keypad embedded in the center of the door. He recalled the numbers and tapped them in: 11, 19, 82. There was a buzz.

"Stop!" cried Zemba.

"Oliver, they're coming!" Tiffany yelled.

Drex had used two codes, but Mr. McGregor had only given him three digits. Oliver tried a mixed combination: 11, 19, 82, followed by 26, 45, 90.

Nothing.

Oliver tapped in 18, 00, 23, followed by 11, 19, 82.

Click.

The door slid up. Oliver and Tiffany slipped into an alcove. Oliver spun around, looking for the keypad, but his sister already had it. She pounded her fist against the button, closing the door. They caught a brief glimpse of Zemba's face before it locked.

"Wow, great idea," Tiffany said. "That was quick thinking."

Oliver held up the e-journal. "Plus, I got something back."

"No way." Tiffany took the e-journal in her hands. "This is great." She unzipped the top of her suit and slipped it in.

There was a thump on the door.

"We'll celebrate later. We've got to hide," Oliver said. Tiffany nodded.

The alcove opened into a laboratory.

"Wait," Oliver said. "There might be security cameras or guards." He moved past his sister and scanned the ceiling and corners of the rooms.

He saw no cameras. There were no scientists or guards in sight. The lab was at most twice the size of the *Phoenix's* cargo bay but not as tall. Though the walls were sterile white, the room was filled with color because of eight-foot-tall glass cylinders of blue, yellow, green, or purple liquid standing throughout the room. Arrays of tubes and cables connected to each of the large glass tubes. Gas canisters and pumps at the other end of the connections hissed and chugged.

Several long tables sat together with row upon row of vials and test tubes arranged in trays. Robotic arms lifted test tubes from the trays, turned them over, then placed them back in place. Multiple monitors sat nearby. Graphs and data formed on the screens, then cleared and formed again.

A large red globe at the far end of the room caught Oliver's attention. It hovered above the ground. A round hatch sat in the center of one side, a black screen next to it. While there were several hazardous monikers across it, five large silver letters stood out: *ZXDNA*. On the wall directly behind it was an all-too-familiar phrase.

"And I give unto them eternal life, and they shall never perish," Oliver read aloud.

There was a thunk on the lift doors behind them.

"We need to hide," Tiffany said.

Oliver started through the maze of cylinders and tables, holding out his hand for his sister. A door at the far edge was the only clear exit from the lab. What was on the other side?

Tiffany gasped. She pointed at the nearest glass cylinder.

Inside was a human body. Deep blue liquid hid most of it, but they could see a face with eyes closed and lips pursed.

"Oliver?" Tiffany asked. "Are they dead?"

Oliver looked at the face, but it was obscured by the blue liquid. He couldn't tell if it belonged to a man or woman.

"I . . . I don't know. This looks like an experiment chamber. It might be anything."

"Can we . . . should we try to let them out?" Tiffany asked. "Maybe they're in some sort of suspended sleep state. They do that with people who are near death from an accident."

"If they're near death, we don't want to interrupt the healing process." Oliver put his hand to the tube. The glass was cold. "We can't do anything now."

A series of soft beeps rang out from one of the monitors. A message in bright green letters flashed on the screen: *Serum complete, 87 percent probability of success predicted.*

Success for what?

The far door hissed. Oliver grabbed Tiffany and pulled her to the ground with him.

3.33

Red Sphere

The door opened. Oliver looked through gaps beneath the tables. The newcomer was alone. He could see the person's pant legs and the bottom of a white lab coat. Guessing by the shape of the scientist's narrow shoes, it was probably a woman, and guessing from the position of her legs, she was not facing him.

She stopped near one of the glass cylinders. There was a bubbling noise. Oliver rose just enough to see across the lab table.

As the scientist held down a lever, purple liquid sloshed around and drained from the chamber. The body within became visible as the liquid lowered.

"Wait here," Oliver whispered.

Tiffany scowled. "What are you going to do?"

But Oliver didn't listen. He crept low along the table. He turned the corner. The scientist was hidden on the other side of the now half-empty glass tube. The liquid had stopped draining, and the upper torso of a man was clearly in view. A harness under his armpits stopped him from slumping. As far as Oliver could see, he was not awake.

The scientist's shoes tapped across the floor, and Oliver ducked back behind the table. She took a breathing mask off a shelf and placed it over her mouth and nose, then acquired a visor for her eyes. She stood near the red globe and pressed her hand against a panel, which flashed yellow. Her handprint remained glowing on the screen while she took a pair of gloves from a container and slipped them on. She opened the round hatch on the globe.

The scientist removed a glowing red sphere and shut the hatch again. The sphere was no larger than an inch across. The handprint image on the screen disappeared as she walked to the table nearest the half-empty chamber.

Oliver moved around the corner again.

The screen that had alerted him to the completed serum now flashed several bar graphs. A hologramic image of a molecule glowed before it.

The scientist's back was to Oliver as she mixed several of the vials that had been in the robotic arm's rotation. An orange haze appeared around her. The glowing red sphere hovered in place a few inches above the table, illuminating the haze like a flashing emergency light.

What was he witnessing? Was this why Mr. McGregor had sent them here?

The scientist moved to the tank with the red sphere in one hand and a beaker of liquid in the other. She placed the red sphere in an opening atop one of the canisters hooked to the cylinder, then opened the lid to another. She slowly poured in the contents of the beaker. A black cloud began to escape the canister, but the scientist quickly sealed it. She hit a button on a keypad nearby, and the black cloud was sucked into a siphon hanging from the ceiling.

The scientist watched a screen attached to the cylinder. Three flat green lines ran across it. Several moments passed, and nothing changed. The scientist removed her mask and visor in defeat, tossing them on a nearby table. She again removed the red sphere, holding it carefully in her gloved hand, and placed it back in the large red container.

THUMP! THUMP! THUMP!

Oliver looked at the startled scientist. He knew what she was going to do; she set the vials back in place and started for the opposite door. He had no choice but to leap up and run after her. His sudden appearance caught her even further off guard, and she screamed, running directly into one of the tables. She stumbled backward from the impact.

Oliver caught her from falling. She fought against him, but he restrained her with his arms. "We aren't going to harm you."

Tiffany ran to his aid, putting her hand over the scientist's mouth as she started to cry for help.

"What now?" Tiffany asked.

"Get me that tubing and some tape."

"Intruders!" the scientist shouted.

Oliver slipped his hand over her mouth, grunting as he used his other to control her two arms. He read the scientist's name badge. "Dr. Green, I'm not going to hurt you."

Items retrieved, Tiffany put the tape across Dr. Green's mouth, and Oliver began securing her wrists with the thin flexible tubing. "Sorry about this," Tiffany said.

Oliver opened the laboratory door in time to see the elevator doors jerk open. Zemba reached an arm inside in an attempt to reach the keypad. Oliver kicked one of the nearby tables as hard as he could. It slid toward the elevator and flipped to its side with a loud racket. Vials of liquid shattered and covered the floor in front of the lift doors. Acrid steam poured up from bubbles that boiled across the floor. What *was* this stuff?

Oliver didn't want to leave without questioning Dr. Green about what was going on, but O'Farrell and his men were coming. "Quick, Tiffany, grab one of those hazardous material bags and put on those lab gloves and your mask."

Tiffany didn't ask questions as she obeyed. Oliver moved Dr. Green toward the red containment unit. The scientist shook her head and tried to hold back her hands, but Oliver forced them to the panel. The screen flashed, leaving the yellow print behind.

"Take it," Oliver ordered.

Tiffany pulled open the hatch and removed the glowing red sphere. She set the sphere in the bag she'd taken and sealed it. She discarded the lab gloves.

Oliver let the scientist go, and she backpedaled toward the wall.

"Now what?" Tiffany asked, pulling her mask back down.

The doors to the lift shuddered open under the Corsairs' force. They were out of time, but how to escape? The door Dr. Green had come through was out of the question. She'd been yelling for help, so there must be guards or other scientists just outside the lab. They'd be walking into a hornet's nest.

A large vent caught his attention. "Over here."

He kicked at the covering. It dented. He kicked again. A crash echoed in the laboratory. With a final kick, the vent crumpled. Oliver gripped it with his gloved hands and yanked it free with all his might.

"Hurry! Go!" Oliver yelled.

"Are you sure?"

The elevator doors spread wide. Dr. Green rammed a keypad near the other door with her shoulder.

"*Go!*"

Tiffany dove in, bag in hand. Oliver followed immediately. His sister barreled ahead, crawling as best she could with her free hand. A cool breeze enveloped them.

Several shouts and a crash echoed in the laboratory. The Corsairs were in. They'd soon be coming through the vent, which split in three directions ahead of them.

Tiffany looked back at Oliver.

"Down," he said. "Use your gloves."

"I thought you would say that," she sighed. She twisted her feet ahead of her and dropped into the vent.

Oliver was close behind. He kept an eye toward the vent opening, but the Corsairs hadn't yet come after them. Were they questioning Dr. Green? Had Oliver missed something? Was whatever Mr. McGregor had wanted him to find now in O'Farrell's hands?

"Oliver," Tiffany called. "Are you coming?"

He made quick work climbing down. The vent soon went horizontal, and the brother-sister duo followed it. There was still no sign of the Corsairs coming after them.

SWOOSH. SWOOSH. SWOOSH.

Oliver recognized the sound: it was a turbine. The temperature in the vent had dropped, and the force of the airflow had grown stronger.

Oliver and Tiffany changed positions through a very tight maneuver.

Ahead of them a large fan was pushing air into their vent. Although it was moving slowly, Oliver wasn't willing to stick his hand or foot into it. He squinted as he got closer to the blades. How would he stop them? They needed to go through; he didn't want to risk going back. Even though he'd not heard them, he doubted the Corsairs had given up pursuit.

3.34

Hidden

The twins and Obbin had remained in their cabin; on the other side of the hatch stood a stiff Corsair guard. They'd played twelve games of chess, of which Mason had won all the games he'd played. Obbin and Austin had debated who was better looking, which had ended in a draw. Obbin decided to return to his fur shorts and go shirtless again, saying he was more comfortable that way. Austin decided to go shirtless as well, which started a sit-ups and push-ups contest. Obbin won sit-ups and Austin push-ups. Finally an Energen-chugging contest took place, which resulted in Austin and Obbin requesting to be excused to the lavatory.

Mason sat in the cabin with Midnight. The guard had found compassion enough within to rescue the cat from Tiffany's cabin.

Mason had not participated in the Energen-chugging contest or discussions of who was better looking, secretly knowing the answer was himself. He smiled. He'd kept his blue shirt on and not joined the sit-ups and push-ups contest. That was a waste of time, if you asked him. Did it really matter who was stronger? None of the boys stood a chance against the Corsairs. No, he'd begun reading through some of the things the Blauwe Mensen had given Oliver. What he'd learned had been surprising.

The Blauwe Mensen didn't know where they'd come from. After many failed missions to discover their past, they'd given up, determining to live in secret and protect their way of life from what was then the Empire.

During their brief foray into Cobalt Gorge, the twins hadn't seen much evidence of any belief system held by the Blauwe Mensen. Obbin hadn't spoken of it, but Mason had noticed some of his . . . *odd* habits. One was to lower his head and close his eyes before they ate and before bed. Obbin also said "Thank Creator" sometimes. Mason hoped he might find an explanation of Creator in his reading.

In the middle of the stack of books, he discovered a tattered leather book filled with handwriting. A journal? It was dated more than a century ago—of course, that was only if the Blauwe Mensen had the same calendar as the Federation. On the front page was a title containing the word he had heard Obbin use: *The Path to Creator.*

This book could possibly give him the information he sought. The Blauwe Mensen had included it in the stack of resources they'd given Oliver, which made it clear Creator was important to them.

Mason was ready to find out more. He flipped the page and began to read.

Rescuer was given to our world by Creator to set us free forever. By following Rescuer alone, we escape from our captivity.

Before the days of our ancestors, there was Creator. First Creator created the universe, and then He created us. We are His, and He is ours. In the days of our ancestors, Rescuer walked among us as one of us. He spoke the truth and accomplished great wonders. When we turned against Him, He died on a cross as a willing sacrifice for our sake, then lived again. By His death and new life, we become free to live forever.

As we await the coming eternity, Creator gave us Helper. Helper works to changes us and guide us. One in the same are the Three. Creator is yours to be known by you, if you only ask. In Him lies the one and only eternal truth.

The text ended. Mason had the oddest sensation. Although the words were written like a riddle, they did not seem enigmatic. He understood them. Creator had created "us," which might mean the Blauwe Mensen or all humans. Rescuer had to be a person because he had "walked among us" and was often referred to as *He* or *Him*—always with a capital *H*. He had died in order to free Creator's people. Now Helper watched over and guided them.

What was humanity freed from? It wasn't an army, because the text made it sound as though people were held captive even today until they followed Rescuer. And how could Rescuer's personal sacrifice stop an army? Mason read the line at the end of the passage again: "One in the same are the Three." That meant that Creator, Rescuer, and Helper were names for the same person. Yet each name fit different actions in a time sequence: first, creation, then wonders and sacrifice, then changing and guidance. Creator created the universe, yet can still be known today? Did that mean he was still alive?

Mason thought of the Übel captain's words that Oliver had repeated: "And I give unto them eternal life, and they shall never perish." If possible, eternal life made sense in this passage, especially since it mentioned becoming free to live forever.

If the title, *The Path to Creator*, referred to a journey, it might mean if you got to Creator, you could live forever. So was Creator a place, and Rescuer was a person? That didn't make sense. Obbin had given thanks to Creator—why would he thank a place? It seemed like an odd custom. But the Blauwe Mensen were far different from any people he'd met before. Then again, maybe Creator was a He.

Mason reread the passage and focused on it without thinking about the title of the journal. It started to make sense. Humans weren't free to live for eternity. They'd been put in captivity. Did that mean that even now Mason was in captivity? Was that what the Übel, his parents, and the Corsairs were trying to find—freedom? Were they looking for someone who had the power to free them?

"In Him lies the one and only eternal truth." Mason shivered with excitement. He held the answer to the quest—to everything—in his hands. This journal clearly spoke of truth. Wasn't that what they'd come to seek on Evad? The truth here could be the same as the Truth there.

He read the text over again. This was good news. No—this was great news. He stood up and looked around.

He had to tell Austin! To tell Obbin! Where were they? Surely they should have been back by now.

3.35

Production

Tiffany was the one who stopped the fan. She pulled a clip from her hair and twisted it into the screw head of the fan's centrifuge. The bolt loosened and dropped out the other side. The fan wobbled and slipped away from them into the vent, the blades clanking against the walls.

"Clear," Tiffany said with a smile, then eyed her hair clip. "I won't be using this again."

"Good work, sis."

"Hey, don't you think it's odd that we haven't heard any alarms yet?"

"Yeah," Oliver said. "Maybe they captured Dr. Green before she could get help."

Oliver led, but Tiffany would have rather. The idea that the Corsairs could be coming down the vent behind them made the hair on the back of her neck stand up. She tried to blame it on the cold air, not her nerves, but she knew better.

A humming sound grew louder as they moved down the tunnel. The vent opened level with the floor of a narrow cylindrical room stretching at least ten stories high. The room was frigid—a cooling chamber of sorts—and she shivered despite her bodysuit. Ice crystals hung from tall arches in the center of the room. The hum was loud as ever, a constant drone.

Tiffany looked around the room. There were literally thousands of vent openings, all pulling cold air from the room and through their respective paths to unseen destinations throughout the Hatchery.

"Look, a door," Tiffany said and started forward. She slipped and barely caught herself as she fell to the ground. The floor of the room was slick with ice.

"Careful," Oliver warned. He crouched, then started forward in a bear crawl. It was quickly clear that he could get little traction. The gripping features on the suit's gloves and boots had little effect on the ice.

Tiffany doubted their bodies could tolerate the cold for very long, especially since their necks and heads were exposed. Oliver's method for crossing the room was too slow. The room was at least fifty feet across.

Tiffany moved against the wall. She turned with her back toward the door, then tucked her body in. She slipped the bag with the sphere inside her jacket next to the e-journal. "Watch this!" she called.

She kicked off from the wall as hard as she could, then lifted her body so only her elbows and one foot touched the floor. She shot across the floor like a toboggan down a chute. The ice was so extremely slick.

Oliver cheered as she passed him and continued to the far wall. She bumped against it a short way from the door. Oliver arduously made his way back to the wall, then mimicked his sister's maneuver.

Tiffany typed in the code she'd seen Drex use before. It worked. The door opened into a bright white corridor. Oliver scoped out the hall and pointed out a security camera facing the opposite direction. It was set to monitor someone trying to access the cooling chamber, not leave.

Oliver motioned for Tiffany to hand him the clip. "I need to disable it."

"Why? Drex said most of the cameras were on a loop."

"We don't know which ones."

"Won't it be more obvious to security if we disable it?" Tiffany asked.

Oliver shrugged. "It shorted out?"

Tiffany didn't buy it. "I think it's better to risk it."

"All right, you're the smart one," he said. "I'll trust you."

The weight of the comment hit her. She and Oliver were contributing equally to the success of this mission. It was a big responsibility, but she was ready.

One side of the corridor was lined with windows. They looked out over an expansive floor with long conveyor belts crisscrossing the room. Varying sizes of cages, all shaped like eggs and white in color, scooted along the belts. It was difficult to make out what was in the barred eggs, and after hearing of the celtyx, Tiffany didn't want to know. A rainbow forest of tall glass cylinders occupied one side of the room.

Oliver recaptured her attention. "This must be where they manufacture all their creatures, like Schlamm's Spike."

"Or the wartocks," Tiffany said. "Austin certainly is brave."

"He is," Oliver said. "I just hope he can try not to be brave until we get back."

"Me too," Tiffany said.

They stopped worrying about the security. Since no guards had appeared and no sirens were wailing, it seemed Tiffany's theory had been correct. Brother and sister traveled down the hall until they came to a fork in the path. A sign displayed two options: *Exit* or *Lift*. Tiffany started toward the exit.

"Wait," Oliver said. "We can't go yet. We have to get to the twenty-first floor and find Dad and Mom."

She stopped. "Don't you think we're beyond that now?"

"No, come on. We can use the lift."

"Are you sure that's even the same lift we were on before?" asked Tiffany. "We might be at one of the ends of the Hatchery where those celtyx things are."

"Did you see how the cooling chamber was built? It's centralized in the Hatchery. This must be the central lift."

"Oliver, I think it'd be better to get back to the boys," Tiffany said. "What if O'Farrell gets there first or signals his men on the ship?"

It was clear Oliver hadn't thought of that. A second passed. Then he shook his head. "No, we're too close. We have to try." His voice carried a need that she'd not heard before. Her heart sank; she couldn't resist. "The boys will be fine."

"Okay," was her simple answer.

They took the hall to the lift and found it unguarded. A closed-for-maintenance sign was posted in front of it. This was the same lift Drex had shut down so the Corsairs could penetrate the security of the Hatchery. It explained why they hadn't come across any guards. The lift was the only point of access to the area, other than the exit. The cooling system was unlikely to be a high-priority security detail.

Oliver touched the keypad. No code was needed this time, and a moment later, the elevator arrived.

3.36

Retaken

ustin had taken a page from Tiffany's knockout tactic and laced every bottle of H_2O in the cryostore with sleeping agent. Unfortunately he'd used most of the supply, but it was for a worthwhile cause. Now he had to remember to tell his siblings not to drink any H_2O from the fridge.

Once the guard assigned to the cargo bay was asleep on a bench, Austin and Obbin located the tools they needed to carry out their plan. The search was a success, partly because the Corsair crates were labeled *weapons, medical,* and so on. A keycard around the sleeping Corsair's neck unlocked them.

Austin and Obbin were armed with Zapp-It-like weapons labeled *StingerXN.* Austin made sure the devices were set on stun, since, unlike the Zapp-It, they contained a lethal feature. The weapons' ability made him nervous, but he had to take back the *Phoenix*, and he needed weapons to do that. They also found several canisters of IZ-KLOZE Vapor inside the weapons crate. It would serve as another nonlethal weapon.

The boys stripped down and covered themselves in a patchwork of weatherproofing tarp. The material was used for protecting equipment on a dig site. The tarps were thin and flexible and easy to slice, then piece back together with adhesive binding strips. The rubber in the material would mute the effect of the shocking weapons the Corsairs carried—at least, Austin strongly hoped so.

Austin and Obbin's objectives were simple: take control of the *Phoenix* and set a trap to snare O'Farrell and his men when they returned.

"Okay, one more time," Austin said.

Obbin grunted but repeated the plan. "You head through the lower level to clear off any Corsairs. I go straight for the guard at our cabin."

"But don't get Mason yet," Austin interrupted.

Obbin nodded. "If I encounter the pilot or copilot, I subdue them. If not, I meet you at the stairs. Together we proceed to the bridge. We rush the door, and I take the copilot while you take the pilot."

"Perfect." Austin looked toward the bay. He took a deep breath. "Ready?"

Obbin hesitated. "Actually, I'd like to say something first."

"Go ahead."

Obbin bowed his head. "Creator, I ask for your protection over us as we fight for our families and subdue the enemy that has beset us."

Austin was confused. Who was Creator? Why had Obbin asked for his help?

The prince's chin rose, and he smiled. "Now I'm ready. Creator will watch over us."

"Who's Creator?"

"I'll tell you as soon as we have the *Phoenix* back to ourselves," Obbin promised. "In fact, I need to tell all of you."

"Fair enough." Austin checked the charge on his StingerXN. It was still set to stun. "How's yours?"

"Good."

He stepped back and looked at Obbin. All that he could see were his bare feet, hands, hair, and face. All else was covered in weatherproofing tarp. He pictured the looks on the guards' faces if they had the chance to see them before the attack came. These outfits were even more comical than the puffy white parkas.

"Let's go," Austin said, and they started around the crates.

The guard at the base of the stairs was still asleep and tied up just as they'd left him. Austin double-checked the knots of the rope he'd used. Still secure.

Obbin moved for the staircase. The sound of his bare feet on the metal stairs was barely noticeable as he ascended.

Confident in their plan, Austin moved into the lower level. "STOP!"

Austin spun around and charged back to the door. His target was still out. He looked up. Obbin was a few feet from the balcony. The guard from their cabin stood with his sword drawn and glowing.

Austin reached for a canister of IZ-KLOZE Vapor and prepared to pull the tab. Obbin was too close, and the gas would likely render him unconscious as well, leaving Austin to carry out the plan himself. Obbin might also tumble down the stairs and get hurt. Did Austin have any other choice?

The Corsair brought down the sword on Obbin, who twisted, throwing himself over the railing of the staircase. He hung like a monkey, then dropped as the Corsair slashed his sword again. Sparks blasted from the staircase railing.

This was Austin's chance.

The lights went off. A siren blared, and yellow emergency lights flashed all around. A voice came over the speakers. "Alert. Level two, cabin four." The message repeated.

Cabin four was their cabin. Something had happened to Mason.

The Corsair seemed confused. Austin took the opportunity to drop the canister and charge up the stairs. The alert message called over the speakers again. The Corsair looked down the corridor toward the cabin.

Austin reached the guard before the man saw him coming. The StingerXN flashed, and the guard slumped into the corridor. Obbin had already rounded the base of the stairs and was on his way up.

The corridor flashed with yellow light.

"What now?" Obbin asked as he came to Austin's side.

"Charge!" Austin cried.

The boys ran down the corridor, their bare feet smacking against the metal. Austin glanced at his cabin door, but it remained closed. He hit the keypad, opening it, but the alert didn't stop.

"What are you wearing?" Mason asked, stepping out of the room.

"Protection," Obbin said.

"What happened?" Austin asked.

"The guard seemed suspicious you'd been gone so long, so I created a diversion when he left," Mason said, pointing to the alarm inside the cabin.

"Two Corsairs left: the pilot and the copilot," Austin called over his shoulder. "The bridge. Stay behind us."

His twin said nothing more as he followed. He had joined the fight.

3.37

Level Twenty-one

Oliver touched the button for the twenty-first floor. The lift jerked upward.

"What are we going to do with this?" Tiffany asked, holding out the hazardous materials bag. "What is it?"

"I don't know, but it seemed like the most important thing in the room. I couldn't think what else Mr. McGregor would have sent us for."

The lift stopped, and Oliver tapped in the code Mr. McGregor had given them—not Drex's code, which seemed to be for less secure areas. The doors separated without any alarms, and they stepped into an alcove. This corridor was not like the ones below. It had dark, wood-paneled walls, sconces with fancy lights, and pictures.

"This looks more like a residence than a laboratory," Tiffany said. "It's like the halls of Bewaldeter."

A door opened down the hall from them.

Tiffany and Oliver jumped back into the elevator alcove. Oliver clenched his fist; he'd have to subdue whover it was. He peered around the corner once he was sure the footfalls were headed away from them.

He gasped and felt a gloved hand over his mouth: his sister's. Tiffany was looking at the people too.

Their parents were headed in the opposite direction down the hall, escorted by a man in a black suit. Oliver assumed it was Zebra Xavier. The fourth was a man Oliver knew and despised: Captain Vedrik.

With the help of his dad and mom, he could take the Übel soldiers. Oliver felt the adrenaline surge, he twitched forward, but Tiffany's other arm pulled him back. "No," she said. "Look."

A short, stout, lizard-like creature clung upside down from the ceiling, crawling along just above their parents. Its back and tail were covered in two rows of long spikes. Its leathery skin was a sickly blue-gray. Oliver assumed it could turn invisible if it wanted but figured the creature's appearance was considered more intimidating than any element of surprise. Clearly Megus had thought so.

Oliver felt a knot in his throat. If not for his sister's attention to their surroundings, he'd have charged into an almost assuredly deadly situation. He berated himself to always look up.

His parents neared the door. They were about to slip away again. It was almost too much for Oliver to bear, but he knew he had to let them go.

Tiffany pointed to a door in the opposite direction. "We can't take on a celtyx. I agreed to come, but now that they've gone, we have to get back to the twins."

Oliver looked at the door his parents had come from. "We have to get into that room first," he said. "It must be Zebra Xavier's office or something."

"We don't have time. We have to get out of here, back to the ship. What if they do something to the twins? O'Farrell said he would."

"They're under communication silence. O'Farrell said they were to act only if they physically saw one of them. He should have been more careful than to make a threat and then let us overhear it being nullified."

A soft beep sounded behind them. Someone had arrived on the twenty-first floor on the lift: O'Farrell and Drex. Apparently Drex's code had worked, which meant the lab was more secure than level twenty-one.

Oliver took off toward the door. He twisted its handle, but it didn't move. "Step back."

They heard the elevator doors start to open. Suddenly the lights in the hall went black, replaced immediately by flashing red strobe lights. An alarm rang out, followed by a voice over an intercom: "Intruders on level twenty-one!"

Oliver had no choice; he raised his foot and kicked the door. It blasted open but remained on hinges. He and Tiffany surged into the room, yanking the door shut.

"Tiffany, help me," Oliver cried.

Tiffany set down the bag with the red sphere. Brother and sister moved to a table and together carried it toward the doorway. They heaved it on end, bracing it against the heavy wooden door.

3.38

Take the Bridge

The door to the bridge remained open, yellow lights flashing within. Were the pilot and copilot still there? They'd not been in the corridor, so Austin hoped they were.

He squeezed his StingerXN, his nerves taking over. He'd considered tossing an IZ-KLOZE canister inside and letting it do the work, but then the bridge would be unusable for a time. What if they had to take off?

No more stalling. Austin dashed into the room. He jumped over the back row of seats and made for the Corsair in the pilot's seat. Obbin was right behind him.

The StingerXN sparked, and Austin swept it to the Corsair pilot's arm. Blue energy flashed. The man slumped in his chair instantly, the jolt just enough to knock him out.

Austin looked toward Obbin.

The prince shook his head. His target was nowhere to be seen.

"Where?" asked Obbin.

Mason looked toward the door. "The lower deck!"

Austin nodded. "I'll take the stairs. You and Obbin go through the cargo bay and loop back."

The boys were off.

Austin slowed as he stepped into the lower level of the *Phoenix*. The corridor still flashed with yellow alert lights. He was alone, and he felt it. Obbin and Mason were at the other end of the ship, and between him and them was a Corsair.

He moved toward the engine room. The door was open; lights flashed within. He listened as he got closer. He couldn't hear anything. He peered into the room. No one.

He turned back and moved toward the server room. He peeked in and jumped back. He'd found his target. Austin gripped the StingerXN. He looked down to be sure it was still set to stun. It was ready. He took a deep breath, trying to calm the nervous shake his hand had developed in the search.

The final Corsair was before him. He had to act. If he succeeded, he would have single-handedly taken control of the *Phoenix*. He cleared the lump in his throat.

Austin swung around the corner, then dove at the spot where he'd seen the enemy. He stopped. There was no one in front of him. A door to the server rack swung loosely.

A mistake.

Austin backpedaled into the corridor. The Corsair might be in any one of the storage rooms along the path to the cargo bay. He saw two silhouettes in the doorway at the end of the hall: Mason and Obbin.

"Austin, behind you!" Mason cried.

Austin ducked, then twisted around. The Corsair's sword sparked as it struck the wall. The copilot kicked Austin square in the chest, knocking the air from him. He fell backward, his elbows first to strike the floor.

Austin gasped for breath as the Corsair lifted his sword, then brought it down for a second strike. He rolled left, bouncing against the wall. Sparks exploded across the floor; one sizzled on the back of his hand.

Austin looked up as the Corsair sliced the sword toward him. A blur of blue flew over him and hit the copilot dead in the chest. The Corsair tumbled backward with his attacker on top. They rolled into the engine room.

Austin scrambled to his feet to go to Obbin's aid. A hand assisted him up. "Thanks, Ma . . ." Austin's voice trailed away as he saw his helper's blue fingers. "Obbin?"

Obbin hadn't tackled the Corsair. The attacker had been his twin. Mason had thrown himself against the enemy, stopping his brother from getting struck.

Austin and Obbin charged forward, but the door to the engine room slid shut.

Mason stared at the Corsair. The man had regained his composure and held his silver sword at the ready. Mason looked at his surroundings. He needed a weapon. Unlike Austin and Obbin, he didn't have one.

There was a thud against the door. The Corsair took a quick look but returned his stare to Mason.

Another thud. Austin and Obbin were trying to get in.

The Corsair shifted apprehensively. Mason looked at him. Was he nervous? Mason certainly was. He didn't want to feel the knockout shock of the sword.

Mason knew there were tools in the drawers directly behind him. But what was he going to do, go hand to hand with the Corsair in combat? There had to be a way for him to use his wits to get out of this. If only he could get the door open or stall long enough for his brother to open it.

"You work for O'Farrell then?" asked Mason awkwardly.

The Corsair's head lowered, his expression hidden behind his mask. He took a step forward; Mason shifted backward. The hum of a generator nearby let him know he was running out of space.

"You're a pilot?" Mason asked.

Still no response.

Another thud against the door.

The Corsair moved forward again, his sword out before him.

Out of the corner of his eye, Mason saw a narrow gap between two of the generators. He'd have to climb over a hose and a few cables, but it was the only place he could go to put distance between himself and his attacker.

He shifted to the left. The Corsair jumped forward. Mason darted for the gap. He hopped two cables, then ducked under a thick yellow hose. There wasn't much space between him and the wall of the room.

At the top of the generators, a series of lights flickered, and large copper coils under glass domes buzzed with energy. His situation could turn deadly if the confrontation took either of them too close to the upper portion of the generator units.

He heard a voice near his feet: a whisper. He dared not look.

"Mason, Austin is coming," Obbin said. "The far wall."

Mason glanced toward the wall behind the Corsair; it was the very vent that Obbin had hidden in.

The Corsair was no more than a foot away from the front of the generator. His stalling made it clear he hadn't decided how to get at Mason.

Mason looked toward the grate. He could see movement. Austin was there. Mason had to distract the guard, or the noise would alert him to his twin.

"What if we make a deal?" Mason said. "I come out peacefully and you take me back to my cabin without hitting me with your glow stick. I'll stay in my cabin and not try to escape."

The Corsair grunted and swung his sword. Either he wasn't buying it or he wanted revenge for the embarrassment of an eleven-year-old tackling him.

Mason had to think of a more mutually beneficial deal.

"You know, you'll need me awake when you take me out of here," Mason said. "You can use me as a shield so my brother and Obbin won't attack you. I'll be your leverage."

There was a metallic squeak from the direction of the vent. The Corsair turned; Mason had to act.

He read the label across the yellow hosing: *Steam.* It was a risk, but he had to take it.

Austin saw the Corsair's legs twist. He had to go now. He kicked his feet against the grate. It buckled. He kicked again, and the grate fell free.

He wriggled out, but before he was entirely clear, he heard a gushing sound and then a scream.

It wasn't Mason, however. It was the Corsair. A cloud of steam engulfed the man as he spun around. His tricorne hat fell to the ground as he stumbled backward. Mason held a hose in his direction; it writhed like a yellow snake, pouring steam from its mouth.

Austin charged forward with his StingerXN ready.

The steam from the hose sputtered to an end, and Mason discarded it.

Austin shoved the StingerXN toward the Corsair, but he dodged right. Mason was charging him from the back. Austin redoubled his attack; he jabbed the weapon forward and missed again. The Corsair swept his sword at Austin. He leaned backward and felt the energy from the sword buzz against his chest, though it hadn't hit him. A lock of his hair flittered to the ground, the ends singed and smoldering.

The enemy jolted to the side as Mason tackled him again. It was a crude attack, but it worked the second time as well as it had the first. Austin was impressed by his brother's willingness to put it all on the line.

The Corsair struggled to aim his sword at Mason, whose hands gripped the sword's hilt also. Austin noticed the Corsair was only using one arm; the other lay limply at his side.

The glowing silver sword swung back and forth between them. Sparks erupted each time it struck the ground or nearby shelving. Austin tried to get close but had to jump out of the way with each swing. Then Mason bent the sword toward the man, and the tip hit the Corsair in the chest. His grip went limp, and he lay on the ground, unconscious.

The Corsair had been subdued.

Austin clapped. It was all he could do.

"Wow!" Obbin said, slipping out from the space between the generators. "That was impressive."

Mason blushed. "Well."

"Good work, brother," Austin said, "but we're not done yet. We need to bind the Corsairs and put them in Drex's cell until Oliver and Tiffany get back."

"Right," Mason said.

"Let's get this guy first and drag him to the bay. Then we'll get the other three," Obbin said.

Mason lifted the man's arm. "Yikes, this guy is heavy." He let the arm fall back down. It clinked.

"Did you hear that?" Obbin knelt over the man and rolled back the damp sleeve of his gray jumpsuit. "What's this?"

Austin and Mason joined him.

"It's metal?" said Obbin.

The arm of the Corsair was silver chrome. Darkened lights lined it. Austin saw an access panel. He recalled how the Corsair had used only one arm after being attacked by Mason. "You shorted it out with the steam," he said to Mason.

"Is he a robot?" Mason asked.

Austin shrugged. He didn't think so. The man's hat had fallen off, and he had a full head of hair.

"Have you ever seen one of these guys without a mask?" Mason asked.

As far as he could remember, Austin hadn't.

"Let's take a look," Obbin said. He leaned over and began removing the mask.

Austin grimaced at what might be underneath but didn't stop him.

Study

The lights in Zebra Xavier's expansive study were still on. A massive bookshelf covered one wall; there must have been thousands on thousands of books. That seemed odd. The Übel at one time had been bent on destroying them all. Most likely this represented decades—if not centuries—of collecting.

Large framed maps covered another wall. Like the books, they looked ancient. The third wall was all windows, and the final contained a cabinet equal in size to the bookcase but filled with a variety of artifacts: statues, crates, keys, and even animal skeletons. Tables throughout the room were littered with various treasures.

Oliver grunted as he heaved a couch toward the door. Tiffany turned to help, but then she saw it: a large desk near the bookshelf. On it sat a device that looked like the e-journal. Its two screens lay open but dark.

"Oliver, look at this," she called.

He didn't answer. She watched as he flipped a couch on its back. He moved toward the door, pushing the couch against the tables.

Tiffany moved to the desk. "This must be Zebra Xavier's e-journal. Can you imagine what research is in here?"

"Sure," Oliver said absently. The couch was apparently the third and final barrier, because Oliver moved quickly to the window. He looked out over the night-covered planet. "We've got to get out of here."

"You were the one who said we had to get in here," Tiffany argued.

"That was before O'Farrell and his men arrived hot on our trail." Oliver tapped on the glass. "It's high, but we don't have a choice."

"Out the window?" she asked. "Are you serious?"

"Very," he said and grabbed an odd-shaped statue from a nearby desk. "It's the only way. We can climb down the side of the building in our suits."

There was a bang on the door. The upended table rattled.

"What are you going to do?"

"Put your mask and goggles back on," Oliver said, sliding his into place. "Stand back," he warned and turned his head as she moved away.

He lobbed the stone statue at the window.

CLANK!

A web of cracks traveled across the glass. The statue bounced to the floor. Oliver retrieved it and threw it again. This time the end of the statue pierced the window, remaining lodged in it. He raised his foot and kicked the base of the figure, which disappeared into the darkness as the entire sheet of glass shattered. Fragments exploded out into the night air, which swept into the room in a warm, sulfur-laced gust.

"Come on," he said as the tables and couch wobbled violently. "They're coming."

Tiffany dashed back to the desk and grabbed the e-journal. "Oliver, the red orb!"

"Where?" he asked, climbing back in through the window.

"The door!"

Oliver ran toward the entrance, where the bag sat on a round table. He swept it up just as the first table toppled over the second and crashed into the overturned couch. The barricade was no more.

Oliver sprinted for the window.

The door burst open.

In rushed Drex and Megus. Tiffany shoved the confiscated e-journal inside her jacket with the other.

"Stop!" cried Drex.

Tiffany wasn't about to. Oliver was already halfway out the window, the hazardous materials bag in one hand.

"Watch the shards," he warned.

Megus and Drex overturned tables as they charged toward them. Artifacts fell to the ground, some shattering. Drex fired his weapon. A silver explosion of sparks flashed near Tiffany's left leg, just missing her.

There was no time for fear. Tiffany placed her hands on the ledge and threw her legs over. She didn't even pause as her brother had. The suit had worked against the cliff; it should work on the building as well. She relied on logic and a bit of hope.

Her feet touched the white exterior and stuck. She released her gloves' grip and started down. Shaped like an egg, the building curved inward as it went down. Soon she reached Oliver. He'd tucked the globe into his jacket. She looked up to see their pursuers, but Drex and Megus didn't appear. Instead she heard a fight break out. Yelling. Crashing. O'Farrell shouting orders.

Übel soldiers had responded to the intruder alert. It sounded as though a battle was taking place between the Corsairs and the Übel. If he were captured, would O'Farrell tell the Übel about her and Oliver, or did he have a reason to keep their presence secret and let them escape? Either way, she wasn't going to wait to find out. There was one way out of here, and it was down.

Red beacons flashed across the exterior of the building, creating flashes of crimson all along it. Sirens rang out across the expansive grounds surrounding the GenTexic Hatchery facility.

Like ants on the underside of a hanging tree fruit, Tiffany and Oliver made their way down the side of the building. Tiffany was soon clinging upside down, the ground almost horizontally beneath her back.

She and Oliver moved quickly toward the underneath of the Hatchery. Then they stopped dead in their tracks. An explosive roar, like the onset of thunder, bellowed out from beneath them. Tiffany looked over her shoulder. What she saw took her breath away.

A lizard of gargantuan size was peering up at her. Its jaws were wide open, its sharp teeth ready to chomp down on its soon-to-be meal. The beast was many feet below, yet it seemed confident that she was about to fall into its mouth.

"Quick! Back up!" Oliver warned. "It looks like there are cages across the entire underside of the building."

ROAR!

Tiffany looked once more. The beast was bucking its head; its narrow eyes drilled into her. She noticed its two scrawny arms, which didn't seem proportional to the rest of the terrible lizard.

Tiffany and Oliver climbed back up the side of the building until they reached the first floor. Oliver pounded his fist on the window, but it didn't budge. He grabbed the top of the frame, placed his feet against the glass, and, using the grip in the palms of his gloves, kicked off. His feet swung back and hit the glass. Still the window didn't move.

Tiffany looked across the side of the building. "Oliver, over there." She pointed to several large hoses coming out from the building. The lines angled down and toward a collection of huge tanks.

"Good eyes, sis," Oliver congratulated her.

They moved across the Hatchery exterior to the sound of the vicious snarls and roars of the beasts below. Zips of green and silver light blasted out through the shattered window of level twenty-one. The battle was still raging.

Oliver tugged on one of the hoses. "Seems secure. Do you want me to go first?"

"No, it's fine. I will." Tiffany took the rubbery hose in her hands.

"I'll take a different one so we don't put too much weight on it," Oliver said.

Tiffany grabbed the hose with both hands and swung her legs up over the cable. She started to make her way down like a sloth on a tree branch. Below her was an empty yard. Tall fences surrounded the expanse, but she saw no creatures.

"You're doing great," called Oliver from a few feet away. "We're almost there."

Ripples of blue energy sparked along the fence as bugs made the unfortunate mistake of flying too close. The charged barrier made Tiffany think twice. Maybe the cage wasn't empty. What was down there? Spike had been part chameleon. Who could know what other sort of cloaking creatures the mad scientists at RepFuse had dreamed up? She'd seen the wartock and the celtyx. A shiver rocked her body, causing her to tighten her grip on the cable. She'd feel much better once they were outside the energized walls of the compound.

The firefight in Building 6 seemed to have ended, and no one had appeared at the window. She wondered what the outcome had been. If O'Farrell and his men had won, surely they'd have come out the window and chased after Tiffany and Oliver like spiders. Again, perhaps not. They might try to beat them back to the *Phoenix*.

A gust of warm volcanic wind swept around Tiffany. She tightened her grasp as she swung back and forth like the basket of a bassinet. The moment she thought she'd steadied, the wind rushed around her again.

This time she began to drop—not because she'd lost her hold on the hose, but because the hose connector had ripped free from the side of the Hatchery. Gas gushed from the end of the hose in a white cloud.

Her feet swung free, but she held tight to the lifeline.

The hose snagged on the fence, slowing her fall to the ground and jerking her body backward like a pendulum. Tiffany swung toward the mesh wall. She twisted and let go to avoid collision with the energized fence.

Her body rolled across the ground, and she threw her hands out to stop herself from hitting the fence. She sat up and caught her breath. The screens in her goggles were full of static, damaged from the impact. Even her mask was making an odd spurting noise. She recalled what O'Farrell had said about the atmosphere: it was breathable but not hospitable. She ripped her goggles from her head and removed her mask.

A crackling noise overhead got her attention.

The gas had frozen a section of the fence, which was now peeling free from the rest of the mesh wall. Blue sparks flashed along the torn edges.

Tiffany pushed to her feet and ran clear as the fence tumbled down, then shattered in thousands of pieces. The fallen hose thrashed like a snake, white freezing gas pouring from the end. She backed farther away.

"Tiffany! Are you all right?" Oliver called from overhead. He was still clinging to his cable. "I'm coming."

Still too high in the air, Oliver couldn't let go. He would have to get to the other side of the fence to climb down. Tiffany was on her own.

A new sound interrupted the blaring sirens, and bright floodlights flared up along nearly the entire surface of the underside of the Hatchery. Every cage was illuminated.

A voice came over the loud speakers. "Sector thirteen breached. Containment teams report to stations immediately. This is a crimson alert."

A series of loud beeps followed, and the message repeated.

A hiss came from behind Tiffany, and she slowly began to turn. She wanted to see what was about to eat her.

3.40

Traitor

Obbin lifted the mask from the Corsair's face.

What was there wasn't entirely robot, nor was it entirely human or normal. Most of the man's face was intact, with the exception of his right eye. In its place was a glowing glass ball that pulsed blue in the rhythm of a heartbeat.

"Biotronics," Mason said. "Cybornotics. I thought the Federation had banned the integration of machine and man."

"These guys don't belong to the Federation, remember?" Austin said.

"True," Mason said.

"Let's check the others," Obbin said.

The twins agreed.

"First let's bind him and drag him to the cell," Austin said.

They used some spare electrical wire from the engine room to bind the Corsair's hands. Then they hauled him to the cargo bay cell, Austin carrying his shoulders and Mason and Obbin carrying one leg each.

They checked the guard whom Austin had secured even before the attack had begun. He was still unconscious. They found no mechanical enhancements after removing the mask and tricorne hat.

Austin patted down the Corsair's arms, legs, and chest, but as far as he could tell, there was nothing but flesh underneath. The sleeping guard was delivered into the cell next to his comrade.

At the top of the stairs, they bound the third guard. There was nothing biotronic or cybornotic under the guard's hat or mask, but when they rolled up his pant leg from the ankle to the knee, the entire segment was plated with chrome. A series of lights ran the full length, bright white light flashing up and down.

"This is biotronic," Mason explained. "Biotronics replaces limbs, organs, or other things like that."

"What was the other type you mentioned?" Obbin asked.

"Cybornotics. It deals with the actual integration of information into a human's brain or nervous system," Mason said. "The first Corsair has an eye replaced and a section of his arm. The eye would likely have some cybornotic connections to the brain, and the arm was plainly biotronics."

"Okay, brother scientist," Austin said. "Thanks for the explanation, but let's get this Corsair locked away and get to the pilot before he wakes up."

The fourth and final Corsair sat in his chair where he'd first been attacked. Removing his tricorne hat, the boys found a metal plate covering the top of his head, but that wasn't all. Both of the man's eyes were glowing blue orbs. His hands were each replaced, and his left leg was made of biotronic replacements from hip to foot.

"Something awful must have happened to this guy if he needed all this work," Mason said.

Austin grunted. "Would you even want to live if you were half machine?"

"Life is valuable," Obbin said. "Perhaps he was not ready to die. Perhaps he did not have hope of eternity."

"So he extended his life through mechanical enhancements," Austin said.

"That reminds me," Mason said. "Just before you released me from my cabin, I was reading a book your people gave Oliver: *The Path to—*"

"Mason, wait. Let's get this guy in the cell first," Austin said.

"Fine, but I need to ask Obbin about this book," Mason said.

"You'll have plenty of time while we wait to spring our trap," Austin said.

"The trap. Part two of the plan," Obbin recalled. He reached up and scratched his scalp. His spiky green hair had become tangled and matted with sweat.

Austin put his hand to his chin. "Yes. It's time to set our trap for O'Farrell and his men. When they return, we'll catch them off guard."

"I was hoping Obbin and I could talk for a minute," Mason interrupted. "I came across something in the books your people gave Oliver," he said to Obbin.

Obbin smiled. "What?"

"A journal, handwritten," Mason said. "I left it in our cabin."

"Really? I want to see," Obbin said.

"Great, let's—"

"No, we can't spend time reading and researching now," Austin said. "We have four prisoners, and O'Farrell might return at any time with three more Corsairs. We need to be ready."

"But, Austin, this is really big. I've never read anything like it. The book spoke of eternal life. I think it's a key to our quest."

"We'll have time soon enough," Austin said. "What you read isn't going anywhere. It was on the pages before; it will still be there after we've captured O'Farrell."

Austin looked at Obbin for backup. The prince looked unsure. It was clear he wanted to see the artifact from his people. Mason's blue eyes were on him as well.

"I . . ." He looked at Austin, then Mason. "I think he's right. We must prepare for the liar's return." It was the first time any of them had used that word to describe O'Farrell.

Mason sighed. "Fine."

The three boys changed into Ultra-Wear in preparation for leaving the ship and returned to the cargo bay. Austin searched through the manifest once again. The list of items in the cargo bay was extensive, but he found what he needed. Austin assigned a crate to Mason and another to Obbin and told them what to retrieve.

Austin's trap was a larger version of one he'd created while hunting rabbits on Tragiws. He'd caught many of the gray-haired, long-eared, white-tailed hoppers with the snare. He hoped the device would work on men too, even crafty evil ones.

The *Phoenix* sat within a forest of tall spiky spires of dark blue rock. The towers of stone helped in the design of his trap, as he'd used tree trunks in the smaller rabbit-catching version. The spires also caused another dilemma: how to ensure that his prey moved where he wanted. The setup would take at least a half hour, if not a full one.

If the Corsairs returned before the snare was complete, plan B was to conduct a frontal assault with IZ-KLOZE and the StingerXNs. Oliver and Tiffany would possibly fall as casualties to the attack, but they'd wake up eventually. Nothing else could be done.

Obbin and Mason located their supplies and Austin his. They also relocated their confiscated mTalks. Though Oliver and Tiffany didn't have theirs, the three boys could communicate with each other.

Austin started to type in the code to open the hatch.

"Wait!" yelled Mason. "Have you checked the atmospheric makeup outside?"

Austin yanked his hand back from the controls. He'd not, a mistake that could be deadly.

Mason grunted and strode to the bay computer console. He worked for a moment, then turned to Austin. "You wouldn't have killed us, but we'll want to wear masks and goggles. The atmosphere has a high level of sulfuric gas."

"Did you say sulfuric?" asked Obbin.

"Yeah."

Obbin's nose scrunched, and he squinted. "Yes, masks, please. Deep in certain caverns near the lava stream that guarded our gorge, sulfur gas was prevalent. My brother coughed for a week after being exposed too long. Plus, his eyes were all red and swollen."

"The levels aren't too high, but they would cause irritation," Mason said.

"You've both made your point," Austin said. "Let's find some masks." He hadn't been entirely neglectful; it wasn't often that planets with unbreathable atmospheres were settled. It made life and work really difficult for the residents. Of course, it made sense to locate a research facility on a less hospitable planet, especially if clandestine activities occurred there.

They soon found masks in the Corsairs' crates.

Austin resumed typing in the code, and the hatch opened.

"Everyone stay close together. We don't know what sort of creatures might be out there," Austin said. This was a concern he'd kept at the top of his mind.

He looked back at the *Phoenix*. The only sign that it was there was the open door of the cargo bay. The exterior of the ship was still cloaked. Without the small remote, he had no choice but to leave the door open. He wasn't sure who had the remote, but he assumed it was O'Farrell.

Mason revealed a LuminOrb. He made it blue, then tossed it near the open hatch.

"Resourceful," Austin said. "Now let's go."

As they walked, Mason spoke up. "Obbin, I read about Creator."

Obbin stopped. "Creator? Do you know him now?"

"Know him?" Mason said. "No. I mean, I've read about him and heard you mention him before."

Austin looked over his shoulder. Obbin started forward again.

"We pray to Creator because he created us. He created everything," Obbin said.

Mason squeaked with interest. "And Rescuer setting us free from captivity by revealing the truth?"

"That's all part of Creator's plan for us," Obbin said confidently. "Our freedom comes from him. He speaks the truth."

This statement stopped Austin dead in his tracks. He remembered what he had learned about the Übel. Brother Sam had said the secret society had destroyed real history and, in doing so, covered up the thing that would set them free.

"Speaks the truth?" Austin asked. "Brother Sam was a follower of the Truth." Mason and Obbin looked at him. "But he called the Truth a *who*."

"The Rescuer spoke truth to humankind," Obbin said with a smile. "He is the son of Creator. My people believe—"

CRACK! SHHHHHBOOOM!

The three boys turned their attention to the sky. A large ship plunged toward the planet. A handful of smaller ships pursued it. Zips of light erupted; trails of flames glowed from the tails of a barrage of missiles. A battle erupted overhead. Austin suspected the Corsairs and Übel were at it again, but the Federation was also a possibility.

"Quick," he said. "We need to set our trap. O'Farrell and his men must have done something to set off an alarm. They'll be coming this way soon."

The conversation about Creator was over. They needed to begin setting the trap. Austin only hoped they had enough time.

3.41

Dinosaurs

Tiffany saw nothing, but the hiss was joined by another, and another. Soon a chorus of growling and snarling had erupted in the yard. Something was working itself—or themselves—into a frenzy. She turned and looked back at the gap in the fence. The hose had stopped writhing. Only a small stream of vapor still poured out; the large storage tanks had been emptied.

She ran. Though she knew in general not to run from a predator, she couldn't see these ones and didn't think it would matter either way. She hoped the fence was down; the creatures' past experiences might make them hesitant to approach the usually charged barrier. Without stopping, she leaped across the hose and over the bottom two feet of fence that remained intact.

"Whoa!" yelled Oliver from where he stood atop the gas tanks. He pulled off his goggles as if to get a clearer view.

Tiffany looked over her shoulder. A pack of lizard-like creatures stalked toward her, not running, but coming. Apparently their movement had made them visible—or the creatures just wanted to frighten her.

Oliver leaped down to meet Tiffany, who approached a cluster of large storage tanks. He held his mask out to her.

She put it to her mouth and breathed in some filtered air, then offered it back. Oliver didn't put the mask back on but held it in his hand with his goggles, each by its strap.

"We need to hide," Tiffany warned him.

"We'll have to squeeze through here," Oliver suggested, nodding toward the storage tanks. It wasn't the safest place, but she couldn't see any other option.

The creatures approached, their heads bobbing with their slow, measured movements. Cautiously, but all the same they came.

They stood on two legs. Sharp claws tipped their feet and hands. Their long necks craned back and forth as they searched the area, sniffing out their prey. A tuft of fur or feathers sprouted atop their beastly, lizard-like heads and continued down their backs. Some were red with purple tufts, some blue with green, and some yellow with orange. Large razor-sharp teeth flashed under the bright security lights each time they opened their mouths to snarl.

Tiffany had heard of ancient creatures called dinosaurs. She'd even seen renderings of them that looked eerily like what she was seeing now. A sign on the side of the intact fence read *Velociraptor Version DS93DE*. A series of warnings were listed directly below the name: *Requires level 89 stun, extremely aggressive, extremely quick, high vertical jump, attacks in pack.*

The pack hesitated at the edge of the fence.

A gasp of air nearby signaled the opening of a hatch to the tunnels. Five men dressed in heavy-duty black biohazard suits marched out from one of the nodes. They didn't see Oliver and Tiffany, instead moving quickly toward the fence. Each carried pronged weapons in their hands; blue sparks jumped across the tips.

It was their chance: Tiffany and Oliver slipped behind the men and into the node. Tiffany closed the hatch. Red lights flashed in the passage, bathing the white walls in crimson.

A low siren continued to roll. An open locker next to the door revealed one more of the weapons the guards had carried. A label read *LX-7712 Phaser*.

There was a series of loud roars outside. The ground shook beneath their feet.

"What was that?" Tiffany asked, but she didn't expect an answer.

Oliver took the weapon from the case. "We may need this."

"Let's go!"

Tiffany and Oliver ran into a still-open hatch from the node and into one of the tunnels. Tiffany swung her palm into the keypad as she crossed the threshold, sealing the door.

BUMP!

The entire hallway jolted, knocking Oliver and Tiffany off their feet. Oliver's mask, goggles, and the phaser slipped from his hands and scattered down the hall. Something struck the roof of the tunnel.

Then again.

And again.

A section of the ceiling crashed to the ground. Oliver hadn't recovered his footing when the head of a velociraptor thrust through the hole and into the tunnel.

Oliver scrambled backward.

Tiffany rolled away.

She looked back at her brother as he reached out for the weapon. There was a shattering crash against the door they'd just come through—another dinosaur, perhaps. The hatch at the far end of the tunnel would not last long. The next door, their exit, was sealed.

She had to open it quickly.

The velociraptor screamed. It reached its claws in and tore at the wall.

Oliver struggled for the gun. Tiffany dove toward him, keeping low to avoid the dinosaur's snapping, saliva-dripping teeth. Her body hit the ground, and she pushed the weapon toward her brother. He gripped it, then swung it round. He tried to fire, but nothing happened.

"The charge," Tiffany cried. The drop must have released the energy. "Recharge it!" She scrambled back toward the door. "I've got to get this open."

As if in confirmation, the door at the other end bulged from another strike. Time was running out.

ZHHHIPP!

The sound of the phaser charging brought momentary hope. Tiffany pulled herself up and tapped the keypad.

A message flashed on a screen: *Access denied.*

"ASHHHRRROAR!" screamed the velociraptor as Oliver blasted it with a surge of energy. But it didn't collapse into unconsciousness; instead, it surged toward them with a renewed vigor. Its claws tore at the tunnel. A section of the wall began to peel away.

Oliver charged the weapon again, this time pushing the power to its max. "Hurry!" he called to his sister.

She tapped in the code again.

Access denied.

A renewed crash against the far hatch.

"What am I doing wrong?" she cried out, more to herself than Oliver.

The phaser was buzzing with electricity. Tiffany looked back. The coil around the barrel and the prongs at the end glowed with bright blue energy. If not for the rubber suits they wore, Tiffany wondered if Oliver would have been fried by now.

ZHHHIPP PROOOM!

The sound was all wrong. Tiffany felt heat on the back of her neck as she turned to look at what had happened. Oliver lay against the far wall, eyes closed, smoldering holes spread across his suit where the blast had melted the material.

There was no beast in sight, only a blackened ring around the torn area of the tunnel. The end of the weapon lay crumpled nearby, the stock of the phaser still intact.

"Oliver?" she yelled.

The left half of the door at the end of the corridor burst open. A second velociraptor snarled and shoved the upper half of its torso through.

"Help," she said. To whom the word was spoken, she was unsure. Only a desperate need to ask compelled her.

The killer beast at the end of the tunnel struggled but couldn't go any farther.

Knowing that going to her brother would cost them both their lives, Tiffany turned to the keypad once more. She started to type the numbers in again and realized she'd accidently switched the order of the two sets in the frantic excitement. She tapped in the numbers Drex had used in the tunnels before.

The door swept open. Tiffany whirled around, grabbed her brother's hands, then pulled. The far door continued to bend as the dinosaur shoved itself farther through. Oliver hadn't moved. She couldn't tell if he was even breathing.

His body bumped as she pulled him across the hatch threshold. The far hatch clanged against the corridor floor as the velociraptor won its battle and surged forward. Its speed was astounding. Claws raised, mouth open, it was coming for her.

Tiffany threw herself against the keypad, and the door closed, then sealed. The hatch shook with a resounding boom as the full weight of the dinosaur crashed against it.

They couldn't stay. They had to get out. Several tunnels led out of the node, but which one was an escape?

Tiffany saw Oliver's chest rise and fall. He was breathing.

Again she took her brother's hands and pulled him along the floor. A trail of blood streaked behind them. She had to get Oliver back to the ship. She had to find help.

3.42

Wounds

Oliver's body weight pulled heavily on Tiffany's arms as she fought to escape their pursuer. The velociraptor hammered through door after door, relentless in its hunt. The crimson trail of blood was luring it on. Sirens wailed, and lights flashed, and Tiffany was losing hope the Übel would get the creatures under control.

Escaping or stopping the beast fell solely to her. She was the only one who could keep them alive.

There'd been no more weapon lockers since they'd first entered. She was unarmed. The signs throughout the corridor were of no use either. Most simply listed access to different sectors and the species of genetically mutated creatures that were housed in that sector: *Tyrannosaurus rex, Stegosaurus, Brachiosaurus, Gir-elephant, Hiposaurus, Arctodus simus*, and so on.

She wanted to check Oliver or stop the blood trail, but his body was heavy, her arms tired, and the velociraptor was still in pursuit. She and the dinosaur had no mutual agreement to take a breather.

Loud explosions echoed all around; roars and screams filled the space between them. How would she ever carry Oliver back across the field of lava fissures and pools, especially if predators roamed freely?

Where were all the guards and scientists? None had come across their path.

After a dozen more doors, corridors, and several nodes, she finally saw a sign that had promise: *Vehicle Utility Node.*

She typed in the borrowed code for the uncountableth time, and the door opened. It was then she realized that she'd not heard the crashing pursuit of the velociraptor for a while. Finally, the break she needed.

The Vehicle Utility Node flashed, as did every other area of the GenTexic facility. The distracting lights were lost on her when she saw half a dozen large, wheeled craft as well as several models of flying craft. Her escape was at hand. She let down her brother's arms and put her ear to his mouth. Warm air blew against her cheek. Alive. She gently pulled back his eyelids: his pupils were dilated. From the little she knew about medical stuff, this was a good thing. She looked him over to find the site of the bleeding. There was no open wound to be found. It didn't make sense, but it didn't matter now. It was time to get them out.

Could she secure Oliver to a scooter so that he wouldn't fall off? Probably, but did she really want to try to fly one, especially one of the larger deluxe scooters? *No.*

Driving a land-bound vehicle seemed like a better option. Though it was intimidating in size, at least they wouldn't fall out of the sky. Plus, the cabin afforded more protection from any creatures that might be roaming loose. Just because she hadn't seen any flying creatures didn't mean there weren't any. The cabin of the vehicle would also protect them from the sulfuric atmosphere.

She walked to one of the massive, wheeled vehicles: unit number five. The letters *CRACU* were etched along the side. Footholds provided a way onto a ledge that crossed over the wheels. She peered inside the cabin. There was enough room for ten or more people inside. Now she had to figure out how to heave Oliver up and in.

If she could lean Oliver against one of the wheels, she might be able to pull him up onto the ledge. Then dragging him to the door would be easy.

After moving Oliver to the third wheel of the vehicle, she wrapped her arms around his torso. With a deep breath, she heaved him up. His chest bounced against the rubbery tires. She hoped she wasn't hurting him more. His body leaned against the wheel. The wide tread held him up.

She started up the footholds when a sharp pain rang out in her leg. Blood covered her left pant leg and her shoe. She sat on the ledge and softly touched her left calf with her hand. Wincing with pain, she inhaled a sharp breath.

The blood trail had been hers. She was the one injured, not Oliver.

She pulled on her sleeve to tear some fabric for a wrap, but the material was too strong. Tiffany limped to the vehicle's cabin and found a medical kit. Inside she found gauze and NumbaGlu; once she had applied these, she returned to her brother.

He remained just as she'd left him, his condition the same. With each pull, his body rubbed against the treaded wheel. Hopefully the suit provided some protection from getting a burn on his chest.

Tiffany dragged Oliver to the cab of the CRACU and laid him on the floor between two rear-facing rows of seats at the back of the cab. He fit snugly in place, and Tiffany hoped his body wouldn't roll around, hurting him further. In the driver's seat, Tiffany tapped the ignition screen. There was a warbling sound, and the headlights came on, casting bright beams before the vehicle. Her path was clear but for a large door. She took the directional joystick in hand and pressed it forward. The CRACU lurched and rolled toward the massive exit.

Tiffany eyed the dash for a control to open her escape, but it was unnecessary. The door began to open of its own accord. The glow of the CRACU's lights illuminated the dark blue ground.

That wasn't all, though. Two massive legs rose up before her.

Tiffany hammered the brake pedal with her foot, bringing the vehicle to a dead stop.

As the door continued to open, the back of a gargantuan dinosaur was revealed. Far larger than the things that had chased her through the tunnels, this creature was nearly twenty feet in height.

The dinosaur didn't even notice her. Its attention was laser-focused on something else. The beast's tail whipped to and fro. Its head bucked as it roared.

BEEP!

Tiffany looked to the center of the dash. Closer to the navigator's seat, a simple message read: *Target identified. Tyrannosaurus Rex, serial M19C90J19P93.* A set of options were listed below the message: *Active Self-Defense: Intimidate, Sedate, Destroy, Ignore.*

3.43

Believe

Mason was exhausted; he leaned against a spire of blue stone. Obbin was still midway up a nearby spire, tying the final knot. After choosing the optimal path of approach to the *Phoenix*, they'd built their trap.

Only Obbin's knot was left, so Austin had moved deeper through the rock forest to spot Oliver, Tiffany, O'Farrell, and the Corsair goons.

The sound of alarms had reached their ears, ringing out from the other side of the spires. The sky battle still persisted, but smaller fighter craft had joined the larger ship in repelling its attackers.

"Got it," Obbin called and began his descent. "The trap is set."

"Great." Mason smiled. "Can you tell me more about Creator now?"

"Of course," Obbin said as he stepped onto the ground. "We're supposed to share the good news."

Mason frowned. "Then why didn't someone tell us when we were in your home?"

"You'd just come to us. We didn't want to overwhelm you," Obbin said. He scratched his head. "Of course, we should have.

Creator is not overwhelming in a bad way. He is relief to us. He brings peace to his followers."

Mason looked curiously at Obbin. He said the words so naturally, with deep conviction. He really seemed to believe this.

"Can I meet him?" Mason asked.

Obbin smiled. "Everyone can meet him. You just have to speak to him. He is always here."

Mason shook his head. This made no sense at all. "What?"

"Creator is not a physical being who walks among us. That is Rescuer."

"Wait, I remember this. The passage I read—it said, 'One in the same are the Three,'" Mason said.

Obbin nodded. "Creator, Rescuer, and Helper are all one in the same. Creator created the universe. Rescuer walked among us, then died for our sins. And Helper is with us now."

"Sins? What are those?" Mason asked. The word was foreign to him.

"It's sort of like when you do something bad," Obbin explained. "Like disobeying your parents or lying. We are all born into sin."

"Born into sin?" asked Mason.

"We have a sinful nature from the moment we are conceived," Obbin explained. "It wasn't always that way. Not in the beginning."

"The beginning?"

"The first humans were made without sin and walked in the garden in the very beginning," Obbin said.

"Garden?" Mason asked.

Obbin frowned. "This is going to take a while, so be patient."

Mason nodded.

Obbin seemed to be pondering where to pick up. "I'll explain about the garden in a minute. First you need to understand that there is a path to freedom from sin."

"Okay," Mason said.

"When Rescuer sacrificed himself for us, he made a way for us to be free from the curse of sin," Obbin explained.

"How does Rescuer's sacrifice give me freedom? Didn't it happen long ago?"

"Rescuer was the perfect sacrifice, given to humanity by Creator for just that reason," Obbin said. "Rescuer was the answer to the first sin in the garden. The first man lived in the garden. He was given a mate, a woman. The woman was persuaded into eating fruit from a tree that Creator had told them never to eat from. But the woman did, and then shared the fruit with the man. That act of disobedience to Creator caused everyone born afterward to be sinful in nature and under the curse of death."

"Curse of death?" Mason asked.

"Without this curse, human beings would have lived forever. That's why Rescuer broke the curse with his sacrifice and why he is the path to eternal life," Obbin said.

Mason was beyond impressed with Obbin's knowledge on the subject. It seemed like something a teacher should explain, yet a boy his age was doing a good job.

"And what about the third one . . . Helper? You said he's with us now?"

"Helper was given to us to speak to us, to be with us every day," Obbin said. "We do not see Helper, though. He guides us after we trust in Rescuer."

Mason looked toward the sky. What Obbin had told him was unlike anything he had ever heard. He should have thought the prince was crazy, but inside him was a deep stirring. He knew the words Obbin spoke were true. The Truth.

"All you must do is ask Rescuer to forgive you of your sins. If you are sincere, he will forgive you and set you free. Eternal life will be yours," Obbin said.

Mason swallowed the guilty lump in his throat. His parents had always taught him to do right, to be kind to others, but still he had done many things wrong. He'd lied before. He'd been disobedient to his parents. He'd even cheated once on a test, though he'd ended up telling the teacher out of guilt. Yet this idea of sin was new—that he was born into it from the beginning, that it was a curse.

"Obbin, I want Rescuer to set me free," Mason said.

Obbin nodded. "You cannot see him with your eyes, but Helper will live within you and guide you."

"Okay." Mason felt the need to bow his head. He'd seen Obbin do it when he spoke to Creator before. "Rescuer, thank you for sacrificing yourself for me. Thank you for taking my sin from me. Send Helper to guide me." A hand gripped his shoulder. He glanced to his side. Obbin was beside him.

Tears formed in Mason's eyes. A relief unlike anything he'd ever felt washed over him. His breathing sped up. The tears began to roll down his cheeks. He wasn't sad, no. He felt happiness and joy. He felt excitement.

Obbin wrapped his arms around him in a hug. He whispered into Mason's ear. "Welcome, brother."

Mason smiled. *Brother.* Obbin had many and Mason had two, yet this meant something different to him. Certainly he didn't know everything there was to know about Creator, Rescuer, or Helper, but he knew he wanted to believe. He knew he wanted to follow.

"Now what?" Mason asked.

"I will do my best to tell you all I know. You have accepted Rescuer's sacrifice and Helper will guide you. Creator is watching over us. He is our strength and protection," Obbin explained.

A grin crossed Mason's face. He was so happy. He felt so good. He wanted to tell his family. He wanted them to experience the same feelings.

"Obbin! Mason!" called Austin, his voice somewhere among the forest of blue spires. "Where are you? I didn't mark the trap's location on my mTalk."

"Over here," yelled Mason.

"Keep talking," Austin called. "I'll follow your voice."

"We're over here. We are over here," Mason repeated. He continued saying, "Over here," until Austin came into view.

"You guys have to see this. You have to see the egg," Austin said.

"The egg?" Obbin asked.

"It's a massive building. It's huge," Austin said. "But even more, there's something major going on. Lights are flashing. Things are exploding. And it looks like there are giant"—Austin spread his arms wide—"I mean, *giant* reptiles everywhere." He turned and started off.

Mason wanted to tell Austin about what he had just learned, but the moment didn't seem right. They couldn't pause to talk with a battle taking place and Oliver and Tiffany unaccounted for.

"Wait, how will we get back?" Mason asked.

Obbin slipped out his knife. "I'll mark our way." And as they went, he gashed his blade across the blue stones, leaving visible scratches.

"That works," Mason said.

3.44

Intimidate

The tyrannosaur lifted its head and roared. Tiffany's seat vibrated from the sound. The dinosaur swung its tail and ducked its head. The CRACU was again rolling forward under her control. She still couldn't see exactly what the beast was opposing.

A decision remained on the screen: *Intimidate, Sedate, Destroy, Ignore.* She couldn't press *Destroy*, regardless of the terrible lizard's appearance. Killing it seemed too much. If she sedated it, she might very well be sentencing it to death by its attackers or the other freed beasts. But *Ignore* might cause death for others or for her and Oliver. *Intimidate* seemed like the best option. Perhaps it would run far away.

Her finger hovered over the flashing option for *Intimidate*, but she didn't press it.

A bright blue stream of energy blasted the tyrannosaur in the chest. The dinosaur wailed and rose to its full height, then charged.

She could see its opponents now: a group of soldiers dressed in black biohazard suits. They held phasers, but it became clear the tyrannosaur would get one of them. Tiffany hit *Sedate*.

DJJJJJJJJOOOOOOUP!

The CRACU shuddered as a series of glowing purple orbs blasted from a weapon atop the vehicle. The purple orbs curved as they zeroed in on their target and struck the dinosaur at multiple points: the head, each arm, each leg, and several places along its back. The effect was instantaneous. The large beast twisted, then collapsed to the ground.

The men looked toward the CRACU. They seemed surprised to see Tiffany, who was clearly visible through the windshield, instead of relieved at being saved from the dripping jaws of the terrible monster they'd faced.

Tiffany knew her troubles were not over. One of the men pointed, and the soldiers charged the vehicle. Tiffany looked for the lock.

The men climbed up onto the vehicle, pulling on doors, knocking on windows. Tiffany was distracted by the onslaught before she noticed a new message and option: *Vehicle integrity at risk.* Beneath the message was the option *Active Self-Defense: Intimidate, Sedate, Destroy, Ignore.*

It was time to try *Intimidate.* After all, these were humans. *Destroy* wasn't an option.

The exterior of the CRACU glowed blue. The entire vehicle shook viciously. Soldiers were thrown to the side; one fell directly in front of the CRACU. Tiffany hammered the brake again. The vehicle stopped.

Life form obstructing path, the screen read. A new option appeared: *Clear path.*

Tiffany tapped it. Two powerful streams of liquid blasted from the underside of the vehicle, turning as they worked. She saw the soldier's body roll out of the way, propelled by the liquid canons. He sat up, looking dazed.

Tiffany pressed the control stick forward, and the CRACU again rolled along. She steered it around the unconscious dinosaur and onto the open blue plain. It was only a matter of time before the men would be after them with scooters, CRACUs, and who knew what else.

BOOOOOOOOM!

Tiffany looked out the passenger window. A massive cloud of green smoke billowed from the earth a half-mile away. Then another. She craned her neck to look up.

A battle. Dozens of spacecraft were zipping around the sky. A dogfight had broken out. The Übel were defending their Hatchery, and the Corsairs were coming to O'Farrell's aid and perhaps to pillage the secrets of GenTexic.

Where were her parents? Were they safe? Had the *Phoenix* joined the battle?

One of the fighters was struck. A man jettisoned from the cockpit; then the ship exploded as it crashed into the planet's dark surface. The fight soon encompassed the space overhead. A white orb of light, a rogue missile, hit a lava pool a hundred feet away and detonated, sending liquid rock spewing into the air. A splattering landed on the exterior of the CRACU, but its exterior must have been built to handle it because no alerts appeared on the screen.

The large, industrious vehicle continued to roll along, un-pursued. Why had she not been followed by the soldiers? She'd seen them enter the Vehicle Utility Node. Had they instead joined the battle against the invaders or escapees? Regardless, she was relieved.

Tiffany drove on. Was she headed in the right direction? A tall blue ridge rose ahead of her, topped by a forest of rock spires, the only landmarks of the sort around. She hoped her brothers were safe inside the *Phoenix* on the other side of the rock formation. She wished Oliver would wake up. She needed him to fly. She needed him to fight off the Corsairs aboard the ship. She needed her brother at her side.

3.45

Approach

Austin watched the large vehicle make its way around the bursting lava pools. The ridge before it was at least a forty-five degree slope and 150 feet high. The vehicle wouldn't be able to come up the ridge, playing perfectly into Austin's plan. Obbin lay on one side of him, Mason on the other.

"We'll need to head back shortly," Mason said.

"Agreed."

They watched the six-wheeled vehicle roll closer. In the distance, the white oval building flashed with red lights. The ship they knew as the *Skull* had landed near it. Its weapons were a blaze of activity, targeting its flying enemies. Smaller fighters, Übel and Corsair, battled throughout the sky. Lizards of all sizes roamed freely around the building; groups of soldiers battled against the creatures. It was a bizarre scene filled with a variety of creatures and vehicles unlike anything Austin had ever seen. He was pleased with the goggles they had found, as they were capable of great zooming.

A massive long-necked animal strode no more than two hundred feet from the vehicle. Its legs were of such size that one step of its foot on the incoming vehicle would crush it. But the gigantic lizard showed no interest. It seemed more concerned with fleeing the chaos at the building.

"Austin, we should go," Mason reminded him.

Austin nodded. "You two go. I want to see who came back. Hopefully one or two of the Corsairs got captured back at the building."

"We should stay together," Obbin said. Mason agreed.

"Then let's give it a few more minutes. It'll take them time to get up the ridge on foot anyway," Austin said.

The large vehicle finally came to a stop just below the ridge. Austin was anxious to see his opponents. He'd taken out four Corsairs, and he had another four to go, including O'Farrell.

Then the door to the vehicle opened and so did Austin's mouth. Although he couldn't see her perfectly, he knew it was his sister from her size. Tiffany stepped out from the cab of the vehicle first. She turned and bent over. Then she pulled someone from the vehicle. *Was that Oliver?*

"Oliver?" Mason echoed Austin's thoughts.

"I think so," Austin said.

They waited, but no one else stepped into view. *Were Tiffany and Oliver alone?*

"Quick, let's get down and help her," Austin ordered. The three boys stood and took off down the slope. In his excitement, Austin nearly tripped and fell down the slope, which might have resulted in broken bones. He slowed himself but continued to lead his brother and the prince in the descent.

"Tiffany," shouted Mason.

Their sister turned in shock. She'd just gotten Oliver down from the ledge on the vehicle.

"Boys?" she asked as they came closer. "What are you . . . ? Never mind. Help me. Oliver's hurt. I don't know how badly. He's been unconscious for a while now." Her voice was strained but not panicked. She seemed in control of the situation.

This was a different sister from the one Austin had known at Bewaldeter less than a month ago.

"Austin, you and Obbin take hold of Oliver. Get him back to the ship. Mason, come with me. We brought a couple of things back from the Hatchery with us. I want to take whatever we can carry from the vehicle."

The boys obeyed, and Austin took Oliver under the arms while Obbin took his legs. The Hatchery was an interesting name, but accurate. The building looked like a white egg, and he knew from O'Farrell that creatures were genetically engineered there.

Up they carried Oliver, their pace a tenth of the speed they'd used running down. Austin watched Oliver's chest rise and fall and heard his wheezing breath. He was relieved that his brother was alive. But the burn spots across his rubbery outfit concerned him, especially as he noticed reddened patches of skin beneath.

Tiffany and Mason caught up to them slowly. Tiffany was limping. Sister and brother each carried an armful of things, and Mason had a satchel slung over his shoulder.

"Austin, great work. Mason told me that the three of you took over the *Phoenix*," Tiffany said.

"Yes, the Corsairs are locked in the cell Oliver built," Austin explained. "What happened to Oliver?"

"I'm not fully sure. We were attacked by a velociraptor. Oliver tried to fire a weapon at it, but the charge backfired or something. The weapon exploded. I don't know if he's been electrocuted or knocked out by the explosion." Concern slipped into her voice.

"What about you?" Austin asked.

"Something cut my leg. I dragged Oliver a long way before we were free of the dinosaur. It wasn't until then that I saw my wound, so I'm not sure what did it."

"I'll take a look at it when we get to the *Phoenix*," Mason said.

Tiffany looked at Oliver. "Not until we attend to him."

"Did you say *dinosaurs*?" Obbin asked.

"Monsters, if you ask me. These scientists must be mad."

"Wow. There are old stories that tell of dinosaurs," Obbin said.

"Austin, can you fly the *Phoenix*?" Tiffany asked.

Austin nearly dropped Oliver. He'd not expected that. "I . . . I don't know."

"Of course you can," Obbin encouraged him.

"I think you can," Tiffany added. "Most of it is pre-programmed."

"But . . . I mean, I've watched. I've never flown," Austin said.

"We just need to take off and land somewhere else," Tiffany said. "We can't have O'Farrell finding us or leading the Übel to us."

"Where are the supremo admiral and his men?" Mason asked.

"I don't know," Tiffany admitted. "But Drex works for him."

"So he wasn't in any hospital bay. He was already back in service," Mason said.

"He might have been there briefly," Tiffany said. "His wounds appeared bad. But they probably have some very sophisticated equipment to fix—"

"Cybornotics!" Mason shouted. "And biotronics. The Corsair soldiers—most of them had some sort of mechanical enhancement."

"I should have guessed," Tiffany said. "When they spoke, they sound—"

"I can do it," Austin blurted. "I'll do it."

Tiffany, Mason, and Obbin looked surprised at the outburst but appreciative of his decision.

"Good, because we don't have anyone more skilled than you," Tiffany said.

"Did you say Drex was working for O'Farrell?" asked Austin.

"Drex had infiltrated the ranks of the Übel," Tiffany said. "He knew the ins and outs of the Hatchery. I'm pretty sure his cover is blown now."

"This way," Austin said as they turned and headed perpendicular to the *Phoenix*.

"We set a trap for them," Obbin said. "Austin's design."

"Oliver and Tiffany got Zebra Xavier's journal," Mason said.

"We haven't looked at it yet. It might be empty or have nothing of use," Tiffany said. "We also got our e-journal back. Plus, we took something from a lab, but I don't want to take it out until we know more about it. The scientist in the lab took many precautions before she handled it, but we were in a rush so we just grabbed it."

The only signs of the *Phoenix* were the blue LuminOrb Mason had placed beside it and a large glowing square, which showed the cargo bay. With the ship cloaked, its silver exterior mirrored its surroundings, but the interior of the cargo bay showed through the open door.

Austin heard voices from within as they approached. The Corsairs were awake. Had they escaped from their cell? To his relief, they had not, but shouted a series of threats as they entered the ship. Austin peered through gaps in the makeshift jail. All four prisoners were accounted for.

Obbin walked toward the cell. He raised his StingerXN and wiggled it at the men as sparks erupted from its tips. This had a silencing effect. Austin could imagine three of them had serious headaches from their shocks.

"Where should we take Oliver?" Austin asked.

"His cabin. I'll tend to him there," Tiffany said. "Mason, check the manifest for more medical supplies. We've used quite a bit from the kit in the galley. Plus, I might need something more extensive than the ship's day kit. Austin, get the ship ready for takeoff, and Obbin, you get these Corsairs off the ship."

"Off the ship?" asked Obbin.

"Tie them up somewhere outside. I don't want them on the *Phoenix*. They are too much of a threat," Tiffany said.

Austin was surprised she'd take such action. She'd voted for keeping Drex previously. Now she wanted no prisoners.

"How will they be found?" Mason asked.

"We'll leave an emergency beacon. Eventually the Übel will come and take them prisoner," Tiffany explained. She clapped her hands. "Now everyone go. I'm going to stash these things from the Hatchery in the library."

This was not the Tiffany he knew, but Austin liked it. He wouldn't have to feel so protective of her. No, he would be able to fight alongside her.

3.46

Burns

Mason set the medical supplies in Oliver's cabin and waited for Tiffany to arrive. Oliver lay unconscious on his bed. He'd groaned a few times, which Mason thought was a good sign, but he hadn't opened his eyes.

Oliver's breathing was labored. The leader of their expedition lay unable to lead, yet Mason didn't feel leaderless. He, Tiffany, and Austin had grown more skillful and independent, yes, but that wasn't it.

A presence filled him that he couldn't explain any other way but by Obbin's words. He knew that he was safe. He knew that he was being guided. It didn't seem logical to him, yet it must be.

Tiffany hobbled into the room. "Did you get the supplies?"

"Here," he said lifting them onto the bed. "Are you okay, though? Maybe I should take a look at your leg first."

"The most serious injuries should be handled first," Tiffany said. "Mine can wait."

Tiffany searched through the medical supplies. She touched a silver pen-like tool to Oliver's forehead, ears, neck, and chest, and above each eye.

"His vitals are fine," she said calmly. She took out a pair of scissors. "Mason, I need you to help me, but we must be careful and patient."

He nodded.

Tiffany cut the fabric at the collar of Oliver's shirt. When she neared a burned patch, she stopped. She cut another path down the side of his suit again, starting at the collar of his shirt and stopping when she reached the first burn area. She did this three more times until Oliver's shirt was divided into sections.

"Now we must remove the shirt. When we get to a burned area, I want you to squeeze some of this at the edge. Then I will slowly pull the fabric clear and cut farther," Tiffany explained. She handed Mason a tube. Its label read *SlickWick*.

The work was tedious and delicate. Oliver never moved, though his skin stuck to the fabric despite the purple lubricant Mason applied. Mason's worry for his brother grew with every passing moment. Oliver's legs, arms, and chest were covered in small burn marks. His skin was red and even blackened in some areas. Only his undershorts remained mostly untouched by the explosion Tiffany had described.

Obbin stopped by the cabin. "The Corsairs are relocated to a spire a fair distance from here. I gave them all masks and left an emergency beacon, which means our location will be evident to the Übel. But I've closed the cargo bay door so we can leave."

"Good work," Tiffany said. "But we'll be a little while yet." Her tone was calm. She seemed unaffected by the mention of the Übel.

"Is he going to be all right?" Obbin asked.

Tiffany didn't speak. Mason knew why. If she did, she might lose control of her emotions; he felt the same way. It was painful to see their oldest brother with his skin bare and marked with so many wounds; the once-strong force in their family was now broken and unresponsive.

Tiffany took out a roll of gauze, NumbaGlu, and a package of FlexSkyn. "We're still working," she said. "He's breathing."

"Mason, there is something we can do," Obbin said.

"What is that?"

"We can pray. Creator will take care of Oliver. We can pray for quick and complete healing," Obbin explained.

This was new to Mason, but so was his knowledge of Creator. Not only would he try almost anything to heal his brother, he also believed in Creator and what Obbin had told him. The recent sensations of courage and leadership he'd received he attributed directly to his acceptance of Rescuer's sacrifice.

Tiffany looked at the prince but didn't say anything. Instead she went about applying the NumbaGlu, then FlexSkyn, then gauze.

Obbin moved to the end of Oliver's bed and knelt down. Mason knelt beside him. Obbin bowed his head and began.

"Creator, we ask for your healing power to come over Oliver. We pray that you keep him safe and give him rest. We know that Oliver is yet unaware of you, but we pray on his behalf and out of our concern for him. Please heal his wounds and awaken him. We trust you are working and trust in whatever the outcome may be." Obbin's voice was soft but deep with conviction.

There was a brief pause as if Mason were supposed to say something. He'd never done this before. Then he heard purring, and something moved against his chest. He looked down and saw Midnight. He smiled.

"Creator, I ask you to heal my brother. Please help his wounds heal. Please help him wake up. We need him. Please, Creator." Mason sniffled. He felt tears streaming down his cheeks. He couldn't lose Oliver. He loved his oldest brother.

"Amen," added Obbin.

When Mason looked up, Tiffany was still working. She said nothing of the prayer, but the look on her face was curious. He wanted to tell her about his new discovery and what it meant. Yet they seemed to have a silent mutual agreement to concentrate on fixing Oliver for now.

"Ship is ready for . . ." Austin started as he stepped into the cabin. His words trailed off. Oliver's bandaged body lay on the bed with Midnight curled nearby as if comforting him. "Ummm . . . the ship is ready," Austin said. "I just need to know where to go."

Tiffany looked at him. "We're going to Enaid. We can't stay here. I've done as much for Oliver as I can. We must continue our quest." She pulled Oliver's sheet up over his legs and chest to his neck.

"But he needs medical attention," Austin said. "Shouldn't we—"

"No, there is no one." Tiffany's voice caught. "I've checked his vital signs, and they are good. He's asleep now. We must wait for him to wake up."

"I'll need your help on the hyper flight," Austin told Tiffany.

Tiffany stood up from the bedside. "Let's go."

3.47

First Flight

Austin quivered, his hands on the controls. His nerves wanted to overtake him like the killer vines on Evad, strangling his ability to move.

The screen flashed with information; a globe swirled before him. Tiffany programmed the coordinates for Enaid. Everything for the hyper flight jump was ready. Now he just had to get them off Re Lyt.

In itself, taking off for the first time was an overwhelming task, but that wasn't all he had to do. Austin had to fly through a gauntlet of enemy fighters, Übel and Corsairs alike. Only after that could he attempt the risky hyper flight sequence.

His sister looked at him from the copilot's seat. "Austin, you can do this," she promised.

"Yeah, Austin, you've always wanted to," Mason encouraged him.

But wanting and having the ability were very different things.

Obbin clapped his hands. "You can do it."

Mason joined him. It was the oddest thing for the two boys to be clapping in rhythm, striking a beat leading up to the liftoff. Yet it was encouraging. It reminded him of playing kugel at Bewaldeter.

Austin saw the icon he needed on the screen. He took a deep breath, and the engines rumbled as he initiated takeoff. He watched as the screen showed his thrust increasing. The engines hummed along at 100 percent power. The *Phoenix* began to rattle, waiting for the freedom to lift into the sky. Austin pulled on the controls. The ship rose.

Soon it was above the blue spires.

"Austin, we are cloaked," Tiffany reminded him. "The enemy fighters shouldn't see you."

That was a good thing indeed.

The Hatchery glowed with fire. A side of the building was aflame. Thick smoke billowed into the sky. The burning cloud flashed from the dogfight that sometimes passed through.

The large Übel cruiser, the *Skull*, still sat in its place near the Hatchery, its guns a blaze of activity. There was no way to know who was winning, though Austin imagined the Corsair escorts were sorely outnumbered.

He turned the controls of the *Phoenix*, and the battle was quickly out of sight. So far, so good. Flying was similar to riding his bike at home—with the exception of altitude, of course.

Austin flew across the planet. Their goal was to exit the atmosphere on the opposite side of the moon outpost on Nmutu-A. The planet was nearly the same all around. No water, no plant life was visible, just large ridges, tall spires of stone, and thousands of craters spewing molten lava. He was surprised that the atmosphere had been breathable at all.

"All right, Austin, take her up here," Tiffany said.

He pulled back on the controls; the black sky sprinkled with thousands of white lights was ahead.

"Exiting atmosphere in three, two, one," Tiffany called aloud.

There was a violent jerk, but the *Phoenix* continued on.

A familiar menace flashed into view.

"Look," called Mason from the second row. "It's the *Black Ranger*."

Having been caught in a battle, his secrecy blown, Austin knew the supreme admiral must have called in help. The large ship paid them no attention. A swarm of smaller ships launched from its sides and blasted toward the planet.

Austin was thankful they were cloaked, but also that they were not caught in the raging battle. He wouldn't have wanted to be aboard the *Black Ranger* or the *Skull*. His stomach lurched. His parents were there, and so were the McGregors.

"Did you see that?" asked Obbin. "Were those all ships?"

"I think so," said Austin.

"Destination set," Tiffany said. "Looks like we're getting out of there at just the right time."

Right, his sister was keeping herself on task. He needed to also.

"Please confirm the coordinates: 102.580 X, 5912.23 Y, 22.0 Z, Enaid," the *Phoenix*'s flight control system said.

"Yes," Tiffany confirmed.

"Hyper flight sequence engaged. Plotting course," the computer said.

Several applications popped up on the screen, displaying the final steps the flight computer was taking for the *Phoenix*'s jump into hyper flight.

"Everyone strapped in?" Tiffany asked. The bridge's red warning light flashed.

"Confirm hyper flight sequence initialization. Projected course is clear," the computer stated.

Austin's finger hovered over an icon that flashed the word *jump*. It was up to him now, though he and Tiffany hadn't had to do much. The *Phoenix* system was highly sophisticated. Between Oliver and the Corsairs, all the necessary settings had already been programmed. Why did he feel such anxiety?

He took a deep breath.

"Jumping," Austin said. He pressed the icon.

The large blue countdown numbers flashed on the screen.

The computer spoke again. "Ten seconds to jump."

Austin remembered the titanium heat shields. He brought them closed with a swipe of his finger.

"Three . . . two . . . one."

A whistling noise filled the cabin momentarily and then ceased. Austin felt a pressing on his body.

Then it was gone.

"Hyper flight stabilized," the computer informed them.

"Great job, Austin!" everyone exclaimed.

His cheeks flushed. It'd gone well, and they were now safely cruising to Enaid. A countdown on the screen showed this flight to be very short. Almost exactly one hour, which he relayed to everyone else.

"Tiffany, I have to tell you and Austin something," Mason said. "Well, Obbin has to tell you."

She turned to look at him. "What is it?"

"It's about Creator," Mason said. "I need to show you something I discovered. Can we go to the library? I want to see if there's more information in the LibrixCaptex."

"Let's go," Tiffany agreed. "I'm going to peek in on Oliver and Midnight."

3.48

Creator

Mason had retrieved the handwritten journal and a few other books. Tiffany had checked on Oliver. There'd been no change. Austin and Obbin were waiting in the library.

Now they gathered around the small round table along with the once-hidden items. There was less than an hour to discuss and search. The first and most important thing Mason wanted to share was about Creator, Rescuer, and Helper.

First he reread the text he'd found. Obbin explained what he and Mason had discussed in the spire forest. Austin listened and shook his head. Mason thought perhaps it was with disbelief, but his brother's response was quite the opposite.

"This has to be what Brother Sam meant. This was what he meant to tell me before we ran out of time." Austin looked at Mason. "He said that during their pursuit to live forever, the Übel had buried the very thing that could set them free. He was talking about the Truth," he said. "You mentioned eternal life and this Rescuer speaking the Truth. Are they the same?"

"I don't know for certain," Obbin admitted. "But they do seem to be. Brother Sam and I never got to specifics, though it seemed we believe in the same person. If he talked about Truth as a person, then I would say we speak of the same Rescuer."

Mason smiled. "Yes, we need to follow Rescuer and his truth."

Austin scratched his ear. "Tiffany?" he asked.

Tiffany hadn't said a word. "It doesn't seem possible . . . yet . . . somehow I am certain it is the only way. I think I've always known there is something greater at work." Tiffany smiled. "Right now I need more than anything to believe in someone who is in control of all this mess. I feel like we are in the middle of chaos." She took a deep breath and then sobbed. Tears rolled down her cheeks.

"Tiffany, it's okay," Mason said and moved to the armrest of her chair. "There is hope. Creator gives us hope."

Obbin smiled. "He is our Creator, our Father, and the One who watches over us."

Tiffany sniffled. "But how do I really know?"

"Faith," was Obbin's simple reply.

"Brother Sam said having faith would lead to the Truth," Austin said. "This is not a coincidence. The Truth is Rescuer. This is what he was leading me to."

"Faith does lead to Truth, to eternal life," Obbin said. "I have never seen Creator, Rescuer, or Helper, but I know in my heart that they exist."

Mason nodded. "It's like crossing the invisible bridge on Evad. It was there, yet we couldn't see it."

"I've always felt as though there's a plan for me," Austin said. "But on Evad it became even more apparent. Brother Sam's words were genuine. He spoke of something greater that I wanted. What must I do?"

Obbin sat next to Austin and hugged him. "It's simple. Tiffany and Austin, you must humbly accept Rescuer's sacrifice and put your trust and belief in Creator. Then you will receive Helper, who will guide you."

"I do," said Austin, his voice choked up. Mason watched as relief washed over Austin's face as he dropped to his knees. "I do. I accept the Truth." He used Brother Sam's word.

"As do I," Tiffany said, her head resting on Mason's chest. "I believe what you've told me. I believe in Creator. I accept Rescuer's sacrifice for me."

Something thumped on the table. Midnight strolled toward them, her purring loud and rhythmic.

"That's it," Obbin said. "We must only believe in the Truth."

His childlike attitude was refreshing to Mason. It wasn't complicated; it was faith. It was believing in someone who loved you enough to sacrifice himself for you.

The path to accepting Rescuer's sacrifice and Creator's plan was clear to any who wished to follow, and Helper's guidance cost nothing.

3.49

Enaid

I t was nearing time to come out of hyper flight. Austin was nervous for one reason: they'd yet to land at a spaceport that required clearance. Oliver had only had to land in places that were secluded: forests and jungles. As far as he and Tiffany could determine from the map, there was no seclusion on Enaid. A network of federal outposts guarded the planet like a fortress.

Austin and Tiffany had looked up all the clearance information for the *Phoenix*. At least they wouldn't raise suspicion by not having the right serial numbers and owner logs.

Obbin had also led him and Tiffany in their first prayer to Creator. It had been a calming experience. It'd made him feel as though he was no longer carrying the weight of everything. That burden was on Creator now.

Mason had brought out the cross necklaces Brother Sam had given them on Evad. Obbin took Oliver's for the time being, since their brother was still asleep.

"According to the Veritas Nachfolger, the cross symbolizes Truth. I think these will serve as good reminders of that," Mason said.

"Yes, but they are only symbols," Obbin said. "They're not the real Truth."

Austin thought that was an interesting point to make. Surely there was more to it: an experience Obbin had had or a lesson he had been taught.

"Of course," Mason said and sat in a seat beside Austin.

It was time.

Numbers flashed on the screen, growing smaller.

Slipping out of hyper flight felt like being pulled forward through a tunnel. An instant later, they were out, and Enaid was before them. Austin couldn't see it with the heat shields still down. But the information on the *Phoenix* screens confirmed it.

"We're there," Austin said. He tapped the console to raise the titanium shields.

"Good work," Mason said.

"Yes, good job," Tiffany said. "I'll handle the access request when it comes."

Why was she dealing with it? Didn't she trust him? Austin started to react but held back. He shook off the notion. Of course she trusted him. She'd asked him to fly the *Phoenix*.

All doubt washed from his mind as the planet appeared before them. It shimmered like sun glinting off the windows of their home at sunrise. He knew why: the planet was one large city. Buildings covered every inch of the surface. The glass and metal structures reflected the light of the nearest sun.

"Did you know that almost twenty percent of the Federation's citizens reside on Enaid?" Mason asked. "And ninety-seven percent of them have never traveled off Enaid."

"No, I didn't," Tiffany said.

"Also, I once heard that there are no plants still rooted in the soil of Enaid. The only plants are grown in rooftop gardens or food production greenhouses," Mason added.

"Would you look at that?" Austin said. More than fifty spaceships dotted the space around him, flashing lights showing their position to other craft.

"Are all these ships on their way to Enaid?" asked Obbin.

"To or from," Mason explained.

"Amazing," Obbin said.

"Complicated," added Austin.

"It'll be fine," Tiffany said. "I've set the coordinates for Simba Intergalactic Spaceport. They should be on your screen now, though our course will be assigned to us by Galactic Traffic Control."

Another message flashed on the screen. *Incoming message.*

"I think they're calling," Austin said.

Tiffany tapped the screen before her, accepting the transmission.

"This is Enaid Federal Outpost A9127. Please identify yourself with ship name, serial code, location of registration, and flight license code," a bored, gruff voice said. This was one of the galactic traffic controllers.

"E4:32 *Phoenix*, 3D4L19E59-1980-12D23S19E59, Jahr des Eises, 11B15D19E83," Tiffany said.

Static on the radio.

Austin could hear Mason and Obbin's bated breaths behind him. He felt the same.

"Clearance granted. Requested spaceport?" the gruff voice asked.

"Simba Intergalactic Spaceport," Tiffany said.

Static.

"Assigned docking station is COAL9192012. Proceed on course US24, watch onboard signals for instructions and current information. Weather in sector I25 is clear. Wind speed is 200 knots from the north," the galactic traffic controller droned on. "Proceed to destination in seventeen minutes."

Austin's nerves were on end. He now had to fly an assigned course, and 200 knots seemed like a high wind speed. Would he be able to control the *Phoenix*?

"Thank you," Tiffany said, but there was no reply. "Austin, the course assigned should appear on your screen with waypoints. Just turn the ship the direction it says and follow the course. I'll pay attention to the signals and let you know if anything affects our flight. The seventeen minutes is count-ing down now."

Austin swallowed. "Okay."

"Austin, you can do this," Tiffany assured him.

"You can," said Mason.

He looked at his sister and nodded. He was nervous, but he wasn't helpless or alone.

The seventeen minutes passed, and they were given the go-ahead to proceed by the same galactic traffic controller as before.

Tiffany was prepared for this mission. While she badly wanted to discover more about Creator, the task of landing was at hand, and she'd not let herself lose sight of the respon-sibility now on her. She had to get her siblings to Enaid and the Cathedral of the Star. She had to reunite them with their parents. This was her goal.

She'd considered turning herself in to the Übel when she thought she was alone on Evad. It would have been a relief to be reunited with her parents, but at what a cost. Even now she hated that at any moment she could lose her parents forever. It would take just one misstep on this quest, one missed clue.

All three groups were now headed to Enaid. The worst possible thing would be for her and her siblings to fall captive to O'Farrell again. Then they'd remain separate from their parents but no longer free.

She would be reunited with her parents, but it would be on her terms. They would be reunited separate from the Übel or Corsairs. They would finish this quest together and for reasons beyond the greedy desires of secretive and ruthless organizations.

It had been devastating to learn that O'Farrell was in charge of the Corsairs and that the Übel had infiltrated so much of the Federation that they couldn't trust anyone. But the past day had strengthened Tiffany more than she ever could have fathomed.

"Austin, there are no warnings. It looks like you're on target," she said. She was watching everything from her seat. Anything regarding the actual flying of the ship appeared before her. Austin had never done this, and while she wanted to build confidence in him, she also knew he was still an eleven-year-old boy with no flight training. He had struggled to remember to do his homework and his laundry at Bewaldeter, and now she had him in control of the Phoenix.

The darkness of space lightened as they entered the atmosphere of Enaid. Soon the city's shining lights formed into massive towers unlike anything she'd ever seen in her travels before. These were called arcologies: massive structures that tens of thousands of people could live and work in. The ones before her were metropolis-arcologies that could house up to a million people.

The horizon looked like rows upon rows of teeth, as most of the arcologies came to points. Heavy layers of clouds lay among them, but she soon wondered if it was actually smog. Above the buildings, lines or dots crisscrossed the sky. The dots looked like ants but were actually flying craft. Some of the dots were intergalactic ships like theirs, while others were only for intra-planetary travel and never left Enaid.

Austin brought the ship down into the line on his assigned course. Before them a cruiser thirty times their size blasted along. Bright purple circles of flaming engine exhaust burned ahead of them.

"Keep your distance," Tiffany said, though she knew Austin probably had figured that out. Midnight purred in her lap, giving her peace and calm.

Simba Intergalactic Spaceport rose high into the sky. Soon Tiffany could see nothing but a wall of large open bays filled with ships of all sizes and shapes. The massive spaceport swallowed the view of everything else. A light flashed ahead as two bay doors spread apart, ready to swallow the *Phoenix*.

COAL9192012 flashed on the screen. It glowed in thin air just before the bay: a hologram.

"There it is," Austin said. He slowed the ship and adjusted the vector of the engine thrust so that they were nearly hovering before they entered the docking station. The bay was very basic: a large enclosed space constructed of metal. Simple lighting lined the ceiling and walls. A series of charging, fueling, and maintenance equipment was arranged on the back wall.

"Lowering gear," Austin said. The *Phoenix* touched down with hardly a bump.

Tiffany smiled. "Great work, Austin." The kid had done it.

"Yes, indeed. Great work."

Midnight leaped down as Tiffany turned in surprise at the voice.

Awake

Oliver awakened shivering, his skin bare. A pile of shredded black fabric lay next to the bed. His body hurt all over. Small bandages amassed across the entirety of his body. His head hurt.

What had happened? He looked and felt like he'd been through a space crash or tornado. He pushed himself up despite the pain of his many small wounds scraping against their bandages.

He swung his feet over the side of his bed and forced himself up. He snagged his cadet hoodie and put it on, then dug out a pair of loose athletic pants that matched. A pair of slip-on shoes completed the outfit.

Oliver assumed that whoever was on the ship would be on the bridge of the *Phoenix*. He started down the hall and glanced in the library. The window didn't reveal black empty space but instead a large gray wall with lights blinking across it.

Where were they? Captured again?

His view of the bridge took those thoughts away. Austin sat in the pilot's seat, Tiffany was in the copilot's, and no Corsairs were in sight. Somehow they'd gotten their freedom back.

Had his youngest brother really piloted the ship from wherever they had been to wherever they were now? He couldn't remember what planet they'd been on.

He heard Austin's voice. "Lowering gear."

"Great work, Austin," Tiffany said.

Oliver felt proud even though he didn't know where they were or what had happened to bring them there or even how long he'd been unconscious. "Yes, indeed," he said. "Great work."

Everyone turned to look at him. Each looked very surprised to see him.

"Oliver!" cried Tiffany as she let herself free of her harness and started for her brother. The three boys did the same. No one attempted to hug him. This meant Tiffany hadn't hidden any of what had happened. She wasn't protecting them from the damage done to Oliver. Instead she was treating them like equals.

"Glad you're awake," Austin said.

"Me too, but Austin did a great job," Mason added.

Obbin smiled. "You are looking better."

"Yikes, I'm worried about what I must have looked like earlier," Oliver said. His throat was dry and scratchy.

"Perhaps it's because we can't see all your wounds," Obbin added honestly.

"Yes, about those. How did I get them? Where are we?"

Tiffany frowned. Clearly his lack of memory concerned her. "We're on Enaid, and you were shocked, I think, or at least knocked out. Either way, you've been out for several hours."

"We escaped O'Farrell and the Corsairs," Austin added.

"Tiffany rescued you," Mason said. "She had to drag you to safety and fought off a dinosaur and a bunch of Übel soldiers."

Tiffany blushed. "It wasn't like—"

"It was too," Austin spoke up. "Without her you'd have been eaten, and we'd be prisoners on the *Black Ranger* again."

Oliver shook his head. "Sounds like quite . . . Thanks, sis," he said, lowering himself into a chair in the back row.

"Are you all right?"

"Yeah, I think so. Just tired."

"Why don't you lie down again?" suggested Tiffany.

"Actually, I'm really thirsty," Oliver said, "and hungry."

"I'll make you something," Austin said. "I could use a bite."

"Me too," Obbin said.

"I'm going to get the journal," Mason said. "I want to show Oliver."

"You got the e-journal back?" Oliver asked.

"You did, actually. You don't remember?" Tiffany asked.

Oliver shook his head.

"Yes, we got it back, but Mason is talking about a different journal," Tiffany explained. "Zebra Xavier's."

Oliver's ears pricked to that. "This I can't wait to hear about."

"Obbin, can you get mTalks for Oliver and Tiffany?" Austin said. "They'll need them."

3.51

Planning

The table was littered with empty and half-full food containers. Oliver felt better, some of his strength having returned to him. The food had helped, but the Insta-Vita shake had really done the trick. The thick chilled liquid had all the essential vitamins and nano-injectors for treating ailments within the body, such as muscle tears or bone fractures.

While he knew he wasn't back to 100 percent, he certainly was ready to continue the quest.

Tiffany had retold the exciting events that had unfolded on Re Lyt, from being shoved out of the *Phoenix*, to seeing Zebra Xavier in person, to being chased by dinosaurs. She'd started to talk about their time on the *Black Ranger*, but Oliver remembered most of that, including Ashley and her parents.

"So, Tiffany, where are we headed now that we're here?" Oliver asked.

"We're going to locate Casper," Tiffany said. "Remember? We found his address in the e-journal earlier. He may have a connection to get into the Cathedral of the Star."

"How do we even know this guy is still here?" Austin asked.

"We don't know, but we have to try. It's our only lead," Oliver said.

"No, we need to get to the Cathedral of the Star before our parents do," Austin said. "We have to create a plan to rescue them. We can't do that without scouting the place."

"I know that," Oliver said.

"But Dad and Mom were denied access repeatedly," Tiffany said.

"So you think this guy has a way to get us in?" Obbin asked.

"Look, the note says, 'Must contact when on Enaid.' I think that's what we should do," Tiffany said.

Mason shrugged. "It's highly possible Casper knows something of the underworking of the city and that's why Dad and Mom were going to contact him."

Austin grunted. "Maybe, but I think we should go to the site of the ruins and look around first."

"Why don't we split up?" Obbin suggested.

"Yeah, the two of us will go—" Austin began.

Oliver sighed. "We should stay together. Splitting up hasn't had the best results in the past."

"It's how we found Ashley and discovered O'Farrell was a bad guy," Austin said. "Besides, we all have mTalks now."

"Working ones too. I wouldn't be here if the twins . . ." Obbin stopped. "You wouldn't have found the map if you hadn't split up."

Oliver weighed Austin and Obbin's argument. They could cover more ground that way. Tiffany and the boys had proven themselves.

Oliver eyed his sister. Her objection to Austin's plan was written across her scowling face.

"We stick together," Oliver said, breaking the tie.

3.52

Casper's Stage

The tops of the massive arcologies appeared to bend to touch each other, nearly blotting the sky from view. Staring up at them made Austin's head spin. In fact, the walkway they were on was elevated nearly fifty floors. The levels and regular floors did not line up; in terms of floors, there were probably more than a thousand. He hated to think what it was like farther down, yet he knew that was exactly where they were going.

A sign and map near the echo-lifts in Simba Intergalactic Spaceport had explained the vertical setup of the city. The map had broken the city into sections like the layers of a cake. The highest was labeled *Crystal Skyline* and accompanied by a warning that only citizens holding crystal passes were granted access. They did not have passes, and according to their parents' contact information for Casper, they were headed downward anyway.

In all there were fifty levels on Enaid: Crystal Skyline being the highest and Larva Lair the lowest. Austin had first read it as *lava* and had thought it meant they'd be so deep below the planet's surface that they'd literally be surrounded by magma. There was no need for a pass to access this level of the city.

After all, who would want to, other than those seeking their kidnapped parents?

The city was unlike anything Austin had ever experienced. He'd been to cities before, but not on this scale. The noise was mind numbing, the smells were stomach churning, the humidity felt like three extra layers of clothing, and the flashing lights made him see spots. How could anyone live here? Yet people did. Austin and the others would be entering the so-called underworld to access the ruins, but it seemed even at level twelve they'd entered a very questionable area.

No, Austin was not a city kid. He loved the woods behind their home on Tragiws and the wide-open plains of golden grass before it. He longed for home. He longed for his room. He longed for his family to again be one.

"Over here," Oliver said. A purple light strip arched around the door. A sign above read *Casper's Stage*.

The five kids approached, Oliver in the lead, Austin bringing up the rear. The order had been established after the many calls to them from shadowy passersby. Oliver and Austin were armed with Zingers, and the other three with StingerXNs, which had been inadvertently supplied by the Corsairs in the cargo. The StingerXNs were placed inside packs so as not to raise suspicion. The Zingers were less easy to conceal. Oliver and Austin had tried many ways but finally had to sling the weapons across their backs and under their jackets. This made wearing a pack slightly uncomfortable, but the protection was worth it. All were reunited with their mTalks. They were ready for the mission into the ruins.

They tried the door to Casper's Stage, but it was locked. They knocked.

A man in a flashy sequined purple suit and large square shades greeted them. The light of the sign above him made the sequins glimmer. "Welcome to Casper's Stage. We don't open for a few more hours. What's your business?"

"We're here to see Mr. Casper," Oliver said.

The man looked over his shoulder. He looked back at Oliver, his expression unreadable with his eyes hidden behind the smokey-lensed glasses he wore. "Who's asking?" He leaned forward, his hands folded before him.

Oliver leaned in. "Oliver Wikk, son of Elliot Wikk."

"Really?"

Oliver nodded.

"I wasn't asking for confirmation," the man said with a chortle. He looked at them with an expression of shock and curiosity.

"Sir, I never caught your name," Mason spoke up.

"Coolz is my name, but my buds called me Coo."

"Coo," Mason repeated. "I'm Mason."

The man looked at the group, and they all said their names.

"One moment. Wait here." Coo opened the door and slipped inside.

A billow of smoke rolled from Casper's Stage before the door closed, and Austin's nostrils flared as the smoky scent of cooking meat caught his attention. His mouth salivated. He always felt hungry these days.

"I'm not so sure this guy will be able to help us get into the ruins," Tiffany said reluctantly. "I mean, this place . . . it seems . . ."

"Shady?" asked Mason.

Tiffany nodded.

"You're the one who said we had to go here," Austin said.

"I know what I said." Tiffany straightened her shoulders.

Austin saw that she was driving off any fear or doubt she'd shown. The sister he'd known, or thought he'd known, a few days ago was hiding, only making brief appearances. The question was which Tiffany would remain when all this was over.

Obbin was at the walkway railing, looking out over the city. "Huge, isn't it?" Austin said, stepping next to him.

"Yeah," Obbin said. "It's so much larger than Brighton."

"Did you go there?"

"Rylin and I never made it. But we would sneak to the edge of the forest and stare through the dome. We promised ourselves we would find a way in one day." Obbin's chin dropped. "I guess we won't now."

"Obbin, don't say that. We're going to find your brother, your whole family. You'll explore with him again. Maybe we'll all get to explore together."

Obbin's turquoise eyes twinkled with what could have been the onset of tears. "I'd like that."

Austin looked back at Oliver, Tiffany, and Mason. The quest was probably a lot harder on Obbin, since he didn't have any of his family with him. He was thankful he had all three of his siblings with him. It made the adventure less lonely.

"What do we do now?" Mason asked.

Oliver rubbed the stubble on his chin.

Growing more impatient, Austin stepped forward and raised his hand to knock, but the door opened. Sweet-smelling smoke billowed out, and Austin coughed.

"Are you cooking something?" Obbin asked Coo as he stepped out.

"Best barbecue around," Coo said with a smile. "Oliver, you may come in. Mr. Casper will see you."

They started forward. Coo held up his hand. "Just Oliver."

"But we're all together, sir," Oliver said.

Coo shook his head. "They'll have to wait right here."

"Will they be safe?" asked Oliver.

"Bruno!" called Coo over his shoulder.

The door opened, and a large, burly man in a white sleeveless shirt stepped out. Red splotches stained his clothes. Austin grimaced. Was it blood?

"Bruno will take care of them," Coo promised. "This be the Wikk family and a friend."

Bruno nodded with a deep grunt.

"Now that we're all acquainted, shall we go?" Coo asked Oliver.

"I'll just be a few minutes," Oliver said. "Austin, keep a lookout for . . . well, you know."

Austin nodded. He was always ready for a security assignment. He was glad that Oliver had a weapon concealed beneath his pack.

Oliver followed Coo through the smoky entrance and disappeared into Casper's Stage. Bruno leaned against the railing of the walkway and looked down at the city below.

Austin heard a growl. Not from an animal—it sounded like a person's stomach. He smirked at Obbin. "Hungry?"

"I know we just ate, but the smell of that food and the mention of barbecue . . . " Obbin rubbed his stomach.

Bruno straightened. "You kids hungry? We've got the best—"

"—barbecue around," Obbin said, "And, yes, I am."

"I could eat too," said Austin. "So this is a restaurant?"

"Sure is, and a stage for performing," Bruno said, "though a lot less of that is done these days." His words were sorrowful.

"Barbecue sounds good," Tiffany said.

"Then come on in," Bruno said.

"What about Coo? He said we had to wait out here," Mason said.

Bruno waved his hand. "Coo, always trying to make this place more exclusive than it is."

"Exclusive?" Austin asked. "Shouldn't the place be higher in the city?"

Tiffany jabbed him in the side, but Bruno just laughed. "That's a reality Coo hasn't been willing to accept," he said. "Do you think he's going to argue with me?" Bruno flexed his biceps and made a serious face.

Austin had to admit Bruno could take Coo in a fight. Bruno was at least a foot taller than Coo and probably twice his weight, Coo being slim and Bruno being . . . well . . . thicker. Still, the Zinger in Austin's pack could handle either of them.

It was clear that Oliver had wanted them all in Casper's Stage, rather than outside on the walkway. Bruno's offer was win-win.

The room they entered was large, with tables and chairs arranged throughout. A thick, meaty smoke hung in the air. Colored lights striped the ceiling, causing the smoke to glow in all the shades of the rainbow and illuminating the smoke's movement as it floated across the room.

"Sweet, sour, spicy, or sizzlin'?" Bruno asked as he seated the four at a large table. They set their packs around. The weapons within were only an arm's length away.

Austin didn't want to take off his jacket and reveal the Zinger. He also knew sitting would be awkward with the weapon against his back. He'd just have to deal with it; if needed, he could hop to his feet and slip the weapon into position. He was prepared.

"Sizzlin'," answered Obbin.

"You, miss?" asked Bruno.

"How about sweet?"

"You?" he asked.

"Sweet," said Mason.

"And?"

"Spicy," Austin said. Obbin jabbed him. "Sizzlin', I mean."

"I'll have them right up," Bruno promised, then started for a counter at the far end of the room.

Oliver was nowhere in sight, but Austin saw a door with extra lights glowing around its edges and a nameplate on it that read *Casper*. He was sure that was where his brother was, but how did they know that they could trust this Casper guy?

Austin considered going to the door and listening, but at that moment Coo came out. He looked at the four kids and hurried over.

"I told you—" Coo started.

"You, Coo!" Bruno shouted from behind the counter. "Chill, I brought them in for some yummy barbecue."

Coo sighed, shook his head, and walked toward the front door. He stopped behind a podium and started typing. He seemed to wait, then typed some more. Pause, typing, pause, typing.

Austin didn't like it. Who was he talking to?

Coo frowned and started back across the room. He looked over the four kids but didn't say anything. Then he took his spot by the door.

Everything in Austin told him to get a look at what Coo was doing, but the man was still in the room, and Bruno wasn't too far off either.

3.53

Zick Star

Oliver sat alone in a round room with black marble walls. His pack and weapon had been acknowledged by Coo but not taken away. This meant they didn't consider him a danger and perhaps were not a danger to him. If they didn't mind his being armed, they weren't planning to challenge him. His weapon leaned against his chair.

A zick stick hung on the wall, and several holograms of a man dressed in a sparkling white suit holding a zick stick glowed on pedestals ringing the room. Zick sticks were played by strumming a series of light beams. Each beam produced its own sound and was preset by the musician, giving each musician a very distinct sound.

Was Mr. Casper a musician? If so, why was his place so deep in the levels on Enaid? The lower the kids had gone in the city, the sketchier it had become.

A door opened opposite, and in walked a tall, slender man in a sequined white suit like the one in the holograms. He had an angular face with short brown hair. He had small diamond earrings in each ear and a pointy nose. He stared at Oliver with a look of interest.

"So, the son of Elliot Wikk has come to Enaid," the man said. His voice was unreadable, but the statement seemed threatening. Oliver was unsure of what to say.

"I wouldn't have thought to see you again," the man said.

Oliver wondered when they'd met before; he didn't remember this guy by sight or by name.

"Aw, you don't recall. You were just three, and your sister newly born," Mr. Casper said. He stared at one of his holograms. The image started to move, and music began to play.

"You think you can't walk away, but your heart won't let you stay!" crooned Mr. Casper's voice from overhead speakers, softly joined by the in-person musician.

Mr. Casper looked back at Oliver, who maintained a straight face.

"Ah, my first number-one single," Mr. Casper said and took a seat across from Oliver. "So, what can I do for you?"

"Mr. Casper, my—"

"It's Lucas Casper. You may call me Lucas. Mr. Casper is not the name of a zick star; it's the name of my father. Lucas will be just fine."

"M . . . Lucas, sir," Oliver began.

"No sir," Mr. Casper interrupted.

"Lucas, I need your help."

"Why, of course you do. Why else would you visit your long-lost uncle?"

The word nearly stole Oliver's breath. *Uncle?*

"Is it money? Have your parents got themselves in a bind again?"

"No . . . I mean . . . well, yes, but not of their own doing." Oliver hesitated. "Did you say *uncle*?"

Lucas Casper leaned back in his seat with shock. "Wait. Are you . . . ? Did you not . . . ?"

Oliver shook his head, but exactly what he was denying was unclear.

"Your father never told you of me?" Mr. Casper sounded exaggeratedly hurt.

Oliver shook his head again. "No."

"I'm not that surprised," Mr. Casper said. "After I moved to Enaid, we lost touch." He mumbled, "I suppose ten or so years of not reaching out to him would do that. I did once . . . Ah, never mind."

"So you're my uncle?" Oliver asked. Anger toward his parents flickered within him. Why had they hidden this relationship?

"Indeed I am," he said.

"But your name is Casper."

"I married your father's sister."

"His sister who went missing?" Oliver asked.

Uncle Lucas stared at one of the pedestals. "Yes, my sweet Shona."

At his words, soft music began to play again. The lyrics were clear: "My sweet Shona, where are you? My sweet Shona with eyes so blue?" The rhythm suddenly changed, a low chord striking out. "Gone, gone, gone. In the dead of night, you were gone, gone, gone."

Oliver's aunt had been missing since he had been a little boy. She had been a diplomat for the Federation, reaching out to newly discovered human settlements and working toward uniting them with the Federation.

Apparently she had never returned from one of her trips to the far reaches of space. Her ship and crew had disappeared. She had been labeled missing, and the Federation had never updated her status. Oliver's father had always been suspicious of that, since it surely meant they knew something that prevented them from declaring her deceased.

The music faded away as Uncle Lucas looked back to Oliver. Oliver shivered under his uncle's blue eyes and the forlorn tune that echoed in his mind.

"A number-one hit. Top of the charts." Uncle Lucas sighed. "Yes, your Aunt Shona was my wife. We had a great life. I was a musician at the top of the charts; she was an emissary for the Federation. Our jobs made it difficult to be together, but we made it work. We each valued our careers, but we valued each other more." His voice was forlorn and truthful. "When she disappeared, I distanced myself from your family." He closed his eyes. "It wasn't my intention, but quickly a month became a year, and a year a decade. I poured myself into my music. It became my one absolute obsession, my way of dealing with the grief of loss. It was a way for me to distract myself from wondering where she might be." A single tear rolled down his cheek.

"Uncle Lucas, I'm sorry. I knew of her disappearance, just not . . ." The words Oliver had been about to say caught in his throat. They were awkward, although the meaning of them hadn't necessarily been hurtful to Uncle Lucas before.

"Not about me." Lucas left it there. "Now, nephew . . . That word felt quite nice to say. Now, how might I be of help?" His tone was polite, with no lingering sense of loss.

"My parents have been kidnapped," Oliver said.

Uncle Lucas stood up. "What? Kidnapped?"

Oliver nodded.

"Money! Those dirty kidnappers. They must have known we were family. Thought to get me to pay a ransom, I suppose!"

"No, no, these guys aren't interested in money."

Uncle Lucas sat back down, his eyes doubtful.

"They are seeking the secret to eternal life," Oliver explained. "They need Dad and Mom to discover a series of clues to a path that is hidden."

"Eternal life?" Hand on chin, Uncle Lucas sighed. "Not money. Mercenaries," he said. "We'll need to get a hold of federal forces. They have a team for just this sort of situation. I should know. I was nearly kidnapped by Corsairs during one of my tours."

Oliver raised his hand. "No, no federal anything. These guys have got their fingers in everything. We're the ones who have to rescue our parents. It can only be us. Recently we discovered that someone we trusted was actually against us."

Uncle Lucas shook his head. "No, no, this sort of thing is best in the hands of trained professionals."

"You can't," Oliver said. "They'll come for you. They'll come for us and take us."

"So why did you come to me? How did you even know of me?"

"You were listed in my parents' contacts for Enaid. A note next to your name said, 'Must contact.' So this was the first place we came."

"Must contact," Uncle Lucas repeated.

Oliver waited while his uncle thought.

"Your dad probably hoped to find out what had happened over the last ten years. I can't imagine any other reason."

Oliver's heart sank. It was logical. His dad had simply wanted to reach out to his sister's husband when next he was on Enaid. His uncle had nothing to offer in the way of rescuing his parents or finding a way into the ruins.

"We've come to find the Cathedral of the Star," Oliver said. "We have the coordinates."

"The what?"

"The Cathedral of the Star."

"Never heard of it."

"Well, it doesn't exist anymore," Oliver said. "It's just ruins buried deep underground."

"Ruins." Uncle Lucas pondered. "Yes, that's it. I once read an article about some archeologists requesting access. I saw your parents' names. I meant to message them . . ." He looked off into the distance.

"Can you help us find it?" Oliver asked.

"No, no . . . I'm not very knowledgeable about ruins and exploring. I don't venture into the depths of the city. I stay on my level for the most part."

"Uncle Lucas, don't you want to meet Tiffany and the twins?"

Uncle Lucas looked at the door. "Ummm . . ."

Oliver frowned. Why would he not want to meet Tiffany, Austin, and Mason?

"I can't."

Oliver's eyes grew wide. "Why not?"

Uncle Lucas was thinking. He looked distraught. How could meeting his niece and nephews be a hard decision?

"Coo!" Uncle Lucas called.

The door opened, and Coo walked in. "Yes, Casper?" he asked. "Six minutes."

"Change of plans. Get the kids. Have Bruno lock up." Anxiety filled Uncle Lucas's voice.

"Sir?" asked Coo with utter surprise.

"'Whispers of the Heart,'" Uncle Lucas said.

"Sir, 'Whispers of the Heart' never even made an album," Coo argued. "Think about the anniversary tour."

"Those days are gone. This is what is important now," Uncle Lucas said confidently.

"What are you talking about?" Oliver asked.

"I'm sorry. I made a mistake. But I'm about to make it right," Uncle Lucas said.

"Sir, five minutes," Coo said, looking toward the door. "The Federation is never late."

3.54

The Silo

"The Federation?" Oliver cried, but he knew what was happening. The Federation had been called to capture them, but his uncle had had a change of heart.

"Go, Coo. We'll take the silo," Uncle Lucas said. Coo left.

"Oliver, I'm sorry. When you showed up, Coo recognized your faces and names from the federal wanted list. They claim you stole something."

This was the first time Oliver had heard that the Federation was after them.

"Stolen?" he asked.

"A valuable artifact or something," Uncle Lucas said.

"Why did you turn us in?"

"A moment of weakness." Uncle Lucas groaned. "A business decision, in fact. I'm about to relaunch my career. Headlines calling me a hero would boost my media attention. My past hits would resurge to the top of the charts. Our last names are different, so no one would have guessed a family connection. But alas"—Uncle Lucas looked into Oliver's eyes—"you are my family. My only family. I wouldn't be able to live with myself."

Uncle Lucas looked at one of the holograms of himself strumming on his zick stick. He sighed.

Oliver opened his mouth to speak, but the door flew open. Tiffany entered, followed by the three boys. Each had their packs. Coo and Bruno carried two large duffle bags each. Tiffany, his brothers, and Obbin looked confused.

"What's happening?" Tiffany asked.

Uncle Lucas moved toward one of the pedestals. "Ready?" he asked.

"No!" Tiffany shouted. "Ready for what?"

"We're on the federal wanted list," Oliver said.

"We are?" asked Austin with a sign of excitement. He pulled off his jacket and held the Zinger in his hands.

A loud crash echoed down the hall.

"Speaking of which, they're here," Bruno said with a backward kick to the door to the pedestal room.

"Who?" asked Mason.

"The Federation," Oliver said. He lifted his pack, shoving the jacket inside, and took hold of the Zinger.

"Let's go. Hold on!" Uncle Lucas slammed his hand down through a holographic image of himself, the one that had played "My Sweet Shona."

The floor dropped below them; the room was a lift, and they were on it. Oliver gripped the edge of the table for balance. He saw Austin steady Tiffany. Mason and Obbin locked arms. Coo, Bruno, and Uncle Lucas looked as though they'd done this before.

The walls flew past. The ceiling shrank above them.

"Keep your arms and hands inside the circle," Coo warned.

Obbin and the Wikks moved closer to the table at the center. Above them, the lights on the ceiling grew smaller. There was a yellow flash.

"Down!" cried Bruno.

Sparks exploded at the edge of the platform.

Bruno ripped open one of the bags and removed a bundle of fabric. He pulled a small cord and threw the fabric above them. It inflated into a massive blimp.

THUMP. THUMP. THUMP. THUMP.

Shots hammered the top of the blimp, which floating higher and higher as they zipped down. What sort of material resisted shots from soldiers?

"At least twenty more seconds until we're down," warned Coo. "They'll jump by then."

"Be ready, everyone. We've got to get through the door right away. Stay close. Don't stop for anything. Just follow me," Uncle Lucas commanded. He didn't sound quite like a musician at that moment.

The lift jerked as it slowed. Oliver heard a tearing noise high overhead where darkness had long consumed the blimp from view.

Bruno took a defensive posture, as did Coo. Oliver followed their lead, aiming his Zinger.

A split second later, three figures dropped into view and landed on the platform. They wore black jumpsuits and helmets. Bruno dove at one and Coo the other. The third landed between Tiffany and Austin. He swept a kick at Austin, knocking the Zinger from his hands, then reached for Tiffany. Austin recovered quickly. He grabbed the soldier around the waist and yanked. The soldier swung his elbow, throwing Austin to the ground.

Oliver climbed onto a table and threw himself at the solider, whose helmet fell free and rattled across the floor. Oliver gasped. The soldier was a woman; she had bright green eyes and black hair. He shouldn't have been surprised; he knew women were in the federal forces.

Oliver hesitated, and the soldier jerked her knee into his chest. His breath caught. She wasn't wasting any time. He grabbed her wrists and fought her back to the ground, but his strength was still lagging after Re Lyt. His opponent flipped him to his back.

Oliver glanced at his remaining allies. Austin and Obbin were unconscious. Coo was on the ground with his opponent standing over him. Bruno held his attacker in the air. Neither could come to his aid. A whizzing sound overhead signified that more soldiers were on their way down via drop ropes. Neither Oliver nor his attacker could get a hand free to grab a weapon.

Oliver wanted his sister and brothers out of there. He might very well end up captured, but at least they would be free. "Go!" he yelled.

Uncle Lucas lifted an unconscious Obbin over his shoulder while Mason took Austin under the arms and began to drag him toward the door.

Tiffany hesitated. "Oliver!" she yelled from the far side of the room.

"Get out of here," Oliver forced out as he continued to battle the soldier. "Now!"

Tiffany turned and started to the door.

Oliver's attacker rolled him to his side and jabbed her leg into his chest. He coughed, and she pushed away from him, then scrambled to her feet. The soldier towered over him, grinning. She grappled at her side and removed an X14-Phaser from its holster. Like the StingerXN and the Zapp-It, it was simply a handheld stun weapon the Federation used.

What was he going to do?

His opponent suddenly fell to the ground. In her place stood Tiffany, holding her StingerXN. She had saved him again.

Tiffany dashed over to Coo. The soldier aimed a kick in her direction but missed. Meanwhile, Bruno dropped his opponent to the ground. He looked at Oliver. "Out cold," he promised, making it clear he'd not killed anyone.

Oliver pushed himself to his feet. He gathered his weapon.

There was a groan as Tiffany landed a StingerXN strike on Coo's opponent. Coo coughed, but Tiffany pulled him up.

Oliver saw Austin's fallen weapon and got a hold of it.

"Let's go before the rest repel down," Bruno grunted.

3.55

Larva Level

In the unlit tunnel, the only indication anyone was ahead of him was the scuffling of feet across a muck-covered floor. The air was heavy with the smell of mold. Mason hated dragging Austin along the floor, but Mr. Casper had made it clear that they could not stop yet. Mason hoped Tiffany and Oliver were coming.

"Left," called Mr. Casper from up ahead.

Mason slowed so as to not miss the turn. His left hand ran against the slimy wall to find the opening. Goop caked his hand, oozing over it. His right hand clung to his brother.

Mason squinted as light flashed on before him. Around the corner, Mr. Casper seemed to glow, his sequined suit lit with thousands of pinprick lights. It was just enough to make out silhouettes.

"Put Austin next to him," Mr. Casper said.

A pattering of feet echoed around the corner. Tiffany came first, then Oliver and Coo.

"Are they okay?" asked Tiffany as she knelt next to Austin.

Coo set down a duffle and started digging. "They will be."

A deafening grinding of stone against stone echoed in the hall. An explosive crash followed.

"The tunnel is collapsed," Bruno called. He lumbered around the corner, a slight limp in his gait. "They won't be coming that way."

"Good work, but we still need to move," Mr. Casper said.

"One minute." Coo held a small white vial under Austin's nose and then Obbin's. The two boys began to stir slightly. "They'll be groggy, but they'll be awake soon enough."

Mason leaned toward Tiffany. "They keep getting knocked out."

"I know," Tiffany said guiltily.

"Tiffany and Mason, meet your Uncle Lucas," Oliver interjected, nodding toward Mr. Casper.

"Uncle?" they exclaimed.

"I was shocked too," Oliver admitted.

"Yes, well, we can chat about it soon," their uncle said. "We have to keep going. They'll alert the city's surveillance force to watch for us."

"Uncle?" Mason repeated.

"Yes. We have to get into the Larva Lair before it's too late," Uncle Lucas reiterated.

"Is that the way to the Cathedral of the Star?" asked Oliver.

"Not exactly." Uncle Lucas sighed. "It's . . . not a place many want to travel. The Larva Lair is where the lowest class lives. It's a place where the federal soldiers will not venture, and it's easy to disappear there."

"Lowest class?" asked Tiffany.

"Have you disappeared there before?" Oliver asked.

"Unfortunately, yes. Tabloids and their phony stories," Uncle Lucas scoffed. "But that's a long story. The truth did come out eventually."

A light flashed on. Coo held up an mTalk. "All clear for light now," he said. He looked at Uncle Lucas. "Though the suit does look good."

Bruno grunted. "Patting yourself on the back a bit, aren't you?"

"One of my better designs, yes," Coo said.

They turned their lights on.

"What do you mean by *lowest class*?" Tiffany repeated.

Mason too thought *class* was an odd word to use in describing the sections of a city. He'd heard it in travel on spaceships or maglevs, but not a city. Sure, in a hotel you could rent the penthouse up top or stay in a less expensive room. But the way Uncle Lucas was using *class*, it sounded like a status. Confirmation came.

Uncle Lucas sighed, his face serious. "Not everyone on Enaid is equal," he said, sounding approving of the notion.

"Like how?" Mason asked. He knew all too well from their mission that the Wikks hadn't been equal in leading their quest. He suspected his uncle wasn't talking about authority or even finances.

"Some people are just superior to others, physically, mentally, charismatically," Uncle Lucas said.

"You don't believe that, do you?" Tiffany asked with shock.

Uncle Lucas cleared his throat. He opened his mouth but didn't speak.

"So doesn't it bother you to be all the way down on level twelve?" asked Mason.

"We weren't always here," Coo said defensively.

"And we'll get back to the Crystal Skyline," Uncle Lucas promised.

"No, we won't," Coo said matter-of-factly. "Not after this fiasco."

Mason knew what he was talking about. Uncle Lucas, Coo, and Bruno were all marked men for helping them escape the Federation.

"We should save the talking until we're clear." Bruno heaved Obbin over one shoulder and Austin over the other. He moved to the front of the line, Mason right behind him. "This way."

After a few minutes, they came to a set of vertical and horizontal metal bars. They'd been in a drainage tunnel. Now they were at the exit grate.

Bruno set the boys down, steadying them with his big arms. They rubbed their heads.

"Where am I?" asked Austin.

"We're escaping," Mason said.

"We'll explain in a little while," Tiffany added.

Austin's eyes were heavy. Obbin was blinking. Neither boy argued. They stood by and waited.

Bruno pulled a tool from his pack. A blue stream of flame spurted from the end of the mini torch. He quickly cut the peripheral bars, and the entire grate clanked to the ground.

"They'll have heard that," Coo grunted. "Why didn't you tell us? We could have held it."

Bruno shook his head. "Just go!"

A gutter led away from the drain grate and toward a wide canal. Black liquid streamed down it, chunks of debris floating past on the rapid current.

Coo ran along the side of the gutter. At the edge of the canal, he pulled out a grapple hook launcher exactly like the one Oliver had used when rescuing Tiffany and Austin from the observatory tower on Evad. Coo aimed the device at the far wall. The launcher gave a soft *pfft* as the hook flew across the canal, trailing a long gray wire, and plunged through the top of the grate directly across. The separate hooks flipped open and locked onto the bars of the grate. Coo yanked on the line; it appeared snug.

Coo unhooked the canister and ran it back to a portion of the grate Bruno had left. He looped the wire through the beams, then tied off the line. He put his weight on it, lifting his legs. "Secure," he said.

Coo produced five hooks with wheels and handed them out. "Oliver, you take Obbin; Mason, you're with Bruno; Austin, you're with me. Tiffany and Lucas are on their own. Let's go."

This assignment came as a relief to Mason. Bruno was the strongest of them all.

Bruno set his wheeled hooks atop the line, swept Mason up in one arm, and with his free hand held the pulley. "Here we go."

"All right." Mason gripped Bruno's forearm.

Bruno pushed off, and away they went across the canal of murky drainage. When Bruno released Mason, he looked back at his siblings on the other side. Bruno ran toward the grate and lit his torch again, starting work on the lower portion of bars.

"You're next," Uncle Lucas said to Oliver.

Oliver nodded. "Obbin, are you okay?"

"I can hold on."

"Good. Get on my back."

Obbin wrapped his arms around Oliver's neck and across they went, followed by Tiffany, followed by Uncle Lucas. Coo took Austin last.

The grate rattled to the floor, and in they went. As before, Bruno collapsed the entrance using small explosives once everyone was a safe distance down the tunnel.

"From here we'll reach a staircase that will take us into the Larva Lair." Uncle Lucas shuddered as if Larva Lair tasted bad on his lips.

Coo opened one of his bags and tossed them each an arm-ful of dirty cloaks. "Throw these over your clothes."

Mason's smelled musty and possibly of animal dung as he put it on.

"Conceal your weapons," Bruno added. "Weapons will give the wrong impression down here."

Mason thought that odd. It seemed they were headed somewhere dangerous. Wouldn't being armed give the *right* impression? Still, they stashed away their weapons.

No more than a hundred feet down, the tunnel curved: at the elbow of the turn stood a rusted door. Bruno wasted no time with the handle and kicked the door in. The metal clanked across the stone floor.

The new corridor wasn't in much better condition regarding a slimy floor and ceiling. However, overhead lights glowed dimly along the tunnel. Most were burned out, but the remaining few gave off enough light to see.

Mason heard talking ahead. Around Bruno's massive frame, he saw something dark scuttle by. They had arrived in an alley. Fronts of buildings, low overhangs made of dirty fabric, and half-boarded windows lined the path.

Mason hadn't ever seen anything like it. He couldn't help but feel bad for whoever had to live down there.

"So this is the Larva Lair?" asked Austin.

"No, not yet," said Coo.

Mason's breath caught. The scene around him frightened him. The few people he saw wore heavy dark cloaks that concealed their faces. All avoided the new arrivals.

Shouting erupted behind them. Mason looked back, sure that the Übel, Federation, or Corsairs had found them. But it wasn't any of them, just an argument. Coo walked backward to keep an eye on the disturbance.

Uncle Lucas, Bruno, and Coo's tense behavior was no comfort to Mason. He'd been in danger before, but seeing adults on edge made it worse. Adults were supposed to have it all together.

A sign creaked as it swung back and forth on one remaining hinge. It read *Larva Lair Descent.*

What an odd way to describe the entrance. *Descent* implied you could go in only one direction: down. Mason froze.

Was that what it meant? Certainly not.

The argument went back and forth in his mind.

They stepped into a narrow stairwell. There was no grime, but there was no light either. The mTalks were essential as they descended. The stairway was so narrow that Mason began to think his assumption was exactly right. No one could possibly pass them coming up.

His claustrophobia started to creep over him. He turned around.

Obbin nearly ran him over. "What's wrong?"

Mason spoke in short bursts, trying to catch his breath. "It's too tight. I want out. I can't . . ."

Obbin wrapped his blue arms around Mason and put his head against his shoulder. "Creator, please come upon Mason. Give him calm. Give him peace. Creator, he is unsure of our future; we are all unsure. We do not know what it holds, but you do. Please let us rest our minds in you. Take our fear from us. Creator, send Helper to soothe our minds." The prince released Mason and looked into his eyes. "You will be okay. We are protected."

During the prayer, Mason had felt something indescribable wash over him. It was a sense of calm, but it was more too. It felt as though someone other than Obbin had wrapped his arms and body around him.

"Thank you," Mason said.

Bruno stopped a few stairs down. Austin and Tiffany stood behind Obbin with looks of understanding on their faces. Had they felt what he had?

"We really must keep moving," Uncle Lucas said from behind.

Obbin patted Mason's shoulder. Mason smiled and followed after Bruno.

The descent was straight. Mason started counting steps: two hundred and sixty, not including the fifty or more they'd descended earlier. The stairwell opened into a circular entryway. A black door marked the only way through the wall.

Bruno knocked.

A yellow eye appeared at the peephole as a shrill voice answered from behind the door. "Who comes?"

"We are travelers. We seek refuge in the depths," Bruno said.

Travelers, yes? Seeking refuge? Mason supposed that was true.

"Why should we grant you access?"

"We bring trades," Bruno said.

"Trades?" the shrill voice said.

Bruno looked back at Mason. Something in his eyes gave Mason grave concern.

"Trades," Bruno repeated with a nod.

The yellow eye seemed to fix on Mason. He had a sick feeling in his stomach. Were *they* the trade? He'd heard that slavery existed in the dark reaches of the Federation, but . . .

"Creator, protect us," he prayed silently.

3.56

Amulet

Bruno lifted his satchel and shook it. He unzipped it, and the eye looked in.

"You may enter," the shrill voice said greedily.

The black door creaked open, and Bruno entered first. Oliver looked back up the dark staircase. This quest continued to take them to depths unknown in their previous life. He'd had no idea that these worlds existed. His parents had never exposed him to this sort of destitution.

Oliver knew his parents had always avoided taking them to Enaid. Had they been sheltering them? He knew the city-planet was filled with rampant greed and immorality.

Oliver looked at the doorkeeper. The sight surprised him. A person half his size stood wrapped in a pure black cloak, his face barely visible. His eyes glowed yellow like a cat's under light.

Oliver had heard of solar retina replacement, but he'd never seen it firsthand. The effect was startling: the doorkeeper's eyes swirled with a yellow glow. The replacements allowed their owner to see in complete darkness. Nano light sources floated within the eyes, providing enough light to see by.

The doorkeeper motioned for Bruno to set down the bag. He began poking around in it with a hooked staff, removing a shiny chain of silver or platinum, a black leather case, and three green bags tied at the top.

The doorkeeper opened the black case, revealing a rectangular piece of reflective material—was it a mirror? The green bags were filled with brown cubes. The scent of chocolate filled the space. A mirror and chocolate seemed an odd trade for entrance into the Larva Lair.

The doorkeeper straightened and waved his staff. A dozen cloaked figures rushed out of the shadows. Some were short like the one at the door; others were taller than Oliver.

Coo slipped another bag from his duffle and tossed it at the feet of the doorkeeper, who unzipped it and pulled out several cylinders. Oliver could just make out a few words on one label. *Hydroponic Tomatoes*. Plants?

The doorkeeper seemed pleased. When he shook his staff, the other guards sunk back into the shadows as if they had never existed.

Austin whispered to Obbin. "Darkness can be a great ally."

Oliver thought of the solar retina replacement. Darkness wouldn't work against them.

"You may go," the doorkeeper said. "But be warned, we watch all. We do not take well to those who cause trouble. We have enough trouble without Uppers' problems."

Uppers?

Bruno motioned for everyone to walk past him. Coo took the lead. They gathered near the beginning of several tunnels. The corridors were wider than the staircase, but not as wide as the one they'd used to escape Casper's Stage.

"Well, where to now?" asked Uncle Lucas.

Oliver looked at Tiffany. "We don't have any more information. We just knew we were supposed to go to the Cathedral of the Star."

"Actually, we were to come to Enaid," Mason said. "Discovering the Cathedral of the Star was research. Tiffany, do you have the e-journal?"

Tiffany handed it to Mason. Mason swept his hand back and forth and tapped away.

"What are you doing?" asked Oliver.

"Here it is," Mason said. "120.1995 Y, 112.1990 X, 620.2011 Z."

"And?" asked Austin.

"Remember Brother Sam's notes?" Mason said. "They aren't space coordinates. They're terra coordinates."

"Since the city has many vertical layers, a Z coordinate works here," Tiffany said.

"Plug it in," Mason said.

Oliver lifted his mTalk, and Mason read off the coordinates. Austin also tapped in the location.

"Mason, you're a genius!" were the only words Oliver could use to express his pleasure in what he saw on the screen. A red dot on his mTalk's map blinked a short distance from their location.

"Good job, kid," Bruno said, giving Mason a nudge that nearly knocked him to the ground. "Sorry."

"Lead on," Uncle Lucas said.

Oliver led with Mason at his side. They didn't have a map of the underground level, so they guessed and took halls left and right to get closer to the location.

They ended in what appeared to be a gathering hall. Long tables stretched out across the room; several booths circled the outskirts. All were piled with odd-looking foods and clothing. A marketplace?

Oliver frowned as he looked at the screen on his mTalk. They were nearly over the coordinate's location.

"This doesn't look like the Cathedral of the Star or any ruins at all," Obbin said.

"It was a good thought, Mason, but I don't think your coordinates were leading here," Uncle Lucas said.

"Wait. Look at that," Austin said, pointing at a battered sign. It read *Truth Is the Way.*

"Truth is how Brother Sam referred to Rescuer," Austin said.

"Rescuer?" asked Oliver.

"Oliver, I'm so sorry," Tiffany began. "It's just that you were asleep, and then we arrived in the city. We haven't told you what Obbin revealed about Truth."

"My people call Truth Rescuer," Obbin said. "But we believe he is the same person. Rescuer is the key to eternal life."

"Don't tell me you believe in that stuff," said Coo.

Tiffany and Mason stared at the man. "You know?"

Coo shook his head. "I've not heard the names you mention. But eternal life, I have. It's a fable. It can't be obtained."

Oliver ignored the man and looked at Mason. "What are you talking about?"

A figure in brown rags stalked toward them. Its mouth and hair remained veiled behind a gray scarf. Only bright green eyes and a narrow nose could be seen.

"Stay where you are," warned Bruno, stepping between the newcomer and everyone else.

The figure obeyed but spoke with urgency. "You must come with me immediately." The voice was a woman's. "We have been waiting for you. They are coming."

"Who?" asked Oliver.

"You know who," the woman said. "The darkness."

Oliver wasn't sure what to do or say. With all the betrayal they'd faced, with all the dangers of this mission, he wasn't ready to blindly trust her. He knew they were being pursued; he also knew his enemies had a knack of already being wherever they were going.

"Who are you?" asked Oliver.

The woman took a step closer, her face still masked.

Bruno put out his hand in warning.

"I'm here to help you," she said. "I know what you seek." She glanced around.

"She's lying," Coo said. "These larva will tell you anything you want to hear if they believe they can get something in return."

"Did you just call her *larva*?" asked Tiffany, clearly offended.

"What of it?"

Tiffany frowned, but Oliver put a hand on her shoulder. "What do you know?" he asked the woman.

"You seek the Cathedral of the Star, the work of a great people—a people who held a secret." Her words were like honey to Oliver.

"Tiffany, she knows," he said.

"Do not be foolish, nephew," Uncle Lucas said. "She probably heard the blue kid say the name of the place when we arrived."

Oliver looked at Obbin, who looked embarrassed.

Uncle Lucas put a hand on Oliver's shoulder. He stared into his eyes with seriousness. "'A great people, holding a secret.' She probably read about your parents' planned archeological expedition just as I did. Don't be disappointed. It was too much of a coincidence."

The woman reached within her rags. Bruno tugged at something within his vest. The stock of a weapon glinted in the dim light.

Oliver put up his hand, and Bruno stayed his.

The woman took from her rags an amulet containing a ruby surrounded by several smaller clear stones. She held it toward Oliver.

"Oliver!" shouted Tiffany, making him jump and recoil from the woman. Bruno pulled his weapon into view.

"Oliver, I've seen that before!" Tiffany said. "The amulet . . . the video . . . the room underground on Evad . . . the man. He wore one. It was pinned on his collar. He had one of those amulets."

Oliver looked back at the woman. "May I see it?"

Bruno relaxed his stance as the woman set the amulet in Oliver's hand. He held it out for Tiffany, who began nodding enthusiastically.

"This is it. This is what he wore," she exclaimed. "She is telling the truth."

In all this, the woman held her composure.

"Ma'am, is there anything else you can tell us?"

"I can tell you much."

Coo scoffed. "Cryptic words of deceit."

A smile crossed the woman's lips. " 'Enter ye in at the straight gate: for wide is the gate and broad is the way that leadeth to destruction, and many there be which go in there. Straight is the gate and narrow is the way which leadeth unto life, and few there be that find it. Beware of false prophets, which come to you in sheep's clothing, but inwardly they are ravening wolves,' " she said.

"I have heard this, or something similar," Obbin said. "These words, they are of Creator."

"He has many names," the woman said. "So you are Veritas Nachfolger?" she asked in a soft whisper.

Obbin shook his head. "I—"

"You know of them?" Tiffany interrupted.

The woman looked around. "May we go somewhere quieter?" she asked. "I fear already too much has been said."

Oliver understood. There were too many ears nearby, too many who might trade information for rewards. Already they'd nearly been turned in to the Federation by their own uncle.

Oliver nodded. "Lead the way."

"Stop. No one is going anywhere," Uncle Lucas said. "You aren't traipsing after some larva in rags."

The name-calling angered Oliver. "Uncle, we must. We are on a quest."

"No, I am protecting you."

"That's not your responsibility," Oliver said. "I appreciate that you want to watch out for us, but you don't understand what we've been through."

"And you do not understand the Truth," Mason said with authority.

Oliver looked to his younger brother. He'd not spoken for some time. Now that he had, Oliver couldn't comprehend the words or the passion in them.

Oliver looked at the woman. "Will you lead us?"

"Yes," she answered.

"Uncle, will you come?" Oliver asked.

Uncle Lucas took in a deep breath and looked at Coo, then Bruno. They seemed ready to restrain the kids. Then Uncle Lucas waved his hand. "Nephew, I will not. If you must go, you must go. But . . ." He looked at Tiffany, then each of the twins. "When you do get whatever you are after—when you find your parents—seek me out?"

Of all the words Uncle Lucas had said, these seemed to hold sincerity and compassion.

Oliver nodded. "We will."

There were no goodbyes. The woman moved to the door from which she'd come, and the five kids followed.

3.57

Serve

"Ma'am, may I ask your name?" Tiffany said.

The woman pulled a key from under her cloak. "My name is Dorothy," she said. The lock clicked and the door opened. "This way."

The kids shuffled into a humble room. A tall fireplace glowed on one wall; a single chair and couch sat before it. A simple pitcher and a bowl of fruit stood on a table by one wall. A corner of the room had a kitchen, and in another there appeared to be a bed.

"This is my home. Welcome." Dorothy moved to a window and slid a shutter over the opening.

"Thank you," Tiffany said.

"You mentioned the Veritas Nachfolger," Mason said. "What do you know of them?"

"I'm a member."

"You are?" asked Tiffany.

"Yes," she said with a smile.

"Then can you take us to the Cathedral?" Oliver asked. "We must get there before—"

"Before the Übel destroy the clue," Dorothy said softly. "We are running out of time. We expected you a day ago." She reached above the door and pulled down a heavy metal door on tracks. It covered the exit. Tiffany saw Austin fidget in his seat.

"We?" asked Tiffany.

The woman smiled. "Soon." She moved to another window and shuttered it.

"Dorothy, why do you live down here?" Mason asked.

"Because we are needed," she said. "Those who most need our help live here and in the levels just above."

"What sort of help?" Tiffany asked.

"We provide medicine, food, clothing. We share the Truth. Those here are most willing to hear it. They receive it and feed from it. The message of Truth gives them hope when they have none. It is our job to nourish those in need both physically and spiritually," Dorothy explained. "It is our call to serve."

"Doesn't the Federation handle that?"

"It tries, but that is not what it is called to do. As Veritas Nachfolger, as followers, we are called to serve and help those less fortunate than us. We also provide something that feeds more than a stomach, something the Federation would never share."

"If you are sharing the Truth openly down here, why don't more know about it?" asked Austin. "Why not share it elsewhere?"

Dorothy sighed. She looked sad at the question. "It isn't time yet. Even down here, there are those who oppose the Truth."

"Isn't that when it is needed most?" asked Obbin.

"My son, you are correct," Dorothy said. "But we are so few, and we could be quickly stamped out."

"But it is written that all will hear of the Truth," Obbin said.

"They will, but that is why we must be patient and wait on him," Dorothy said. "The Truth will reveal the time of revival to us."

The words were so foreign to Tiffany. They made little sense, but she was hungry to find out more—to understand them.

Oliver cleared his throat. "Dorothy, I don't wish to be rude, but may we go? You said we have little time left. Can't we talk about this while we walk?"

"Oliver, my son," Dorothy said, "time in this realm is limited indeed. You know not of the limitless time your brothers and sister have chosen."

Oliver shook his head. "What?"

There was a knock on the wall at the back of the room. Dorothy walked over to a tall bookshelf and touched the surface of a mirror. The reflective surface changed to an image, but Tiffany couldn't make it out from her location.

"Enter," Dorothy said. The fire in the hearth extinguished, and the back wall dropped into the ground with a soft grinding sound.

3.58

Reunion

"Brother Sam?" asked Austin.

"Mr. Krank?" asked Oliver.

The newcomer wore a deep red cloak and sandals. He bowed his head and removed the hood as he straightened. "One and the same."

"You know him?" Austin asked.

"He was at the parts shop in Brighton. He gave us the cloaking device," Tiffany said. "This is your Brother Sam?"

"Yes," Austin said.

Obbin shook Brother Sam's hand. "I did as you told me."

"You did wonderfully. Great work," Brother Sam congratulated him.

Austin wondered what exactly Obbin had done.

"Now we must go," Brother Sam said. "We have little time."

Dorothy nodded. "I will be ready."

"Thank you, sister."

Brother Sam motioned to the fireplace, and the kids filed through after him. Sister Dorothy remained.

The tunnels they traversed grew darker and darker with fewer overhead lights and narrower walls. Several doors stood between them and their destination, but none were locked.

Occasionally they climbed over piles of rubble and squeezed through areas where the walls had crumbled in, loosing dirt into the tunnel. No one would venture this way without a very good reason.

During their trek, the kids filled in Brother Sam on the past couple of days' adventures. First they confirmed that Brother Sam had been the one to drive off the enemy ship on Evad. Then they told of the distress call that had led them back to Jahr des Eises and O'Farrell's betrayal. Brother Sam was unsurprised and confirmed why he'd given them the cloaking device. They told of the attack on Cobalt Gorge and Obbin's people. They talked about Re Lyt and the Hatchery and Zebra Xavier. Brother Sam didn't say much then. Austin got the feeling he was considering the Übel leader, perhaps trying to recall information he might know about him. Tiffany talked about her escape from the Hatchery and praised Austin's ability and courage in flying the *Phoenix*. That was all they could say before they arrived at a door that blocked the path. It had no handle.

"Austin, would you open the door?" Brother Sam asked.

Austin looked at him curiously.

"Your cross," Brother Sam reminded him.

"Ah!" Austin smiled. He'd forgotten about it, but the key had been around his neck since Mason had returned it to him when they were coming out of hyper flight.

Austin slipped his hand under the neck of his shirt and pulled the chain and pendant free. He pushed the cross against the indentation in the frame. The door slowly slid open.

Brother Sam waved everyone through. The door closed.

Before them was a cavernous room. Stairs led down into a sunken floor. Torches burned throughout the room, illuminating a massive mural of grand design on the far wall. The paint was flaking. Its colors brightened and darkened in the flickering light, but Austin could still make out images. It appeared to be a timeline. Hundreds of scenes were painted across it: a garden with two people and a snake, a boat surrounded by water, a silver cup, a giant and boy . . . but most significant was a cross.

Near the middle of the mural, the large cross stood with a man on it. Red liquid swirled out from the man and spread out in lines that reached into the rest of the mural. The symbolism seemed odd, but Austin was sure there was a reason. In fact, he knew there was. Was this Truth? Was this the sacrifice of Rescuer that Obbin had explained?

Large, ridged columns held up a second mural that covered the ceiling with stars and planets. Austin imagined that the painting had probably been very realistic in its earlier years.

His brothers and sister had stopped in awe at the sight of the image. Brother Sam smiled, giving them a moment to take it all in.

"This is our history. This is the true history of humanity," Brother Sam explained. "This was done by the Veritas Nachfolger many centuries ago. It is all that remained when the Cathedral above was destroyed. We have worked hard to protect it all these years."

"It's beautiful," Tiffany said.

"Yes, but it's much more. It reveals the Truth. It brings forth the story of creation and the gifts given to us."

"Is this the sacrifice, Obbin?" Austin asked, his eyes on the man on the cross. "Is he the Truth? The Rescuer?"

Brother Sam looked at Austin with a bright smile. "You know?"

Austin nodded. "I know the Truth. I believe in him, and so do Tiffany and Mason."

"Obbin told us about Creator and Helper," Mason explained. "We understand. We believe."

Brother Sam glanced at Obbin. "Good work, my boy. Your people remained true to our beliefs even after these years of separation. When we see your parents again, I will thank them."

That was all the confirmation Austin needed. His brother's suspicions that the Blauwe Mensen were linked to the Veritas

Nachfolger—or at least were part of the story of the search for Ursprung—rang true.

Brother Sam looked back to Austin. "I brought you here to explain what I couldn't on Evad. It appears my task has already been completed."

"You can still tell us. Oliver doesn't know," Austin said.

Brother Sam looked at the oldest Wikk. "Oliver, do you wish to know?"

All eyes went to Oliver. "I think I do. I think I know already." His voice cracked. "It's as if someone were whispering in my ear and explained the pictures ahead of us."

Brother Sam put his hand on Oliver's shoulder. "My son, Someone is whispering in your ear. That Someone is calling you to himself. That Someone wants to watch over you. That Someone wants to lead you."

"Oliver, I've never felt such peace," Mason said.

"Me too," Austin added.

Oliver turned to Brother Sam. "I want that."

"It is yours, if you simply believe in the Truth. You must only accept his sacrifice," Brother Sam explained. "You see, in the beginning of time, the Father created our universe. But the first man and woman disobeyed our Father. Their disobedience was so great that there was nothing any human could do to make up for it. So our Father made a way through his Son, the One we call Truth. He spoke the truth, and he told of the only way to eternal life. He shared the plan our Father had for us, and then he willingly sacrificed himself on a cross to cover over our disobedience." Brother Sam swept his arms outward as if displaying the red paint swirls that spread out from the cross. "The Truth's sacrifice was our way to eternal life, our only way. The Father gave us the Spirit to help us and comfort us. The Spirit is all around us, within us. He is unseen but here at all times." Brother Sam placed his hands on Oliver's shoulders. "Do you see?"

Oliver cleared his throat. Austin watched with pent-up excitement. He saw his brother look toward the mural. He knew

Oliver was focused on the cross with the man, the image of the sacrifice made long ago. The images, the explanation by Brother Sam, they were so clear.

"Truth, I believe. Thank you for your sacrifice." Oliver exhaled a great sigh of relief.

The words had barely left his lips before the kids surrounded him in an embrace.

Brother Sam stepped back and smiled. He looked toward the ceiling. "Thanks be to you, Father."

"Sir," Obbin began, "what do we do now?"

"My young friend, you must retrieve the necessary information to begin your journey to Ursprung," Brother Sam said. "Look at the mural and the map above. You will have what you need to find the *Ark*."

"The *Ark*?" asked Tiffany.

"The *Ark* is how we escaped Ursprung in its final days," Brother Sam explained. "It alone holds the way back."

"Can't you just tell us how to get to the *Ark* or even take us there?" asked Austin.

"I took an oath that allows me only to bring you as far as this room. Your destination from here must be discovered by you alone," Brother Sam said. "This journey is yours."

"But why?" Mason asked. "Don't you want us to find Ursprung?"

Brother Sam smiled. "I do, my son, but that is not the purpose of the Veritas Nachfolger. Our job is to protect the truth, to share what we can, and to teach and allow those on the quest to grow. Growth is essential to your faith and your belief in the Father, Son, and Spirit. Look, and you will find." He pointed at the mural ahead. "Ask, and it shall be given."

Obbin smiled. "I've heard that before."

Brother Sam's mTalk beeped. He looked down at it. His lips curled in a frown.

Austin had been with Brother Sam when he'd gotten a warning on his mTalk; soon after, he'd gone to rescue Oliver and Tiffany.

"I will return shortly," said Brother Sam.

"But what about our parents?" asked Mason.

"They will be here soon. That's why I must hurry. Whether we can free them from the Übel is yet to be known," Brother Sam said. "Now look."

He walked to a door at the far end of the room and left. The kids were alone to search.

Austin led the way down the wide staircase into the room. To see the whole mural, they needed to remain near the entrance to the room on the ledge. To see the details, they had to get close.

"We must capture the whole image and then get as much as we can up close," Tiffany said. "Mason, go to the stairs. Take as many shots as you can over the whole mural. Austin, you start down there." She pointed to the far left of the mural, where perhaps the beginning was. "Oliver, you start at the far right and move toward Austin. Obbin, start capturing as much of the ceiling as you can."

Tiffany took a deep breath. "I'm going to scour this for a clue. I suspect that's where I should start." She pointed to a circle surrounded by a haze of gray with bursts of flames spotted across it. It was to the right of the cross but not quite at the end of the mural.

She had the e-journal out. Its screens glowed.

Ark

T ime was running out, and no clock could tell her exactly how long she had left. Tiffany only knew the Übel would be there soon, and Brother Sam had yet to return.

All of the artwork, wall, and ceiling had been captured. The mural contained two mentions of the *Ark*. One was a wooden boat surrounded by water. It was at the far left of the mural. The other was a spaceship of immense size, closer to the right side. The most logical *Ark* was the one on the right side. It seemed to be traveling to a small blue-green dot, away from a planet covered in gray clouds and bursting with flames. The fiery planet was labeled Terra Originem, not Ursprung. This excited her. The books Rylin had taken as a bartering chip had been called *The Chronicles of Terra Originem*.

It appeared that Ursprung and Terra Originem were one and the same. Everything was fitting together like a well-designed puzzle. The path of the *Ark* ended at the blue and green globe, but there were no coordinates, and the name of the place wouldn't come up in a search on the e-journal. It made sense. If Tiffany's parents had been there or known about the planet, they would have put information about it in their e-journal. This was a sign that the planet was the place they sought, its coordinates still unknown.

A shot rang out from Austin's weapon. "Drex!"

Oliver swung around and fired in the direction Austin was aiming.

Tiffany looked but saw no one. She dove as a purple flash zipped in their direction and exploded in sparks across the marble floor.

Austin and Oliver fired again.

Tiffany and Mason ducked behind a pillar; Obbin slipped behind another one nearby. Oliver was on his belly, his weapon trained and firing. Austin crouched behind a pillar, leaning over and firing, then tucking back behind the safety of the pillar.

The purple return fire ceased. Oliver and Austin's barrage did not.

"Quick! We have to get him!" called Austin.

Without any opportunity for discussion, Oliver wordlessly agreed. Tiffany watched as her oldest and youngest brothers sprinted toward the exit in pursuit of their enemy.

Before leaving, Oliver turned. "Find the clues. We'll be back."

"But Mr. Krank?" Tiffany called. There was no answer. Oliver and Austin were already gone.

She didn't like that Oliver and Austin had taken off after Drex, but she knew why. Being alone, Drex had been probably sent ahead to scout. He would lead the Corsairs to them. But how had they escaped Re Lyt? Had the *Black Ranger* extracted the Corsairs from the Hatchery? Had they rescued the Corsairs they'd kicked off the *Phoenix*?

"We have to hurry," Tiffany said. "Not only are the Übel likely nearly here, but the Corsairs are here, and if Oliver and Austin can't stop Drex—"

"We get it," Mason said bluntly.

The three went back to work. Not even a minute passed before Mason called for her.

He was lying on his back, staring at the ceiling. "Come here. You have to see this."

Tiffany walked toward the center of the large room. As she lay down, the ceiling moved. "Interest—"

"What was that?" asked Obbin.

"I don't—" Mason started. He pushed himself up.

The three looked around cautiously, but no shaking followed.

"We should get out of here," Obbin said.

"Not yet," Mason said. "We have to figure this out. If this place is destroyed, we'll have nothing." His voice held a note of desperation. Everything they were discovering built together. One missing piece might mean they'd never find Ursprung.

Tiffany shook her head. "Nothing fell. We need to finish."

"Let's hurry," Obbin said. He had always shown fearlessness, but Tiffany sensed something had shaken that trait.

She shrugged. "So what did you find?"

Mason pointed. "You see that planet there; it looks exactly like the one the *Ark* ends at on the mural." He held up his wrist and showed her the picture of the mural on his mTalk.

She looked back to the real mural, then to the ceiling. He was right. "A clear match," she said, "but we still don't have any coordinates."

"We do, actually. The constellation was on one of the maps you took from Evad," Mason explained. "You and Austin found them in the observatory."

"That's great!" Tiffany held out the e-journal and took a picture. "I'll cross-reference with those maps."

"I've already done that," Mason said. "That was how I got the matches in the first place."

"Matches?" asked Tiffany.

Mason smiled. "You remember Mom's entry about Dabnis Castle, when Dad took pictures of a solar map on the ceiling of a library?"

Tiffany nodded.

"That map matched with eighty percent confidence. I think the fading of the image is the only reason it wasn't 100 percent," Mason explained. "It is called YelNik Eisle. We have to—"

A loud rumbled echoed above them. The ceiling shook briefly, loosing dust from the ceiling. The room didn't seem to be in danger of collapsing.

Tiffany looked toward the exit.

"Earthquake?" asked Mason.

"No. I think it's worse," Obbin said. "I think they're here."

"Extinguish the torches," Tiffany commanded.

They took off in different directions, like a coordinated assault team, their targets the flames.

The pockets of light disappeared one at a time but quickly.

Standoff

They'd lost Drex almost immediately, but his footsteps echoed loudly through the stone corridor. They twisted around a corner, and Oliver shoved Austin to the ground. A spray of purple sparks bounced from the wall as Drex's shot just missed him.

Oliver fired. Austin lifted his weapon and fired too. Drex took off running again, outgunned and outnumbered.

The ground shook beneath them, and the two stopped abruptly.

"Did you feel that?" asked Oliver.

"Yes."

"Maybe we should turn back and get the others."

"Don't leave now," said an unwelcome voice.

"Austin, run!" Oliver yelled.

"Not another step," warned O'Farrell. He turned sideways as two lizards hobbled forward, muzzles across their mouths and long leashes in the hands of Corsair guards. The wartocks were about to be unleashed. Austin doubted his trick would work so well this time. The creatures hissed. One of the lizards disappeared, leaving only a metal collar remaining. Every inch of its red bumpy body reappeared as the yellow one next to it went invisible and reappeared.

"Surrender," called O'Farrell.

Oliver looked at Austin. Austin knew the question on his mind. He forced a smile and nodded.

Oliver fired at the red lizard, Austin at the yellow one. A green sphere of light flashed around them, deflecting the shots to the ceiling. The red wartock's black, forked tongue shot forward as if it were trying to suck energy from the field before it. Its bright green eyes bulged and zeroed in on Oliver.

There was nothing left to do. In unison, Austin and Oliver turned and ran. Each fired over their shoulders as they blazed away. Austin knew they wouldn't be able to keep this up. He heard the creatures' pounding feet as they rounded the corner.

Oliver turned and fired his Zinger. *Whoop!*

Austin ran ahead. He stopped and turned. "Go!" he yelled.

Oliver dashed past him. He repeated the maneuver. "Go!" he yelled.

A flash of blue exploded from Oliver's weapon. Austin heard the *whoop*, then *shoop shoop*, as two small projectiles zipped past him.

Without hesitation Austin spun and ran. He fired a stun shot over his shoulder. A short way past Oliver, he turned again and fired. "Go!"

Green orbs illuminated their now-invisible targets with each shot. The creatures were enshrouded in some sort of protective electromagnetic field. Only their metal collars marked them. The lizards were loosed on them without restraint. Austin could tell they were hungry from the vicious hisses.

He fired. *Whoop!*

Oliver started toward him, then fell to the ground and cried out. He twisted to his back and shoved the Zinger forward, firing the weapon.

A blast of blue erupted a foot from Oliver. A green half-circle flashed.

RHARRR RHARRRRRR!

The beasts were on them.

Oliver yanked his leg to free himself from the unseen creature's grip. He kicked back at the beast. His foot struck the metal collar, and it snapped open. The wartock hissed, and the collar dropped off and clanked to the ground.

Oliver scrambled to his feet, limping heavily away. Austin ran toward him and slipped under his shoulder.

"Fire!" ordered Oliver. Austin turned and fired. Oliver turned and did the same. They sent a barrage of blazing stun shots into the empty space. A blizzard of cries and snarls erupted with no green flash of protection. Had they taken one out?

"Run!" yelled Oliver.

Austin helped his brother hobble down the long hall.

HISSS!

He heard a scratching against the stone floor behind him. The second wartock was still in pursuit. If only Austin could get the silver collar off. It was dangerous, but he had to try.

Oliver shoved Austin's arm off him. "Go, Austin. Just go!"

"I'm not leaving."

"You are." Oliver leaned against the wall and aimed his weapon, then fired. "Now go!"

Austin looked toward the exit. He could never leave his brother.

"No, we go together or . . . or we don't go," Austin said. He lifted his weapon and fired.

RHARRR!

"We're all going," said a voice from behind them.

A man and woman in a red cloaks swept toward them: Brother Sam and Sister Dorothy.

Brother Sam threw two silver canisters down the hall.

ZCHBOOMP! ZCHBOOMP! The two canisters exploded. Thick white smoke poured from either end of the grenades.

"Come on," Brother Sam ordered.

They ran to the far end of the corridor. No one looked back. No more snarls. No more shots from the Zingers.

"Go with Sister Dorothy," Brother Sam said. "I must get the others."

"But our parents?" Austin asked.

"The soldiers of darkness are near," Sister Dorothy said.

Brother Sam nodded. "They can't be surprised now. The Corsairs' arrival has interrupted that plan. The five of you must go on. You must remain free."

"Sir, we want to rescue our parents," Oliver said. "We can't leave."

"Son, you must go," he said. "I will make every attempt to rescue your parents. But Phelan's arrival endangers your safety. Loosing those beasts on you has shown me his desperation. In his mind, if he loses you, he loses his wife, though how he planned on stopping those beast from . . ."

"His wife?" Oliver interrupted.

Austin shivered. He knew Brother Sam's next words would have been *eating you.*

Brother Sam shook his head. "Not now. Another time. I must get to your sister. Even now the Corsairs may be headed there."

"Come," said Sister Dorothy.

Austin grabbed Oliver's arm and pulled him along. But he too hoped to find their parents before they left.

3.61

Stunned

The door exploded, landing on the sunken floor with a resounding clatter. Three men rushed forward and spread out. Light beams from the barrels of their weapons swept back and forth as they searched the room.

Tiffany knew the uniforms of these men. She held her arm across Mason and Obbin's chests. They were gathered out of sight behind one of the large columns. It was a good thing they'd extinguished the torches.

"Clear!" cried one of the men.

A second later, a fourth man walked in. Tiffany jerked her head back behind the column. Captain Vedrik had arrived.

"Tiffany," whispered Mason, "is it them?"

She nodded, but the action was hidden in the darkness of the room.

"Tiffany?" Mason asked.

"Yes," she whispered. "It's them."

Tiffany peered back around the column. Her parents moved into the room. She smiled. Seeing them—seeing that they were safe even if they were prisoners—made her feel happy. The happiness soon changed into longing. She felt the tug in her chest. She missed them so much.

"This way," Obbin said, but she couldn't see where he was pointing.

"Mason, take his hand," she said as she took his.

Mason pulled her along, and they dashed to another column. They were headed toward the door Mr. Krank had gone through, and later Oliver and Austin.

Where was Mr. Krank? Where were Oliver and Austin?

Tiffany looked toward her parents. She gasped again. Mason's hand shot up over her mouth.

"Quiet, sis," he warned, then whispered. "What is it?"

"It's the McGregors, but . . . there's no sign of Ashley."

"The McGregors? That means the *Black Ranger* was taken by the Übel," Mason said.

"Maybe," chimed in Obbin. "Or . . . maybe they've all joined forces."

"Perhaps."

"I don't see my father or mother," Obbin said.

"Maybe they're still on the *Skull*," Mason suggested.

"We need to get out of here," Tiffany said. "Your parents are most likely still on the *Skull*. That's probably where Ashley is too." The statement was self-reassuring. "Obbin, lead the way."

Again linked by their hands, they scurried toward the far end of the room.

The room glowed. A multitude of flares and LuminOrbs had been cast around it. Unfortunately, the trio was still in the middle of the large room.

Mason stopped dead in his tracks, but Obbin broke away. Tiffany nearly fell over her younger brother. "Keep going," she urged him.

"Over there!" shouted one of the soldiers. Light washed over Tiffany and Mason. Obbin was already behind the next column.

"Come on," Tiffany shouted. Mason didn't move. She grabbed his arm and pulled. He stumbled after her.

Whoomp! Whoomp! Whoomp!

A chorus of shots from the stun rifles echoed out, zips of green light blasted their direction. Tiffany and Mason dove to the ground. She looked back at the Übel and her parents. Her dad had already dived at one of the men, as had Rand McGregor.

There were far more Übel. They fired another volley of shots. Tiffany scrambled toward the column. Obbin rushed back toward Mason. He reached out and pulled him to his feet. They ran toward the column.

Whoomp! Whoomp! Whoomp!

Everything moved in slow motion. Tiffany opened her mouth to scream, but no sound came out. A green glow struck Mason right in the side. His body slumped, and he tumbled to the ground in a roll. Obbin turned and ducked, but it was too late. A stun hit him right in his thigh. He fell sideways and slid across the floor.

Decisions flashed through Tiffany's mind. Nothing was in slow motion anymore. This was real. This was live. And this was dangerous.

Tiffany dove toward the fallen boys. She grabbed a hand of each and yanked with all her might. The boys slid her direction. Shots blasted around her. Mason and Obbin's limp bodies each took a few more stuns. She didn't know how that would affect how long they were unconscious.

Tiffany pulled again, and the three were behind the column.

How could she possibly drag them the rest of the way to the door by herself? Only one other column provided a waypoint between herself and the door. Übel soldiers were spreading out through the room. Her hiding places were disappearing rapidly.

Too quickly, an Übel soldier appeared to her right and fired. She slipped farther around the column, but her brother and the prince remained in the line of fire.

She had to get them. Tiffany started forward, but a hand gripped her arm and pulled her back. "There's no time," Mr. Krank said. "We must go." She looked at the man to argue, but his blue eyes were calm, honest.

Whoomp! Whoomp! Whoomp! Green flashed all around as the stuns struck the column and floor.

Mr. Krank guided her toward the door, keeping himself between the Übel and Tiffany like a shield.

Through the door they charged. Tiffany looked back at her parents one last time. Her dad was holding her mom, who was crying. Two soldiers restrained them with their presence. The McGregors were close and under guard.

Übel soldiers charged toward them, led by Captain Vedrik, his Luger raised.

"Monk! I will stop you!" he screamed with rage.

BANG!

The shot rang out across the room.

ZING!

It ricocheted off the nearest wall. Tiffany knew it had not been a stun shot. Vedrik wanted to stop Mr. Krank dead in his tracks.

Mr. Krank swung his silver cross toward the indent, and the door slid shut. An Übel soldier appeared, but too late. Tiffany followed. Her breaths were short and heavy. She pictured Mason's limp body. She pictured Obbin.

"They'll be with their parents now," Mr. Krank said as if he had read her mind. "Do not worry for them. You must stay free. Oliver and Austin need you."

They ran down long corridors and through many rooms that had once been part of the Cathedral of the Star.

Mr. Krank opened a final door.

The *Phoenix* sat in a tall cylindrical tower. Dust swirled as the engines idled. A glowing dot high overhead was the only sign of an exit.

Oliver and Austin ran from the ship.

"Tiffany! Are you okay?" asked Oliver.

"Yes," she said. "But . . ." Her voice caught. Tears filled her eyes.

"Where is Mason? Obbin?" asked Austin.

Oliver held Tiffany close.

"They have been captured," Mr. Krank explained.

"We have to rescue them. Those Corsairs—" Austin began.

"Not by the Corsairs, by the Übel. Mason and Obbin are with your parents now," Mr. Krank explained. "You must use what you have discovered from the murals. It will lead you to the Eochair."

"Eochair?" asked Tiffany.

"Your quest is far from over. To unlock the *Ark*, you must have the Eochair and the crosses from the valley," Mr. Krank said.

"The valley?" asked Austin.

"Your parents knew it as the Valley of Shadows," Mr. Krank said.

Tiffany looked at him curiously.

"O'Farrell told me much. Remember, he and I were friends," Mr. Krank said. "I kept track of his work with Archeos."

Oliver recoiled.

"Do not be concerned. He has chosen a different path," Mr. Krank said. "He chose it long ago, and our friendship suffered greatly. He is the reason I knew of you and your parents. He has not accepted the Truth yet."

"Sir, what about the planet that the *Ark* travels to?" Tiffany asked. "We found maps that seem to show the same planet, or so . . ." She paused. "Or so Mason thought. It was called YelNik Eisle."

"That is your destination," Mr. Krank said. "But first you need the crosses and the Eochair. Those clues are also within the map and mural."

"Why can't you tell us?" asked Austin.

"My son, when you take an oath, you do not break it."

"Aren't you at least coming with us?" asked Tiffany.

"No. You will take the *Eagle*," Mr. Krank said.

Tiffany looked at the ship and noticed the name. It was the ship Mr. Krank had flown on Evad to rescue them.

"What about the *Phoenix*?" asked Oliver. "All our supplies, the artifacts—they are all on the *Phoenix*."

"My cat, Midnight?" asked Tiffany.

"Sister Dorothy and I will take care of everything. We will rendezvous with you soon."

"Where?" asked Austin.

"I will find you. Now go!"

3.62

Distress

Oliver took his place in the pilot's seat. The ship seemed empty with only himself, Tiffany, and Austin inside. He missed his brother; he even missed Obbin. He held on to the fact that they were both with their parents and Helper was guiding them now.

The *Eagle* was almost exactly like the *Phoenix*. The only real difference was the layout of the cabins. They were not as personalized as each of the Wikks'. The interiors were standard and simple.

Tiffany was searching the mural and maps. Her mission was unstated: find the location of the Eochair.

The *Eagle* lifted with a solid wall before it. Up, up, and up. All at once, the cityscape lay before them. The vertical path had taken them right up the center of an arcology and out.

Two icons flashed across the screen: *Planetary Travel* or *Galactic Travel?*

Oliver tapped on *Galactic Travel*.

A voice droned on the speakers. "This is Enaid Federal Outpost A9127. Please identify yourself with ship name, serial code, location of registration, and flight license code."

"Tiff?"

Her fingers fluttered on the screen before her. "Sending."

The information appeared on his screen.

"I40:31 *Eagle*, 10K4G20E09-2007-6E20M20E11, Jahr des Eises, 5A6J19M85," Oliver read aloud.

"Clearance granted. Proceed on course I74, and exit vector 8-19-20-11."

Oliver saw the course appear on his screen with waypoints, and he followed. He watched the radar for enemy ships but doubted the Übel or Corsairs would take such a risk—at least, not in such a heavily guarded airspace. Of course, with their limitless reach, he wasn't sure the Übel wouldn't be able to follow them. He also wondered why security hadn't locked down flights in and off the planet, especially if federal forces were searching for them. Then again, the value of finding a few children was small in comparison to the havoc of grounding or delaying space travel from Enaid.

"Do you have our destination?" Oliver asked.

"No, not yet," Tiffany said.

"Do you think Mason is okay?" Austin asked.

Oliver hadn't thought about how Mason's capture would affect Austin. Though they were all siblings, Mason and Austin were twins. They had a bond that Oliver sometimes didn't understand.

Tiffany answered for him. "He's with Dad and Mom. He's with Obbin. Obbin and Mason know Creator, and I believe we'll all be together soon."

"You're right," Austin said. "I just wish he was with us. We've all found our place on the mission. I mean . . ." He paused. "I mean, we're a team now."

Oliver smiled. "We are indeed."

The ship slipped out of Enaid's atmosphere seamlessly. "I'll take us into a holding pattern, but we need to go somewhere. We can't wait here. If the Übel or Corsairs are coming, they'll find us."

"We can't just jump into hyper flight," Austin said. "We'd waste too much time."

"You're right, but—"

An urgent message appeared on the screen. It said it had been forwarded from the *Phoenix*. Had Mr. Krank already taken off in the *Phoenix*? Oliver tapped it.

"Oliver? Tiffany?" It was Ashley. She sounded distressed. "We've been attacked. I ... I escaped. But ..." Her voice trailed off. He heard sobbing. "I'm alone. I got into an escape pod. I'm on some moon. The Übel took my parents. I'm all alone. I need help!"

The transmission cut out. A set of coordinates appeared on the screen, as they would for any distress call from an escape pod.

Oliver went to tap in the coordinates for their hyper flight jump, but it was unnecessary: Tiffany already had.

"Let's get her," Tiffany said.

There was no discussion, no thought of getting to the Eochair first. They were headed to rescue their stranded friend.

Visual Glossary

Academy, Federal Star Fleet: The Academy provides top-of-the-line education while creating future leaders for the Federal Fleet. All males in the Federation must participate in the Federation's military service for at least five years. Most begin at age eighteen but a select few are admitted early at age sixteen.

Archeos Alliance: An organization that exists to unlock the past that has been lost. Founded as nonprofit, but receiving both private and federal funds, the organization has become a battleground for special-interest groups. Mr. and Mrs. Wikk often receive grants through this organization and are considered employees. They report their findings to Archeos, and then Archeos makes official reports available to the Federation and other groups.

Bewaldeter: A private boarding school and premier K–12 establishment. A majority of Archeos employees send their children to Bewaldeter. The school provides a curriculum that allows kids to focus on their interests. Tiffany, Mason, and Austin Wikk attend it, and Oliver did too until he was selected for early admittance to the Academy.

Biotronics: The replacement of limbs and organs with mechanical devices. Banned in the Federation.

Black Ranger: The flagship of the Corsairs. The ship is self-sustainable and never needs to dock on a planet or space station. Heavily armed and swift, it has been in more than a hundred engagements with Federal Forces.

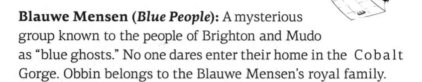

Blauwe Mensen (*Blue People*): A mysterious group known to the people of Brighton and Mudo as "blue ghosts." No one dares enter their home in the Cobalt Gorge. Obbin belongs to the Blauwe Mensen's royal family.

Bliz-Zero Gear: A brand of winter outerwear, coming in parkas, pants, and facemasks. The Wikks' outfits have a gray and white camouflage pattern. With proper hand and foot coverings, Bliz-Zero can sustain the wearer through sub-100-degree temperatures.

Brighton: The capital of Jahr des Eises after the Federation annexed the planet. The city's main purpose is to act as a base for the large-scale logging operation on the planet.

Building 6: The sixth floor of the Hatchery. A specialized laboratory filled with glass cylinders containing human bodies. A red globe is also stationed in the room.

Captain Fritz Vedrik: An agent and captain of the Übel forces, who attended the Übel's Raven's Nest Academy, on planet Babylt. Fritz Vedrik never knew his father. His mother died when he was just five years of age. He was enrolled into the Düsterkeit Boys School for pre-military training, which specialized in math, virtual war games, and endurance and survival techniques. He went missing from the school for several years, and was eventually found and brought back. Shortly afterward he was sent to the Drachen Bach colony for further training and re-education. He excelled and quickly rose to the top of his class. At age seventeen he was given his first secret mission. Having gained top-level security clearance, he conducts clandestine missions on behalf of, but off the record of, the Übel high command. Capable of going rogue, he often works for himself. He is dangerous.

Cavern Haven: An underground city, built as the Blauwe Mensen's sanctuary in times of danger.

Celtyx: A creature created from synthesizing the DNA of a lexovisaurus into the genes of an attack dog. The mutants are able to walk on ceilings and are some of the deadliest guard creatures ever engineered.

Cobalt Gorge: Home to the Blauwe Mensen. The gorge is well protected from the weather and from outsiders. The Blauwe

Mensen devised a series of drains that dump water deep into the planet and create steam. The steam then rises into the gorge and forms thick clouds over the city. The clouds create a warm humid environment that turns the gorge into a jungle, habitable through the time of Eises. The city's external protection from intruders consists of a drawbridge, a deep crevice, and a cave protected by large doors and guard towers. The gorge has been home to the Blauwe Mensen since they arrived on Jahr des Eises as the first settlers of the planet.

Corsair Goggles: Eyewear with night vision and navigation capabilities that provide directions and information to the wearer. They can zoom in on targets.

Corsairs: Also known as pirates, corsairs plague trade routes in the far reaches of the Federation and are a constant burden to Federal forces.

Corsair Swords: Weapons with black handles and blades that glow silver with energy. Strikes can either stun someone or give a warning shock.

Cryostore: A refrigeration and freezing appliance in the galley of the *Phoenix*.

Cybornotics: The actual integration of information into a human's brain or nervous system. Banned in the Federation.

Dabnis Castle: An abandoned castle where several clues and artifacts were found during the Wikks' last archeological dig. The clues provided what the Wikks believe is the missing step on the path to Ursprung.

Drex's Ship: A gray ship unlike the black Übel fighters. A globular canopy sits on a fuselage with short rounded wings and three tailfins. It is armed with ion torpedoes for disabling other craft.

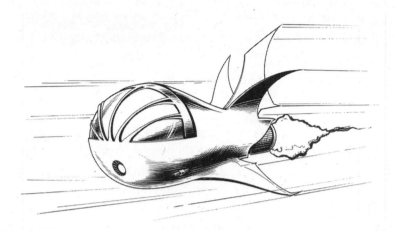

e-Journal: An electronic notebook in which Mr. and Mrs. Wikk store all their archeological notes. The notes consist of maps, statistics, pictures, videos, reports, coordinates, contacts, and much more. The information contains clues that may help unlock the path to Ursprung via a complex tapping method that traces links and makes connections. This tapping method is known only to Mr. and Mrs. Wikk and Tiffany.

e-Papyrus: A single-screen tablet for drawing or writing. Sketches or notes can be transferred to journals or computers. Does not have a high storage capacity.

Eagle: A sister ship to the *Phoenix*. Piloted by Brother Samuel, it was used to help the twins escape from the Übel.

Eochair: Brother Sam states that this is needed to unlock the *Ark*.

Eises: A harsh winter storm that turns the planet of Jahr des Eises to ice for an entire year. The storm releases its frigid breath after a two-year cycle of spring, summer, and fall. It occurs as the planet travels away from its star (sun) and becomes the thirteenth planet by passing Vor Eis. Two layers of clouds form, an upper layer that is heavy and purple, and a lower layer that is wispy and pink. Warm gusts of air, or updrafts, blast upward from the pink layer as it is charged by lighting strikes. This causes violent storms and drastically lowers the surface temperature of the planet.

Empire: The government preceding the Federation, ruled by an emperor of unknown origin. The Empire expanded, through war, annexations, and clandestine revolutions. This was also the time when the truth of Ursprung was lost.

Enaid: This planet was the site of the beginning of the Empire. While not the capital of the Empire or the Federation, the first settlements, then cities were built here. Located at 102.580 X, 5912.23 Y, 22.0 Z, Enaid is somewhat centrally located in the current boundaries of the Federation. The planet is small and controlled by one major city. This city is thought to be one of the most dangerous in the Federation, even with its ample police force. Instead the governor of the planet has allowed bribery and corruption to influence every facet of the planetary government.

Energen: The boys' favorite drink. It provides a jolt of energy and is 100 percent natural.

Evad: A planet previously explored by Mr. and Mrs. Wikk that became part of their search via a clue found at Dabnis Castle. The only habitable planet in the Rel Krev system, it is covered in lush green tropical plants, some of which can be deadly. The atmosphere is breathable, but hot and humid. There are many wild animals, some of which are unknown due to the loss of historical information.

Federal Star Fleet: The militaristic arm of the Federation that stands to protect and serve its citizens. Half of the entire force is dedicated to the expansion of the Federation. Expansion occurs through either the colonization of uninhabited planets or annexation by a vote of the inhabitants of a non-federal planet. The Federal Star Fleet has taken a peaceful approach to expansion. All males must serve five years in the federal service.

Federation: Established when the childless emperor Albert the XI ceded rule to the senate by declaring, "The people should decide their fate." The Federation consists of 1,983 planets, asteroids, or stations. Governed by a president and senate, the Federation is currently enjoying a time of great wealth and expansion.

FlexSkyn: A faux skin patch made of plasma containing nano-bots. The nano-bots take the patient's DNA and embed it into the skin cell framework within the plasma patch.

GenTexic: A genetics company funded by many organizations, but controlled by the Übel. Mr. O'Farrell has invested in the company as well. GenTexic owns the Hatchery, and RepFuse is a subsidiary of GenTexic.

GlobeX Glowmap: A disc that expands and turns into the form of a planet, asteroid, moon, or other orbital location when the user speaks the name of the place he or she wants to see. The disc generates a fully detailed map of the location's surface. The location information must be loaded into the GlobeX Glowmap.

Griffin: The sister ship of the *Phoenix*, built as an identical twin. It was given to Rand and Jenn McGregor to use on the quest for Ursprung. The ship, attacked by Corsairs and traded to Schlamm, is currently stored at his warehouse in Mudo on Jahr des Eises.

Hatchery: A large oval-shaped building set atop seven arched supports. The primary laboratory for GenTexic, located on Re Lyt. The bulk of GenTexic's lifetime-enhancing genetics research is carried out here. Through cloning, biotic growth, new species development, and crossbreeding, it is hoped life can be extended indefinitely. The Hatchery's massive energy requirements are met by unlimited access to Re Lyt's thermal heat as a power source. The egg energy systems used by the Übel were created here as well and use a microbial substance to create energy.

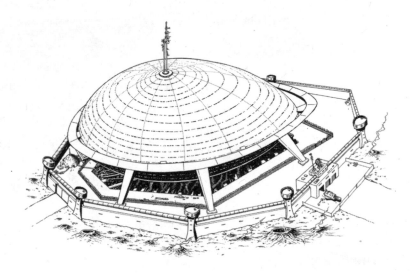

Hover Board: Used in several sports, including kugel, the hover board can levitate as high as ten feet above the ground. The rider gains altitude by leaning back and drops in altitude by leaning forward. A simple tap on the front of the board propels the hover board forward.

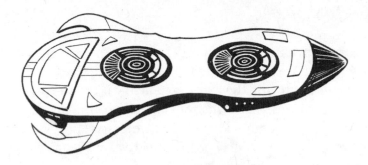

Hovermats: Bedding that hovers off the ground, allowing air to provide an extra cushion of support.

Hyper Flight: Space-flight navigation at extreme speeds, considered very dangerous for inexperienced pilots. The route of hyper flight must be entirely clear for the duration of the trip, otherwise the ship will smash into another object and be obliterated.

Insta-Vita Shake: A thick, chilled liquid with all the essential vitamins and nano-injectors for treating ailments within the body.

IZEE-150 Boots and Gloves: Subzero winter wear needed for exploration in frigid climates.

IZ-KLOZE Vapor: A canister of vapors used to knock out anyone who inhales the gas mixture.

Jahr des Eises: A small forest planet. Initially the planet was discovered and settled by the Blauwe Mensen. These people however remained hidden and are not officially known to the

Federation. An outpost, Mudo, was established by a resource exploration company as a base for logging operations. When the planet was annexed by the Federation, the city of Brighton was established.

While covered in a thick forest of gargantuan trees, the planet suffers from ice storms called Eises, every three years. In the two years of growth, the logging industry is in full operation. During the Eises, those who remain behind are sealed within the dome of Brighton. Phelan O'Farrell, a wealthy donor to Archeos, and the Wikks specifically, lives on Jahr des Eises in the city of Brighton.

Kinetic Plasma: A modified mixture of mammal blood and molecular compounds that is used not only as food, but as a control over the vast majority of RepFuse creations. Without kinetic plasma, the creatures will perish. Production and sales of kinetic plasma are exclusive to GenTexic and a major source of recurring revenue.

Kugel: A sport consisting of hover balls, hover boards, and three teams, with fifteen players per team. Austin and Oliver both played at Bewaldeter. There is a federal league with more than six hundred teams.

LibrixCaptex: A scanner created by Archeos that instantly scans the contents of a book. It allows exploration teams to quickly search texts for possible clues that might lead to further discovery on their expeditions. Though books are rare, LibrixCaptex devices are provided to all archeological teams in the event that one is discovered.

LOCA-drone: A small silver disc with a screen embedded in its top. The LOCA-drone uses magnetism and negative energy to propel itself to a position over a designated area. Often used for search and rescue, it can also be used to mark locations and coordinates. Each device is assigned a unique encrypted access signature code.

LuminOrb: A small orb that glows when squeezed, often used to mark paths or designated rendezvous points.

LX-7712 Phaser: A tubular weapon with prongs at the end. Used to subdue and render creatures unconscious. Voltage can be turned up to a fatal level.

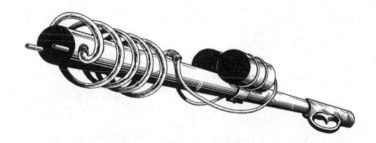

Maglev: A train type vehicle that travels along a single magnetized rail using magnetic repulsion to reduce friction and reach high speeds. The maglev on Jahr des Eises is used for delivery of newly felled timber to the processing facility and then to the spaceport for distribution throughout the Federation.

Magnilox: A tool that uses magnetism to seal and unseal things.

mTalk: Worn on the wrist like a watch, the mTalk has many useful features, including a built-in video call feature, flashlight, navigation, video camera, and other features still unknown to the Wikks.

Mudo: An outpost on Jahr des Eises established by the Resource Exploration Company XPLR Corp. The outpost quickly became a rough community of loggers and opportunists looking to make a quick buck. When the first winter after Mudo's establishment arrived, XPLR Corp. failed to provide the needed supplies to their workforce, and rather than evacuate, forced them to make do. Management quickly lost control and the workers revolted. Some attempted to flee the planet via the large colonization ships that were being used for housing, operations management, and timber processing. Only two of the twelve ships actually launched successfully. The remaining ships were either not in appropriate condition, or were not flown by workers with flight experience. The outpost was left in shambles, and although XPLR continued to harvest lumber, it did nothing to repair or renovate the broken village.

Nano-injectors: Small robots designed to look for ailments in the body such as muscle tears or bone fractures.

Nmutu-A: A pink moon that orbits Re Lyt. It is a primary source for a mineral used in building materials and mined by XPLR Corp. A security outpost on Nmutu-A provides protection for the Hatchery.

Nos Idam: An orange moon that orbits Re Lyt. Its atmosphere is actually on fire. Its surface is coated in a thick layer of ash, continually kicked up by high winds. The ash smolders and smolders.

NumbaGlu: A rubbery strip of adhesive that is laid next to an area of human skin or tissue that needs to be numbed. The numbing agent's effects are nearly instant to allow little delay in treating the patient.

Ontdekking: The space ship that brought the Blauwe Mensen to Cobalt Gorge. The nose is a domed windshield, which allows the passengers to look out into space. The surface of the craft is a bronze color. Landing skids sweep out from the side of the craft like wings but curve toward the ground. Five engines run along the underside of the ship. The bridge is under a glass dome that provides the crew a 360-degree view. The ship is capable of carrying up to one thousand people and supplies, including livestock.

Phoenix: A spaceship donated to the Wikks to facilitate their research on their quest for the origins of mankind. The ship's sleek silver skin and forward-swept wings give it a unique appearance. But those features are nothing compared to the secret capabilities of the ship that Oliver will have to discover. The ship consists of a bridge (cockpit), four cabins (sleeping quarters), a galley (dining room/kitchen), three lavatories (bathrooms), a library/office, an engine room, an electronics suite, a two-story cargo bay, and an artifacts room.

Polkin Powder: A highly toxic poison with no antidote. Death is instantaneous if ingested by a human. However, because of the genetic makeup of a celtyx, it only acts as a sedative to the creature.

Ppank System: The solar system in which Re Lyt exists.

Re Lyt: A planet of deep blue earth, pocketed with millions of lava fissures and pools. The inner core of the planet threatens eruption at any moment. The hostile environment was one of the reasons the planet was selected by GenTexic to build the Hatchery. Re Lyt provides an abundant source of free thermal power to fuel experiments and supply the containment fences.

RepFuse: A subsidiary of GenTexic.

RepFuse Facility: The laboratory for RepFuse in the lower portion of the Hatchery. Most of the RepFuse mutations are contained in a series of large electrified fences directly below the building. A labyrinth of tubular walkways connects the cages and allows scientists access to their experiments.

RetinaX Goggles: Protective eyewear that provides a display of information on the lenses when activated.

Simba Intergalactic Spaceport: A spaceport on Enaid. The Federation's largest by passenger and cargo traffic as well as in size.

Skull (**Übel cruiser**): The cruiser is one of the primary craft in the Übel's small fleet. The communications bridge rivals the technology and power of a Star Fleet frigate. The cruiser's exterior is black and heavily armored with thick nano-carbon skin. It is armed with plasma blasters, phaser torpedo canisters, and skeleton-missile launchers. Housing a full battalion of soldiers, it also carries star fighters, and ground equipment.

Sky Scooter: This small craft seats two and has multiple storage compartments. It can hover up to twenty feet above the ground and can reach speeds of one hundred miles per hour. The scooter is ideal for short commutes.

SlickWick: A purple lubricant used for medical needs.

Solar Retina Replacement: A process by which nano light sources are injected into the eyes, providing enough light to allow the recipient to see even in total darkness.

Spectrum Scope: A device that produces desired wavelengths of light. Critical for most archeological research in the biology field.

Spike: A seven-foot hybrid chameleon-iguana. Genetically engineered and bred by a company called RepFuse. Spike is virtually invisible when he changes colors and blends into his surroundings.

StingerXN: Similar to a Zapp-It, this weapon can be set to fire a lethal level of energy.

StunShot Rifle SI: This rifle features the ability to either be lethal with standard bullets or utilize a stun option that fires a green orb of energy. SI stands for "standard-issue," as this rifle is widely manufactured and used amongst the soldiers of the federal fleet.

Towers of Fire: Towers with arms on which silver bowls hang, with flames that light the Blauwe Mensen gorge as well as Cavern Haven.

Tragiws: The planet the Wikks call home. Its climate is dry and arid, but not a desert. The Wikks' home sits on the edge of the Plains of Yrovi near a deep cavern. The planet is small and sparsely populated.

Tyrannosaurus Rex: Genetically modified versions of pre-historic dinosaurs created by Gentexic's RepFuse subsidiary. By studying "true" dinosaurs the company hoped to modify and enhance these creatures into versions that could be used for military or security reasons. Because of the T-Rex's size, RepFuse instead began harvesting genes for implantation into smaller mutations. (See also Velociraptors.)

Übel: A secret order/society composed of renegade forces. Captain Vedrik is an agent of the mysterious society. The society's handiwork is threaded throughout the history of the Federation and Empire, but is not publicly recognized. Their reach and influence is unknown, but thought to be vast. Their financial resources are second only to the Federation.

Übel Deluxe Scooter: A roofless craft with two rows of seats, one for a pilot and copilot and one for passengers. It is also known as a skiff and is armed with two plasma blasters.

Übel Scooter: Unlike the Wikks' scooters, Übel scooters are armed with dual plasma blasters. They can carry up to two soldiers.

Ultra-Wear Pants: Invented by the Wikk children's grandfather, the pants are made of titanium-flex fabric. Water resistant, flame retardant, and temperature controlled, the pants are great for the adverse conditions the Wikks sometimes face on expeditions.

Ultra-Wear Shirt: Titanium-flex shirts invented by the Wikk children's grandfather that can maintain a consistent temperature, keep the wearer dry, and are inflammable. Other features include electric-shock protection and puncture protection in the case of sharp branches or animal bites. If the shirt is pulled over one's head it can filter poisonous gases.

Ursprung: A fabled planet believed to be the birthplace of mankind. Its discovery is sought by many.

Velociraptor: The modifications to the Velociraptors caused an even more dangerous beast that forced RepFuse to triple the strength of its enclosures. The program to enhance the Raptors is on hold until cerebral modification technology can be used to control the dinosaurs. Currently Raptors are too dangerous to be used outside of their enclosure.

Veritas Nachfolger: A group of people who are guardians of the Truth. They remain to keep it alive and guide those on the quest for Truth. The Veritas Nachfolger symbolize Truth by a cross and use it as their symbol and insignia. They integrate the cross and many other symbols into their daily lives. The Veritas Nachfolger have been seen wearing red cloaks, and understand the Übel to be the forces of darkness.

Wartock: Lizards that are five generations newer than Spike and the size of full-grown men. RepFuse created this more advanced version to hunt instead of guard. Sharp spikes line the ridge of their backs. Their skin is bumpy and covered in a slick oily substance. The lizards can be red, yellow, or grey. Their ability to change their skin to appear like their surroundings means they can seem to disappear.

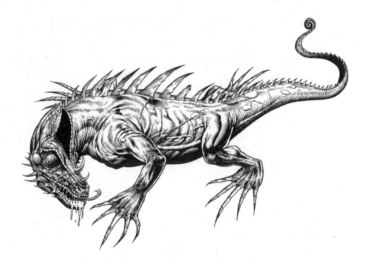

XPLR Corp: A large resource exploration company. Mr. O'Farrell worked for them in his early days. They have many outposts and subsidiaries operating within as well as outside the Federation.

Yeldah: The moon closest to Re Lyt. Its atmosphere is a source of voletic gas used for the creation of plutox torpedoes, which are highly volatile and toxic. The voletic gas gives the planet its purplish hue.

Yth Orod: The city that the Veritas Nachfolger inhabited while on Evad. Set within the Ero Doeht basin, the city was surrounded by a high ridge that acted as an extra layer of protection. The city was settled in 1397 with a population of five thousand, and within ten short years the large ziggurats and cross-shaped pool had been completed. Meant to serve as a symbol and beacon to the Truth, many other secrets were also laid within the depths of the city in order to preserve the path back to Ursprung.

Zapp-It: A small defense device that uses an electric shock either to deter or stun an assailant.

Zick Stick: An instrument played by strumming one's fingers across a series of light beams. Each beam produces its own sound. The note produced is preset by the musician and can be changed, giving each zick stick musician a very distinct sound.

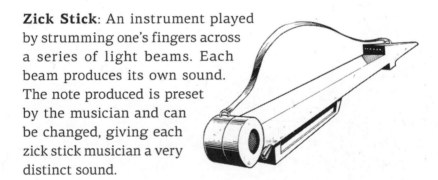

Zinger: A larger version of the Zapp-It that has the ability to shoot small projectiles at a target. Once connected, the projectiles give off a series of disabling shocks. The military has a more powerful version called the TW414.

Recipe for Blauwe Mensen Chocolate Scotcharoos

BARS

Ingredients

- 1 cup honey
- 1 ½ cups peanut butter
- 6 cups Rice Krispies

Directions

1. Combine honey and peanut butter in a quart pan.
2. Cook over medium heat stirring until mix begins to bubble.
3. Remove from heat.
4. Add Rice Krispies then press into a greased 9 x 13 pan.

FROSTING

Ingredients

- 2 cups chocolate chips
- 2 cups butterscotch chips

Directions

1. Melt in double boiler slowly until creamy. Remove from heat immediately.
2. Frost the bars and place in refrigerator until cool.

Prayer to Receive Jesus Christ

In The Quest for Truth series, I use other words to name Jesus, God, and the Holy Spirit. My characters come from a different time and different cultures and have different words to refer to God, just like Christians in other cultures today have names for God in their own languages. The Truth/Rescuer is Jesus Christ, Creator is God the Father, and Helper is the Holy Spirit.

If you've never asked Jesus into your heart to be your Savior, why don't you do that right now? All you need do is pray the prayer below and believe with your heart.

Dear Lord Jesus, I feel lost, and I need a Savior. Please come into my heart and help me to change and be obedient to you. Thanks for dying on the cross for me. Amen.

If you have decided to give your life to Christ, please let us know. We want to pray for you. Contact us at info@Brock Eastman.com.

Brock Eastman lives in Colorado with his wife, three children, and two cats. Inspiration comes on his morning drives to work with America's Mountain in view. Growing up in the Midwest, Brock enjoyed autumn most and misses the chilly sweatshirt morning air and colorful leaves.

Brock works at Focus on the Family as the Odyssey Adventure Club producer. He is the author of The Quest for Truth and Sages of Darkness series and writes for The Imagination Station series. You may have seen him on the official *Adventures in Odyssey* podcast and *Social Shout Out*, informing *Adventures in Odyssey* fans about the latest news.

He enjoys getting letters and artwork from fans. You can contact him at BrockEastman.com by clicking on the Connect & Contact link.

To keep track of what Brock is working on, connect with him at

Twitter: @bdeastman
Facebook: http://www.facebook.com/eastmanbrock
YouTube: http://www.youtube.com/user/FictionforAll/videos

MORE FROM BROCK EASTMAN!

BOOK ONE — THE QUEST FOR TRUTH

"Taken is a riveting tale of just how far mankind is
willing to go . . . for the ultimate prize."
—**Wayne Thomas Batson**, Bestselling Author of *The Door Within* Trilogy,
The Berinfell Prophecies, and *The Dark Sea Annals*

THE QUEST FOR TRUTH series follows the four Wikk kids in their
desperate race to find the mysterious planet Ursprung and stop
the Übel renegades from misusing its long-lost secrets. Ancient cities,
treacherous villains, high-tech gadgets, The Phoenix—encounter all of
these and more on this futuristic, interplanetary adventure!

BUY *TAKEN* WHEREVER BOOKS ARE SOLD.

WWW.BROCKEASTMAN.COM   WWW.PRPBOOKS.COM

Start an adventure!
with Focus on the Family

Whether you're looking for new ways to teach young children about God's Word, entertain active imaginations with exciting adventures or help teenagers understand and defend their faith, we can help. For trusted resources to help your kids thrive, visit our online Family Store at: